Totally Bound Publishing books by Makayla Roberts

The Royal Gordanos
A Royal's Touch
A Royal's Pursuit

I0691657

The Royal Gordanos

A ROYAL'S PURSUIT

MAKAYLA ROBERTS

A Royal's Pursuit
ISBN # 978-1-913186-20-3
©Copyright Makayla Roberts 2019
Cover Art by Erin Dameron-Hill ©Copyright September 2019
Interior text design by Claire Siemaszkiewicz
Totally Bound Publishing

Published in 2019 by Totally Bound Publishing, United Kingdom.

A ROYAL'S PURSUIT

Dedication

To my parents, for their unwavering love and support.

Prologue

For countless years, I've been at your side. I've fought beside you. I've cried with and for you. I know you better than anyone, better than you know yourself.

When you suffered, I suffered. When you smiled, I smiled. When you fell apart, I picked up the pieces. And when the gods of death demanded your life, I gave mine instead.

My love for you runs deeper than any ocean. I will sacrifice everything I have if it means you can continue living.

You are the reason for the breath in my body.

You are my truemate.

Unfortunately, you can never know. Fate will never allow it.

Not again.

Vivinna

Chapter One

St. Louis, Missouri

Contrary to its elaborate name, The Golden Crown was nothing special in appearance. It was decent enough, with its green wooden exterior and tin roof catching the soft glow of the moon, which was partially hidden behind snow clouds. The two-story building had the sort of welcoming air meant to attract the local demons.

However, the Irish-inspired pub was at the bottom of the barrel compared to its competitors in the nearby city. The beverages were cheap and ofttimes flat, the food was bland and the layout was rather simple — a rustic bar with a handful of worn stools, metal tables clean yet unadorned and a small stage where amateurs belted out karaoke songs.

The pub catered to those who didn't care for the over-the-top glim and glam that most demon establishments had. It had been created for those who just wanted to get out of their lairs, caves or nests for a casual night out.

Whether it was fancy or modest, Siovon would much rather spend her nights curled in front of a fireplace to exercise her art skills or brew new potions to add to her collection of medicines. She wasn't an introvert, but as a rare demon whose ancestors had been wiped off the face of the earth centuries ago, making friends and enjoying a night out were next to impossible if she wasn't careful.

Tonight, however, she was on a mission, and until she completed it, her hobbies would have to wait.

It'd been ten years since she'd been separated from her beloved younger sister. Ever since she'd escaped Mikhail's clutches a few months before, she had been searching high and low for Calysta, a task that was proving to be far more difficult than she'd hoped.

Out of habit, she touched the golden hoop at the top of her right ear. One of five enchanted earrings, the cold metal didn't do a damn thing to improve the worry twisting in her gut.

At one point in time, she'd been able to touch the hoop to locate her sister — and vice versa. It connected them, so even if they were on opposite ends of the world, they'd always be able to find one another. Of course, like all magic, it needed to be refilled every few months to keep its effect. But since they hadn't seen each other in a decade, the magic was long gone, rendering the earring a useless piece of jewelry. So, she'd had to bust out her rusty tracking skills and search for Calysta the old-fashioned way.

After spending weeks with no results, Siovon had caught a break when an old friend had informed her of a rumor about a siren with a healing voice working at The Golden Crown. It was a long shot, but it had been her only lead, so she'd traveled from the coast of South Carolina all the way to the outskirts of St. Louis to investigate.

To add to her mounting annoyance, the rumor had turned out to be true, but Caly was long gone, right along with Keegan, who'd likely held her against her will. Siovon didn't believe for one second that Calysta would use her singing voice for something as simple as entertaining a crowd of greedy demons.

What was worse, Siovon had learned that some vampire leeches were trying to find her as well. Whether it was for her blood or to use her unique gift for their own heinous plots, as Mikhail had done to Siovon, the sooner she found Calysta, the quicker they could go back to living their lives under the radar from the wretched demon world.

Siovon had first ventured to the pub a few weeks prior, but she'd had to leave after being harassed by two huge vampires. She'd eluded them, but several days later she'd run into them again, and when she'd learned they were looking for Caly, she hadn't hesitated to kick their asses and send them on their way with a clear message—'*Back off.*' It wasn't until after they'd left the pub unguarded that she'd returned.

After a quick look around the imp Keegan's office to find any clues to their disappearances, she crept past the bouncer, who was dead-asleep in a rocking chair next to the door.

Siovon rolled her eyes. *Some guard.* She didn't even have to tiptoe. A parade of elephants could come tromping through and the schmuck would snore right through it. *Lazy-ass trolls. Always more brawn than brain.*

She returned to the bar downstairs, drawing her hood over her head. Then, sticking close to the shadows, she made a swift exit. She took out an ink pen and a folded piece of paper from her pants pocket and scratched *The Golden Crown* from the list. There was nothing in the imp's office to indicate where he or Calysta had vanished to, but she had a few addresses to places he frequented.

With any luck, she'd find the jackass, catch him off guard and do what was necessary to get some answers. If he didn't have Caly, he had to know something.

Shaking her head, she jogged across the snow-covered fields back toward the city. She willed her adrenaline to kick into gear to keep her warm against the cold December air. Not for the first time, she was thankful for her disciplined — some might say cruel — mercenary training growing up. She'd learned to tolerate hours and hours on end of strenuous exercise, including running long distances without losing breath. Her drills had been good for something, at least.

Siovon grimaced at the dark memories threatening to rise and she shook her head again. Now was not the time to reminisce about her less-than-cheery childhood. Besides, those days were behind her. She was a new person. She was a healer, dedicated to the sick and dying.

A pacifist.

She snorted at the absurd statement. Well, she was an *aspiring* pacifist. She'd been trying to channel her inner peace and not be so hasty in resorting to violence to resolve every issue. *I let those two vamps live, after all.*

Sure, she'd roughed them up a teensy-tiny bit, but she could have killed them if she'd wanted to. Hell, in another day and age, she *would* have killed them.

She was learning to focus on blue skies and sunshine. That kind of progress had to count for something.

When Siovon made it to the city a little while later, she kept to the alleys as she zigzagged her way to her hotel. Even in large cities filled with varying scents to wash away her own, she was wise enough to cover her tracks. It was second nature to be cautious. As much as her newly birthed pacifist soul wanted to be trusting and look for the best in people, like Calysta could, she wasn't stupid.

Still, having a vehicle to get around in would have made everything a hundred times simpler — and faster. *And warmer.* She made a mental note to find a local car rental service before nightfall.

Her hotel was an old building, but it was up-to-date with an air of cleanliness. That was a must for Siovon. She liked to keep a low profile, but that didn't mean she had to slum about in rinky-dink motels to keep her privacy. *A lady has needs, after all.*

She took the stairs two at a time until she got to the fourth floor. It was her preferred method. When it came to choosing between a cement stairwell with a sturdy structure or a metal cage waiting to get stuck in a shaft, it was a no-brainer.

Polite pass on elevators, thank you very much.

Exiting the stairwell, she pulled out a keycard when a sudden chill filled the air, making her hair stand on end. The humans inhabiting the hotel would assume the dramatic drop in temperature was a result of the snowy weather outside and resort to cranking up their individual heating units.

Siovon, however, knew the source was something far more alarming than the threat of catching a cold.

There was a damned vampire approaching — and a powerful one, at that.

Cursing under her breath, she unlocked the door to her room and ducked inside, bolting the locks. *Yeah, as if that will keep out a bloodsucker,* she thought. They had the uncanny ability to get past any obstacle that wasn't made of pure silver.

Of course, there was no guarantee that the particular vamp was after her. It was possible he had his own room, was meeting someone or was up to any number of things.

Possible, but not freaking likely.

After her run-in with the other leeches, it wouldn't surprise her if they'd sent someone to avenge them. Or perhaps it was Mikhail looking to continue where he'd left off.

Either way, the vamp was far too close for comfort. She'd already escaped one maniac.

It was a good thing she was quick on her feet. If one plan failed, it would take only moments for her to develop another.

As the ice prickles from the vamp's power danced along her skin, she grabbed her prepacked bag and darted for the window. She'd just pushed the glass open when the leech worked his powers to unlock her door.

A handy skill, no doubt, but Siovon had no interest in staying to admire his efforts.

She stood on the window's ledge, gritting her teeth against the cold. *Christ...* She didn't know which was worse—Missouri's winter air whipping at her face or Frosty the Vampire's powers creeping over her skin.

Her window faced an apartment building with a fire escape seven feet away, and below her was a dark alley with a solid forty-foot drop. A human would have been screwed.

Fortunately, she was a siren, which meant the demon blood in her veins provided a substantial amount of strength and speed.

She bent her knees and, with a strong spring of muscles, leaped across the distance and grabbed hold of the rickety fire escape, her light weight giving it only the slightest of creaks in protest. She pulled herself over the railing and planted her feet on the rusty landing.

Siovon shivered as she pulled off the jacket that had kept her warm for the past few days. With nothing more than a tank top covering her torso, she fought to keep her teeth from chattering. Hell, she'd endured worse. She'd once had to survive stark naked for a week outside in the snowy mountains in Siberia as part of her training. She'd endured great levels of frostbite and hypothermia before her natural demon healing could kick in gear, but she'd made it.

This Missouri weather? Easy-peasy.

Stiffening her spine, she tucked her bag inside the jacket and dropped it to the ground. Assuming her plan worked, the stalker would follow her scent.

She dashed up the crisscrossing stairs to the roof. Once there, she ducked behind the brick ledge and peeked over just in time to see a large figure peering outside her room window.

She twisted her lips in grim amusement as the schmuck looked around in confusion, trying to determine which way she'd disappeared to.

* * * *

As Lucian entered the hotel room, he had to swallow a groan as the overwhelming scent of sweet cherry blossoms hit him. He'd been tracking the fairy ever since coming to St. Louis a week before, and with every passing day, her scent was growing on him more.

His sole mission was to locate a mythical siren whose singing voice could heal anything. It was the most ridiculous, insulting use of his skills.

The job was a tedious matter better suited for the Guard, the uber-elite group of vampires who acted as the Secret Service for Cyrus, the king of all vampires, except they were bigger, meaner and far more intimidating. There was nothing in the world or the depths of hell that would halt them from protecting Cyrus or carrying out whatever obscure missions he sent them on.

So why was he—the first in line to the throne and a powerful clan chief of Chicago—the one performing the menial task of searching for a woman who may or may not exist instead of the almighty Guard?

The answer was simple. Annoying, but simple.

The fey woman had gotten the upper hand on Lynx and Caesar. Not only had she been able to disarm and rough up a couple of the most lethal vampires around, she'd done so *and* eluded them. Twice.

It was pathetic.

Thus, instead of sending others with nothing better to do with themselves—that is, any one of his five brothers—*he* was the lucky one. *Yay.*

His objective had been to track down the source of the rumor and determine if it was true. If it were false, he'd return to his territory and continue with his life. If it were true, he'd been ordered to find the woman and somehow convince her to travel with him to Chicago to heal his youngest brother from a lethal disease.

It was so simple that it should have taken a few days...tops.

Unfortunately, things could never be that easy. All he'd gathered were the same few rumors of the siren who'd disappeared, along with the owner of the establishment. To his dismay, so long as he had no solid proof the woman wasn't real, he'd have to stay.

Lucian then turned to tracking down the missing imp, charming lesser demons to spill what they knew about the man. He'd just finished his interrogation when he'd run across the most tantalizing scent he'd ever smelled. He'd latched onto it and followed the creature all throughout the city until he'd caught up to her at the hotel.

When Lynx, the leader of the Guard, had described the woman who'd attacked him, all he'd remembered was a specific scent and her height. The woman had concealed her identity, but both men stated she'd been short. Lucian knew it was embarrassing as hell for them to admit they'd been bested by a little fairy, but if either of them had been distracted by the woman's sweet scent like Lucian, he couldn't very well say he blamed them.

However, he wouldn't allow some woman to get the upper hand if it came down to a fight. He'd faced women who were as beautiful as they were deadly, and none of them had ever sidetracked him from his purpose. Tonight would be no different.

Except, in a way, it already was. He had strict orders not to approach the woman without provocation, but Lucian had convinced himself that it was necessary. After all, she *could* be a siren, just not the one he was looking for.

Not to mention she could very well have been Mikhail's ally. Her scent was similar to the blood they'd found in the Apennine Mountains after their fight with him several weeks before. They'd hypothesized that Mikhail had used siren blood to create a band of Rogues to control, though they had no solid proof, just a bunch of 'maybes' and 'what-ifs'. If the woman he was following was a siren who was tied to Mikhail, she would need to be brought in to be held accountable for her actions.

Cyrus wanted to admonish anyone who'd been a part of Mikhail's schemes.

As Lucian strolled down the narrow corridor, common sense told him to turn his ass around and not waste any more time. Another part of him argued that the woman reappearing couldn't be a coincidence. She had to have some information, and the sooner he figured out her role in everything, the sooner he could be done with this ludicrous ordeal and return to his lair.

In truth, it was the curious part of him that sought out the fairy. Her scent was intoxicating. He was damn near two thousand years old, so he'd come across more than his fair share of demons of all shapes and sizes. He could differentiate the blood of a wood sprite and a dew fairy from a mile away, and the two were almost impossible to tell apart.

All fey tended to have a sweet fragrance with a hint of something outdoorsy. But hers was far more potent than a normal fairy's. There was an underlying sense of power in her scent that tugged at his more primal instincts.

Plus, he wanted to see what kind of woman could defeat a couple of vampires well over six feet tall. She had to be some sort of Amazon warrior with god-like strength. Sure, Lynx and Caesar had said the woman was tiny, but they'd also said she moved fast, so they could be mistaken.

Yes, that's it, Lucian thought with confidence. *They only thought she was small, but in truth, she's built like a Roman gladiator.*

When Lucian heard a soft *thump*, he rushed to the window.

He frowned in disbelief at the darkness below. Not even his night vision could pierce the thick shadows, but he smelled the woman down there. If she was a swift healer like most demons, the fall wouldn't have killed her, but it would likely have broken a bone.

Amazon, he thought again. *She's an Amazon.*

He was convinced, and a lick of excitement flared within him — not just at the woman's delicious scent but also at the idea that she would prove to be a challenge to him.

And, by the gods, it'd been so long since he'd had a good rumble.

His title was boring, more often than not. He no longer felt the need to expand his territory. He'd created an air of peace and wealth in his domain, a place where his vampire brethren could escape the small clan wars that still broke out from time to time.

So he looked forward to seeing what the fairy was capable of.

Not that he truly believed she was a fairy, but until he discovered the truth, the name would stick.

In a smooth manner that not many creatures could match, he leaped and landed in a crouch. The snow crunched under his shitkickers as he ambled to where the woman's scent was strongest.

Far too late, however, he realized he'd been outwitted. He glared at the backpack wrapped inside a jacket. There was no other scent telling him she'd taken off down the alley, nor were there any footsteps in the snow, which meant she'd never jumped in the first place. He took a step back, unable to believe her cunning.

Lucian glanced up in time to see a pale limb push from the rooftop high above him. Curling his lip in annoyance, he caught the fire escape and hauled ass up the old railing.

With his blinding speed, it took all of ten seconds to reach the top. He cursed his ignorance, but he couldn't help the tiny smile playing at his lips. He'd already known the woman was intelligent from the clever way she'd backtracked throughout the city to cover her tracks, but to pull off such a move—on him, no less—was rather impressive.

Too bad for her it only made him more eager to face her. And once a vampire was on the hunt, there wasn't a force in hell that could stop him.

Once at the top, Lucian scanned the surrounding buildings and concentrated on her sweet scent. He dashed through the snow, leaping over two more rooftops before coming to a stop.

Blood tainted the air—not enough to cause alarm, but enough to make him wary—especially when the very scent made his fangs lengthen and his gut clench with hunger.

He followed the trail of small footsteps. He narrowed his eyes as he neared a large vent, spotting a corner of the cold metal stained with fresh blood. He drew a dagger from his boot and rounded the corner, pausing when he saw a woman lying face down in the blanket of snow.

For just a moment, he eyed the curve of her lower back expanding into a rounded ass defined by tight black jeans. He shook his head and used the toe of his boot to roll the woman over onto her back.

For all that is holy…

Lucian went hard as a rock. Her barely-there shirt outlined a tight, flat stomach and full breasts that could fill his hands. Judging by the straps on her shoulders, she was wearing a black sports bra, yet even through the fabric, the cold temperature had her nipples in tight peaks.

His fangs throbbed as he trailed his gaze up the slim column of her throat to a serene face. Smooth, ivory skin stretched over high cheekbones, a dainty little nose and the delicate line of her jaw. Her bow-shaped lips were pink and damp, and her lashes lay motionless over blushed cheeks. Short dark hair peeked from under the black beanie she wore, and swooping bangs lay across her eyebrows. There was a small stain of blood from a gash on her temple.

He snorted. The daft fairy must have tripped and hit her head in her haste to escape him. Such clumsiness made it far too easy for him.

Then again, nothing about her thus far had indicated she was anything short of intelligent.

He eyed the tattoos covering her arms. On one inner forearm was a short sword crossed over a jagged dagger, both with worn hilts.

The shimmering tattoo on the other arm was far more elaborate. It was a black serpentine dragon with iridescent golden scales, two bat-like wings tucked close to its body, four short legs baring sharp talons and sea-green reptilian eyes that seemed to be glaring at Lucian. Its tail curled around her index finger while the rest of its body wrapped around her arm from wrist to elbow. Its head was nestled on her inner biceps.

For several moments, Lucian was stunned. He'd never seen a tattoo so...lifelike. It was as if he could stroke the creature and feel its scales rising from her skin.

As for the rest of the woman, she was exquisite — tiny and delicate with soft curves made to be kissed and caressed. She didn't seem capable of taking down a man twice her size.

With a frown, Lucian scanned the rooftops again. It had to be a trick, some kind of sorcery to fool him into lowering his guard. The Amazon he'd chased was no doubt lurking in the shadows, and somehow she'd used magic to create an illusion of the woman lying on the ground.

It was that thought that had him bringing his dagger up, coiling his body in preparation for an attack. He'd fallen for the wench's trap once. He wouldn't do it again.

On the verge of sending his power out to freeze anything in the shadows, he didn't notice the sudden shift in the air, not until a kick strong enough to crack his ribs caught him in the middle of his back. He sucked in a sharp breath and whipped around in time for the pint-sized female to deck him in the jaw.

For such a tiny thing, the blow hurt like a bitch. He tasted his own blood. Surprised and annoyed, he caught one flying fist in his hand, then her leg in his other when she attempted a kick. It took more strength than he would have liked to admit to detain her. She was strong as hell. And fast.

Just as Lynx and Caesar had described.

With her balanced on one leg, he smirked down at her face hidden in his shadow.

She sneered in return. Before he could guess her intention, she jumped and wrapped her free leg around his waist, using her weight to bring him down on top of her. Stunned, he allowed her to roll him onto his back. She straddled his chest with her knees pressing into his forearms to hold him in place.

Lucian stared with a mix of surprise, frustration and...lust—a hot, unexpected wave of lust.

Hard violet eyes with a small upward slant flashed down at him in triumph. It was the cold tip of a dagger at his throat that had him snapping out of his stupor.

"Why are you following me?" she growled, sounding sexy rather than frightening.

"The answer is pretty obvious," he drawled.

She narrowed her beautiful eyes. "I've done nothing to warrant the attention of leeches."

A bitter scent filled his nose. For her to outwit him twice, she was far too intelligent not to know vampires had the greatest senses in the demon world. They were masters at studying the body language of their prey. Most of them, including Lucian, could even *smell* when they were lying.

He lifted an eyebrow. "You attacked two of my men."

Her eyes widened in disbelief. "Are you kidding me? Those two brutes attacked me first. Am I not allowed the right to defend myself?"

She was telling the truth. Well, not that they'd attacked her. From what Lynx had reported, he and Caesar had tried to speak with her, but she'd grown defensive. Even Lucian knew the men had such imposing presences that they appeared threatening, even if they weren't.

"Maybe so, but those two happen to be members of the Guard. For you to lay harm to them is to challenge the king's authority."

As predicted, she went still above him. Non-vampires weren't under Cyrus' command, but that didn't mean he was any less terrifying. Vampires were at the top of the demon hierarchy chain, and Cyrus sat on a golden throne at the very tip. Lesser creatures scurried away in fear, while greater ones bowed at his feet.

And though he chose to live his life instilling peace among his people, he was still every bit the powerful Etruscan warrior he'd been millennia ago.

The woman above him swallowed hard, and Lucian found his eyes glued to her throat. His fangs throbbed with the desire to see if her blood tasted as sweet as she smelled.

She made a sound of disgust. "I barely even touched them. There's no way they were harmed."

Lucian fixed her with a disbelieving stare. By the time he'd met up with Lynx, the great warrior had already healed, but he'd been nursing a broken nose, a bruised jaw and a few broken ribs. Meanwhile, Caesar was recovering from a dislocated shoulder and a dagger protruding from his foot. After several bags of blood, they were healed within the hour, but there was no repairing their wounded pride.

He could see now why they had been so embarrassed to admit what had happened. The woman was half their size, but she packed one hell of a punch. Gods, his own cracked ribs and jaw repairing themselves from her assault still ached.

He should be furious that she'd dared to attack him. He had a reputation for being a cold-hearted bastard, a lethal foe only those with a death wish were foolish enough to take on. He was a man who preferred action to diplomacy, and he'd kill anyone who ever tried to disrupt the peace of his clan or family.

Point. Blank. Period.

However, as he lay on a bed of ice with an angry waif of a woman perched on his chest, he was far from pissed.

His body heated as his lust stirred, and, above all, he felt a great amount of amusement.

And it had been many, many years since he'd felt anything other than pure boredom or disdain.

How peculiar.

Chapter Two

If Siovon didn't know any better, she would swear the male was laughing at her. Not aloud, of course.

That chiseled face bore a callous mask that seemed to fit him. He didn't look like a man who smiled often or showed any emotions. However, within the depths of his steel-like eyes, she was almost certain they were flashing with amusement—which only pissed her off.

What the heck is so funny? With just a flick of the wrist, she could slice his throat open. It wouldn't kill him, but it'd hurt like hell. Plus, it would give her just enough time to escape and cover her tracks.

So why am I hesitating?

For one, the bloodsucker wasn't an ordinary vampire. As skilled as she was at fighting, she wasn't invincible. If he wanted to, he could squeeze the life out of her or drain her dry in less than a minute. His power alone told her he was of importance, rather than a stray.

For two, she wished she could claim it was due to her newfound pacifism that she refused to kill him—or the sheer knowledge that, if she did, she'd suffer the wrath of his fellow vampires. Leeches were solitary creatures, but if one member of their clan was killed, there would be hell to pay.

No, her hesitation had everything to do with the fact that the man was freaking gorgeous.

Christ. Everyone knew vampires possessed enough beauty to make angels weep in envy. And they weren't above using their looks to seduce their prey.

Frosty, however, had her heart stuttering as if she were a teenage girl with her first crush. If his accent hadn't given it away, she could look at him and tell he was of Italian descent, with his black hair tied at his nape, smooth tan skin and proud Roman features. Well, his accent was more like a strange mix of Old English and Italian. Latin, if she could recall.

Given that it was impossible to determine how old a vampire was, she guessed he had been around before the common romance languages had been created.

His eyes were pale like the moon and just as mysterious, threatening to pull her in with no hope of ever escaping. His lower lip was full, making her want to draw it between her teeth and suck on the soft flesh.

Whoa, where did that come from? she thought with dismay.

His lips twitched with amusement.

She gritted her teeth and tightened her hold on the blade she'd conjured. Beautiful or not, she wasn't about to forget that this cretin had followed her for God knew how long then to her hotel room.

"Did you track me down to avenge your leech buddies?" she demanded.

That mocking little smirk remained in place. "You sound rather concerned. Are you afraid, *fatina*?"

"Of a pack of bloodsucking parasites? Hilarious."

His nostrils flared again, as if scenting whether or not she was lying. Another handy trick, no doubt, but it was a nuisance to her. Her words were only half-true. She wasn't afraid of death, but she'd be damned if she wouldn't see her sister safe and sound first.

"Then you *are* afraid of me," he said in assurance.

She scoffed. She knew she should hurry to incapacitate him in order to escape. Idle chitchat could get someone killed. Even knowing that, she couldn't resist her taunting words. "Don't flatter yourself. It seems you're the one who should be afraid. From my vantage point, I have the upper — "

The words never got the chance to leave Siovon's lips. In the blink of an eye, she was on her back, her dagger flying somewhere across the roof. He wrapped his arms around her, shielding her back from the snow while pinning her own arms in place.

His face was a few inches from hers, while the rest of him pressed against her in the most intimate of ways. Her body seemed impervious to the cold as a white-hot cloud of lust exploded inside her.

Holy hell. Frosty was her enemy. She didn't know him, and he no doubt had some godforsaken plan to use her against her will. It went against everything she believed to accept her body's treacherous response to him.

"You were saying?"

"Get off," she bit out, annoyed that she was powerless to do anything. *Jeez, with all those solid muscles, the man weighs a ton.* Her hand was still sore from punching his jaw.

One corner of his lips turned up as he peered down at her with such a hungry look that she didn't know whether to be excited or terrified.

"Only if you'll get off with me, sweetness," he murmured, flashing perfect teeth that were as white as the snow around them, along with a pair of long, razor-sharp fangs.

No one deserves to be that beautiful.

Catching on to the sexual innuendo, heat rose to her cheeks. "Never," she breathed, wriggling against him in a failed attempt to get free.

He dipped his head and she froze in horror, expecting to feel the pain of his fangs ripping out her throat, so she was unprepared for the cool press of his sinful lips touching a tender spot below her ear.

Siovon stifled a moan as a shudder wracked her body, causing her to ache for a man she hadn't known for five minutes. It was embarrassing.

"Don't you know to never say never?" he whispered. He trailed his fangs down the length of her neck before kissing a scorching path to her collarbone.

Siovon squeezed her eyes shut to fight her body's response to him. She counted to fifty. When that didn't work, she tried to focus on the snow beneath her, willing it to cool her body, anything at all to not focus on the heat pooling in the pit of her stomach. "Do you often go around kissing women against their will?"

"Hmm. Only if they smell this delicious," he murmured against her skin. "So sweet."

"You smell like ass," she ground out with far less conviction than she'd like.

He chuckled. "I can smell your every lie. I can hear the mad beat of your heart. I can almost taste the sweet scent of your arousal." As if to prove his point, he caught her earlobe between his teeth and drew it into the warm cavern of his mouth. The combined feeling of his hot breath and wet tongue in a place she never knew was so sensitive made her give a small cry of pleasure.

"Please," she whimpered, tilting her head to the side. "I..."

Hell if she knew what she was going to say. With every passing second, Frosty drilled a frantic need in her that had lay dormant for years. She didn't know whether she wanted to pull him closer and beg him to ease the sweet ache or push him away and kick his ass for causing it.

His erection strained against his leather pants as he nuzzled the curve of her neck. She wanted to spread her legs to allow him to settle between them.

"I wonder if the rumors are true," he murmured.

"Rumors?" she breathed.

He licked over the vein throbbing in her neck. "The blood of a siren is far richer than that of any other fey."

As if an imaginary vacuum had been turned on, the lust-filled fog clouding her mind vanished. She stiffened at his words. Sensing her immediate withdrawal, Frosty pulled back to peer at her with eyes that had darkened to a smoky gray, revealing he'd been just as aroused.

When he saw her horrified expression, he frowned. "What is it?"

"I'm not a siren," she said, forcing strength into her voice.

It was useless, of course. His eyes widened a fraction, his nostrils flaring at the lie. *Shit, shit, shit*, she thought, trying not to panic. *This is not good. This is so not good.*

Siovon and Calysta were the last remaining sirens that she knew of. Many, many centuries before, sirens had been like the precious gems of the demon world. They'd been the most sought-after of creatures, because of their unique powers and ability to create potent medicines and poisons from a mix of their blood and the earth. When the demand for them grew on the underworld black market, their people had been kidnapped and wiped to the brink of extinction.

Siovon had never met another siren outside her family. It was why she, Caly and their mother had remained under the radar for decades, forced to hide their blood so they could travel around without ever being caught.

That is, until Mikhail Nilsen ruined everything.

Now her mother was dead, while she and Calysta were exposed to every demon, human, alien and whatever else was out there that wanted to get their hands on them. Through their fey magic, the earrings were meant to last for several months until they needed a refill, so they could stay in communication. However, both of theirs had long worn off—at least, Siovon's had—making them both sitting ducks.

Calysta more so. She hadn't endured Siovon's combat training. Siovon had always been the one to protect her.

Siovon shook away the negative thoughts. Frosty was scrutinizing her as if she were a bug underneath a microscope. "Get off me," she commanded, resuming her wriggling to get a leg free. Even with his size and strength, she'd learned that a well-placed kick to the groin could bring even the most powerful of men to his knees.

He released a small hiss when she rubbed against his erection. "Woman, unless you want me to take you right here, right now, I suggest you cease with the movements."

Siovon sucked in a sharp breath at his words, pissed at the way her body threatened to melt against him at the mere image of him doing just that. *Christ, I need to get laid.* Clearly she was long past due, if she was desperate enough to allow a bloodsucker to get her hot and bothered.

Forcing the heated thoughts away, she freed one of her legs. She brought her boot's heel down on the back of his calf. Hard. He choked out a curse, and before she could do it again, he stood, bringing her with him.

"What—?"

"As much as I wouldn't mind continuing this game, I have things to do," he cut in, his expression smoothing over to one of pure frost. Siovon blinked, wondering how the hell he'd pulled that kind of trick. It was like someone had just flipped a switch from a sexy and teasing lover to a menacing block of ice.

"As do I," she muttered, stepping away from him. She made a dismissive gesture with her hands. "So, while you run along and do whatever it is you leeches do, I'll be on my way. Send your little buddies my condolences." *As if.* She couldn't give two shits if the bloodsuckers had been hurt or not. She hadn't killed them, so her pacifism was still intact.

With a mocking half-bow, she had every intention of turning away and returning to her very warm, very cozy hotel room. But of course, it couldn't be that easy.

Frosty blocked her path with that annoying vampire speed. When demons moved that fast, she could at least catch their shadow or sense the shift in the air or *something*. But Frosty was just...there. One moment he was behind her. The next, he was standing in front of her, his hands on his hips while he looked down his elegant nose at her.

"You and I aren't finished."

Siovon took another step back. "I already apologized for fighting those two knuckleheads. It won't happen again, so long as they stay the hell away from me. Satisfied?"

He raked his gaze down her body in slow appreciation. "I'm far from satisfied, *fatina*. But, for now, I only need answers."

She crossed her arms to hide the hardened peaks of her nipples. It wasn't because of the searing heat of his gaze sending tingles of excitement through her. It was because of the cold air. *That's all, dammit.*

Siovon made a rude sound, shifting her weight to one leg. "I don't know anything, and I didn't see anything. Can't help you."

"I doubt that. You may look innocent enough, but there's an acute intelligence in your eyes that tells me you know far more than you're willing to admit."

Siovon kept her expression guarded. He was far too perceptive for his own good. She didn't want anyone poking and prodding at her. That was *her* job.

"I'm just passing through."

"Again, I doubt that. Sirens died out ages ago, yet not one, but two so happen to appear in the same city — at the same pub. That's far too much to be a mere coincidence."

Siovon stiffened, her blood running cold. *He knows about Calysta being here as well? Is he looking for her too?*

She'd known the other two Guards had been searching for Calysta, but she hadn't bothered to get more information from them. She would kill them all before allowing any of those bastards to use her sister as they had her. *Pacifism be damned.*

Despite her pissy attitude, she made sure to match Frosty's air of indifference. Vampires read body language with ease. She had to be careful. She studied her nails. "I wouldn't know. I'd heard whispers of one siren being here, and like many others, I went to see whether or not it was true. I haven't heard anything about there being a second one."

His nostrils flared. It wasn't a lie, but it wasn't the full truth either. She hadn't heard anyone talk about a second siren. So long as she kept up with these half-truths, she might get away without revealing too much information.

"You seem dead-set on trying to convince me you aren't a siren. Why?" It was a demand rather than a question, as if he expected her to answer without hesitation. *Fool.*

She lifted an eyebrow. "You seem dead-set on trying to convince yourself I am. Why?"

He curled his lip in annoyance. He walked a slow circle around her. "You aren't an imp, fairy, sprite or nymph, yet you carry fey in your blood. However, it's more dynamic than the traditional scent. More...potent. That tells me you aren't a half-breed either."

She shrugged. "What does it matter what type of demon I am? I'm not a vampire, so it's none of your concern."

After making a complete loop, he stopped in front of her. His eyes were callous, no doubt trying to intimidate her into spilling her secrets.

Fat chance, that. Vamps weren't the only ones capable of being dark and mysterious, nor were they the first to try to use their mind games and oversized physiques to bully her. She might be pint-sized compared to him, but she was living proof that looks could be deceiving.

"It's interesting," he said, his voice laced with a bit of an edge. "A few weeks ago, a number of us flew to the Apennine Mountains in Tuscany to take down a traitor named Mikhail Nilsen. Sound familiar?"

Siovon kept still, but her heart gave a wild leap. She knew where this conversation was heading. She didn't bother to deny knowing of the insane Slavic vampire who'd tried to overthrow his king. Frosty would just smell the lie.

Instead, she lifted her hands in question. "I've heard the name."

"Indeed. You may have also heard that he believed he could create a new race of vampires and establish an empire through Rogues. He'd even manipulated a man we all trusted into betraying us. It is the king's command that anyone who was involved with Nilsen be brought to him directly—vampire or otherwise."

Siovon dropped her arms. "What has that to do with me?" she demanded, though her voice let out a guilty tremor. Trepidation crept over her skin.

He stepped close to her. His eyes were narrowed and dangerous, glittering in the moonlight to reveal the lethal predator lurking beneath the aloof beauty of his face. "In one cave, we found an iron-lined cell, and there were old blood stains. The scent was several weeks old by then, so we were unable to track it. However, two members of the Guard came across that very scent little over a week ago." He trailed a long, cold finger down her cheek. "That same delicious scent just so happens to be surrounding me as we speak."

Though Siovon's heart thundered in her chest, she was unable to breathe. The soft caress held an underlying threat that made her take a wary step back. She tried to wipe away the lingering feel of his touch. "Are you implying that the blood belongs to me?"

"No." He followed her steps, once again getting in her personal space. "I am stating it."

"I—"

She bit off her words and flinched, peering over her shoulder into the looming darkness. The familiar tingling in her veins told her magic was being used nearby. It was a sense all fey had. She would have been thankful for the distraction if not for the immediate prick of danger.

"What is it?" Frosty demanded.

"A portal was just opened nearby," she said, frowning. "Something's coming this way."

He paused for several moments, tilting his head back to test the air. "Rogues," he growled, procuring two wicked daggers that were long enough to slice off her head. He shot her an accusing glare. "Your doing?"

She crossed her arms. Why she felt the need to explain herself to him, she had no idea. "First off, Frosty, I can't use portals. Second, even if I could, you were watching me the entire time."

He grunted and stood in front of her as three forms removed themselves from the shadows, glaring at them with glowing red eyes. "We'll have to finish this conversation after our battle."

Our battle? Siovon let out a dry snort. Rogues were the lowest-ranked vampires, but they weren't any less lethal than the others. They were the insane ones who'd given in to their bloodlust, turning them into mindless, hunger-crazed animals. There was no talking with them, no bringing them back once they'd tipped over the edge.

Siovon had no doubt that the man before her was even more dangerous than the rabid beasts. It was evident in the freezing drop in temperature he'd caused.

Siovon procured another dagger from her boot. However, instead of moving to his side to fight, she inched toward the edge of the building.

Frosty caught her out of the corner of his eye. "Where the hell are you going?" he demanded.

One female leaped forward and Frosty released an icy blast of power, sending her flying backward.

Siovon flashed a taunting smile. "As we've established, I have my problems to tend to, the same as you."

He glared at her, dodging the next Rogue that attacked. "You're going to leave me fighting these bastards alone? What happened to that bravado you displayed moments ago?" He rammed his blade into the chest of the other Rogue.

"You seem more than capable of handling your own, my dear. Besides" — she drew an invisible X over her heart with the tip of her blade — "I'm a pacifist."

He choked out a sound of disbelief. "Pacifist my ass."

Her gaze dropped to the well-formed muscles flexing beneath his leather pants. *A nice ass indeed.*

She placed two fingers to her forehead in mocking salute. "Adios, amigo."

Frosty slashed his blade across one Rogue's neck, then kicked him into one of his comrades. He had just enough time to send another glare her way. "I'm Italian."

She waved that aside. "Then, *ciao.* I would say it's been nice meeting you, but I try not to lie often."

He scoffed and resumed fighting. "When I catch up to you again — and believe me, I will — you'd better pray I'm in a good mood."

Siovon shrugged and leaped over the edge. The building wasn't high, but she grabbed the nearest windowsill halfway down, stopping her descent mid-fall before dropping the rest of the way. There was no sense risking a broken limb that would prevent her escape.

She returned to the alley outside her hotel. She picked up her discarded duffel bag and donned her jacket, pausing for a second to savor the warmth of the soft fur lining the inside. Then she slung the bag over her shoulder. She gazed up at her open hotel room window, pouting. She wanted nothing more than to take a hot shower and curl up in the bed to catch a few hours of sleep before continuing her search. She cursed Frosty for interfering. Now her precious bath would have to wait even longer.

With a sigh of resignation, she took off running.

She felt a tiny flare of guilt at leaving the silver-eyed hunk to defend himself, but she squashed it right away. He'd said he would take her to Cyrus if she was somehow tied to Mikhail, and since she'd played a pretty vital role in his plan, Frosty wouldn't hesitate to throw her over his shoulder and deliver on his threat. He couldn't be trusted.

Siovon didn't care what happened to him. He would kill those Rogues and come after her. And from the look of his skills, his fight would be over soon.

She only hoped she could get far enough away from him before then.

Chapter Three

Illinois

Slinking through the shadows of a long-forgotten neighborhood wasn't Salvator Gordano's idea of a good time. He'd much rather be back at The Lotus, the latest nightclub he'd opened little over a week ago. It was already the talk of the demon world. All his clubs were known to be exotic, luxurious and, some might say, downright promiscuous. The Lotus wasn't much different.

He should be in his office reveling in yet another successful night. His celebration would include a bottle of his most expensive Scotch and a beautiful woman — or two or three — all lying naked and ready for an night of endless pleasure.

But no. He was instead forced to put aside his personal needs to join two of his brothers in a ridiculous quest for his sister.

Well, guilt-tripped was more accurate. Ava had pulled the waterworks on him. And, as ever the woman-pleasing gentleman, he'd agreed to lead Cassander and Marc to an isolated location some fifty miles south of Chicago where wolopus demons resided. They were ugly creatures with tentacle-like arms and legs. During the winter, they spent more time in a giant mating ball than anything else, leaving the rest of their lands unguarded.

Even so, no one was stupid enough to venture into their territory. The creatures were harmless but territorial. When spooked, they shot out a dark inky substance that aided in their reproduction. Simply put, it was their species' version of sperm. *Who the hell wants to walk around with that shit on them?* It wasn't harmful, but it was disgusting and slimy and fucking horrendous.

With a shudder of revulsion, Sal led his brothers past an old farmhouse. *All this creeping around for a damn jar of berries,* he thought. *Freaking berries.*

The wolopus were frugivores. To be specific, they only ate woloberries, a demon fruit that was native to the wolopus territory. It was sweeter than a plump grape and said to hold tremendous prenatal and reproductive benefits for every species.

Of course, being three months pregnant, Ava had demanded them. It was thanks to his idiot brothers, Julius and Darius, that she'd known about the berries to begin with. They'd told her all about the precious fruit before disappearing, claiming to have business meetings elsewhere. However, Sal knew damn well that those two had planted the thoughts in her head and run away before being stuck with the duty of fetching the berries.

Marc, eager to please his new mate, had offered to do it. However, he didn't know where to go, and being a new were-cougar, there was no telling what kind of trouble he might happen across. Someone needed to keep a close eye on him, and, of course, none of them wanted Ava to risk herself or her unborn child. For that reason, Cassander had decided to go—but only if Sal came along.

As expected of anyone with a sane mindset, Sal had declined without hesitation. He had no interest in sneaking around a crumbling neighborhood belonging to hideous, sperm-shooting demons. However, his conniving sister had made herself cry, weakening his resolve.

She'd done the same thing as a teenager, whenever she'd wanted something but was told no. She'd learned that tears made all her brothers rush to please her. It seemed to be a skill of hers that still affected them decades later.

And so there was Sal in some godforsaken land in the name of siblinghood. Him. A powerful Royal vampire with a reputation for being as sensual as he was lethal, brought to his knees at the mere sight of his little sister shedding a few false tears. It was pathetic with a capital P.

Damn the gods.

His one saving grace was that if he got her the freaking berries, she'd be indebted to him. It wasn't the fairest of deals for him, but he'd take it. After all, her unique gift to see and alter the memories of anyone she touched might come in handy one day. No matter who it was or for what purpose, she could not refuse his request.

With an annoyed shake of his head, he quickened his pace, knowing his brothers would keep up. He followed the sweet scent of the berries. Then, turning the corner of another decaying farmhouse, they came to a large field of bushes.

He took in the surroundings, grimacing in horror at the ten-foot-high ball of writhing bodies of at least twenty wolopuses. It was a thing of nightmares, like a snake mating ball, only bigger and slimier with a mix of humanoid bodies and wriggling tentacles.

He glanced at Marc, who shared his look of revulsion. Cass' expression was as guarded as ever, but Sal could tell by his clenched muscles that his elder brother was disgusted.

"What the fuck?" Marc breathed, keeping his voice low on the off-chance that the giant orgy ball several yards away would hear him.

"This is what happens when you're pussy-whipped," Sal growled, folding his arms. "We warned you about this exact scenario. But did you listen? Hell no."

Marc bared his teeth at Sal. "She's my mate. If it makes her happy, I'll do anything." He shook his arms out and cracked his neck from side to side.

Sal gave a slow, sad shake of his head. He respected the male's determination and eagerness to please Ava, but if doing stupid shit like this was what it meant to have a truemate, then Sal would pass.

He remembered the agony Cyrus and Cass had gone through after losing their truemates. He never wanted to go through that shit. Besides, he was comfortable with his life as a bachelor. At least he didn't have to live with the pain and worry over losing a mate or acting like a love-struck adolescent.

No, having casual lovers was more his speed. It was a reputation he'd gained over the centuries, and he had not a single regret.

"Leave him alone, Sal," Cass commanded. His voice was meant to be soft, but given his large size and gruff nature, it had come out like gravel.

Sal shrugged and leaned against the wall. "There you have it, Marc. Try to keep out of sight while you get the berries. And if one spots you, run like hell toward the front gate."

Marc shot him a look of surprise. "You're not going to help?"

Sal lifted a disbelieving eyebrow. "Absolutely not. I agreed to come along. Not once did I say I would participate in the actual berry-picking, like a little girl."

Cass shook his head while pulling out two twelve-ounce plastic jars from the bag slung over his broad shoulder. "I'll go."

Marc nodded in relief. Sal didn't blame his wariness.

Having already been informed of the nature of the wolopuses and their disgusting means of defense, Marc crouched low to the ground, one jar in hand. He moved with a smooth, effortless prowl. Although he'd transitioned from human to shifter a few months before, Sal admired the male's quick adaptation to demon life. Cass also moved in silence, doing his best to stay low.

Sal snorted at the ridiculous sight. Out of all seven of the Gordano men, Cass was the largest in height and bulk. He was a barrel-chested, solid wall of muscle, yet somehow he always moved with a fluid grace that never failed to amaze Sal.

Then again, he was pretty much a walking shadow.

When a good thirty minutes had passed, Sal straightened when he sensed the two men returning.

"Can we leave now?" he demanded. After such a waste of his time, he was ready to crawl into bed and call over a couple of fey beauties who would be more than willing to spend a few hours beneath him...and on top of him...and beside him.

As the three men returned to their SUV, which was parked outside the gate of the small neighborhood, Sal imagined the feel of lips, fingers and silky hair from his soon-to-be lovers trailing over his body. He was so lost in his fantasy that he didn't notice his brothers had dashed to the side just as they reached the edge of town.

Not until Marc yelled, "Sal, look out!"

Shaking himself from his thoughts, Sal turned to see a seven-foot-tall wolopus raise one tentacle at him. It happened so fast that he didn't have time to move. The slimy ink caught him in the face and hair, sliding down his head to his expensive silk shirt.

Frozen in a mix of shock and horror, he watched the wolopus turn away and saunter off into the shadows, refusing to cross the line separating their territory from the rest of the world.

Long after the creature had disappeared, Sal continued to stare after it. Marc and Cassander approached him, crinkling their noses in disgust. Then, seeing Sal's expression, the two of them fell to the ground laughing.

Seconds turned into five minutes, then ten minutes. Yet, they continued to laugh, tears streaming from both their eyes. Sal opened his mouth to curse, but when the salty substance of the ink-sperm touched his tongue, he puked everything he'd ingested over the last several days.

Which was a grand amount of blood and alcohol.

That made his brothers laugh harder, and when Sal straightened, he shot them both glares that could freeze over the hottest layer of Hell.

"What the fuck is so funny?" he snarled, his muscles tight with the desire to tear them both to shreds.

"Dude," Marc gasped, clutching his side as he tried to control his laughter. "You…you're covered in…"

"You just got creamed," Cass finished. The two fell into another loud round of guffawing.

Sal wanted to leap across the distance and rip their throats out, but he twisted his face in disgust and retched up the rest of whatever was in his stomach.

Damn you, Ava, he growled in his mind. *You owe me big time!*

He just prayed he could convince these two baboons to keep their traps shut about the humiliating situation.

Gods, if the twins found out, he'd just have to kill himself. They would never, *ever* let him live it down.

* * * *

St. Louis, Missouri

After starving and sleeping very little over the previous few days, it was no surprise to Siovon that she'd overslept after escaping Frosty the Vampire. It was also no surprise that in her failure to take better care of herself, she hadn't noticed when said demon entered the old, musty barn she'd hidden in for the day—not until a pair of muscular arms wrapped around her, tucking her against a sturdy chest.

The scent of fresh pine filled her nose. She raised her eyelids, and for several confusing moments, she gazed up into his beautiful eyes. From the close proximity, she noticed he had small pupils and that his eyes were blue, but they were so pale that they appeared silver. It was mesmerizing.

His pupils expanded, darkening the irises to a smoky gray as hunger filled them. Her body heated in response, and it was that reaction that had her blinking away what she thought was a pleasant dream.

With a gasp, she slapped her hands against Frosty in an attempt to pull away. "You creep," she rasped, more annoyed with herself than his cuddling her. "What the hell do you think you're doing?"

Looking far more comfortable than he should, the beautiful leech gave a faint smile, tightening his arms and pressing her against the erection that was poking her thigh. "You looked cold, so I thought I'd offer you some warmth, *fatina*," he murmured, his eyes twinkling with mischief. "By the way, you sound like a hibernating bear when you sleep."

She drew her lips back in a snarl. "I bite like one too, asshole."

His smile broadened, revealing sharp, elongated fangs that could rip the bark off a tree. "I bite harder. Would you like to see?"

Her heart fluttered because, though it was a mere taunt, the offer was far more tempting than it should have been. "I'd like to see you with a stake shoved up your ass."

"So bloodthirsty for a pacifist."

She continued pushing against him, but she may as well have been trying to move one of the Easter Island stone heads. "Don't mock me."

He chuckled. "A pacifist who attacked me and my men. Forgive me if I find that a bit laughable."

She tilted her chin to a defiant angle. "We're allowed to defend ourselves when the time calls for it. Not even you leeches can be so arrogant as to think we lesser demons are supposed to fall at your feet."

"You attacked me first. I had no intention of harming you."

She rolled her eyes. "That's all your kind ever wants."

He stiffened as if she'd managed to offend him. As if. He was a vampire. They had enough pride to share with the entire galaxy. "Why do you think that?"

"Why do you think?" she gritted. With another surge of strength, she slapped her palms against his chest and pushed, her muscles straining.

She could push and push all night long and he wouldn't budge, not unless he wanted to. *Damn his rotten soul.* That is, if vampires even had souls.

That icy mask fell back into place, but he kept his arms locked around her. It was hard to be intimidated when he was holding her as if she were his lover and not a complete stranger who'd beaten up his men. "Let's finish our conversation from last night."

"Let's not and say we did," she retorted.

The sun was setting, its last rays peeking through the small cracks in the rotted wood and shining down on them. To her disappointment, he wasn't sizzling or bursting into flames.

"You are rather stubborn," he chided.

"I just don't like you."

His eyes glittered with humor while his face remained stony. "You don't have to like me, but your body doesn't seem to mind." As if to prove his point, he dragged one big hand down the curve of her back to her ass and squeezed.

Siovon sucked in a sharp breath, her temper going up a few notches at the fact that he was right. Stranger or not, her body wanted this man in the most primal of ways, and there wasn't a damn thing she could do to stop it. "Do you make it a habit of groping women against their will?"

"If it was against your will, you wouldn't be so aroused right now."

"It's because you're using that vampire mojo crap on me."

He cocked a raven brow. "Vampire mojo crap?"

She released an impatient sound. "You know what I mean. You people have been using your charm and looks to lure prey since the very beginning. As old as I'm sure you are, of course it'll have some effect on me."

His head shot back as if she'd slapped him. *Pity.* She wished she had. *Wait, dammit. Think pacifist thoughts. No violence, even if he deserves it.*

His forehead creased, and yep, he was offended. "Old? What makes you think I'm old?"

Siovon hid a smile, feeling like she'd touched a nerve. Of course, he looked no more than mid-to-late twenties, as all vampires did. However, it took centuries to gain the prickling power that surrounded him like a cloak. "Lucky guess."

He didn't look pleased with her answer, but she didn't care. He was the one following and harassing her. She had every right to act bitchy. "Listen, Frosty... I really do have important things to deal with. What is it going to take to get you to return to your coffin and leave me alone?"

"Frosty?" He pretended to consider for a few moments, giving her ass another squeeze. "What is it that you're offering?"

She had to hold her body stiff as a board to keep from rubbing against all that hardness. "What do you want?"

A slow, sexy smile curved his lips. "Oh, the possibilities are endless."

"Money?"

"I have my own considerable amount of wealth."

She didn't doubt that for even a moment. Something about him screamed that he was rich and privileged.

"Blood? Sex?" She shook her head. "Not gonna happen."

"Yet," he murmured, dipping his head to trail his lips across the pulse leaping in her throat. "I have questions."

"Then you'll let me go?"

"That depends on whether or not I'm satisfied with your answers."

She frowned. "That doesn't sound reassuring."

"It wasn't meant to be." He lifted his head to stab her with that intense gaze.

She huffed in annoyance. "At least let me up so we can chat like normal people. You being in my personal space is — "

"Distracting? Arousing? Tantalizing?"

"Revolting."

He chuckled again, shaking his head. "I have your word you will not attempt to fight me, run away or anything of the sort?"

She pursed her lips. "No."

"Then I'm afraid we will remain in this position, *fatina*." He rolled his hips into her, rubbing his hard-on against her belly. "Or we can try another position, if you prefer."

"Stop," she commanded, her cheeks burning. "You have my word I won't fight you or run away for the next hour."

He scoffed. "An hour?"

She shrugged. "It's all you get, Frostbite. Take it or leave it."

He studied her before giving a single nod. If he was smart, he'd figured it was the best he was going to get out of her. He kissed the tip of her nose and stood. She rose as well, albeit with far less grace. She brushed hay from her body before crossing her arms and meeting his flat stare.

She was sure she looked laughable, given that he was over a foot taller than she was, but she stood her ground. "Well? Let the interrogation begin."

His lips twitched, though there was more annoyance than amusement in the movement. He was a man who was used to getting his way and having everyone do his bidding—no questions, no hesitation, no refusal. The fact that she was pint-sized and didn't cower must rub his overinflated ego the wrong way. *Good.*

"Let's start with your name," he said. "And remember that I can smell any lie coming from you."

She rolled her eyes at the dramatic words. "Siovon."

"Shuh-vawn." He dragged her name out as if testing the way it sounded on his tongue. "Siovon."

"And you are? Or should I continue calling you Frosty?" Which she was going to do anyway. She wanted to annoy him.

He lifted his chin to an arrogant angle, his gaze turning prideful. "Lucian."

Siovon's mouth parted. Then, she clucked her tongue. "Of course it is," she muttered.

His brows snapped together. "I beg your pardon?"

"Don't you watch movies or read books? There's always some supernatural, badass bossy-pants whose name is Lucian, Lucius or Luc. It's so cliché."

Confusion shone in his eyes. "My mother chose my name," he grumbled, obviously offended. "I don't know what the hell you're talking about, but I'm almost certain it wasn't a compliment."

Siovon flashed another sickly-sweet smile, refusing to acknowledge his claim. "Next question."

His frown deepened. "What type of fey are you?"

Of course he'd ask that. "What do you think?" she demanded.

He dropped the temperature around them as if the air outside weren't cold enough. "*I'll* be asking the questions."

A muscle ticked in her jaw at the authority in his voice. She wasn't one of his mindless servants. Had she been anyone else, she would have been shrinking under the aloof gaze or the threatening stance he took, as if the moment she gave an answer he didn't approve of, he'd strike.

But she wasn't anyone else. She was Siovon, someone who'd sworn to never again be at the mercy of anyone, regardless of fangs, fur or claws. She had long ago gotten rid of her fear of demons more powerful than her. However, she couldn't spend every second hiding from Frosty.

"Siren," she snapped, glaring at him. "I'm a siren."

Chapter Four

Lucian had known the answer to his question before Siovon had answered. Her body language, her reaction to his mentioning it earlier, her scent that told him she wasn't an ordinary fey — everything had pointed to her being a siren. However, he had to be certain. He wanted her to admit it aloud, to see if she was lying.

She wasn't.

Frowning, he did his best to ignore his body's response to her. Gods, it'd been many years since he'd last reacted to a woman in such a way. Even in bed, he was a cold lover.

However, sometime in the last few days, Siovon's scent had clouded his brain, and when he'd caught sight of her in the wee hours of the morning, he'd been filled with lust. The need to have her near him, to have those lush curves pressed against his body, was as shocking as it was unwanted. She could be his enemy, yet all he could think about was having her enveloped in his arms with her heat draping his aching cock.

Oh, if his family could see him now, they'd poke all kinds of fun at him.

With an inner shake of disgust, he eyed her with his signature glare. He'd have to be sure not to let his demeanor fall. She was tiny, but she wasn't half as fragile as she looked. There wasn't even a twitch of muscle as she met him glare for glare. She possessed a startling amount of courage, and he couldn't decide whether to be annoyed or impressed. Very, very few were able to stand up to him in such a way. Even his siblings knew where the line was drawn.

Something told him there was far more to her skills than just managing to get by in her life. She couldn't be self-taught. The type of evasive maneuvers she'd performed to throw him off her trail had been executed with absolute precision.

He wanted to know more. She was intriguing.

"A real siren," he murmured at last. "Prove it."

She raised a single eyebrow, crossing her arms. Her breasts were hidden under the thick jacket she wore, but he remembered all too well how those creamy swells looked when she'd unintentionally pushed them up. "That isn't a question."

He inhaled a deep breath. She might be a delicious temptation, but the woman had an annoying habit of forgetting she was the inferior one. Hardening his tone, he asked the question that was pressing in his mind. "Was it your blood we scented back in the Apennines?"

She scowled, though it was hard to tell if it was because of his tone or his question. "How am I supposed to know what *you* smelled if *you're* the one who smelled it?"

Smart. Ass. "You know what I am referring to. Were you there all those weeks ago with Mikhail?"

She paused, and for several moments he could see her debating whether or not to answer. Then, she gave a curt nod. "Yes."

He knew it, but it still felt like a sucker-punch to the gut. "So you were in allegiance with the traitor."

Her eyes widened in surprise before turning angry. She spat on the ground as if the memory brought on a bitter taste. "In allegiance? No. Forced against my will into complying with that asshole until I could escape? Yes."

She was telling the truth. Not only could he sense it, but the amount of hatred in her voice couldn't be faked. Still, he wasn't ignorant enough not to know that he could on very microscopic occasions be wrong. "A likely story."

She bristled, clenching her fists on her arms as if to prevent herself from launching across the floor. He hid his amusement. She could claim to be a pacifist all she wanted, but there was no denying the dangerous fire flashing in her violet gaze. "I don't care if you believe me or not."

"You do not seem the type to be captured, nor are you easily found. So how is it that he managed to get his hands on you...and for what purpose?"

She tilted her chin down, her pride likely wounded. She was reluctant to answer, but too bad for her. He could be just as stubborn. He'd stand there for the next decade waiting for a response if he had to. He wasn't a very patient man, but when it came to getting what he wanted, he was as immovable as a mountain.

After several minutes, she blew out an exasperated breath, causing the silky strands of her bangs to flutter. "Has anyone ever told you how much of a nuisance you are?"

He suppressed a smile. "Never to my face."

"Well, allow me to be the first."

Lucian shook his head. He wondered if Siovon knew just how powerful he was. No one was foolish enough to speak to him the way she was. He supposed he was even more foolish for tolerating it. "Very few possess your insane courage."

Impervious to the insult, she rolled her eyes. "And so modest," she drawled.

He shrugged. It was the truth. What was the purpose of being so powerful if he couldn't brag on himself? "You failed to answer the question."

Her feisty expression returned. "Pass."

"This isn't *Family Feud*," he growled in warning. One moment he wanted to sink himself inside her, the next he wanted to throttle her for aggravating him. *Must every few seconds be a fight with her?* "Who is the other siren to you?"

She stiffened. "Who said she's anything to me?" Her voice held the slightest tremor that gave her away.

Interesting. "How do you know it is a female?"

Her ivory skin went a shade paler. "Rumors," she lied.

He stepped toward her, employing his size for intimidation. Not that he expected her to be afraid, but he wasn't above using exploitation to get the answers he needed. He was a vampire, after all. It was one of their means of survival, right along with utilizing their charm and seduction.

Lowering his voice to silken tones, he stroked a finger down the curve of her cheek. "I believe you know this siren very well." He took another step, so close that their clothes touched. He tried convincing himself it was all a part of the mix of seductive manipulation, but, in truth, he just wanted to be close to her. Her scent was far too tempting, her skin too silky to resist.

Tread carefully, a voice in his head warned.

Her troubled gaze didn't meet his. Instead, she focused on the leather pocket over his breastbone, which was eye-level for her. "What makes you think that?" she murmured.

"For one, two sirens in the same city when there have been no whispers of your kind for many centuries is far too much of a coincidence. Two, when you attacked my men, it seemed your defense had nothing to do with your own safety. It was more like you were trying to distract them. Like you were protecting something — or someone."

Siovon drew her lower lip between her teeth. Lucian slid his fingers to the vein pulsing in her throat. His fangs throbbed with the desire to take her sweet essence into his body. "You know who this siren is, don't you?" he continued. "A friend, perhaps. Or maybe a relative." Her pulse under his fingertips gave a wild leap. "Ahh, a relative. Your mother? Child? Sister?"

The beating beneath his fingers jumped again, giving him the answer he needed. He thought about the woman Ava had seen in Mikhail's memories, wondering if she was the one he'd been sent to find. Time to bring out the big guns. "Who is Lila to you?"

Of course, there was no telling if Siovon knew who he was talking about, but her reaction confirmed his suspicions.

The throbs of her pulse ceased beneath his fingertips. He had to strain his hearing until he heard the faint, barely-there beat of her heart.

When she met his gaze, the soul-deep sorrow in her eyes tugged at something inside him. For some reason, he regretted bringing out that grief.

He opened his mouth to apologize before stopping himself. *What the hell am I doing?*

He was a vampire who was renowned for his cold composure. He had never been the type to care about hurting someone's feelings or even something as frilly as comforting them.

With shaking fingers, Siovon wrapped her hand around his wrist where his fingers still touched her neck, and for just a moment, she looked as though she wanted to lean into him for support. Then, her expression hardened and she shoved his hand away. She dropped the appendage as if it were made of acid.

"The siren is my sister. What do you leeches want with her?" she demanded, her voice holding an edge that told him she wouldn't lower her guard again.

Lucian frowned. He didn't like the aching sadness she'd just shown him, nor did he like this tough side of her. Strange, given that under normal circumstances he couldn't give two shits. He straightened. "This is *my* interrogation."

Her lips curled in annoyance. "Your hour is nearly up."

"Nearly, but not yet. Will you not honor your word?"

She blew out a long, deep breath. The tension and frustration drained from her features, leaving behind a mask of indifference. "I always honor my word," she stated in a flat tone.

Still frowning, he gave a solemn nod. "How and why did Mikhail capture you in the first place?"

In the same tone that was beginning to grate on his nerves, she said, "It was the only way I could protect my sister. He would have killed her had I not complied."

"Why didn't he want both of you? Sirens are beyond rare. I would think having the only two alive would have him eager to detain you both."

A haunted look flashed in her eyes before disappearing. "All sirens possess different powers. My sister's didn't appeal to him."

Lucian grew suspicious. Somehow Mikhail had created dozens upon dozens of Rogues he was able to control. They knew he'd used the blood of a fey named Lila to create this 'new race', but according to Ava's vision, Mikhail had wanted to know where her daughter was. It was possible that the daughter in question was standing next to him.

Strange how he was reluctant to mention Lila again, though. He was a hardened asshole, yet seeing that dark look in Siovon's eyes made him want to kiss her sadness away.

He forced the thoughts from his mind. He needed answers and she had them. "Does your ability have anything to do with the Rogues he created?"

Siovon twisted her lips in distaste. "It has everything to do with those poor creatures." At his confusion, she sighed. She removed the black beanie and ran a frustrated hand through her pixie-cut hair. Metal glinted in the fading rays of sunlight, and for the first time, he noticed her ears were pointed and the right one held five small earrings with intricate fey symbols carved into them. That, mixed with the tattoos on her arms, added an edge to her delicate profile.

He liked his women soft and compliant, with less attitude and longer hair. Siovon was none of those things, yet she was far more exquisite than anyone he'd ever come across. He was...bewitched.

Siovon strolled over to a block of hay. Unable to help himself, Lucian licked his lips as he watched the frustrated twitch of her hips in her tight jeans before she flopped down. She glared at him, catching him red-handed. "Were you looking at my ass?"

"Absolutely," he said without a shred of guilt. It was a very nice ass.

She rolled her eyes in exasperation, but pink stained her cheeks. She might continue to deny her attraction to him, but her body wanted him with the same ferocity that he wanted hers. Perhaps if he got the answers he wanted, he could have a taste of her before returning to Chicago.

She flicked her bangs out of her eyes. "Before I tell you anything else, answer this. Why are you looking for my sister?"

Lucian went quiet, debating how much to reveal to her. Vampires were secretive, even among their own. To admit that Cyrus' youngest son lay sick and dying a slow death gave any number of their enemies a reason to exploit that weakness.

"My brother is ill," he explained in a cool tone that defied his inner feelings. The thought of Andreas dying presented a fear that refused to disappear. "When it was discovered that there was a siren whose voice had the power to cure all but death, we wanted to know if it was true. Originally, those two Guards were sent to investigate the rumors, but they were...thwarted."

She tilted her chin at the accusing tone, pride flashing in her eyes. Then, those beautiful gems narrowed. "If you'd determined the source to be true, what would you have done?"

Lucian shrugged. "We were to convince her to come with us without harming her." When she opened her mouth, he held up a hand. "We are vampires, but not all of us are monsters. However, I admit there is a level of desperation to heal my brother. I will shoulder any hate to do whatever is necessary if it means saving his life."

Siovon muttered something under her breath about not trusting leeches. No doubt she could very well figure out what 'whatever is necessary' meant.

Instead of blowing up and threatening him as he expected, she softened her gaze. She toyed with one of the hoops in her ear. "Calysta can't help him," she murmured.

Lucian tensed. He disliked hurting women without reason, but when it came to his family, he would do what he needed to make sure they were taken care of. "There is no other way," he growled.

Her compassionate expression remained in place. "I know better than anyone that duty to family comes first. What kind of illness plagues your brother?"

He clenched his jaw. "It was caused by an abaddon."

She gasped in horror. That was the common reaction. Even among demons, abaddons were feared. With a single scratch, one was able to infect its victim with any number of diseases, anything from a common cold to something far worse than the Black Plague. The disease affected both humans and demons. Someone could die in moments. Or, as was the case with Andreas, it would be a slow death as the virus ate the host from the inside out until nothing but shreds of skin and bones remained.

Whichever the situation, the ending was the same. It was an agonizing death and the only cure was from the same abaddon who'd inserted the disease. However, Mikhail had killed the creature before any of them could catch it. The sick bastard had planned the whole thing, and now they were forced to sit back and watch as Andreas withered away.

Siovon sighed again, this one drawn out with a hint of pain. "I'm telling you... Calysta *can't* help him." She rose from her seat. "She has her own curse."

He jerked back, snapping his brows together. "What kind of curse?"

"Black magic. Every time she uses her gift, everyone around her becomes healed of everything — mentally and physically — but an inch of her life is cut short. She's had it since she was a child." She ran her hand through her hair again, making the spiky strands stand on end. "I've done my best to keep her safe, but after Mikhail..." She grunted in frustration.

"After Mikhail what?" he questioned, not liking where this was going.

"I've been separated from her for ten years. There's no telling what's happened to her or how much singing she's done or..."

Sensing she was about to have a panic attack or some kind of meltdown, Lucian crossed the space between them and took her hands in his. "Calm yourself," he directed. Waiting until her rising panic diminished, he gave her hands a small squeeze, even as his own heart lurched.

If what she said was true, then even if they found her sister, they couldn't force her to heal Andreas, not without killing her. Lucian shouldn't care about the stranger before him. He shouldn't care that he would be hated by her, so long as his brother was healed.

So why the hell am I hesitating?

Siovon sighed, withdrawing her hands to take a step back. She paced while biting her nails. He watched her the entire time until she came to a halt with a grunt. "Look... How about we make a deal, Frosty?"

First she wanted me gone. Now she wants to make a deal. Whatever game she was playing made him suspicious.

"What kind of deal?" he demanded.

She chewed her bottom lip between her teeth, nervous energy surrounding her, as if weighing her choices. At last, she blew out an exasperated breath. "I hate, hate, *hate* to admit it, but you leeches have greater tracking senses than most other demons. I'm no exception."

He lifted an eyebrow. "True."

She paused again, waging some kind of inner war in her mind. Whatever she wanted was tearing apart her pride. "My sister is out there somewhere, but me going about it alone is taking far too much time that she may not have. And I lack the ability to track a scent."

Ahhh, I know where this is going. Lucian hid his smug smile and folded his arms. "I fail to see what point you are trying to make, *fatina*."

She shifted her weight to one leg, then the other. "I..." She licked her lips and his gaze was drawn to the pretty bow. "I will help your brother if you help me find my sister."

He lifted his other brow. "*You* will help him? You possess your sister's healing powers?"

Her eyes darted to the side before meeting his. "Not quite."

"Then how can you possibly be of assistance?"

"I've spent years creating potions, herbs, creams and countless other medicines for varying illnesses...for humans *and* demons."

"An interesting hobby, but not helpful. We've had some of the most powerful demon doctors try. There is no cure. They've only been able to infuse their powers into an amulet that will slow the process and ease his suffering."

She frowned. "My mixes are stronger than average demon remedies. Even if it's from an abaddon, if I can locate the source of the disease, I can concoct an antibiotic to fight it."

"How do you create a cure for a disease that not even a doctor with a thousand years of practice could create?" His tone was a bit harsher than he'd meant for it to be, but hell, they were talking about Andreas' life. He didn't need any 'maybes' or possibilities. He needed absolute facts, and if he didn't have those, he couldn't have blind hope. Hoping only led to disappointments.

"Because everything I create is made from my blood," she admitted with a great amount of reluctance.

"What does that mean?" he choked out, though his body was hard at the image of her writhing in pleasure beneath him while he took her blood. By the gods, he needed to have her to satisfy the near-obsessive craving. The sooner the better. He was afraid that if he went back to Chicago without just one taste of her, he'd spend the next decade dreaming up what-ifs.

Impervious to his blast of desire, Siovon explained, "Sirens are earth fey with varying abilities, but we all have blood that can create different medicines and poisons that you wouldn't be able to find anywhere today. My...*gift* specifically gives each of my mixes a greater effect than the ordinary ones."

"And just what kind of gift is that?"

She was still reluctant to reveal such a thing about herself, not that he blamed her. Royal vampires each had their own special powers that no other vampire had. For instance, Ava could see the memories of anyone she touched. Julius could command animals to do his bidding. Darius could manipulate the earth.

For Royals, revealing their power to anyone was like giving their enemies a way to find a weakness. They preferred to have the upper hand by holding the element of surprise. No doubt the same could be said about sirens.

"It's complicated," she muttered. "It would be easier to show you."

Before she could, she stiffened and looked past him toward the barn door. Sharp needles prickled down his spine, telling him that something dangerous was nearing.

"What is it?" he demanded, facing the door.

"It's the same as this morning. A portal was just opened nearby."

"More Rogues," he growled, catching the familiar scent in the distance. "How the hell are they able to travel by portals?"

"Obviously someone is helping them," she retorted, standing at his side. She held a dagger in front of her. "Mikhail used an imp to send him and his Rogues through portals."

Lucian stepped out of reach, glaring. He assumed the weapon had come from a hidden sheath in her boots, but he hadn't heard a thing. "Where did that come from?"

"Later," she promised. "Do we have a deal or not, Frosty?"

"It's Lucian. How do I know you can be trusted?"

"Right back at you," she countered. "Shall we make a blood oath?"

And have her tantalizing scent leading the Rogues right to their location? Hell no. "We have a deal," he groused.

"Good. Can you tell how many there are?"

Keeping his attention on her lest she dared an attack, Lucian tilted his head to sniff the air before shaking his head. "They're too far away, but they're moving fast. We need to leave."

"Yeah, no shit."

"They're the same type of Rogues that Mikhail had. Several escaped after we killed him in the mountains, but that doesn't explain who the fuck is sending them through portals after me."

Her eyes widened, apprehension tightening her features. "You killed Mikhail? Are you sure?"

He snorted. "I watched the bastard disintegrate to ashes after a silver bullet to the head. He's quite dead, *fatina.*"

She looked far from pleased. "Just him?"

It was his turn to frown. "And most of the Rogues he'd hidden there. Is that a problem?"

Before she could respond, he scooped her small frame into his arms. "We can chat about it later. Right now we need to leave. Unless your poor pacifist heart can survive fighting what could be at least a half-dozen Rogues."

She glared at him, wriggling to get free. "Put me down. I have two legs."

Yeah, but he enjoyed holding her against him. She just...fit. "We can move much faster this way. Not even the Rogues can keep up with a Royal on the go."

Her eyes flew wide. "A Royal?"

Before she could piece the puzzle together, he gathered her bag from the hay and dashed toward the door. Then, with a blinding speed, he took off into the night.

Chapter Five

Siovon had to clench her jaw to keep her teeth from chattering as the brute of a vampire carried her to who knew where. The biting cold was just as brutal as it had been earlier and being held in Lucian's arms didn't make it any better.

The man was like a walking freezer. The very air around him was far colder than it should have been, no doubt thanks to whatever power he possessed. There were vampires she'd met who were able to raise or drop the temperature around them when they were pissed, but it seemed to be natural with Lucian.

After an hour of him leading them away, she'd threatened and cursed for a solid thirty minutes to get him to put her down. When that didn't work, she'd had to concede with an annoyed huff.

It was freaking exasperating. She wasn't some fragile damsel in distress. She might not possess the muscles or height her fellow guild members had, but she carried her own well. Hell, she'd even been offered the title of guild master before she'd gone off the grid after her contract had ended. She'd declined, of course, but her skills hadn't gone away.

With a sharp shake of her head, she tugged the collar of her jacket over her mouth and nose as the blur of the city lights passed them by. She tried to gain command over her bunched muscles that shivered in the cold air, but it was a wasted effort. Most fey were in sync with the weather of their home environment. Given that she'd been born in some humid cave on the coast of Malaysia, cold weather wasn't her cup of tea.

What she needed was a platter of honey-dipped strawberries and a tall glass of wine — oh, and a tub filled to the brim with hot, bubbly water. While her muscles relaxed under the soothing water, she'd have her drink in one hand and let her mind escape to a different world where she could be at total peace.

The imagery was beginning to work at heating her body, but then it shattered when the wind whipping at her face stilled. Blinking, she realized Lucian had stopped running. They stood on a path winding through a large park that was likely bustling with activity during the day. At night, however, it was dark and empty, with only the faint sounds of wood sprites dancing through the nearby forestry.

Frowning, she glanced at Lucian, refusing to acknowledge the way her heart gave a sharp squeeze as she studied his profile. His shoulder-length hair was still tied at his nape without a single strand out of place. Past the tan beauty of his face, he looked like a cold-blooded Roman general.

As with most vampires, his very presence was enough to send lesser demons scurrying away in fear. And in the bedroom, he wouldn't be the warm, cuddling type. No, he'd be rough and quiet as he took his partner, dominating her and sating her every need before walking out of the door without a backward glance.

Well, that was what Siovon assumed. She was having trouble figuring him out. One moment he was kissing and touching her in ways that set her body on fire, and the next he was looking at her like she was a bug he'd found stuck to the bottom of his shoe. Talk about bipolar. Either the bastard wanted her or he didn't.

If he did…hell, her body was reacting at just the memory of feeling his lips on her. Good lord, the man was skilled — or she just hadn't been touched in far too long. Whatever the case was, he sent white-hot licks of pleasure through her, which further pissed her off because she didn't know whether she wanted to shove a stake through the center of his chest or wrap her legs around his waist and let him sink himself into her dripping wet —

Blinking, she realized she'd once again been staring at Lucian, and judging by the arrogant tilt of his lips, he was very much aware of her sudden arousal.

Shit.

In an attempt to hide her embarrassment, she shoved her hands against him and wriggled to get free. "You can put me down now, leech."

Lucian chuckled, but he didn't budge except to tighten his arms around her and continue scanning their surroundings.

Annoyed, Siovon used her thumb and middle finger to flick him in the forehead. Hard. He grunted and set her down, then rubbed the growing red spot between his brows while glaring at her. "What the hell was that for?"

She fastened her bag to her back. "I told you to put me down. You disobey and you get scolded."

He flashed his fangs at her. "Oh, and if I obey, I get a treat? I'm not some damned mutt for you to train."

"No, you're a damned leech. There's hardly a line drawn between the two," she drawled.

Lucian straightened his shoulders to appear taller, perhaps in an attempt to intimidate her with his larger size. *Fat chance, that.* If it hadn't worked the other times he'd tried it, he should know it wouldn't work now.

"Stop calling me a leech."

She feigned indifference by studying her nails. "Very well. Mosquito is more fitting for you. Or perhaps flea. They're all pesky little suckers."

He leaned down to be eye-level with her. "Vampire," he growled, the air around him sending a shiver down her spine. "I am a vampire, and you will do well to remember it. I am not someone to be taken lightly."

Siovon didn't doubt that at all. He was a man whose power could crush her in a matter of seconds. Funny, though, how she wasn't afraid of him. She was wary and untrusting, of course, but that was natural for her. After the life she'd lived, any fear left in her was long gone.

Well, other than her fear of losing Caly. That would always remain.

She tilted her chin to a stubborn angle. "If that's a threat, you're going to have to do better, Frosty. Your arrogance will be your downfall."

"And your mouth will be yours," he grumbled, tracing a cool finger across her lips. "It isn't arrogance if it's the truth."

Siovon struggled to breathe as his light touch sent shockwaves of pleasure through her. "You might have the ability to kill me, but I will not let it be easy."

Just like that, his annoyance was replaced by humor. "Killing you is far from what I want to do to you, *fatina*. Very far."

"Stop calling me that. I'm a siren, not a fairy."

A ghost of a smile touched his lips. "You speak Italian?"

She shrugged. "I'm not fluent, but I know enough to get by."

"Another interesting bit about you. You continue to surprise me." He fingered the rings adorning the shell of her ear. "This is a fascinating fashion choice."

She rolled her eyes at the less-than-subtle hint of derision. So what if the aggravating pest didn't like her earrings? "As if your style is any better, Mr. Tall-Dark-and-Gloomy." She took in his shitkickers, leather pants and leather jacket half-zipped over a black shirt.

God, can he be any more of a cliché? A lethal demon dressed head to toe in black garb with a sword angled across his back, not to mention that she detected at least a half-dozen other hidden blades strapped to him.

Well, either he was a cliché or she'd been watching far too much television. Still, he was tall and yummy and she wanted to have a taste or two.

Wait… No I don't. She didn't want anything to do with this…bug except for him to help find her sister. After that, she'd hold up her end of the deal then she and Calysta would be on their way, never looking back. Simple.

"What are these for?" he questioned, giving one of the hoops a small tug.

"Haven't you seen a woman with earrings before?"

"Yes, but usually in both ears. And these have fey writing on them, which tells me they're more than decorative jewelry."

She wondered if there was anything those pale eyes ever missed. Doubtful. "You're pretty damn nosey."

"I prefer the term 'curious'."

"Well, you know what curiosity did to the cat—or vampire, rather."

A small sound escaped his lips, almost like a sigh. "Can you answer the simplest of questions without giving me a headache?"

That made her smile. "I can, but what's the fun in that?" She pushed his hand away and pointed to the three bottom hoops that were made out of faux silver metal. "These are dampers. They conceal my scent so that even in a room full of demons, I won't stand out. Very few will be able to tell I'm anything other than a lesser imp." She pointed to the black one above them. "This one helps me heal faster than normal."

"So they hold some kind of spell?" he asked with a grimace.

His disgust for magic was no surprise. Most vampires hated anything dealing with magic, because they couldn't sense it. It was their one true kryptonite. Many demons knew it, but very few were brave enough to attack a vampire, no matter what rank they were.

"Yes, but not traditional magic." At his blank look, she blew out a breath. "All fey are magical creatures. It's like how imps can use portals or how fairies can grant certain wishes. Most of us can enchant different objects and give them certain abilities for a short amount of time. Once the magic wears off, we need to go through the process all over again to give the object a 'refill'. If you've ever been to a demon auction, you'll have come across some of these artifacts. They're nothing special."

He gave a stunned shake of his head and tapped on the golden hoop at the top of her ear that was far smaller than the rest. "What does this one do?"

A pang of sadness coursed through her. She turned away from him, stroking the earring as if she could feel something other than cold metal. "Calysta has one to match. It was a beacon that connected us."

Lucian brushed his fingers over her nape in the softest of caresses, something she didn't think someone so cold was capable of. "I'm assuming the magic has worn off, and that is the reason you cannot track her on your own?"

She bit off her sarcastic words. "I stopped sensing her years ago."

"Did she ever try to rescue you from Mikhail while you were held captive?"

She gave a humorless snort. "Of course she did, more than once. But after the last time, I made her take a blood oath to never attempt it again. Mikhail would have killed her, and even though I knew it crushed her not to be able to save me, I preferred to know she was out there surviving rather than suffering the same fate as I was."

At Lucian's thunderous expression, she held up her hand to prevent any further questions. "Drop it, Frosty. I'm done talking about it. Why are we here?"

Still looking as though he wanted to say more, he shoved his hands into his pants pockets. "The imp rents an apartment close by. We're starting our investigation."

Anger forgotten, she straightened and turned to peer at a nearby high-rise apartment building with twinkling lights. "There?" She pulled the folded list from her pocket and studied one of the addresses before flashing the paper his way. "You know about these?"

He gave an easy shrug but didn't comment.

She frowned, a twinge of envy flaring in her. In a matter of days he'd managed to do what had taken her weeks to accomplish. No matter how good she thought she was, she didn't have a vampire's freakish mind control or their frightful presence to get people to talk. She had to sneak around or use blackmail to get the answers she sought, when all Lucian had to do was show off his fangs.

Just another unfair perk vampires had over lesser demons.

A white cloud formed past her lips when she sighed. "All right, Frosty. Lead the way."

He scowled. "Why the devil do you insist on calling me Frosty?"

"As in *Frosty the Snowman*. It's a fitting name, don't you think?" She paused. "Except the snowman was jolly and cheerful, while you're…well…*not*."

His frown deepened when she whistled the tune for the *Frosty the Snowman* song. "You could put my brothers to shame with the level of how you piss me off," he grumbled.

"Brothers? There are more than you and your sick brother?"

"There are six of us. Seven, if you include my sister."

Siovon almost tripped over her feet. "Seven?" she choked out. As if the demon world wasn't filled with enough vampires as it was, but six annoying, beautiful, cold-hearted brutes like him, plus a female version?

Holy shit.

Then, the pieces started to fall into place. He'd mentioned that he was a Royal vampire. From what she knew about them, there were only a few left. Cyrus Gordano, aka the leech king and his children.

His six sons and one daughter.

With a gasp, she stared wide-eyed into Lucian's amused gaze. "Problem, *fatina*?"

A wave of sickness rolled through Siovon. *God, I should have known better.* No ordinary vampire could carry the amount of power she sensed within him, not unless they had some sort of high-ranked position among the other vampires.

And from what Mikhail had ranted about all those years, the name Lucian had popped up more than once. She'd just never thought it would be of any importance, especially since she'd never met or seen a Royal vampire in person.

Surveying Lucian, she chewed on her bottom lip, realizing second by second just how dangerous her situation was. Cyrus' Guard had been looking for Calysta, and when that had failed, the king's own son had been sent in their place. Since Lucian had said his younger brother was the one suffering from the abaddon's disease, that meant she'd agreed to heal one of the Royal princes.

And if she failed, she'd have made an enemy out of all vampires. There wasn't a single rock in Heaven, on Earth or in Hell she could hide under to escape their wrath.

Freaking hell.

"Is it too late to back out of the deal?" she squeaked.

The damned pest's smug look didn't make it any better. "I assume you've figured out just how precarious your situation is. If you no longer wish to pursue this agreement, then I cannot stop you. However, my only other option is to find Calysta."

"Even knowing of her curse, you'd still force her to use her powers?"

His face smoothed over to his previous icy mask, one she was sure was his preference. "I will shoulder your hatred if it means my brother can live. Nothing is more important to me than saving his life."

It took an immense amount of resolve to keep from launching across the few feet separating them and ripping his heart from his chest. Calysta was also the most important thing to Siovon. The thought of anyone forcing her to risk her own life to save some wretched leech was enough to make Siovon itch to turn violent.

"What'll it be?" he demanded.

Siovon snapped her teeth together and closed her eyes, reaching deep for a sense of inner peace. If she had to choose between her life and Calysta's, that was an easy decision. She'd fight to the very death and suffer any amount of torture and pain for her sister's sake. They were all each other had, and Siovon had sworn ages ago to never allow Calysta to suffer if she could help it.

Caly's heart was too pure to go through anything like that. Meanwhile, Siovon was used to the corrupt darkness of the world. She could take it.

Even if she had to risk the entire nation of vampires coming down on her head, she could live with it—or sacrifice herself—so long as her dear sister was out of harm's way. Hell, since she'd played an active role in creating Mikhail's Rogues, she was already doomed. Cyrus hadn't earned his powerful name by ignoring his enemies' actions.

Stiffening her spine, she turned a glare on Lucian. "Leave my sister out of this." Then, with leaden steps, she walked past him. "Don't go back on your word, leech."

"I can say the same to you, fey," he shot back.

* * * *

St. Charles, Illinois – Cyrus' lair

Andreas awoke with a cough that filled his chest with fire. Reaching for the glass of water on his nightstand, he gripped the cup with a shaking hand.

When he brought it to his lips, he cursed as he spilled more water on himself than he drank.

Hell's fucking bells. If he had the power to bring the dead to life, he'd reanimate Mikhail Nilsen and kill the asshole a thousand times over. It wouldn't cure him of the disease plaguing his body, but he would gain some form of satisfaction from ripping the man apart.

Instead, a single gunshot wound to the head had ended him. *Pathetic.* He didn't deserve that kind of mercy, not after what he'd done to him, not after what he'd done to Ava and not after what he'd done to hundreds of others.

Andreas didn't blame his family for killing the bastard by any means necessary, but still...

It pissed him off to no end that he'd been unable to do a damned thing during their battle in the Apennines. He hadn't even been conscious.

Even now he couldn't do anything. Though his father's healers had suspended the disease, the damage that had been done prior was irreversible. He'd lost an assload of weight, his muscles no longer had the bulge he'd worked hard to maintain and most of his organs were turning to mush.

His natural healing had taken a severe blow as well. The disease was attacking his immune system faster than his body could keep up.

With a small growl, he returned the empty glass to the nightstand hard enough to crack it. At the feel of something cold pressing into his bare chest, he peered down at the amulet keeping him alive.

The brass pendant was the size of a small child's fist and felt like a block of gold weighing him down. It was further proof of his failing strength.

It damn sure wasn't permanent. It was meant to stave off the disease until they could find a definite cure, but the magic wouldn't last forever. In truth, it was already losing its power day by day.

With a twist of his lips, he slid off the bed and braced himself against one of the posts. He couldn't tell his family about the failing amulet. It would raise alarm, and he'd have to endure several more magical experimentations. His family had just gone back to their normal ways without fretting over him every moment.

He didn't want to send them into another full-blown panic—especially not Ava, what with her being pregnant. She didn't need any additional stress. Besides, they were still rejoicing over having her back in their lives. He couldn't snatch away that joy.

He knew deep down that he wouldn't last much longer. His family would tear the world apart to find a cure, but something told him it would be for nothing. The disease coursing through him had only one other documented case.

There was no cure.

He still had a number of regrets, and it tormented him to no end that he'd never learned of his true heritage. That was just the cruel bitch fate was, he supposed.

A tightening in his chest had him doubling over as another painful cough tore his lungs apart. He covered his mouth as the coughing continued on and on until a warm liquid sprayed into his hands.

Blood. A lot of blood.

With a shuddering sigh, he forced himself upright and shuffled to the connecting bathroom. He grew colder by the minute, his teeth chattering. He set the water to a near-boiling temperature and stepped under the spray, using a bar of soap to scrub away the blood on his hands and chest to hide the scent of it.

His vision blurred as tears streamed from his eyes, mingling with the hot water he could no longer feel striking his naked skin.

Damn it all to hell. He'd already accepted his fate, but he didn't want to die. Not yet. He'd always known he wouldn't live forever, but he had hoped he'd live more than a couple of short centuries. Even a tiny, very faint side of him had been hoping Lucian could find the singing siren and get her to heal him before it was too late.

However, as a small sob wracked his body and blood trickled down one corner of his mouth, he slid down the wall and pulled his legs to his chest. He was forced to accept that there was no such thing as 'before it was too late'.

He'd already run out of time.

Chapter Six

St. Louis, Missouri

Lucian should have been focused on his surroundings, looking for clues to Keegan's and Calysta's disappearances, but he couldn't help that his attention was drawn elsewhere. To be exact, he was fixated on a short siren with sharp violet eyes and delicate features.

Pretending to be reading a stack of papers he'd found on the marble countertop of the imp's rather impressive kitchen, he peered over the top of them to watch as Siovon circled the connecting living room, studying every nook and cranny for some sort of clue.

She was pissed at him, but that was no surprise. The woman seemed to have an endless supply of irritation directed his way. Watching her dressed in the same tight jeans and knee-high black boots, he found it impossible to tear his eyes from the swing of her hips as she walked this way and that. When she bent over to inspect something on the bottom of a bookshelf, he swallowed a groan as he imagined her bent over, wearing nothing but those sexy boots, baring herself to him.

He was beginning to suspect that being near Siovon was far too much of a distraction. More often than not, he pictured having her lying with her legs spread wide, welcoming him to take her and satisfy the painful craving that refused to let him be.

Good gods... He'd never been drawn to anyone as much as he was to Siovon.

The realization was far more dangerous than anything he'd ever faced. His driving need to be with her made him realize she could very well be his truemate, the woman he was bound to mate with for all eternity. It was either that or the last several years he'd gone without taking a lover were catching up to him. He'd much rather that be the reason.

Siovon was beautiful...and intelligent. And she possessed enough strength to make her a dangerous adversary. That explained his attraction to her, but not the deep-seated urge to have her wrapped in his arms while he kissed the dark shadows from her eyes. The desire to comfort her, to expel the haunting pain within her and have her smiling was something he'd never felt the need to do, not for anyone.

It was that feeling that had him straightening and putting some much-needed space between them. She wasn't his truemate. She *couldn't* be. Those kinds of thoughts were hazardous.

He had to keep in mind that there were far more important matters to settle first. Only when they found somewhere to rest and hunker down to wait out the hours of daylight would he attempt to satisfy one or two cravings, just to be rid of the hunger plaguing him.

Afterward, he would help her find Calysta, bring her to his father's home in St. Charles to heal Andreas and forget this ridiculous journey had ever happened.

Shaking his head, he flowed through the narrow hall. It was clear Keegan had a taste for the finer things in life.

This high-rise apartment had floor-to-ceiling windows that offered a spectacular view of the St. Louis city lights. The wooden floors were polished until Lucian could see his own reflection, the walls creamy white with expensive paintings hanging several feet apart.

Lucian wondered what the imp did on the side to accumulate the money to pay for his apartment, because there was no way he was bringing in that much wealth from The Golden Crown alone. From the information he'd gathered, the apartment was one of two of Keegan's residences. The bar was the only establishment he owned and the other three addresses were just his frequent hangout spots.

Entering a room that had been converted into a private office, Lucian circled the area, taking in the black bookcase lining one wall, the L-shaped cherrywood desk tucked in the corner and a dark chaise lounge on the other side.

He neared the bookcase, eyeing the various business management, engineering and marketing textbooks, a few encyclopedias and a handful of other books organized alphabetically behind the clear glass. There were a few unexciting trinkets as well—a framed picture of a kitten playing with a ball of yarn, a small glass vase, an autographed baseball and a bronze mini statue of a cat.

He moved to the desk, taking in the framed picture of another cat — *what is with him and cats?* — a tray of manila folders, a closed laptop, a small pile of neatly stacked papers and a motionless Newton's cradle with metal beads sitting near the edge of the desk.

The scent of cherry blossoms filled the room, and Lucian's pants grew tight. By the gods, Siovon's scent was so sweet that he could drown in it. What was worse, he wasn't sure he'd want to be saved.

"Find anything?" she demanded in a sour tone that contradicted her scent.

Hiding his reaction to her, he half-turned to face her, frowning at the odd pressure in his chest as his eyes met hers. She was watching him with that ever-present wary glare. Though they were temporary allies, she was cautious enough to know not to fully trust him, despite his oath not to harm her.

He understood her caution as much as the next demon, but he didn't like it. He wanted her trust.

"Nothing yet," he murmured, peering at the desk. He scanned through the folders, though nothing stood out — just bank statements, recipes and a list of employees for his pub. Oh, and a complete shopping list of cat supplies.

He sensed rather than heard Siovon move farther into the room. She was light on her feet, not making a sound as she approached the bookcase. It was another skill of hers that made him question her upbringing. Only vampires and very few other demons were able to move with such silence, though it took years of training to do so.

Lost in his train of thought, he blinked when she waved her hand in front of the glass enclosure. "What are you doing?" he demanded, his tone one that he knew grated on her nerves.

Sure enough, her shoulders tensed, but she didn't spare him a glance. "Searching," she drawled.

He crossed his eyes and counted to five at the simple answer. It seemed she'd figured out how to do the same to him. *Sneaky woman.* "Searching for what?"

"Something."

"Something like *what*?" he snapped.

When she turned around, he thought it would be to snap back at him. To his amazement, she just smiled with mischief. "You, sir, need an attitude adjustment."

He needed an attitude adjustment? She was one to talk. There had been maybe a total of five sentences she'd given him that hadn't been filled with disdain or irritation or insults.

Then again, he suspected it was a defense mechanism for her. She was feisty, but she didn't seem like a pent-up ball of anger as he'd first thought. There had been a few times when she'd seemed almost...kind.

Narrowing his eyes, he stalked toward her. Her smile vanished as she backpedaled until she was pressed into the wall. He leaned one forearm against it, above her head. She feigned a look of indifference, but she couldn't cover the way her eyes darkened with a hunger that matched his own.

He hid a smile. It was good to know that the desire roaring to life within him wasn't one-sided.

The top of her head reached just under his chin, and he dipped his head to level his eyes with hers. "You drive me to be this way," he murmured, inhaling her rich scent. "Your scent and your sharp tongue."

Speaking of tongue, he dropped his gaze to her mouth when the little pink tip darted out to dampen her lips. When she spoke, he caught the flash of even teeth. "I don't believe I have any such effect on you," she said in a rush of breath.

He brushed his lips over her ear. "Believe this, *fatina*." He pressed into her, causing her to gasp at the feel of his erection against her belly. He cupped the back of her neck. "You make me want you this much."

A soft sigh escaped her lips when he pulled her earlobe into his mouth, giving it a soft nip. Her arousal spiked the air, clouding his mind with its sweetness. She grasped the opening of his leather jacket, and for a moment he froze out of fear that she was going to push him away — or toss him out of the nearby window.

No matter how much she wanted him, her mind would tell her that he was the enemy.

To his relief, however, she pulled him closer, smoothing her hands over his chest. Groaning, he crushed his lips to hers. The kiss was explosive and demanding, and with the way he'd been craving her, there was no such thing as gentle. There was no slow buildup of tension that would torment them both.

Lucian slipped his tongue past her soft lips, reveling in the sweet taste of honey. She dug her nails into his chest in a way that had him hissing in pleasure. He slid his hand from her neck to the hem of her jacket before jerking it over her head and tossing it to the floor. He drank in the sight of her in the tiny top, the creamy swells of her breasts on display. He palmed one full mound from under her shirt.

Lucian's fangs lengthened with the desire to take her blood. He refrained, though. Giving blood to a vampire was an act that required total trust and surrender, two things that he was certain the beauty in his arms wasn't ready for. Besides, he had a nagging sense that if he mentioned it, the lusty spell around them would break and she'd retreat back behind her walls.

Siovon went on her tiptoes and circled her arms around his neck. With another small groan, he cupped her ass in his free hand. In a quick motion, he picked her up. She wrapped her legs around his waist while he used his body to pin her back to the wall, grinding into her.

By the gods, he'd never wanted anything so bad. He felt as though he was at the end of a short leash when it came to Siovon. With the way he'd been hungry for her, he feared he wouldn't last very long. He needed to have her in this exact position, only naked.

He'd just begun to reach for the bottom of her shirt to yank it off when a sharp pain pricked the side of his neck from under her arm. "Fuck!" he shouted, pulling away from her. He dropped her on her feet and slapped his palm to his neck.

Siovon blinked at him in confusion, but he wasn't falling for the bullshit. "Woman, did you think to kill me while I was distracted? Maybe try to seduce me to get me to lower my guard?" It explained her eager response to his touch when she'd been pushing him away the entire time.

"Woman?" she echoed. "What the heck are you talking about?"

He flashed his fangs at her. "Do not play me for a fool. You cannot convince me that some invisible force stabbed my neck."

Her eyebrows snapped together in a glare. She crossed her arms, forcing her breasts upward. It took all Lucian had in him to keep his eyes from dropping to them. "Newsflash, Frosty, you're the one who came on to me. And if I wanted to kill you, I wouldn't need to distract you to do it."

Well, she had a point there. Two points, really, but he wasn't going to tell her that.

"Maybe so, but how do you explain this?" He flashed his hand at her, showing her the blood on his palm. The wound was small and had already healed, but it still pissed him off. "I didn't do it to myself."

She looked surprised but huffed with indignance. "Well, neither did I..." She trailed off as a slow realization crossed her face. "Oh."

"Oh, what?"

She bit her lip, shuffling her weight from one leg to the other. A sure sign of unease. "I can explain."

He scoffed. "You stabbed me."

"No. Well, not *me*, per se..."

He shook his head, his patience wearing thin. "Siovon—"

"You wanted to know what my powers were, right?" Before he could snap at her for trying to change the subject, she shoved her arm out, showing him the dragon tattoo on her arm. He eyed it. When he'd seen it the other morning, it had looked calm. Normal, even.

At the moment, however, its eyes were narrowed, as if glaring at him. Its mouth was pulled back on a silent snarl, baring teeth with *his* blood staining the pointed choppers. "What kind of tattoo is that?" he demanded, never taking his eyes off the creature. "It...moved."

"This is a fragment of my powers," she explained. "His name is Thor."

Lucian fixed her with a flat stare. "You named your tattoo. Interesting."

She rolled her eyes. "Just watch."

She closed her eyes and murmured words in a language he'd never heard. A whisper of wind flowed past him, and he widened his eyes in amazement when the dragon writhed and detached itself from her skin. It took on a 3D form the size of a chihuahua, then gave its wings a sharp flutter before perching on Siovon's shoulder.

"Devil's balls. It's about damn time you summoned me," the tiny thing fumed in a masculine voice that had a thick Irish brogue. "Honestly, it's like my existence means nothing to you."

Lucian took an abrupt step back. "What the hell is *that*?"

The...'thing' swung its head at him, its sea-green eyes narrowing to slits. "I could ask the same of you, *stook*. You taste like shite."

Lucian touched his neck. "That was *you*? You *bit* me?"

Several tiny, pointy teeth were revealed as the creature grinned. "Are you daft? Of course I bit you. It's my duty to protect my master from fiends like you."

Lucian looked between the creature and Siovon, annoyed at how casual she appeared. "Explain."

"My blood has the ability to...animate things, if you will." She indicated the dragon, who was still glaring at Lucian. "Just watch me." She pulled an ink pen from her pocket, found a notepad on the desk, then tore off a blank piece of paper.

"What are you doing?"

"Shut up and pay attention," Thor snapped.

Lucian growled, his hand twitching with the urge to wring the creature's neck. It was Siovon waving him over that caused him to refrain. Baring his fangs at Thor, Lucian peered over Siovon's opposite shoulder and watched her draw a simple butterfly. She lifted her index finger to the dragon, allowing him to bite into the skin hard enough to draw blood. Lucian opened his mouth to protest but stiffened as she traced over the sketch with her bloodied finger.

With another hushed whisper of foreign words, the butterfly rose from the paper, took on a 3D form and began flying around the room.

Lucian held out his hand and the butterfly landed on his knuckles, smelling of faint cherry blossoms. Despite its black-and-white color, it looked so real.

Anger forgotten, Lucian found himself smiling. Everyone knew sirens possessed unique powers that could either give or take away life some way or another. One could heal any animal with just a touch. Another could use their powers to bring the dead back to life. Another could kill victims with just their voice. He'd never once thought he would get to witness something so…breathtaking.

"This is amazing."

Instead of looking pleased with the compliment, Siovon lowered her lashes. "I suppose once upon a time it would have been."

His smile transformed into a frown, his chest tightening at the sadness in her tone. Of course, having such amazing powers would be nothing more than a burden to her. Sirens had gone extinct centuries ago because of their blood.

"You're able to give life to any picture?"

"Only pictures I draw or paint myself," she stated. "Sometimes I can 'awaken' small statues or sculptures. However, it only works on things that can take on a living form."

"Just like that? Just sprinkle a few drops of blood and you can bring an entire monument to life?"

She snorted. "There is no 'just like that' about it. The amount of blood needed depends on the size of the object. And, of course, no magic is without a price. Even using my powers on something as small as that butterfly is draining me by the minute."

"I see," he murmured, eyeing the dragon. "What about that thing? What's the purpose of having it if it drains you?"

The thing in question hissed at him, but Siovon spoke first. "Thor is...different. Even I don't know how he came to be. He was a painting of mine from decades ago when I first started using my powers. Over the years he grew a mind of his own, and now, no matter how long he's left free, I never feel drained."

Lucian raised his brows at that. "Do you think it's because he's an older creation of yours? Maybe in the past you've given him enough blood and life to sustain him on his own."

She thought it over before shrugging. "It's a possibility, but who's to say what the true cause is? I've learned to count my blessings as they come."

He shook his head, glaring at Thor. "It's a wonderful gift, but I wouldn't consider that nasty vermin a blessing, *fatina.*"

"Says the soulless bloodsucker," Thor shot back, his forked tongue snaking past his teeth.

"Knock it off," Siovon commanded. She muttered another set of foreign words and the butterfly dissolved, reappearing as a mere drawing on the piece of paper. "Thor, I need a favor."

"Anything for you, luv," Thor drawled.

"A portal was opened in the living room not too long ago. I need you to find out who used it and where they went."

"It can do that?" Lucian asked, a hint of surprise in his tone.

"Of course I can," Thor said, puffing his little chest. "I am a creature of many talents." He leaned closer to Siovon's ear, lowering his voice to a loud whisper. "Honestly, Siovon, it's like feeding biscuits to a bear with this one."

Lucian took a threatening step forward. "Siovon, your pet has a death wish."

Thor's tail twitched in annoyance. "Pfft, as if I'll ever fear a parasite."

"Just go," Siovon urged. With a flap of his wings, Thor rose from her shoulder and headed for the door.

"I'm going. I'm going. I'll let you know what I find."

When he was out of sight, Lucian shook his head. "And you say I need an attitude adjustment."

Siovon's lips twitched into a small smile. "He means well. He's just a bit prejudiced against vampires after... You know."

"Understandable, I suppose." He shot her a questioning look. "He was with you when you were held captive by Mikhail?"

She grimaced. "No. Thor and I share a mental connection, but somehow Mikhail was able to block it."

Lucian shook his head in bewilderment. "This is baffling. Thor is able to track portals like you do?"

"Actually, I can't track them. I can sense when one is opened or closed nearby — or if one was recently used. However, Thor is able to sense all traces of magic and track portals anywhere." She shook her head. "It's still a mystery to me how he has powers that I don't even possess. It's like he's a real demon instead of a painting I brought to life."

"He might be an aggravating pest, but it's still miraculous how he's alive. Do you have any other creations like him?"

"He's the only one. When I first used my powers to awaken him, he was like the butterfly — no personality, no powers, nothing. He was just a flying dragon. However, it's like you said. The more blood and magic I gave him, the more he absorbed until he became...him. Now he has a life of his own. He's also bound to the night. When the sun rises, he's forced to return to his original 2D form until the sun sets."

"Can he be killed?" he drawled, eliciting a glare from her.

"I doubt it. Every time he's dealt a killing blow, he returns to his regular form until he heals. He's faced fire, water and decapitation, but nothing is fatal." She narrowed her eyes. "Lay one finger on him and I'll drop you."

He shrugged, unconcerned with the threat. "The creature could test the patience of saints, *fatina*, and I am no saint."

She raked her gaze over his body. "No, you definitely aren't."

The look was more wary than sexual, but it still made him harden in response. *Merda*, all she'd done was glance at him and he was panting like a dog in heat. It was so pathetic. "I'm curious. Why the hell did you name an Irish dragon Thor?"

She cracked a smile at that. "He's made from Irish paint, so I think that's where the accent comes from. However, Caly and I had a mild obsession with Norse mythology at the time, so..." She trailed off with a shrug.

Lucian shook his head, baffled by the whole thing. "So your power to animate things is why Mikhail wanted you. I don't understand how it allowed him to create Rogues — or to get them to follow his command."

She ran a hand through the back of her hair, her eyes darkening with pain. "There was a wizard practicing black magic who helped him. For the healthy vampires, he would starve them for weeks at a time. When they were on the verge of bloodlust, he'd give them small amounts of my blood, just to take the edge off, before making them go more days without feeding. When they were so starved and crazed that they turned Rogue, he mixed my blood with his own and made them drink it while the wizard cast a binding spell that essentially morphed them into one of my creations. Except, instead of me, Mikhail had total power over them.

"The process was the same with the Turnbloods," she continued. "As you know, humans turning vampire is a delicate process that has a fifty percent success rate. With my blood added to Mikhail's, it was poisonous to most of them, and their bodies rejected the combination." She squeezed her eyes shut, scrubbing her hands over her face. "There were so many. Yet the ones who survived the transition never even had a chance to fight their hunger or learn what they'd become."

With a disgusted shake of his head, Lucian strolled to the large window to stare at the city blanketed in snow. For the love of the gods, Mikhail had truly been a monster. They had known full well that whatever he'd done to create those Rogues had involved some sort of magic, but to hear about it in detail was just sickening.

The thought of Siovon being forced to do something so heinous disturbed him. He wasn't a 'feelings' type of man, so the painful clenching in his chest shouldn't exist. She'd already proven that she could handle her own, but beneath that hard-boiled shell was a fragile woman who deserved better than that.

Once more, he didn't hear Siovon move from her spot, but he caught sight of her from the corner of his eye. He watched her reflection as she peered out of the window with sad eyes.

"How did you come to know of Lila?" Her expression was tight with a hint of vulnerability.

He wanted to pull her in his arms and kiss her pain away, but he knew the moment he twitched his fingers she'd withdraw from him. She didn't want to let anyone in. It was a type of intimacy she wasn't ready for — and neither was he.

So he settled for answering her question. "My sister has the ability to see the memories of anyone she touches. A long time ago, she ran into Mikhail and saw Lila in one of his visions. All we know is that Mikhail used her blood to create a new race of vampires and that he wanted to know where her daughter was, for whatever reason." He studied her delicate features, memorizing every curve. "You do know her, don't you?"

She blew out a shaky breath. "She was our mother."

Lucian had already guessed the relationship between them, but hearing the pain in Siovon's voice caused an odd tenderness to open within him. Unable to help himself, he traced the line of her jaw with a light touch. "Mikhail separated the three of you?"

"We were separated before then. She knew someone had been hunting her, so she left us in order to lure the enemy away." She tapped the golden piercing at the top of her ear. "Lila had one of these as well. I always knew she was fading away, but one day the magic just ended. Calysta and I were still connected to each other, but not our mother. The only explanation was that she'd died."

He continued gliding his fingers over her in what he hoped was a comforting way. "Had she mentioned Mikhail to you before?"

"No, but I learned of him afterward through some associates."

He fingered the hoops lining her ear. "Associates?"

"That's a story for another day."

Secret meaning—never. Lucian sensed her retreating behind her forces. He leaned in to press a swift kiss to her lips before stepping away. "Thank you," he murmured. "Let's continue looking around until your lizard comes back."

Chapter Seven

After another hour and a half of inspecting the fancy apartment from top to bottom, Siovon met Lucian back in the private office. She'd done her best to focus on finding anything out of place.

However, the memory of the hulking vampire pressing her against the wall and touching her in ways she'd never been touched before kept surfacing, steering her attention from the task at hand. Jeez, she should have kicked his ass instead of responding to him like some wanton harpy. It was freaking embarrassing.

To make matters worse, she'd opened up to him about her past, something she'd never done for anyone except Calysta and her friend Naomi.

Lucian was the enemy. She couldn't forget that he would hand her to his father for taking part in Mikhail's crimes. Even if the king took mercy on her and believed that she had been forced, Lucian could kill her once he realized she wasn't able to heal his brother. Just because they were temporary allies didn't mean she had to trust him.

As for getting physical, she couldn't do that. How long had it been since she'd allowed herself to feel the touch of a man?

Pfft! Never. She couldn't even recall a time when she'd felt such awareness for someone. It was distracting, annoying and far too dangerous. She feared that if she ever decided to give in to her body's demands and sate her pleasure with Lucian, just one or two go-arounds wouldn't be enough. She'd be stuck thinking about him long afterward.

And in her life, courting such a perilous desire would only lead to letting her guard down. After that would come death.

"Other than a portal, what else did you find?" Lucian demanded.

Siovon frowned, shaking herself from her musings. She needed to focus. "Only a rather unhealthy obsession with cats," she stated, recalling the multiple framed pictures and statues of felines. "You?"

He shook his head. "It's strange. Everything seems in place, as if no one has been here to disturb anything. And yet there isn't a single speck of dust, which suggests there is regular cleaning."

"Well, someone has been here. The portal is barely a day old." She looked around, frustration bubbling. "Do any of the scents stand out to you?"

He lifted a dark eyebrow. "Is there a scent in particular I'm supposed to notice?"

"My senses aren't as sharp as yours, but there must be a trail other than Keegan's if he's had visitors. And if Calysta's been here, she's always smelled like snickerdoodles."

Lucian looked genuinely confused. "What in God's name are snickerdoodles?"

She lifted her hands. "Cinnamon and sugar-flavored cookies. Come on. You've never had a snickerdoodle?"

"Siovon, I would question my status as a hetero man if I ate something with a frilly name like 'snickerdoodle'."

Siovon parted her lips, but she was struck speechless.

Ignoring her, he opened the laptop. "The bedroom and kitchen smell of ripe lemons, as did the imp's office at the pub. I'm guessing that's his natural scent. I don't smell any cookies, but there's a fresh scent of bleach and cleaning chemicals. The others are too old for me to detect." He frowned. "If Andreas…"

When he trailed off, she tilted her head to the side. "Who's Andreas?"

He disregarded her for several moments, so long that she feared he wouldn't answer. That was understandable, given that he was far from the sharing type. However, it was only fair, since she'd revealed a piece of herself to him.

Seeing that she was still waiting for an answer, he admitted, "He's my brother, the sick one. Even if a scent is weeks old, if he catches on to it, he can see whatever happened at the time—kind of like a flashback in his mind."

Her eyes widened. "That's incredible. Is it something vampires can do?"

Lucian shook his head. "Similar to how every siren has a different gift, Royal vampires have a special power that goes beyond what lesser vampires can do. I mentioned my sister can see the memories of the people she touches. Some of us are telepaths, some elementals, et cetera. It varies among us."

Siovon was amazed. "What's your gift?" she asked, more out of curiosity than anything else.

He gave her a look of obvious suspicion. Again, it was understandable. Like it was for her, revealing his gift would take a great deal of trust. She knew firsthand that anyone could use that same power for their own malicious intent.

But then, he pointed one finger to the floor. She gasped when beautiful crystals of ice formed around her feet. She took a step back.

His powers explained why the air around him was always colder than normal. "Now *that's* amazing," she breathed. "So the weather outside doesn't even affect you, does it?"

His expression didn't change, but she caught the flash of pride in his pale eyes, as if her interest in him and his powers pleased him. "My body can adapt to even the most extreme temperatures."

"Lucky," she grumbled, peering back at the ice. It dissolved into a puddle of water before evaporating into the air. "Fey are bound to the environment they are born in."

"I'm guessing your homeland isn't known for cooler weather?"

She gave a wry snort. "Ever been to Malaysia in the middle of March?"

He thought about it before shaking his head with a small smile. "No, but I can imagine."

Siovon walked around the desk to peer over his shoulder at the laptop. Of course, the lock-screen background was the image of a basket of kittens. "This Keegan guy has some serious feline issues," she muttered. She liked cute little animals as much as the next person, but this was a bit extreme. "I don't suppose any of those vampy powers of yours include hacking into a computer?"

His lips twitched with amusement. "No, but I know someone who can help."

She eyed him as he pulled out his phone and tapped away at the touchscreen. "Who?"

Before he could answer, her own buzzed in her pocket. Blinking, she pulled the cheap throw-away out and peered at the screen. It was a text message from an unknown number that contained a series of numbers with letters and symbols dispersed between them. To anyone else, it would look like a random code from a spam caller.

However, Siovon recognized it for what it was. There were a small, select few of her associates who had the means to contact her through her burner phones, and each of them had different cyphers to keep their messages private.

Someone was telling her to call right away. She glanced at Lucian, who was watching her with an unreadable expression. Those piercing eyes didn't miss a thing, damn it. "I need to take this. Excuse me."

He gave a simple nod, as if giving her permission. She would have bristled if not for the urgency to leave.

Naomi was one of her old comrades from the guild. More than a comrade, actually. She was the one person in the world Siovon could trust her entire life to. It was thanks to Naomi that she'd even escaped from Mikhail.

However, Naomi wouldn't risk herself being exposed over the phone unless it was something of utmost importance.

Once outside the apartment, Siovon checked both ends of the hall. Keegan had the penthouse apartment, and since his was the only one on the floor, there was no reason for anyone, even the humans inhabiting the building, to be lurking about.

Satisfied that everything was clear, she dialed the number hidden in the text message.

Naomi answered on the first ring. "Siovon," she said, her husky voice holding a Spanish accent.

"What is it?" Siovon didn't bother with a preamble. Niceties and warm greetings weren't Naomi's thing.

"I found him."

Siovon's heart stopped for several seconds in her chest. She had to clench her free hand at her side to keep from shaking with the fury brought on by those simple words.

She didn't have to ask who Naomi was referring to. After helping her escape the mountains all those weeks ago, Naomi had offered to track down everyone who was involved with Mikhail's plans.

Well, she hadn't offered. She'd *insisted*. Naomi was reserved and cold most of the time, but she was protective of the rare few people she considered a part of her circle.

And Siovon had been a part of that circle for years.

So when the opportunity had arisen to hunt down Mikhail's last living associate, a vampire named Jarek, Naomi had been right on top of it. "Where?"

"Alleman, just outside of Des Moines, Iowa, heading east."

"East?" Siovon frowned, picturing a map in her head. "You think he may be heading toward Chicago?" It was, after all, where Mikhail had launched the last of his Rogue attacks before retreating to the Apennines in Italy. He'd known Cyrus and his brood lived there.

"Your guess is as good as mine. However, he's been hunkering down in this abandoned schoolhouse for a while. I will try to get closer to get more intel."

"Don't. It's not safe."

There was a small pause. Then, "You doubt my skills, Siovon?"

Siovon was smart enough to swallow her laugh of disbelief. Naomi had once led two others to take out an entire cave of mountain trolls. As the story went, once her bloodlust kicked in, she'd shredded the beasts. It had gotten to the point where the entire ground had been littered with blood and internal organs. It had been a disturbing feat, given that mountain trolls were damn hard to kill.

"Of course not," she said, considering her words, "but I know you well enough to know that you'll pounce the moment you lay eyes on Jarek. And with all the Rogues he'll have surrounding him, you can't go alone."

There was another pause before Naomi released a faint sigh. "Fair enough, I suppose. What would you like me to do?"

Siovon paced to the opposite end of the hall to peer out of the large window. The snow was peaceful as it fell over the city lights. "Just keep watch for now. I'll send Thor your way after he's done tracking a portal for me. He can slip past the vamps and gather intel to relay to you. You know he's undetectable to most demons."

When Naomi spoke, there was a smile in her tone. "Ah, very well." Despite Lucian's claims of Thor being a pest, Naomi had taken a liking to her little dragon — and vice versa. Then again, Thor was often adored more by women than men. It just added to his inflated ego. When Naomi spoke again, her voice had a surprising softness to it. "Any luck on finding Calysta?"

Siovon twisted her lips. Naomi had taken Calysta under her wing in the years Siovon was held captive, but Calysta was so stubborn that she'd ended up leaving on her own, and all Naomi could do was respect her decision. However, even Naomi had admitted it'd been about five years since she'd last seen Caly.

"No, but we're at the imp's penthouse looking for clues."

"We?" Naomi demanded.

Oops.

She hadn't meant to say that. Siovon wasn't the type to allow just anyone in her business, and, as far as Naomi knew, none of Siovon's other associates were even in America to help. "It's a long story," she muttered.

"My ass," she hissed. "Is there someone I need to kill?"

Despite herself, Siovon smiled. "No. Not now, anyway. He's proving to be a useful hunting tool." She wouldn't tell her that Lucian was one of the sons of the vampire king or that she had agreed to heal his brother if he helped her find Calysta. Naomi was even less fond of vampires than Thor was.

Naomi wasn't pleased with the explanation, but she didn't question Siovon further. They knew each other's boundaries. "Fine. I will let you know if anything comes up."

"Same. Stay safe, Naomi."

"Where's the fun in that?" Naomi questioned before disconnecting the line.

Siovon shook her head. Naomi knew more about her than Calysta did. She knew of her dark past, of her being raised to be nothing more than a cold-hearted killing machine. Calysta knew Siovon had been an assassin, but she didn't know all the gruesome, gory details of her upbringing. Naomi, however, knew everything. She knew because her childhood had been just as dark. Worse, even.

But, like Siovon, Naomi had been a fighter. She had shown potential, and when Siovon had taken her in, it wasn't surprising Naomi had become one of the deadliest members in the guild.

It was a well-known rule not to get close to anyone, even fellow members. Every day was a battle of life and death. It kind of made it hard to get close to people when any moment could be their last, yet Naomi and Siovon had had each other's backs from the start.

Siovon rubbed the center of her chest, the hollow sadness an all-too-familiar feeling.

Ever since leaving the guild, she'd dedicated her time to turning her life around, only killing and fighting if she needed to. Of course, since then, she'd needed to do so far more than she would have liked, but at least she'd tried to avoid conflict. She'd even spent several decades learning her people's old ways on how to create all sorts of herbs, potions, creams and medicines for hundreds of illnesses before traveling from town to town, healing those who were ill, both humans and demons.

Calysta had a pure soul, and her big heart had rubbed off on Siovon over the years, making her also want to help others in need. It had been all she could think of to atone for everyone she'd killed. Not that it relieved any of the guilt, but it had been *something*. While most of her targets had been people who didn't deserve to live, she'd grown sick of playing God.

Siovon sighed and returned to Keegan's living room, wondering if Lucian had managed to hack into the laptop. She froze, however, when more than one male voice could be heard coming from the office.

She stiffened, the hair on her arms and neck standing on end. Though her nose wasn't as sharp as other demons', she still caught on to the strong masculine scents that hadn't been there before she'd stepped into the hall. There was Lucian's scent of pinewood, mint and fallen snow. It was a heady combination that stirred something in the pit of her stomach. Damn, but the man smelled amazing.

The other two were foreign to her. Both were rich, musky aromas, but one was overpowered with a spicy cologne that, while it smelled nice, was far too pungent for her liking. It reminded her of the times she'd gone to the gym and mortals would spray an entire bottle of cologne on themselves after working out instead of taking a shower. She thought it was an odd human trait, and the combination of odors had made her crinkle her nose in disgust. Most demons had their own natural aromas, so why the intruder felt the need to hide his made her curious.

With a shake of her head, she decided it didn't matter. There was no mistaking the rush of power in the air. Lucian wasn't the only vampire here.

She whispered the magical fey words binding her powers to her skin. There was a familiar tingling on her forearm, and she didn't need to look down to see the ink of the short sword tattooed on her was fading away, taking a 3D form as a much larger weapon in her hands. While her awakening powers only worked on images that could be brought to life, she'd found a way to have weapons tattooed on her person and conjure them for short periods of time.

Holsters were a thing of the past. She could be butt-ass naked in front of an enemy and they would never suspect she had a weapon on her until she summoned one. Along with the two on her arm, there was a blade tatted to the back of her right calf and another on her left hip.

With light footfalls, she followed the rumble of voices as they grew louder. Lucian spoke, though he wasn't as concerned with the intruders as she was. The casual, familiar way they spoke to one another told her Lucian knew them. That didn't, however, make her feel any more at ease. She clenched her hands around the hilt of her sword in annoyance. The bastard had invited company over without even giving her a heads-up.

How the hell had they even slipped inside the apartment without her knowing? She'd been in the hall the whole time. If they'd used their creepy vampy skills to sneak past her, she would still have sensed them. And since they were more than two hundred feet off the ground, there was no way in hell they'd climbed up the building to slip through the window.

Steeling her nerves, she cursed herself for not donning her jacket earlier. She felt vulnerable with nothing but the tiny tank top on that molded to her breasts and stomach.

The memory of Lucian snatching it over her head and kissing her with fevered passion sent a fresh wave of desire through her, causing heat to rise in her cheeks. Good God, the man knew how to work those lips. No doubt he also knew how to work his fingers and tongue and —

With another sharp shake of her head, she banished the thoughts. Now was not the time to be distracted.

Stepping into the doorway with her sword pointed down, she assessed her surroundings with narrowed eyes. Lucian was standing near the desk with his arms crossed, his face set in hard lines. Behind the laptop was a man who seemed far too large for both the chair and the desk. Even while sitting down he was tall, but his torso was even broader and more massive than Lucian's, which she hadn't even thought was freaking possible.

Jeez, he must bench-press Slug Bugs for a living, she thought with a grimace. Still, he wasn't at all bad looking. His black T-shirt looked like it had been spray-painted on him, every stroke of his fingers on the keyboard and mouse causing the muscles of his forearms to ripple. His eyes were an intense pale blue and glued to the screen with a laser focus, his hardened features handsome under the soft glow of the room light. His thick hair was platinum blond and pulled into a series of half-braids down his back, making him look like a Viking warrior.

The other male leaned against the wall, dressed in an outfit that likely cost more than the entire apartment. From the polished leather shoes to the pressed black dress pants, to the full-length mink fur coat covering him from neck to knees, he was all calm elegance. His silver hair was a bone-straight river of silk pulled away from an angelic face, his eyes the same intense, pale blue as the male sitting at the desk. He was a couple of inches shorter than Lucian and leaner, but even under the elegant getup, she sensed dangerous power swirling beneath the surface.

He was the exact definition of wealth, grace and raw sensuality. Siovon hoped the man never crossed paths with Naomi. Based on looks alone, he represented everything her dear friend hated in a man, and she wasn't afraid to show it.

All three men were so beautiful that it was near painful—Lucian in a cold, distant way, the blond in a rugged warrior kind of way and the silver-haired one in a fair, elegant way. Any other woman would fall to her knees and thank every god in existence for allowing her to be in the presence of such gloriousness.

Siovon, however, wasn't any other woman. She scowled at the unexpected invasion. She didn't like surprises.

As if sensing her menacing glare at once, all three pairs of pale eyes turned to her, two of them widening in surprise. She squashed the childish urge to duck behind the wall separating the office from the hallway, instead meeting their curious gazes with one of fearlessness.

The one behind the desk spoke, his voice laced with the same Latin accent as Lucian's, only deeper, as if his very tone could threaten the building's foundation. "*This* is the woman who fought Lynx and Caesar?"

Lucian's lips twitched in amusement. His gaze turned prideful. "Astonishing, isn't it?"

"She's...tiny," the Viking said in blatant disbelief.

Siovon snapped her fingers. "*She* is standing right here."

"Yes, I'm well aware of her stature," Lucian drawled, ignoring her.

"Forgive me if I find it hard to believe."

Siovon battled back the annoyance surging within her, not at all an easy task when the three hulking men regarded her as if she'd crash-landed in their backyard. "Would you care for a demonstration?" she demanded of the Viking. "I could kick your ass and toss you out of the window before you can say 'undead'."

A golden eyebrow shot upward. The silver-haired vamp threw his head back and laughed with glee. "Lucian, she is a delight." He turned to her, his eyes twinkling as they roamed her body in a way that would make any other woman melt into a puddle.

Again, Siovon wasn't any other woman. She already had one drop-dead gorgeous, aggravating vampire that made her body boil. One per century was her limit. She narrowed her eyes at him as he stalked toward her.

"Sal," Lucian warned, his tone holding power that should have had the other vamp scrambling away in terror.

Sal ignored him and closed in on her. "Such delicate beauty can only belong to the fey," he murmured in silken tones. "Tell me, *bella*. Does your blood taste as sweet as you smell?"

Faster than Siovon could track, Lucian was suddenly standing before her, shielding her from the other male. Rage rolled off him in waves, and she knew he was baring his fangs. "Back. Off," he commanded, his voice little more than a growl.

Rising to the tips of her toes to peer over Lucian's shoulder, she watched as surprise rippled over Sal's beautiful face. Then, he smirked. "My, this is startling. Why so possessive, *fratello*?"

Brother? As Siovon studied him closer, she only then noticed that all three men indeed shared a striking resemblance to each other. Though the other two had lighter hair and fair skin compared to Lucian's black hair and tan-colored skin, the proud lines and shapes of their faces were all similar.

"You have a disturbing habit of touching things that don't belong to you," Lucian bit out.

"Does the siren belong to you?" Sal demanded, his nostrils flaring as if scenting the air. "She doesn't carry your mark, so I'd say she's fair game."

"She doesn't need my mark to be mine," Lucian shot back. "She's under my protection. So, for the time being, I won't let anyone, especially *you*, lay one finger on her."

Ugh. There they go again, talking as if I'm not here, Siovon thought with a roll of her eyes. *And what the hell is with all this* mine *and my* crap?

"Hey, assholes. Once again, I'm standing right here." She punched Lucian in the middle of his back, eliciting a satisfying grunt from him. "Last I checked, I am *not* some piece of property for either of you to claim, so shut it with this whole possession thing." She punched him again, this one hard enough to make him hiss. "Also, you can take your protection and shove it up your—" She reared her fist to throw another punch when Lucian whirled around and caught it in his hand.

His eyes were hard, his face twisted with pain. "*Merda*, woman. Stop hitting me."

She failed to yank her arm from him. "Not until you quit acting like a freaking caveman just because some random guy looks at me."

"Random guy?" Sal murmured in offense.

Lucian ignored him. "My brother has a reputation for seducing women into being at his mercy. Had I not interfered, you would have been begging him to take you in the next room."

She sucked in a sharp breath, hurt that he assumed she was some mindless sheep that would *baah* at his brother's beck and call. He was beautiful, but so were hundreds of other vampires. "Damn you," she growled, dropping her weapon from her free hand and raising her fist to strike him in that perfect face. She grunted in annoyance when he caught that hand too. "First of all, ew. Pretty boys are not my type."

"Pretty boy?" Sal asked, once again offended. "I'm most certainly not —"

"Second," she continued, ignoring the aggravating wretch, "even if I wanted to sleep with him, you don't have any say over who I can and can't fuc —" She let out a squeak of surprise when Lucian dipped his head to capture her lips in a fierce, demanding kiss.

It was swift, yet there was no mistaking the stark possessiveness. When he pulled back, it was to glare at her. "No other man will touch you so long as I am working with you. I will kill anyone who tries."

It wasn't a threat. It was a promise. A dark, dangerous promise that she knew he would carry out.

A rush of excitement tingled through her, but she didn't let it show. She couldn't give him the satisfaction of knowing his touch had any effect on her.

Tilting her chin to the stubborn angle she knew irked his nerves, she glared right back at him. "You really are a freaking nuisance."

His eyes shimmered with amusement, though his face, of course, remained impassive. "Isn't there some modern saying about the pot talking to a kettle?"

Siovon snorted, battling back a smile. "We'll finish this later, Frosty. Let's hurry and get back to our search."

He nodded before turning back to the other men, who were watching them with astonished eyes. "What?"

Sal and the Viking shared a look between each other. The bigger male's lips were quirked in an odd smile, a pleased look settling on his face. Sal gave a dip of his head to her and Lucian, who was still half-guarding her behind his back. "I may have overstepped my bounds," he murmured, though his tone was unapologetic. "Forgive me." He stepped back, returning to his spot leaning against the wall, his lips twitching in amusement as he looked between them.

"Are you able to get into the computer?" Lucian demanded.

The Viking pressed a few more buttons and waited several seconds before giving a satisfied nod. "It's unlocked." He rose from his seat, the metal of the chair giving a pathetic squeak, as if on its last legs. *Pun clearly intended.* "Next time, remember that this can be done over the phone."

"As if you weren't eager to meet the siren who roughed up Lynx and Caesar," Sal drawled.

The Viking rolled his big shoulders on an unrepentant shrug. "True." He winked at Siovon. "A woman who managed to batter the pride of two of the king's most skilled warriors. How could I pass on the opportunity to meet such a rare creature?"

Siovon flicked invisible lint off the strap of her shirt. "I was defending myself," she stated, not even pretending to be apologetic. Those two brutes had deserved it. They'd come at her, cornering and interrogating her with the good-cop-bad-cop routine, threating to turn her in to their king if she didn't cooperate, all because she smelled *similar* to the person whose blood had been found back in the caves.

Granted, it *was* her blood in the end, but still... She'd escaped, but then they'd found her again a few days later, and that was when she'd learned they were looking for Calysta. After what she'd gone through with Mikhail, she wouldn't let the vampires or anyone else use her sister for their own greed, so she'd kicked their asses and sent them on their way with some minor cuts and bruises.

Okay, maybe that last part was a lie. They'd had a few broken and dislocated bones, but nothing life-threatening.

But now that she knew it was because Lucian's brother lay sick and dying, Siovon couldn't help but feel the desire to help somehow — not because she cared about Lucian or anything...

Well, maybe there was a teeny, tiny, microscopic side of her that didn't want to see him hurt, but there was also that damnable soft side of her that Calysta had caused. She'd made a promise to turn her violent life around.

It was all a part of her pacifism. She wasn't perfect, and she didn't possess Calysta's love for all creatures undead or alive, but dammit, she was trying. However, no matter how strong her determination to turn over a new leaf, it was impossible to shake all those years of training and killing that had hardened her soul, making her defensive to anyone she came across. She just wasn't ready to throw caution to the wind and pretend everyone had good intentions.

"If that's all you needed," Lucian drawled, bringing her from her musings, "you can go now."

The two men shared another amused look. "Yes, yes, we're going," Sal muttered.

The Viking stepped around the desk and approached Lucian. He leaned in, whispering something too quiet for Siovon to hear. Whatever he said made Lucian stiffen. He then clapped him on his back with a chuckle and moved to Sal's side. Sal flashed Siovon another wide smile, one that was meant to be charming, no doubt. "Call me when you get tired of playing with ice, *bella.*" He blew her a kiss, and Lucian growled in warning.

"Gag," Siovon drawled. "I'd rather spend a night in the wolopus territory." Her words were spoken with sarcasm, but something she said made his face go pale.

Sal's eyes widened in horror, while the Viking choked back a laugh. "What did you —?" Sal broke off his words with a growl of frustration. Then he and his brother vanished out of sight.

Siovon blinked, taking a step back. *Whoa.* There wasn't a flash of light, a puff of smoke, nothing. Just...poof... There one moment and gone the next.

Then she recalled Lucian telling her that one of his brothers was able to teleport. She shook her head, because even though she'd seen it with her own eyes, it was still difficult to accept that her life was growing stranger by the minute.

And dammit, she'd had plenty of strangeness in her hundred-plus years of life.

Chapter Eight

"What did the Viking say to you?" Siovon asked, following Lucian around the desk.

Lucian allowed her to take a seat in the chair that was far less plush than it had been before Cass had sat in it. It wasn't the first time his brother's bulk had damaged some kind of furniture or another. The male was six-foot-six and built like an avid weightlifter. Not one of those guys whose arms were so big they couldn't wipe their asses, but not too far from it.

Lucian lifted an eyebrow at Siovon. Something tightened in his gut—a feeling that was becoming far too familiar when he looked at her. Her beauty was enough to knock the breath out of him, trite as that may be. "The Viking?" he echoed.

She gave a helpless lift of her dainty hands that he only then noticed had multiple scars marring the ivory perfection. "The big blond guy who looks like he can tear the bumper off a car...with his teeth. Who needs that many muscles?"

Lucian fought a wry smile as he realized she was talking about his brother. He wasn't surprised. He, Cassander and Salvator shared the same mother. She was of Norse descent, and his two brothers had received her fair hair and skin. Sal's hair was more silver than blond, while Cass' was pale blond. Despite the modern day and age, both preferred wearing their hair long, but Cass' had always been kept in a series of braids like a Viking warrior. It was a style that fit him, given that he'd gone pillaging and plundering a time or two in the olden days.

"Nothing of importance," he murmured, making sure to keep his tone neutral in hopes she wouldn't catch the lie. By the dubious look in her violet gaze, she didn't believe him, but she only shrugged and turned her attention to the laptop.

In truth, his brother's words to him had made him stiffen in both shock and dismay. *'Looks like you've found your truemate, fratello,'* he'd said. *'Congrats.'*

Lucian had already had a feeling Siovon was the woman he was destined to spend eternity with, but he'd expelled those thoughts from his mind. Finding a truemate was very precious to a vampire. For older ones like himself, they were a blessing. After many centuries, even millennia of being alone, truemates provided endless comfort and peace to their jaded lives. They brought back the desire to live. They were a refreshing splash of color in a fickle world of black and white.

Lucian had longed for a truemate after seeing the joy they brought his father and Cassander and so many of his other vampire brethren, but he'd given up the desire to find true love. No woman was good enough to stand at his side. He'd wanted a mate who was as docile as she was understanding that his duty as a clan chief and heir to the throne came before anything else, a woman who wouldn't disobey him, talk back or be any kind of thorn in his side.

And he'd found women who fit that description to a T, yet he'd felt...nothing.

Except bored...and disappointed.

There were none of the common signs that had told him they were his truemate—no mysterious compulsion to be at their side, no extraordinary amount of lust, no sudden burst of emotions, no mind-blowing sex, no return of his long-absent hunger for anything more than blood. There had even been a few tales that some of the others who'd found their truemate could *feel* their partner's emotions before bonding. His brother-in-law Marc had felt Ava's pain and exhaustion from three hundred miles away, as if it were his own.

Lucian had never come close to feeling a thing for those women, yet, in the past week, he'd experienced half the signs. It was more disconcerting that Cass and Sal had noticed the change in him as well. He was a grumpy old fart, as Ava would say. Had anyone else talked to him or treated him the way Siovon did, they would have been introduced to the bottom of his boot in a heartbeat.

Instead, he'd allowed her to belittle and assault him, and in return, he'd kissed her, argued back and shown obvious signs of jealousy when Sal had made a move on her. His brothers had never seen him act that way.

Siovon brought out a side of him that hadn't existed before, and, in all honesty, it worried him. If she was his truemate, he had a feeling she wouldn't be easily persuaded into believing they were destined to be together. She was the I-choose-my-own-fate type.

With a faint shake of his head, he once again cursed his father for sending him on this journey to find Calysta. If the man had chosen someone else, Lucian would have never stumbled across Siovon's delicious scent, and he would have never felt the compulsion to seek her out. Now he was stuck wondering whether or not she was his truemate—and whether or not she could heal Andreas.

That was another thing that bothered him. Though she'd said she could find a cure, he'd seen the uncertainty in her eyes. He didn't doubt she'd spent numerous years studying and creating healing concoctions, but an abaddon's disease had only one cure. Calysta had been their last hope, and he should very well be out searching for her. Even with her curse, he should possess the resolve to do what was necessary to get her to heal his brother.

However, he had to admit that Siovon's ability to sense magic had been helpful. Even with his age and power, he was one of many vampires who couldn't sense it. He didn't trust anyone outside his clan and family to accompany him. Ava was able to sense magic, due to her half-fey blood, but there was no way in hell he was bringing her along. Not only would Marc have foamed at the mouth at the mere suggestion, but he wasn't about to do a single thing to risk her or her unborn child.

So if he hadn't brought Siovon along, he would have never known a portal had been opened. And it was a bonus that her damnable pet dragon was able to track it.

That didn't mean he would tell her that, however. He was far too proud a vampire to admit his faults.

A sharp gasp drew him out of his musings. Alarmed, he stood at Siovon's side. "What is it?" he demanded, spreading his senses to locate the threat.

She pointed a slender finger at the computer screen and he leaned forward, stifling a groan as her sweet scent filled his nose. Freaking gods, he wanted her so bad. She was so close that he could hear the blood rushing in her veins, could almost taste the sweet substance sliding along his tongue as he drank from her.

Forcing the thoughts away, he focused on the computer screen. He'd left the snooping to Siovon to give her something to do other than nag him with questions. And in truth, it was also because he wasn't very tech-savvy. Unlike his siblings, he wasn't interested in keeping up with the ever-changing modern technologies. He'd often been accused of being stuck in the stone age. His home was updated with the latest security systems, and even then he didn't oversee them. He left that to his hired clansmen who guarded his home throughout the day and night.

Siovon's probing had pulled up a hidden video file. It was paused, and the laptop's camera was centered on a woman who could have passed as Siovon's twin. She was just as beautiful, with the same slanted violet eyes. Unlike Siovon, however, her brown hair was long and curly, her nose and cheeks dotted with pale freckles and her skin was a shade darker, as if she spent a lot of time in the sun. Also, while Siovon possessed the same wide, innocent eyes as the woman on the screen, it was clear that life had hardened hers in a way that didn't seem to have touched the other woman.

"It's Calysta." Siovon turned worried eyes to him, revealing the vulnerability she fought hard to conceal. It was that fragility that tugged at Lucian's heartstrings, making him want to pull her into his arms.

"Press Play, *fatina*," he encouraged, offering her the strength she was too proud to admit she needed.

With shaking fingers, she did as commanded. The video came to life, and when Calysta spoke, her voice was lighter and softer than Siovon's, with a hint of urgency.

"Siovon, I don't have much time to talk," she stated, drawing another sharp gasp from her sister. "If you're watching this, then you know I've been with Keegan. Don't worry. He hasn't forced me or hurt me in any way. He's been protecting me. I just..." She paused and gulped. Then, she straightened and lowered her voice to a monotone. "I think Jarek's following me. Rogues keep appearing and Keegan uses portals to get us away, but I don't think we can keep going. I'm going to buff it out and stay strong." There was a sharp sound, like something crashing, and Calysta ended the video.

Siovon was as still as the tattoo on her arm for several minutes. Lucian sensed the different emotions within her — fear, worry and stress. The video was dated over a week prior, and there was no telling what had become of Calysta.

"Siovon?" He brushed his fingers over the back of her neck.

Squaring her shoulders, she snapped out of her stupor and deleted the video, then proceeded to erase more files. "What are you doing?" he questioned, rising to his full height.

"Deleting all traces of the video," she said in a calm tone.

"I think we should let Cassander — the Viking — go through the computer to find more information. Though he doesn't look it, he's the go-to man for anything dealing with technology. He might find something we haven't."

"No need."

Satisfied with her work, she shut the laptop off and closed it before standing. Lucian frowned and grasped her arm to make her face him. He peered into her eyes, frowning even deeper when she didn't look half as concerned as he knew she was. "You don't have to be stubborn. He can —"

"I'm not being stubborn," she cut in, a small smile curving the corner of her lips. "I know where Calysta is."

He lifted a dubious eyebrow, searching her face for some kind of answer. "She didn't say anything about her location."

Siovon pulled away and gathered her discarded jacket. "She did, actually." She pulled the garment over her head, concealing the sweet curves he wanted to taste. A pity. "She said she's going to *'buff it out'*."

He looked at her as if she'd grown two heads, his impatience rising. His father always spoke in cryptic messages, never outright saying what he wanted to say. It pissed Lucian off to no end, and Siovon was doing the exact same thing. "Gods, woman, do you have to speak in circles? What the devil is that supposed to mean? Is it some kind of new-age terminology the kids are saying these days?"

He paused, only then realizing it must have been some coded message between Siovon and her sister. Seeing the revelation on his face, Siovon's smile expanded. "Buffalo, Iowa. It's one of the homes we used to live in on the Mississippi River."

Stunned, a reluctant smile tugged at his lips at the ingenuity of the two women. "Very clever." She beamed at the compliment then proceeded to the door. "Wait," he called, stepping around the desk. "Who is this Jarek that she thinks is following her, and what do Rogues have to do with it?"

Siovon paused mid-stride, and even from a distance, he could see her muscles bunching in tension. She faced him and stared for several moments, as if contemplating how much to tell him.

Realizing there was no way he was going to let it go, she answered him with caution. "Jarek Nilsen...as in Mikhail Nilsen's son."

Lucian froze, the temperature around him dropping. "Mikhail's son." His voice was as cold as the expression he was sure was plastered on his face. "He had a daughter who died centuries ago. He had no son."

Siovon hesitated before nodding. "Yes, he did. Along with the dark wizard, there were imps and his biological son, Jarek. And, of course, there were several women he would...indulge himself with, but as far as I know, they never survived a night with him. Mikhail would kill everyone except Jarek." She grimaced, then shrugged.

The way she explained everything, as if she were talking about the weather, had Lucian grinding his teeth. He stepped forward, ice forming around his boots. It was a sign of his temper. "You're just now mentioning this why?"

Confusion crossed her features before she straightened, her eyes flashing with fire at the anger rolling off him. "I don't owe you any kind of explanation, Frosty. Besides, what does it matter? You already killed Mikhail."

He took another step. "It matters because he is the son of a traitor, and he was a part of Mikhail's plot. He is to be held accountable for his actions."

"Oh."

That was it. Just *'Oh.'*

He growled. "Were you protecting him?" he accused. "Is that the reason you withheld this information?"

Her eyes widened with outrage. "Protecting him? Have you lost your mind?"

"I assure you that my mind is perfectly intact. You knew very well we killed Mikhail because of his actions, and I told you anyone involved with his dealings was to be turned over to the king. Instead of telling me right away about this son, who we had no idea existed, you kept that tidbit to yourself. It makes me question your involvement."

She almost appeared hurt, as if his accusations had been offensive. "Hold your horses there, pal. When you told me you killed Mikhail, if you'll recall, I was questioning whether or not it was *just* him. Before I could explain he had a partner, you stepped in and carried me off like some barbarian when the Rogues were getting close. After that, I just forgot about the whole ordeal."

That much was true, at least. He remembered the odd look on her face as she'd interrogated him in the barn. Still, he wasn't foolish enough to believe she was innocent. "He and his father held you captive for ten years. Forgive me if I find it hard to believe you just *forgot* about his existence."

Her eyes once again flashed with fire, and she crossed her arms. She clutched at the fabric covering her biceps.

He was beginning to learn it was her way to keep from attacking him.

Yeah, some pacifist.

"Forgive me if I don't give a shit what you do or don't believe," she snapped. "I never once said I'd forgotten he existed. Those two bastards deserve to die, but I've seen and caused enough bloodshed to the point where I want to be far away from it all. Seeking revenge is pointless when it won't change the past."

Her words surprised Lucian. There was some hidden meaning to them, but he didn't question it. Yet.

Instead, he asked, "Where is he now?"

"I don't know."

She was lying. The scent was bitter in his nostrils.

Baring his fangs, he crossed the distance between them. He wouldn't hurt her, though with anyone else he wouldn't have hesitated. Just the thought of laying a harmful finger on Siovon was...wrong.

However, he wasn't in the mood for her games. "Tell me," he commanded. It was not something he was willing to look past. Mikhail had died far too easily. Even months later, there had been no justice for his actions. There was someone else who could be held accountable and the fact that Siovon was withholding information was like a stab in the gut. It felt like betrayal, even knowing that the woman owed him nothing.

She wasn't afraid, of course. For someone so tiny, she possessed enough courage to share with the whole demon world. Perhaps it had something to do with the fact that her strength and fighting abilities were dangerous enough to pose a threat to most enemies. Or maybe it had something to do with the bloodshed she'd mentioned. Whichever the case, her bravery was one of the many things he respected about her.

"He's just outside of Des Moines, in Alleman," she conceded, though he knew better than to think it had anything to do with his attempt at intimidation.

He sucked in a sharp breath. "How do you know?"

She dodged the question. "He's been heading east for quite some time. I have eyes on him, and I intend to send Thor to creep past his Rogues to gather more info on what he's plotting."

"If you have no interest in seeking bloodshed, then why are you tracking him?"

"A friend of mine happens to have a stronger thirst for revenge than I do, FYI. And now that I know he could be after Calysta, it seems you should be thanking me for this knowledge." She smirked. "Ah, that explains why you're so mad, because I knew something you didn't. Figures."

He clenched his hands at his sides. His voice was little more than a growl. "I'm furious because he and his damnable father are the reason why my youngest brother lies dying from a fucking abaddon's disease."

She blanched, her taunting look turning to horror. "*They* summoned the abaddon?" she rasped.

Lucian gritted his teeth. Her shock was genuine. She'd had no idea what those monsters had done. Perhaps Mikhail had summoned the creature after she'd escaped. He relaxed just a little. "Yes, and a vampire who betrayed us led Andreas right into its trap. I take it this Jarek is the one who's been sending Rogues through portals after us."

She worried her bottom lip. "The time on the rooftop was the first time it's ever happened to me. It's hard to say if he's after me or you. However, if he's trying to get to Calysta, it's possible he wants to use me to get to her. That's how Mikhail did it."

Lucian frowned, straightening to his full height. "If he's heading east, he could be planning another attack on my family in Chicago. I need to get back and prepare my clansmen."

"Prepare your clansmen? You mean your brothers?"

"No, my clansmen. If there's a fight coming to my territory, they need their chief to guide them."

She took a sharp step backward. "Prince of the leeches *and* Chicago clan chief? Yet you accuse me of withholding vital information?"

He shrugged, unconcerned. "Consider us even."

She grumbled a rather unladylike curse in Russian. *Strange.* "Well, don't let me stop you from carrying out your duties, Your Majesty. Now that I'm closer to finding Calysta and you have your own problems, there's no need for us to continue on together."

He frowned. He didn't like her eagerness to be rid of him, not when there was a dangerous foe looking for her. If he were honest with himself, even if there was no danger, he didn't want her to be separated from him.

"We had a deal," he stated. "We have not found your sister, and you haven't carried out your promise. We'll remain together."

If he wasn't mistaken, there was the faintest flare of relief in her eyes before it was replaced with disdain.

"Well, we can't go to Buffalo and Chicago at the same time, genius."

He pulled out his phone and went to the GPS app. After some quick calculations, he devised a plan, then he checked the time. It took all of ten minutes, yet Siovon watched him with growing impatience.

When she couldn't stand it any longer, she let out a loud, aggravated huff. "What *are* you doing?"

Lucian was wise enough to hide his amused smile. "Buffalo is almost dead center between Des Moines and Chicago. It'll take us about four hours to get there, but it'll be sunrise by then. I'm going to have several of my men meet us there after the sun sets."

Of course, she wasn't pleased. "Why? It doesn't take that many people to search for Calysta, and I damn sure don't want a bunch of rotten leeches stinking up a place we call home."

He heaved an exasperated sigh. "Hopefully, Calysta will be there by the time we reach your home, and there will be no need for a search party. However, you have to accept the possibility that she may not have made it — or that Jarek has her. Alleman is only two hours or so away from Buffalo, and if he's holed up in one spot, he could be expecting you to seek him out. If Thor finds Calysta, we can plan our next move. If he doesn't, I'll send my men ahead to Alleman when the sun sets and have them close in on him. Now that we know where he's hiding, he will not be able to make another escape."

Siovon still didn't look pleased with him, but her anger gave way to worry. "You think he has her already?"

Lucian frowned as he brushed her bangs from her eyes. "Whether he does or doesn't, we will find her, *fatina*. I can promise you that."

She swept her violet eyes over his face for several moments, searching for…something. *Reassurance? Hope? Hell if I know.* But the vulnerable look in her eyes returned, and if vowing that he'd scrape the entire ends of the Earth to find her lost sister was what she wanted, then by the gods, he'd do so.

Pathetic, yes. But he didn't care.

Somehow she'd managed to touch a spot in his heart, and as the hours passed, it was beginning to thaw the ice he'd spent centuries forming.

Truemate or not, Siovon's feelings and wellbeing had somehow become his top priority, and though he should have long ago deserted her, there was no turning back. She'd bewitched him.

"Come on," he murmured, taking her hand and leading her toward the front of the apartment. "We'll take my car to Buffalo. We'll work out more details on the way."

"Okay," she muttered in response. And whether it was a sign of her starting to trust him or just her concern for her sister distracting her, for once, she wasn't resisting him.

Chapter Nine

Chicago, Illinois

Transferring a half-dozen bags of groceries from the shopping cart to the trunk of her car, Ava scowled at her mate as he took the last of them from her and placed them inside.

He flashed her that sexy, dimpled smile that never failed to make her heart stutter. "Don't look at me like that, love. I don't want you doing any heavy lifting."

She raised a disbelieving eyebrow. "You've seen me lift a grown man off the ground by his throat," she drawled. "These bags weigh nothing."

He shrugged and splayed a big hand across the tiny swell of her belly. He used his free hand to tap the tip of her nose, as if she were a small child he was patronizing. "Yes, love, you're a big scary vampire, but I don't want to take any chances."

She nipped at the index finger waving in her face, drawing a lusty hiss from him. "Don't mock me, jerk."

His golden eyes darkened, and he stepped so close to her that she could feel the heat from his skin wrapping her in a comforting embrace. "Don't bite me unless you want me to strip you naked and take you right here in this parking lot."

Ava's fangs lengthened and heat pooled in the pit of her stomach. They'd been mated for a little over two months, and not once had that passion lessened. If anything, it had intensified.

There had even been a few embarrassing times when they'd had to rush out of the room her family was in before they attacked each other right then and there, without a care for who was watching.

Marc settled his hand on the side of her neck where the mark of their mating lay in the crook of her shoulder. He pulled her in for a sizzling kiss that left her breathless. It was an hour past midnight, and only a handful of other cars were parked in the snowy lot, most of them belonging to the overnight employees of the twenty-four-hour market.

Even so, Ava forced herself to pull away from him, chuckling at his whine of displeasure. It was her turn to tap him on the nose. "If you want any more than that, you'd better hurry and get us home."

With a grumbled curse, he showed his demon speed by pushing the buggy away to where the others were lined up, then ran to the passenger side and opened the door for her to get in. She smiled when he growled for her to move faster.

"By the way, babe, thanks for those berries," she murmured, taking her time to annoy him. "They were delicious."

His eyes widened. "You ate them all? I just got them two nights ago."

"I didn't. The second jar is in the fridge, still full. I'm trying to hold back from eating them all in one go."

He smirked, humor twinkling in his eyes. "I'm sure your gratefulness will in no way comfort Sal."

At that, Ava frowned. "Is he mad at *me*? He hasn't returned my calls since then."

Marc chuckled. "Let's just say he blames you for his up-close-and-personal encounter with one of the wolopuses."

Ava gasped when realization hit her. "Oh, that poor man." She laughed. "That is just rich. Do the twins know?"

"Not yet, but it's killing me not to tell them."

Ava grinned, about to say something, but she paused in the middle of sliding into the seat when a faint cry sounded. She tilted her head to Marc, knowing he'd heard it too by the way he'd gone still. He scanned the shadows that the light of the market's blinking sign didn't touch.

Given his years as a human cop, he was already in tune with his surroundings, always searching for anything that might be amiss. Ever since his demon blood had been awakened and he'd turned into a full cougar shifter, his senses had sharpened to those of a skilled predator.

After several more moments, the soft cry sounded again, though it was much closer. Marc opened his mouth as if to tell her to get in the car, but she ignored him. She rose, pulling a hidden dagger from her boot. Despite the threat of Mikhail being over, she never went anywhere unarmed.

"Ava—" Marc started in warning, only to break off with a curse when she darted past him. She didn't want to spend time arguing with him that it was too dangerous for her to be wandering around and *blah-blah-blah*. She'd heard the same speech from her father, her brothers and even Duncan—Marc's partner and closest friend—at least five hundred times in the past two months.

Good gods. She may be pregnant, but she wasn't helpless, not to mention the cry had sounded like it came from a child. Ava was an empathetic Royal, meaning that along with her telepathic powers, she could sense strong emotions from afar.

And the person who was crying was feeling a colossal amount of fear and sadness.

Marc was at her side, drawing her gloved hand into his, though he managed to walk a smidge in front of her. A small smile tugged at her lips. Even as a human, knowing she was far stronger and faster than him, he still acted all macho, as if to prove his masculinity. He was a protector by nature and it was just one of the many things she loved about him.

They rounded the back of the market and passed a couple of alleys before coming to a stop at a darker one between two closed businesses.

"It's a child," Marc breathed.

Ava stared into the darkness, straining her eyes until she could make out the little ball curled between an empty trash can and a dumpster. "You can tell from this distance?" she asked, surprised. Not even her vampire vision could pierce the darkness, which was something to do with her mother's fey blood running through her veins. Though she was a Royal, she was still lacking in most skills that full vampires were given.

Marc gave a solemn nod, peering at her with suspicion. "I would tell you to wait here, but why do I get the feeling you won't listen?"

Ava flashed a sweet smile and kissed him on his cheek. "Because you're a smart man." She frowned as she looked onward. "Besides, most children tend to be more relaxed around women than men."

With an exasperated sigh, Marc accepted her reasoning and led her down the alley. As she drew near, Ava could better make out the tiny, malnourished form dressed in tattered rags for clothing, sickly-pale skin that was as white as the snow around them and innocent, terrified orange eyes that seemed to glow under the light of the moon.

When they were mere feet away from the child, she backed away to bolt. "Wait," Ava soothed, sheathing her dagger and holding her hands up in a gesture of peace. "We aren't going to hurt you."

The child hesitated, and when she looked like she was about to run again, Ava crouched to appear small and non-threatening. Behind her, Marc did the same.

The child's eyes were wild as they darted around, unfocused and petrified. When Ava spoke, she laced her voice with charm to ease the child's fear. "It's all right, little one. You're safe. I'm Ava. This is my husband, Marc. He's a police officer. Do you have a name?"

The girl's nose scrunched, and Ava frowned as she realized the girl was fighting against Ava's charm — and winning.

Odd. She'd never had to use it on a child, but it should have been easier to charm children than adults. Their minds were weak and susceptible to these kinds of things. Mortals were more so than demons, so perhaps the girl was a demon.

After another moment's hesitation, the child whispered, "Anais."

"Anais," Ava repeated, using what she hoped was a motherly tone. "That's a beautiful name. Why are you here by yourself? Where's your family?"

Anais' eyes widened farther, and the fear and sadness rolling off her clogged Ava's senses, causing her heart to bleed for the child. "I have no family, not anymore."

Ava turned to Marc with a frown, and he also appeared sympathetic. Marc had been a foster child until he was a teenager, then he'd been adopted by an old couple. She and Marc had talked about buying a bigger house and opening their doors to strays, runaways and other kids who needed love and a place to call home. Actually, they were scheduled to meet with a real estate agent in the next week.

Ava returned her attention to Anais, who had started to cry again. "I'm sorry, Anais. I lost my mother when I was little. I know what it's like to be alone and afraid."

"I also lost my family at a young age," Marc murmured, his deep voice just as soothing as Ava's. "However, you don't have to be alone anymore. We'll take care of you." He paused when Anais eased out of her hiding spot, though she was still tense.

"When's the last time you ate, sweetie?" Ava questioned.

"I-I don't remember."

Ava's heart broke as she eyed Anais. The poor girl was so skinny, and her cheeks looked a little hollow. She couldn't have been any more than ten years of age.

She also wasn't human, going by the way her eyes flashed in the darkness.

"I don't want to hurt you," Anais croaked. "I'm not normal."

Hurt us?

Ava gave a comforting smile. "Trust me, sweetness. We aren't so normal either." She held out a hand. "Come on. We'll take care of you. How does a hot meal and a warm bath sound?"

The girl's eyes filled with longing as she took more tentative steps toward them. "And...a bed?"

Ava's smile returned. "Of course. A bed with soft sheets and fluffy pillows. Anything you want."

Anais sniffled and wiped her eyes with the heels of her hands, all the tension seeming to leave her little body. "You promise not to tell Master I ran away?"

Alarmed, Ava fought the urge to reel back in shock. *Master? What...the hell?* "Your *master*?" she inquired.

Anais nodded, fear creeping back into her voice. "He's not a nice man," she whispered. "He kills people who run away."

Ava's heart gave another painful lurch. Slaves of all types were sought-after in the demon world—even humans. She knew that firsthand.

With shaking fingers, Ava drew an invisible X over her heart. "You have my word that I will let no harm come to you, Anais. Marc and I will protect you."

For odd moments, Anais just watched the two of them with a sharp stare that made her look older than she was. It was as if she were looking *through* them rather than *at* them. At last, she relaxed and shuffled toward Ava. When she was within reach, she stunned Ava by wrapping her frail arms around her neck in a hug.

"You both have beautiful souls," she said with a sniffle. "I can trust you."

Ava was again surprised, wondering what the girl meant, but then Anais' exposed skin touching her bare neck sent a myriad of memories flooding through her mind.

They were horrifying.

After several minutes of shocked stillness, Anais' body went limp and her heart settled to a slow, steady pace as she fell asleep—just like that, holding on to Ava's neck, as if afraid to let go.

"Ava? What is it?" Marc demanded with worry.

With wide eyes, Ava stood while cradling Anais in her arms. The poor girl couldn't have been more than fifty pounds. Marc wiped her cheeks with his fingers, making Ava realize she'd been crying.

The memories replayed over and over in her mind until she felt sick to her stomach. There was so much bloodshed, so many screams of terror, so much pain.

And Anais had watched it all, had watched her entire family slaughtered before her very eyes. Then everything had gone blank. The bloodcurdling screams, however, had never vanished. Anais had been rendered blind, but she could still hear everything.

But what was even more pressing was that Anais wasn't just any demon child, as Ava had thought.

A familiar darkness spread through Ava's chest, the need to go into one of her Purging episodes making her shake where she stood. It had happened a handful of times in the past. Whenever she'd get a prolonged peek inside Cyrus' head, the dark emotions from his past memories would flow into her, her empathic powers absorbing it until her body could release the darkness. The memories would remain on repeat, sending her to a dark place in the back of her mind.

When Marc's warm hands framed her face, she blinked at him. "Talk to me, love," he urged. Through the shared connection of their mating, he could feel every last one of her emotions. No doubt he sensed her feelings fading away, giving in to the soul-deep depression that was taking over her mind and heart. "What did you see?"

Her mouth worked, but it took several tries before she was able to form words. The darkness was swiftly sinking her into an abyss far deeper than anything she'd ever encountered.

"P-purge. Take me to my f-father," she stammered, her voice sounding distant to her own ears. "Anais is a Royal."

* * * *

Siovon sat in the passenger seat of Lucian's Jag, staring at the fading darkness beyond the tinted windows. After leaving Keegan's apartment, he'd once again carried her through the city until he came upon where he'd parked his car. They hadn't spoken much in the three-hour ride since then. He'd taken the hint that she didn't want to be bothered and had settled for listening to soft Christmas music.

The cheery jingling melodies did nothing to ease the strain on her mind. Calysta's video had been a week old. She prayed her sister had made it to their hidden cabin in Buffalo, safe and sound.

Maybe it was intuition or a premonition or whatever the hell they called it, but somehow she just knew Caly wouldn't be there. If that were the case, she hoped her sister had found another place to hide away until Siovon could find her. If she didn't have that bit of hope, she had nothing.

Sighing, she ran her hand over her right forearm. Though Thor couldn't be killed, she still worried over him, too. He wasn't just her creation. He was a piece of her. He was her friend, and she cared just as much for him as she did Caly.

When he'd telepathically told her that the wielder of the magic had been some imps from a demon housekeeping company, she'd sent him to Alleman to be with Naomi.

With Lucian's clansmen heading there in the evening, Naomi would not react with kindness. Siovon had taken it easy on those Guards, but if Naomi felt cornered, she would go down fighting, bringing down as many people as she could with her. It didn't matter in the slightest that the vamps were allies.

Siovon shook her head, a soft smile curling her lips. Naomi was pretty misunderstood. She had a certain look that made people wonder if she was counting the ways she could kill them, but she wasn't entirely cold. What outsiders didn't know was that she was caring and tender-hearted to those in her circle and would battle Satan himself to protect them.

She'd never admit it aloud, of course, but the feelings were there. It was what made Siovon just as loyal to her as she was to Calysta.

"Why are you smiling?" Lucian asked, his baritone jarring her from her thoughts.

Startled, she turned to him, having forgotten he was even there. She'd been too distracted by her thoughts, something she'd do well to avoid in the future. She never got sidetracked. She was always aware of her surroundings.

Yet somehow Lucian made her feel...safe, like she could relax.

It was a dangerous notion, considering they'd only known each other for a brief time and he'd see her as an enemy soon enough.

"I was just thinking," she muttered, scolding herself for her ignorance. "Nothing important."

"Hmm." His eyes remained straight ahead as he sped along the road. Dawn was only an hour away, but there were very few other cars traveling along the old road. "How did you gain an interest in healing?"

Siovon frowned, trying to figure out whether or not he was asking to converse or to be nosey. Caution was her middle name, so she didn't bother hiding her suspicion. "Why?"

He glared out of the corner of his eye. "Must everything be a fight with you?"

She grunted. "No, but you don't strike me as a man who indulges in idle chitchat, so I want to know why the sudden interest."

"There are a lot of things I've done out of character this past week," he muttered under his breath. Before she could question it, he said, "I'm curious, *fatina*. I'm having a hard time figuring you out. You have eluded and incapacitated a couple of the best warriors I've ever met, yet you claim to be a pacifist. I want to know how someone who has been well-trained in martial arts chooses instead to claim a life of peace and studying healing properties. It seems contradictory."

Siovon twisted in her seat to sit still as a statue as she peered straight ahead. She didn't want him to see how uncomfortable the question made her. "Women are allowed an air of mystery, aren't we?"

His lips twitched again, but he shook his head. "I suppose so. Forgive me for my intrusion."

She rolled her eyes at the stupid flare of guilt. "Tell you what, Frosty. For every bit of information I reveal, you give me something in return. And it has to be of equal significance. Deal?"

He cut his eyes to her again before giving a small nod. "I should have known that would backfire on me. Very well, *fatina*. What would you like to know?"

She didn't hesitate. "How old are you?"

The car swerved into the neighboring lane before he jerked it back into position with a small cough. His face was twisted into a grim expression.

"What the heck?" she demanded, clutching her chest to still her pounding heart. "You almost ran us off the road over that question?"

"It was a squirrel," he lied, shaking his head. "Bloody hell, woman. You aren't supposed to ask a vampire their age."

"That's an odd thing to be insecure over. If you want honest answers from me, I want the same."

He grunted. "I was born about a hundred years before the fall of the Roman Empire."

Siovon did a mental calculation. "Good lord. That would make you almost two thousand years old."

He tightened his grip on the wheel. "My age is something I'd prefer we not talk about."

"Wow," she murmured, sitting back in her seat. She'd known he was old, but not *that* old. He was freaking ancient. "Jesus Christ."

"Your turn."

She shook her head. "When I met Calysta and Lila, they kind of just rubbed off on me. They were both healers, so I wanted to contribute to their practices."

His eyes widened at her words. "When you *met* them? They are your blood sister and mother, correct?"

She frowned, turning in her seat as unease slid through her. "Yes." She waved that away. "It's a long story. I don't want to bore you with the details."

Without looking over at her, Lucian placed a hand on her knee. Nothing sexual, but it sent a jolt of heat straight to her core. "Siovon, I doubt anything about you is boring."

His intimate tone made her even more uncomfortable. She was not used to feeling so vulnerable. She brushed his hand away from her. "The three of us *are* related, but I didn't meet them until a little after my hundredth birthday."

When he sucked in a sharp breath and glanced at her with shock, she gave a solemn nod. "I told you it's a long story." She could tell he wanted to ask more questions, but she held up a finger. "It's my turn for a question, Frosty."

He nodded in reluctance. "Very well."

"I've heard stories of how vampires were once uncivilized, and I know Cyrus came to be your king, but how? I can't imagine him strolling along wearing a crown and commanding people to bow to him."

His frown deepened. Siovon wondered if it was a touchy question, but she hadn't meant for it to be cruel. She was genuinely interested in learning more about his kind. As an assassin, it was vital to learn about her target's species. As a healer, she wanted to learn about vampires to aid in her studies. It might even help her find a cure for Andreas.

That was doubtful, but she wouldn't tell Lucian that. She'd be killed the moment they realized she couldn't really help Andreas—but she was prepared for that.

"Long ago, before my father became king, there was a council of five Ancients who ruled before him. They cared only for themselves and caused death and destruction everywhere. Our people were feral beasts who hunted and killed one another without mercy. Of course, humans and other demons were no exception. They were seen as livestock. It was a time of chaos, a time of constant war and fear. My father wanted better for our kind, and so pulled together a clan of vampires to battle the Ancients."

"I'm sorry. Who were the Ancients?" Siovon asked.

"Ancients are what we call the earliest vampires. They were all Royals. They were the very first vampires ever to walk the Earth thousands of years ago."

"Ah, so they're the creators of vampires?"

"Essentially, yes. They are the Adams and Eves of our kind."

"Gotcha. So they weren't nice rulers?"

"Nice couldn't even come close to describing them. "

"Why didn't the Imperials step in and do something if they were so bad?"

The Imperials, after all, were the supreme justice dealers of the demon world. If there was a problem that couldn't be handled by the individual rulers of each demon species — if there was an issue between two or more or if there was someone posing a threat to humans — then the Imperials took over. Not even the most brutal of demons wanted to get on their bad side. Punishments dealt by them were unspeakable.

"There was nothing they could do without destroying our entire race," he muttered. "My father went to them for help, even knowing there was nothing they could do. However, he received advice to take matters into his own hands."

Siovon lifted her brows at that. "Advice?"

He smirked. "A subliminal message encouraging him to make a change to those in power."

"In other words, kill them."

Lucian gave a single nod. "Mikhail's father, Vladimir, was my father's closest friend. Together, they formed a clan strong enough to lead into battle. It was a battle that went on for years, and many of their own were killed—including Vlad, in the end—but my father's clan proved victorious. Cyrus landed the killing blow to the last of the Ancients, and since none of them had any direct heirs, he was, by the laws of nature, the next in line to rule vampire-kind. Even if he hadn't been the one to kill them, his clansmen selected him as king, regardless. It was a position he didn't want but accepted in order to bring peace to our people."

"Wait a minute," Siovon cut in. "Cyrus is a Royal, and from what you're saying, Royals are all descended from the Ancients. So, if there were only five Ancients, wouldn't that make them his own family? And he couldn't have been the only Royal during that time, so how was it that he alone became king and not any others?"

"The council was made up of five Ancients but there were others. However, the council members had similar ideals of ruling, and any Ancient who opposed them was killed." Siovon gasped at that and Lucian nodded. "As I said, they cared only for destruction. My father was birthed by a couple of the opposing Ancients, and he had siblings, but he was the only one to survive a home invasion."

Siovon was poised on the edge of her seat with eagerness. She felt like a kid attending a reading of an urban legend, one that was compelling enough to make her heart race with anticipation. She was so invested in the story that she'd forgotten what she'd asked him in the first place.

Lucian continued. "As you can imagine, it was impossible to expect change to happen right away after vamps had run amok for thousands of years, but Cyrus was patient—and adamant. He set his laws into motion, the first being a need for clans. Every clan needed a chief. Gladiator wars were set up, and only the strongest of the strong were able to obtain the title. It was considered a great honor."

"I bet," she murmured. She knew of the more common gladiator games during the days of the Roman Empire, but somehow she figured that was a mild, innocent version of what the vampires had been forced to go through. "How old is your father?"

Lucian tilted his head to the side in consideration before shaking his head. "Truth be told, no one knows for sure. I doubt even he remembers. All we know is that he was born around the time when the Etruscans migrated from Libya to Rome, some three thousand years ago."

Siovon inhaled a sharp breath. *Holy freaking moly. Lucian's ancient, but Cyrus is freaking prehistoric. He's so old he doesn't know how old he is.*

"Wow," she breathed.

Lucian snorted. "Each time a clan chief was appointed, they were sent with groups of hunters loyal to Cyrus to conquer their preferred lands. Along with the clan laws, we could no longer kill humans without just cause, all Rogues were to be killed on sight and a handful of other mandates that had been necessary at the time but aren't so much anymore. There were those who opposed these laws, of course, and tried to kill him. A good number of them had been other Royals who'd felt they'd be better suited to rule as king or queen—or who preferred the old way of living. Also, no one was forced to join clans. Anyone who wanted to remain clanless was free to do so, but they did not have the protection of a clan to keep them safe from outsiders."

He continued. "My father lost so many people, including his truemates, just to see our people prosper. Even today, there are those who are uncivilized, as you say, and there are still clan wars and other things that make it seem like we are all monsters. But compared to how life was for us before then, we have come a very long way, all thanks to Cyrus and his determination. He can be colder than me at times, but beneath it all is a man who set out to conquer his people to lead them to a life of peace and prosperity. When he steps down and I take over as king, I can only hope to continue his legacy with pride."

Siovon watched Lucian for several minutes, admiring him. Despite his callous exterior, he adored his father. Who wouldn't, after listening to that story? Cyrus had been an ordinary Royal among a chaotic world of vampires, and with sheer willpower, he'd set out to accomplish his goals and provide his people with balance. That had taken an immense amount of resolve and strength. Now she understood why he was called Cyrus the Conqueror.

"What's a truemate?" she asked.

Lucian twisted his lips in displeasure. "It's my turn."

Siovon blinked in confusion. "Your turn for what?"

He glanced at her with humor. "A question, *fatina*. Remember? We are getting to know one another."

Siovon blinked again, realizing she'd indeed forgotten. Again. "Right. Ask away."

He pondered, as if trying to find the right words to ask. "How come you didn't meet your mother and sister until you were over a hundred years old?"

Chapter Ten

Lucian was patient as Siovon considered answering his question. He knew she'd be disinclined, but even so, he continued to wait. For once, it wasn't to seek information to benefit himself. Everything about her amazed him. She was as intriguing as she was beautiful, and with every new bit of information he discovered about her, he was left with more questions.

She was a mystery he wanted to solve.

When he peered at her again, she was toying with the drawstring of her hoodie. He didn't think she was the type to have any nervous habits, which made him more curious.

He dropped his gaze to the slim, graceful column of her neck, his stomach tightening in hunger that had as much to do with him wanting blood as it did sex.

But not just any sex, not just anyone would do.

No, he wanted one woman only, something that terrified him far more than anything else, because if Siovon wasn't his truemate, it would mean he'd developed feelings for a woman who could never be his.

And such an outcome was just...sad.

Forcing the thoughts away, he returned his focus to the road as a wave of fatigue washed over him. The sun hadn't yet risen, but it wasn't far off. He was able to withstand the rays of the sun, but to do so he'd have to feed more, and the portable cooler full of bagged blood he'd brought wouldn't last forever.

It was for that reason that he tended to avoid the sun unless necessary. He was a vampire. He was strongest at night, when wrapped in total darkness.

Besides, such was the norm with Royals and Aristocrats. The older they were, the more their humanoid bodies became...well, vampire-y. They lost their taste for human food, they grew less tolerant of sunlight, they were grumpy more often than not and, for most, sex became boring as hell. There were very few things to excite them anymore.

That was until they found their truemate to make them feel again. It was like they'd reached maturity all over again.

Lucian thought of all the times he'd tried and failed to resist touching Siovon. Whether it was to kiss her soft lips, trace the lines of her face or just to stand close to her to inhale her rich scent, he'd felt as if he needed to do all of those things. They pleased a deep part of him.

He let out an inaudible sigh. He hoped she would forget asking him what a truemate was. He'd have to answer truthfully and doing so made him want to cut his own tongue out. If he were being honest with himself, a small piece of him was nervous to hear what her opinion would be on such a matter. She'd scoff at the idea, no doubt.

Just when he was sure Siovon wouldn't answer his question, she blew out a harsh breath. "It's a pretty dreadful story. My mother gave birth to me on the coast of Malaysia in the 1800s."

"Without your father?"

"My father was a human whom my mother fell in love during her travels."

Lucian was surprised. "A human? You don't smell..."

She shrugged as his words trailed off. "Sirens haven't been around for centuries, so not many people know our secrets. Our children are born purebloods — either pureblood siren or pure whatever the other parent is. There are no half-bloods."

That was news to Lucian. That was just another reason why they'd been so desired to the point of extinction. He could envision other races of demons who were on the verge of dying wanting to breed with sirens in the hopes that their spawn would be able to repopulate their kind. Hell, if she was his truemate, there was a possibility she could birth pureblood Royals and save his people.

He frowned. Would she even want children one day? Lucian had always longed to start a family of his own. Though he knew any children he fathered wouldn't be full Royal, he would love them regardless. Others would never guess it, but he loved children. He couldn't wait for Ava to give birth. Right alongside his father and brothers, he was going to spoil his first niece or nephew rotten.

"So you and Calysta were born sirens," he murmured. "Were there any others?"

She shook her head. "No, thank God." When he shot her a surprised look, she shrugged. "Being a siren isn't all peaches and cream, Frosty. I wouldn't wish this life on my greatest enemy."

When he remained silent, she continued. "My parents' marriage didn't last when my father realized he could turn a profit by selling pureblood siren children to the UBM."

"UBM?" Lucian questioned. Gods, as if he wasn't old enough, her new-age terms made him feel it.

"Underworld black market."

Lucian damn near ran off the road again. When he settled the car back into the lane, she was glaring at him. "Another squirrel," he breathed, his temper flaring. "The human—your own father—wanted to sell you to the under...uh, UBM? Was he not in love with your mother?"

Siovon's lips twisted with bitterness. "I suppose he was at first. However, as is the case with many people, greed filled him. During that time, money wasn't easy to come by in their region, and after my mother made the mistake of telling him how rare a demon she was, he'd gone behind her back and set up bids before I was ever born."

"That bastard," Lucian growled, his knuckles turning white on the steering wheel.

"My words as well," Siovon muttered. "One night, while my mother was recovering from giving birth to me, my father sold me to the highest bidder. I wasn't even a week old yet. From what Lila told me, he came up with some crafty lie about how their home had been broken into and bandits had stolen me away. He even went as far as to hire someone to beat him up to make it seem as though he'd put up a fight."

"And your mother believed him?"

149

Siovon snorted. "She was in love with the man, in pain from giving birth and grieving over losing her first child. You'd be surprised to learn how fragile a woman's heart can be after such things." She paused. "Not that I have any experiences to go by, but I at least tried to understand. Anyway, the man who bought me was a Raptor. I suppose that alone is enough to explain my upbringing."

Instead of swerving and risk sending them crashing into the nearby trees, Lucian eased the car to the hard shoulder and set the gear to Park. He turned hard eyes on her, but she met his look with a blank one.

Gods above.

Raptors were an elite group of assassins who made even the Guard look like innocent Cub Scouts. They were the types that could kill their target in broad daylight in front of a crowd of people, yet no one would ever know who'd done it. They were impossible to find unless they wanted to be found and they were even harder to kill. What was worse, they worked for the Imperials, both in the human plane and in Hell, thus making them some of the deadliest demons in more than one realm.

One must have done something of pure evil to have a Raptor sent after them or have made the mistake of making an Imperial their enemy.

He studied Siovon. Leaving no room for her to dodge the question, he asked, "You were raised by a Raptor?"

"Yes."

"So you are one of them?"

She shook her head. "No. My mentor never allowed me the chance."

"What is that supposed to mean?"

"No one can just walk up to the Imperials and ask to become a Raptor. You have to be referred by a current member. If the Imperial who oversees such things is interested, he will come to you and test your skills to see if you're worthy of the title. My mentor trained me to be just like him from the day I took my first steps until I turned twenty. He wanted me to follow in his footsteps, and I did so to make him proud. He'd give me targets, and I'd do what I had to do with absolute precision. However, no matter how skilled I became, he never once thought I was good enough to become a Raptor. Not that I wanted to be one, mind you, but it was like he didn't see the potential in me. Well, that's what I thought, at least."

She lowered her eyes, likely to hide the pain that surfaced. Unable to help himself, Lucian laid his hand over hers in her lap. She flinched at the contact but didn't pull away. He took that as a good sign.

"Why didn't he?" Lucian questioned, sick to his stomach. The thought of Siovon growing up and living that kind of lifestyle made his skin crawl. Not that he was a goddamn saint himself, given the horrible choices and number of people he'd killed and tortured in his day, but unlike him, she had a vulnerability in her that made it hard for him to picture her being so...cold. It just didn't fit her. "You seem adequate enough to me, *fatina*. *Merda*, you broke several bones of my father's men and outsmarted them — and me, if I'm being honest."

She snorted. "That's a compliment I don't want, Lucian. One night he just upped and left, leaving only a letter behind. He'd written that I would have been the perfect Raptor, but he didn't want me to lose my heart." She shrugged at his confused look. "I didn't understand it either. Still don't." When she spoke, she appeared casual, but there was a hint of bitterness in her tone. "It's not like I've seen the man since then to ask him what was up with that."

Lucian shook his head and continued their drive. "He left one night with only a letter addressed to you. That's it?"

"Yep."

"Do you miss him?"

"After the hell he put me through to become a cold-hearted killing machine?" She gave a harsh, bitter laugh. Then, in a much softer, unexpected tone that touched his frozen heart, she murmured, "Of course I miss the old bastard. He didn't have a nurturing bone in his body, but he was the only father I ever knew. Besides, it wasn't all bad. There were times when I saw him as more than a mentor. He was quick to squash it, of course, but deep down the feeling was still there."

Lucian squeezed her hand. His father had been in his life since the day he had been conceived. As much as Cyrus pissed him off, he couldn't imagine life without him. So many had come and gone in all his years, but his family was the one thing that had stayed. They'd lost some — like his mother and the twins' mother — but they'd made it. It was why he'd been so devastated when Ava had run away all those years ago. Like Cyrus always said, as long as the Gordanos had each other and stood as one, there was no pain so great that they couldn't overcome it.

The words were corny, but there was a vast amount of truth to them. So long as he had his family, life was worth living. It was boring as hell most times, but worth living.

"So what happened after you received that letter from him?" Lucian asked.

"He left a decent amount of money and his home to me, should I decide to stay, but we both knew that wouldn't happen. Siberia wasn't a place I wanted to live any longer than I had to. There was an address written at the bottom that I was to seek out if I wanted to venture into the world. There was a woman waiting for me, and I'd learned she was a scout for a local assassin's den. They weren't friends of my mentor, per se, but they were people he'd trusted once upon a time before becoming a Raptor. He'd arranged it so she could test my skill if I wanted to join them. With nowhere else to go and no-one to turn to, I stayed with them for the next eighty years or so."

"And that's when you met your sister and mother?"

A small smile curved her pretty lips, making Lucian swallow a groan. They were having an intimate moment of trust, something he didn't think he'd get from her again any time soon. He didn't want to ruin it with admitting to his lust, powerful as that may be.

"Yes. One day I was finishing a job in Romania and slipped into a popular town to do a bit of sightseeing. It was by chance alone that this woman came up to me and hugged me. She couldn't have been more than a few years younger than me. When she pulled back, she was confused when she realized that I wasn't her mother, whom she was there to meet. But when I looked at her, I would have thought she was a doppelgänger, if not for a few moments later when her real mom caught up to her, apologizing for the misunderstanding. When she got a good look at me, though...honestly, we could have been mistaken for triplets."

Lucian smiled, recalling how much Calysta had looked like Siovon in the video. Hell, even in the vision Ava had shown him, Lila had appeared pretty similar, though she'd been on the verge of death. "Calysta and Lila, I'm assuming?"

She chuckled, the sound like tinkling bells in his ears. Such sappy fucking thoughts, but he didn't care. She had a beautiful laugh. "Yes. It was so weird. Calysta and Lila had been separated for a few weeks and had planned to meet up in that particular town, and I suppose by fate I happened to drop in as well. It was strange at first, as we all just kind of stared at each other. Then Lila started crying. It freaked the hell out of me, but she kept hugging me and crying. It made the entire situation even more awkward."

"Did she explain it all to you?"

She nodded. "She told me everything, about how my father had sold me as a babe. She hadn't known until a few years later when she'd given birth to Calysta and caught the bastard trying to do the same thing. She killed him, but no one knew how to find me, so while she'd grieved for me all those decades, she'd kept hope alive that one day we'd meet again. I had trouble believing everything at first, but I came to terms with it. The resemblances between the three of us were too precise to be a coincidence, and the timeline of her story matched up. To make an even longer story short, I continued as an assassin for several more years until my contract was up, and instead of renewing it with the guild, I joined my mother and sister on their travels as they went from city to city, country to country, working to heal those who were sick. As you can imagine, after spending a century killing, not trusting anyone but maybe one or two people, it was hard to break away from that lifestyle. It still is, to be honest, but I'm learning."

She turned to him, her smile turning sly. "So, to answer your first question, I've been an assassin for the first half of my life and only in the last eighty or so years have I turned pacifist. Well, mostly pacifist. I slip up from time to time."

He snorted, then drawled, "I hadn't noticed."

She rolled her eyes, but it was in good humor. "I'm trying. I haven't killed anyone in decades."

Lucian cracked a smile. He was still trying to figure her out, but she was telling the truth. She continued to surprise him. "Sure. Whatever you say."

He was pleased to note that the air around her had eased. Perhaps opening up about her past had relieved some unknown burden from her shoulders. Lucian liked it. He wasn't the laughing or joking type, but it felt so natural to do it with Siovon.

"Hey, I left those two Guards alive, didn't I?" she asked. "I'm a pacifist in training."

Lucian chuckled. "I don't think that counts, *fatina*. Either you are or you aren't, but I admire your desire to change."

At that, her smile waned and she straightened in her seat. "Calysta dedicated herself to doing what she could to help others. Lila, not so much, but I didn't blame her for her bitterness at the world. However, Caly always had a pure heart. Even if she couldn't heal people with her voice—you know, due to the curse— she still worked hard to learn about as many herbs and potions as possible. She had so much love for all living creatures that I couldn't help but want to be like her. So the three of us found a way to conceal our blood while we traveled all over Europe to provide healing to those in need."

Lucian tilted his head. "You grew up in Europe, yet your accent is American."

When she spoke again, it was in fluent Russian. "It is because I have learned to adapt. Otherwise, this is what I would sound like."

He translated it as she spoke. Lucian grinned. The accent fit her just as well as her American one. It was, dare he say, adorable. He could also change his dialect to blend in with his surroundings, but he had no need to. Everyone knew him or knew of him. There was no sense hiding the old Latin accent. "Fair enough. So after traveling around, that's when Lila had to leave because Mikhail was hunting her?"

He sensed her mood darkening, and she grew quiet again. When they approached a turnoff, she murmured, "Take this exit, then the first left."

Lucian did as instructed. As the minutes passed, the roads nearing the small town of Buffalo grew narrower with each mile, the copse of trees lining the roads becoming thicker and darker as they traveled through the boonies.

"My mother didn't have any powers," she said at last. When he raised his eyebrows at her, she didn't look at him, instead choosing to focus on the passing landscape that was beginning to lighten from the rays of dawn. "From the stories Lila told, we sirens have blood that can create or enhance either medicines or poisons, but no one could do both, if that makes any sense. My family through Lila's side were all healers, so Calysta and I inherited the same blood, therefore our powers have some 'awakening' abilities — like how she can sing to heal others or I can give life to inanimate artworks.

"Lila didn't have powers, but what she lacked in that department, the healing properties of her blood more than made up. A single drop of her blood could be a sole cure for most human diseases. When Mikhail gave chase to her, he'd thought any healing siren would do in order to reanimate the Rogues he wanted. However, it became evident that Lila's blood was awakening a few Rogues but killing the rest. Not only that, but he couldn't bind the Rogues to himself. He'd figured out she wasn't the one he needed. I'm not sure whether he tortured the answers out of her or not, but he came to learn about my powers and decided I would be better suited."

Lucian gave her hand another gentle squeeze. He recalled the vision Ava had shown him. "Siovon, I don't think your mother ratted you out. Even if she'd been tortured, the sheer devotion she had to you in Mikhail's memory was that of a mother who'd suffer any amount of pain to protect her children."

He heard rather than saw her give a hard swallow. He knew his words had touched her by the unconscious way she gripped his hand in return. "Thank you."

He flashed her a warm smile. "So after ten years, how did you manage to escape Mikhail? I know he had you in an iron cage, which is a weakness for fey, but why do I get the feeling you could have escaped even that?"

Siovon's eyes glinted with pride, but then she groaned. "There were a few times when I could have escaped him, but I refrained because I knew he had eyes on Calysta for that very purpose. When he realized he didn't have me as securely as he'd thought, he went searching for Darkmist on the UBM."

Lucian shook his head. "What the hell is Darkmist?"

Siovon hesitated. "It's crushed poison hemlock mixed with micro-shards of iron, meant to paralyze fey if inhaled or ingested. Mikhail would try to mix it into my food, but when I recognized the smell, he went with using a needle. For months at a time, I just lay there while he used IVs to draw blood from me, wait for me to replenish what was lost and repeat. I was too weak to even lift my hands ninety percent of the time, let alone strong enough to escape."

Disgust and anger twisted his gut. He didn't realize he was growling until Siovon squeezed his hand in her much smaller one. She continued talking. "As I told you before, he always had a pet imp. When one failed a task or was no longer useful, he'd kill them and find another. The last one was a male named Lee. He wasn't too bright, but he was one hell of a spellcaster. One night I used my blood to awaken a minion to do some spying while I had strength. I found out Mikhail had long ago lost track of Calysta, and from there, I planned my escape.

"I feigned weakness until Lee gave me another dose of Darkmist. I kept him distracted long enough until my minion managed to sneak his phone away from his belt. As I said, the imp wasn't too bright and had his phone clipped there. When he left, I called one of my old comrades, Naomi, and left a message for her about how to find me. From then on, everything was placed in her hands, as I was powerless to do much else. She saved me before Mikhail returned, but as for Lee..." She grimaced. "I have no idea what happened to the poor schmuck, but I don't think it was anything good."

Lucian brought her hand to his lips and pressed a kiss to her knuckles. "This Naomi seems like a trustworthy friend to have risked herself to save you from a cave full of Rogues."

Siovon smiled at that, giving a small laugh. "Yeah, she's one of a kind, all right. She's the one person I can count on to always have my back."

It was on the tip of Lucian's tongue to say she could trust him in such a way, but he refrained. He knew it would cause her to slink back behind her defenses, and that was something he hoped to avoid.

Their conversation ended there. She didn't say anything further, only continued to guide him along the creepy roads until he turned down a thin dirt path woven between thick brush and trees. He would never have seen the pathway had she not pointed it out to him. It was well concealed, though he couldn't tell if it was due to overgrowth throughout the years or if Siovon and her sister had set it up that way.

More than once he cringed on the inside when twigs and low branches scraped along the sides of his car. He wasn't as materialistic as Salvator, but he damn sure had a lot of pride in his fancy Jag. It was his baby. He was nervous to even check to see what kind of damage had been done.

Lucian slowed his car to a crawl, then a full stop, as they approached a two-story wooden cottage that had long ago given in to the surrounding nature. Browned vines and weeds traveled up the sidings, and snow-covered moss draped the slanted tin roof in a frozen blanket. There were three short steps leading onto the screened porch, the surrounding forest bare and covered in snow.

A shiver slid over his skin and a feeling of disgust washed over him since he'd turned down the path. "Why do I feel like I'm about to be chopped up and fed to a family of inbreeds?"

Siovon snorted with humor. The two stepped out of the car and met at the front bumper. She started to walk ahead of him. "What's wrong, Frosty? Big, bad vamp scared of a few trees and little ole me?"

Lucian caught her around the waist with one arm, drawing her back against his chest. He went hard as a rock at the feel of her soft body molded to his, making him annoyed at the layers of clothes separating them. He leaned down to whisper into her pointed little ear, the one holding the earrings.

"Ever heard the saying, you mess with the bull, you get the horns?" he growled, smiling at the violent shiver that shook her body. "The same could be said about big, bad vamps, *fatina*." He licked over each of her earrings, teasing the bits of skin between them. "Only you'll get the fangs."

She sucked in a sharp breath, her arousal a potent aroma in the air, making him shudder with the need to be wrapped in her heat.

With a startling amount of control, he pulled away from her, plastering a smile to his lips when she turned to him, her eyes glazed with passion. Gods, he would take her right now if he could, right there in the middle of fucking nowhere with only the snow on the ground as a cushion.

However, he forced himself to behave. When he made love to Siovon—and he had every intention of doing so—it was going to be on a proper bed.

Funny how he'd never cared about such things with previous lovers, but somehow this was important. He wanted to take his time with Siovon, to explore every perfect inch of her, from the top of the short silky strands of her hair to the feet he knew would be as cute and dainty as the rest of her.

Though his body begged him to pull her against him and ravish her like a starved animal until they both climaxed, that would be far too swift for his liking. The passion would be over long before it started. He wanted this beautiful woman to open herself to him so he could touch, kiss and lick away every last one of the dark shadows in her eyes.

Glancing at the sky as it continued to lighten, he tested the air, though what he sensed was the continuous feeling of disgust. Recognizing it for what it was, he frowned at her. "Repellant spells?"

She blinked, realizing she'd been staring at him. Lucian was wise enough to hide his smile as a blush rose to her cheeks before she turned away. "Yes. Put there to keep out"—she peered over her shoulder, sending him a glare that had no conviction in it whatsoever—"unwanted pests."

Lucian winked. She rolled her eyes and walked to the front door. Lucian dropped his gaze to her backside, and he licked his lips at the seductive sway.

It really was a beautiful ass—high and firm with muscle yet rounded in a way that was made to catch a man's attention. And he was certainly attentive, he acknowledged, shifting himself in his leather pants as they grew tight.

When Siovon stopped just before the bottom step, Lucian thought he'd been caught red-handed. But when her shoulders tensed, he stiffened.

"What is it?" he questioned.

"Someone's inside."

"I can't sense anything."

"Of course not. The spells would dampen your senses. However, they are linked to Calysta and me. So long as we're standing inside the barrier, we can sense intruders."

He nodded, though he hadn't a clue what the devil she was talking about. He didn't know shit about magic and he had no desire to learn something he couldn't use.

Scanning the cabin, he took in the windows sealed by heavy shutters, but even with strained ears he could hear only the gentle breeze flowing through the naked forest and the distant flow of the Mississippi River.

The short sword that had been tattooed on Siovon's forearm materialized in her hands. He shook his head in amazement, wondering if he'd ever get used to seeing that.

"Do you think Calysta is inside?"

Siovon was glued to the spot, one foot on the bottom step as she concentrated on the front door. Her eyes were narrowed, fixated with such intensity that Lucian half-expected the wood to erupt in flames.

At last, she heaved a disappointed sigh, tightening her grip on her sword. "No," she said with annoyance. "I can't sense her. Humans can't get past the spells and neither can most lesser demons, so this could very well be a trap. We'll need to split up."

Chapter Eleven

The words hadn't even left Siovon's lips when Lucian said in a flat tone, "No."

Siovon scowled, shifting her weight to one leg. "This isn't up for debate."

She was pissed to learn someone was inside just waiting to launch an attack on them. There was a possibility it was Jarek.

Then again, she doubted that. There was only one person inside the cabin, and Jarek was far too much of a coward to go anywhere without his Rogues for protection. He and Mikhail had been afraid of her. They'd had more than enough of her blood over the years, but they'd feared she would seek revenge the moment she was free.

Perhaps that was the reason Mikhail had rushed to launch his attack on Lucian's family when she'd escaped. No doubt he'd been afraid she would come back and ruin their plans.

So, yeah, Jarek might be Mikhail's son, but the little prick wasn't half as bright as his father, nor was he brave enough to take her on alone — or a clan chief who happened to be the eldest son of the king of vampires. Whoever was inside had some balls to think they stood a chance.

Even though she wasn't afraid, worry twisted her gut over the knowledge that Calysta hadn't made it to Buffalo. Siovon was, yet again, back at square one. She just hoped Calysta had left another clue somewhere for her to find.

Ignoring Lucian, she fiddled around until she found the fist-sized stones buried in the snow next to the steps. She overturned them all until she found the spare key hidden there. She glared at Lucian. "Why are you still standing around? Go scope out the back."

His eyes flashed with silver fire. "I said 'no'. We'll go through the cabin together."

She straightened and placed one fist on her hip, holding her sword at her side in the other. "You are the great clan chief of Chicago and almost two thousand years old. You know better than anyone else that the best way to catch an enemy is to close in on them from all exits to make sure there are no other means for escape."

"Yes, but—"

"And," she cut in, "you are a master vampire. With your speed, it will take no more than five minutes for you to check your end."

"Yes, but—"

"*And* we both know I can handle my own against someone even twice my size. There's one person inside, and I'm armed. This is me being logical, while you are being stubborn. So get your ass going and stop wasting more of our time, Lucian Gordano."

Lucian's mouth parted, though the rest of his features were in a deep scowl. Siovon didn't miss the flare of admiration in his eyes as he stepped back. He stroked a gentle finger down her cheek. "Very well, Siovon. You win this one. I am but a shout away." With that, he took off to follow her orders.

What a stubborn male, she thought in exasperation. Why he felt she needed protection was beyond comprehension. She was a pacifist, but if her life depended on it, she could fight back if evasive maneuvers didn't work.

Shaking her head, she unlocked the door. The thick panel opened with an eerie creak, reminding her of those cheesy horror flicks she and Calysta used to watch. The inside was dark, thanks to the shuttered windows. It didn't take long for her vision to adjust to the darkness.

Had it not, she knew her surroundings as well as the back of her hand. On her right was a straight set of stairs, and on her left was a living room, decorated with the sort of comfortable, rustic feel she'd always loved. There was a brown sofa with plush pillows and a homemade throw blanket hung over the back and a matching armchair. The sofa was angled to face an old floor-model TV, as well as a stone fireplace that she felt a sudden desire to light. It had been many years since she and Calysta had visited the place, but she had so many fond memories of sitting on the floor in front of a roaring fire, the two of them brainstorming new recipes to try for their medicines while they binged on hot chocolate and snack cakes.

Past the living room was an open kitchen with a small round table for two. A narrow hall that contained a full bathroom and a private room ran perpendicular to the kitchen. It was first meant to be a spare bedroom, but since she and Calysta slept upstairs, they'd converted it into a walk-in storage room for all their potions, herbs and medicines, plus the tools they used to brew them.

Lucian was silent as he entered the back door, but his movements caused the spells to send vibrations through her body like a thousand fire ants marching down her spine. She resisted the urge to shake out her jacket. Though she couldn't cast spells or weave magic like other fey or even human witches and mages, Calysta could, so she'd created a type of inner security system for each of their homes. It worked so that the two of them could sense intruders if they were on the premises. It was a lot cheaper and far more effective than the digital systems of the modern world.

Entrusting the downstairs area to Lucian, Siovon ascended the stairs, willing her steps to be as silent as possible. Not hard under most circumstances, but the wooden stairs were old and hadn't been tended to in many years. When she stepped on one plank, it let out a loud creak. She paused mid-step.

After several beats of not sensing anything, she continued. She was three steps from the top when her weight brought on another loud groan from the rickety wood. She paused again at a separate vibration thrumming in her chest, telling her that someone other than Lucian was near.

She froze and tightened her fingers on the hilt of her sword. She wasn't afraid of death, but she didn't like surprises.

Funny, given that she'd used the element of surprise to kill her targets dozens of times.

With a deep but silent inhale, she continued and turned the corner once on the landing. There were a total of three doors. The first on her left was Calysta's bedroom, one that would be decorated in multiple pastel colors.

Go figure that along with her pure heart and sunny disposition, she liked all things bright and girly. Not that Siovon disliked feminine things, but décor-wise she enjoyed rural, earthy tones.

The first door on her right was her own room. The last door was facing her at the far end of the hall, wide open to reveal another full bathroom.

Siovon inched forward, and when she stepped close to Caly's door, the vibrations intensified before vanishing. That was where the intruder was hiding.

She frowned. She hoped she wouldn't have to kill him or her. Enemy or not, she had plenty of blood on her hands as it was. The idea of adding one or two more bodies to her count shouldn't have bothered her, but it did.

Siovon gave a mental count to three. Gripping her sword, she swung the door inward.

Having already expected an attack, she ducked under the swing of a dagger. The blade from her attacker lodged in the doorjamb where her head would have been. Siovon struck out with her foot, kicking her attacker's feet from under them. Instead of losing balance and falling to the ground, the assailant landed in a smooth crouch and jumped to their feet to swing another blade at Siovon's head. She leaped to the side, but before she could bring her sword up for an attack, her opponent launched at Siovon, sending them both to the floor and knocking her weapon from her.

Siovon landed with a hard thump. A flash of silver glinted as the invader prepared to bring it down on her. She caught her opponent's wrists in her hands, surprised at how thin they were despite the other person's strength.

A woman? she thought. She inhaled the scent of exotic chocolate spices.

After a cautious beat, she asked, "Naomi?"

The woman above her hesitated. "Siovon?" came the husky response. The woman shuffled around a few moments and Siovon squeezed her eyes shut when a flashlight shone on her face. "*Dios mio.* Why didn't you say it was you?"

Naomi backed away and held out a hand to help Siovon to her feet.

"Considering this is *my* home and *you* are the intruder, I didn't think I needed to announce my presence."

Naomi grunted an apology. "I needed a place to lie low, and this was the closest. I thought someone had followed me."

Siovon shook her head, about to respond. However, a sudden chill in the air had them both stiffening. Naomi stood in a defensive position, holding her dagger steady as Lucian stepped into the room and flipped the light switch.

Lucian's eyes were narrowed at Siovon's and Naomi's disheveled looks. He bared his fangs at Naomi, but Siovon eased between the two of them before the room became a battlefield. Lucian was a powerful clan chief who would kill anyone he thought was an enemy, and Naomi was a lethal assassin who would do the same, just for the hell of it. The woman was just as skilled as Siovon, if not deadlier, due to her defensive nature.

"Who is she?" Lucian demanded.

At the same time, Naomi growled, "Who is he?"

Siovon looked between them, biting the inside of her cheek as she contemplated how she was supposed to go about this without causing bloodshed. Neither of these demons was trusting, and both were kill-first-ask-questions-later types.

"Oh, hell," she muttered in annoyance. *Talk about being stuck between a rock and a hard place.*

"Lucian, this is Naomi, a friend of mine," Siovon said in a steady tone. "Naomi, this is Lucian, the one who's been helping me look for Calysta."

In truth, she was nervous as a dew fairy as she stood between the agitated demons. Lucian held his sword in front of him, his eyes hard and unwavering as he scrutinized Naomi. Likewise, Naomi was poised, swaying from side to side like a cobra about to strike.

As was her usual style, her deep brown hair was pulled into a high ponytail falling to her waist, with silver bands clamped every five or so inches. A pitch-black veil of fabric covered the bottom half of her face, concealing her full identity. The skin from her hairline to mid-nose bore a natural sun-kiss from her Latin heritage.

She was dressed head to toe in a black Spandex bodysuit that clung to her tall, slender frame like a second skin. She had some kind of leather armor around her forearms and chest, and leather boots up to her knees. With the skin-hugging getup, it was clear to see the half-dozen blades sheathed along her body, as well as the two handguns tucked into straps hanging under her arms.

Never let it be said that Naomi wasn't war-ready. And going by the bloodstains marring what bit of skin was showing through a number of tears, she'd already had one battle.

Siovon frowned. "Are you hurt?"

Naomi didn't look away from Lucian. "Nothing that won't heal."

Even with her mouth covered, her words were clear rather than muffled. However, her voice held the tiniest of strains that had Siovon been anyone else, she would have never caught on to. Despite the strength Naomi was displaying, she was injured, though she'd never show such a weakness to an enemy.

And, to her, Lucian was undeniably an enemy.

Not wanting to embarrass her friend, Siovon faced Lucian. "Will you wait for me downstairs?"

He didn't even look at her. "No. She attacked you." He sent a pointed glare at the dagger still lodged within the doorjamb by his shoulder.

Siovon rolled her eyes in exasperation. "She didn't know it was me."

"*Cazzate*," he growled. "Your looks are very distinct, *fatina*."

Her lips twitched as she fought a smile. She wasn't sure whether or not it was a compliment but chose not to dwell on it. She also wasn't about to mention that Naomi couldn't see very well in the dark, despite being a demon.

"Look," she said on a sigh. "Naomi has been a trusted friend of mine for many years. She has never betrayed me."

"That doesn't mean she won't start today."

Okay, now I'm getting annoyed.

Glaring, Siovon marched forward. She jabbed a finger into his chest—his very muscular, rock-hard chest that she *really* wanted to rub against. "Listen, Frosty. You might not trust her, but I do—just like I didn't trust your damned brothers but I tolerated them." He opened his mouth to protest, but she jabbed him in the chest again. "If I was patient enough to put up with them, you can at least show the same respect and back the hell off. So suck it up and wait for me downstairs." Then, she softened her tone. "Please."

He fixed her with a hard look, but amusement flared in his silver eyes. There was a wicked promise in those beautiful depths, a promise that sent a delicious shiver down her spine. It felt like she'd known him for ages, which was ridiculous. She should be cautious and wary. Instead, she'd opened up to him about her past and was even now willing to give in to the passion that had been burning since she'd first laid eyes on him.

That didn't mean she was ready to throw caution to the wind and declare eternal love for the leech.

Lucian grunted and gave a grudging nod. "Very well." He glared over her head at Naomi. "But if she lays one finger on you, she's dead."

"Better than you have tried, bloodsucker," Naomi growled.

With one last glare, Lucian stalked out of the room and closed the door. He didn't leave right away, and when Siovon yelled at him to go, he grumbled before heading downstairs at last.

She shook her head, a small smile tugging at her lips. *Stubborn vampire.*

When she turned to Naomi, her smile disappeared at the incredulous look from her friend. "What?" she demanded.

Naomi straightened, the tension draining from her muscles as she flopped onto the wooden floor. "*Fatina*?" she mocked, lifting a slim eyebrow. "The Siovon I know would have kicked a man's balls into his scrotum for calling her such cute names."

Siovon crouched in front of Naomi, balancing her weight on the balls of her feet. "I'm a pacifist."

Naomi snorted in derision. "Keep telling yourself that. Old habits die hard." She grimaced. "*Really* hard. What's going on?"

It was Siovon's turn to lift a brow. "I should be asking you that." She eyed Naomi's unhealed wounds. "You were in Alleman tracking Jarek earlier. What happened?"

Obvious frustration had Naomi's brows snapping together. "I was waiting on Thor to find me, but I grew impatient." Waving away Siovon's annoyed glare, she continued. "I tried to get closer to the schoolhouse, but I must have tripped whatever magical alarm was set, because suddenly a portal opened and the imp who's been helping Jarek stepped out with a fuck-ton of Rogues."

Siovon frowned at the news. The imp couldn't have been Lee. Mikhail would have killed the poor bastard the moment it was discovered he'd let Siovon get away. "So, he has a pet imp just like Mikhail."

"I'd say more than a pet," Naomi drawled. "The bitch looked like she'd been in the middle of shooting some cheesy porno." Under the mask, Naomi's nose was scrunched in disgust. "Seriously, who comes to a fight dressed in a skimpy schoolgirl's uniform and high heels? Or maybe she thought I was a male who would drop to my knees and drool at the mouth upon seeing her."

Siovon bit the inside of her cheek to hide a smile at her friend's obvious contempt, not about to point out that Naomi's own fashion choices had men drooling. It wasn't intentional, but she just had that effect. Hell, there'd been plenty of times when Naomi had been covered head to toe, yet she was able to instill lust in dozens of men at a time. She was half-succubus, after all. She oozed sex appeal without even trying.

"You escaped," Siovon murmured.

Naomi lifted a shaking arm, glaring at the sluggish bleeding as her skin struggled to knit itself closed. Siovon frowned, lowering her voice to a whisper. "When's the last time you...um...recharged?"

Naomi ignored her. "Those pesky bloodsuckers were pretty damn fast, and that bitch didn't make it any better when she threw some spells at me, not to mention that I lost my favorite dagger. That thing was irreplaceable."

"Naomi," Siovon said, her voice stern as if she were talking to a child, "how long has it been?"

Naomi rolled her eyes, no longer trying to change the subject. Nor did she ask what Siovon was referring to. "It's been a while, okay? And before you ask, yes, it's the reason why my wounds aren't healing. I came here because it was the closest place you owned, and I was hoping to find some medicine so I wouldn't have to... You know."

Yes, I do know.

Naomi was half-succubus and half-fury, a combination that had given her nothing but shame and misery. Furies were a small race of female demons who were fierce and extremely reserved, so reserved that they only bred through human males, but there was no penetration involved. To reproduce, their kind became pregnant through artificial insemination so they would remain 'pure maidens'. In addition, all their children were born pureblood fury and always female.

As the story went, Naomi's mother had been seduced by an incubus pretending to be human. When she gave birth, no one had known Naomi was a half-blood until she'd reached maturity and her succubus powers had been revealed. To make a long story short, she'd been sold to the demon slave trade by her own people. With no knowledge of how to control her urges, she'd been forced to give in to her lust or else her body would cramp with a near-crippling pain that could lead to death if she didn't take care of it.

That was, if she didn't lose her mind and attack the closest male to her.

It was the reason why her wounds weren't healing. She despised what she was. She hated needing sex in order to survive, so no doubt it had been many weeks since she'd last had any. She always waited until the pain became unbearable before seeking relief.

Siovon had so much sympathy for her dear friend, but she couldn't show it. Naomi hated that, too. She didn't like to be seen as weak in any way.

"I'll see what I can whip up in the storeroom," Siovon murmured.

Naomi blew out an impatient breath. "Great," she muttered with disdain. "You gonna tell me about the leech now or what?"

Siovon grunted, rocking back on her heels. "Beautiful, isn't he?"

Naomi wasn't amused. "They always are. To misquote the old proverb, 'Beauty is the root of all evil.'"

"You're beautiful, though," Siovon countered. "And you're not evil."

Her words, though honest, were meant to keep the mood light, and they had their desired effect. Naomi's eyes widened and she made a 'tsk' noise before jerking her head to the side. If the mask hadn't been covering her face, her cheeks would have been flaming red. Yet another secret about Naomi was that she was insecure when it came to her looks. Even without the succubus pheromones she tended to release, she was a really beautiful woman, scars and all.

"There's nothing beautiful about me," she groused. "Unlike you, I still kill for a living. That hardly makes me a saint."

Siovon's smile turned wry. "No, but unlike me, you've never killed an innocent. Still, you can always quit and become more."

Naomi lowered her lashes. "I'm not like you, Siovon. This life saved me. It made me stronger. It's all I know. Without it…"

Siovon shook her head and changed the subject to avoid bringing forth Naomi's dark past. "I'll tell you about the vampire, but I need your word you will refrain from attacking him."

Relief crossed Naomi's features before she met Siovon's gaze. "That's a joke, right?"

She shook her head again. "Do not take this the wrong way, but you are no match for him." When Naomi definitely took offense, Siovon lifted her hands to calm her. "I'm not saying you're unable to kill him.

What I mean is, he isn't just another leech. He's Lucian Gordano."

Those caramel-colored eyes widened once more, this time in horror. "You're lying."

"I'm not. He's the eldest of the Gordano sons and the Chicago clan chief. Killing him is a powerful death wish."

"*Dios*," Naomi breathed. "Is that why you're with him?"

Siovon was silent for a few moments, contemplating her words. In the end, she wouldn't ever lie to Naomi, not for anything. "We have a deal."

"What kind of deal?"

"He's to help me find Calysta, and in return, I'll do what I can to heal his brother from an abaddon's curse."

Naomi breathed a long string of Spanish curses, none of them ladylike in the least. When she spoke again, her voice was a low hiss. "You are a siren, not a goddess. No one can heal an abaddon's disease."

Siovon paced, scrubbing her hands through her hair. Her own voice was a harsh whisper. "I know that, but I couldn't track Calysta on my own. Not to mention the vamps would find her long before I ever could, and they would have done everything to get her to use her powers to cure him."

As expected, Naomi stiffened. "No," she growled and stood as well. Her eyes flashed red and her body shook, though whether it was from her weak state or rage, Siovon didn't know. A mix of both, she was guessing. "I'll kill them before they put their hands on her."

"My thoughts too," Siovon muttered. "However, I'd like to avoid bloodshed if it's possible. I vowed long ago that if it ever came to choosing her life or mine, I would never hesitate over the decision. I know what would happen to me should I fail. I just hope Calysta is long gone and safe by then."

Naomi clenched her hands at her sides. "I'd rather neither of you loses your life. It's the two of us against one leech. I've heard about his reputation, but if we catch that bastard by surprise, we can knock him out, secure him with silver and hold him hostage until the king makes a blood oath to leave the two of you alone."

Siovon paused in the middle of the floor, tilting her head in disbelief. "Naomi, I'm not even going to begin to touch on how stupid that plan is, let alone how much it will not work."

"True, but I still say we should knock him out. I've been yearning for leech blood, and those Rogues were just appetizers."

Siovon snorted. "You're in no condition to fight anyone right now, least of all a Royal clan chief."

Naomi didn't deny it, only heaved an exasperated sigh. To hide her shaking legs, she sat on the edge of Calysta's bed.

Thank God Calysta's spells had worked, so their home remained as clean as the day they left it, no matter how many years had passed. It would stay that way until Calysta either died or released the spells. The fact that they were still in place provided assurance that her sister was still alive.

"I don't like him, and I don't like this plan of yours."

Siovon offered a soft smile. She stood before Naomi and gave her hand a gentle squeeze. The contact was awkward, considering neither of them was the touchy-feely type, but she'd learned from Calysta that the smallest touch could provide comfort, even for social outcasts like them. "That's because you don't like anyone—"

Naomi snorted. "True."

"Or most of my plans, but they always work. Besides, I've already given my oath. I will not go back on my word, not even for a vampire."

Naomi observed Siovon for several long moments. There was a stern calculation in those caramel orbs, a look that made Naomi appear every bit the dangerous warrior she was. "You like him."

It was a statement rather than a question. Even so, Siovon walked toward the shuttered window, shivering as the winter air outside seeped through the glass. The cabin was modern enough that it had basic utilities, but she'd been too distracted searching for an intruder to bother with turning on the heat.

Naomi's words bounced around in her head. She might as well be honest with herself. She liked Lucian…a lot. He was stubborn and annoying as hell, but he had a strange pull on her that made her desire him in a way she'd never felt before. He was cold and demanding, but when he kissed her, there was nothing but a scorching heat. He set her body aflame.

She'd never given her body to another. Every time she'd kissed a man or let him touch her, there had never been a spark of desire, just loathing and disappointment. Her embarrassing and awkward attempt with a woman had been worse. With much frustration, she'd come to accept that she'd forever be celibate, only able to find satisfaction from her own hands.

Ever since meeting Lucian, however, desire had struck her unlike anything she was accustomed to. He wasn't even in the same room as her, but she wanted to seek him out and see if he'd be the one to ease the longing she'd suffered for years.

What was even more maddening was that she wasn't sure if it was a mere matter of lust. In such a short time he'd managed to rile her up, get under her skin, earn a fair amount of her trust and make her smile. She was unaccustomed to those feelings, and she didn't like them.

The emotions Lucian stirred within her were strange and terrifying. She no longer considered him an enemy, though she knew that when all was said and done and it came time for her to try to heal his brother Andreas, he would hate her for being unsuccessful. She'd be lucky if his clan or family allowed her to make it out alive.

She shouldn't care. She really shouldn't. Hell, hours ago she hadn't. Just as long as they left Calysta alone, she would have accepted their hatred of her.

So what changed? And when?

Just when the hell did I become so soft?

A sudden urge for that long soak she'd been daydreaming about earlier in the evening had her shaking her head. There was no wine or honey or strawberries, much to her displeasure, but at least there was a tub with hot running water. There should also be some non-perishable food items in the cupboards in the kitchen. She was starving.

Maybe that was what was wrong with her. She must be having some kind of food withdrawals. Hunger made people act out of character. Like how there were people who became grumpy while hungry, maybe the same could make someone…emotional.

The reasoning sounded ridiculous, but she was sticking to it, dammit. She was hungry, horny, stressed and there was no way she was falling for a vampire. Her exhaustion was just catching up to her.

There was nothing wrong with indulging in one's carnal desires every once in a while, not after damn near two hundred years of celibacy. That was the way of the world, after all. Sex was the one primal instinct all demons, humans and animals had.

She hoped Lucian wouldn't be another disappointment. If so, she'd just have to concede the fact that God had cursed her to be some kind of freak of nature unable to get off with anyone.

Jeez, why was she overthinking things anyway?

Siovon turned back to Naomi, who was looking straight ahead of herself with a blank stare. It was her RBF—or Resting-Bitch-Face, as she called it. Other people would take her expression as being pissed off or contemplating killing them, but Siovon knew her friend was just lost in her own thoughts. She tended to space out a lot.

Siovon strolled to the door. "We will have to wait here until the sun sets and Thor awakens to see if he's discovered anything. It'll give us plenty of time to eat and rest. You need it."

Naomi blinked to the present and shrugged. "Very well, but don't think this means I trust your vampire."

Siovon grunted. "He's not my anything."

"Yeah, sure, *fatina*," she mocked.

Siovon shook her head. "You're more than welcome to join us downstairs. I'm going to find something to cook as well."

Naomi just stretched out on Calysta's bed. "Not a chance. With the way I'm feeling right now, I can't guarantee I won't stake his ass."

Siovon snorted. "Right. I'll be back to check on you. Make yourself comfortable, and if you want to bathe and change clothes, feel free to raid my wardrobe or Calysta's."

Naomi said nothing, just folded her arms underneath her head and gazed up at the open-beam ceiling. Siovon stepped into the hall and closed the door.

The vibrations linked to Lucian had lessened minutes ago, making her aware that he was outside somewhere close to the edge of the property. No doubt he was scouting the landscape to make sure no one else found a way onto the land. It wasn't necessary, since she'd feel any trespassers, but she wouldn't correct him on it. The man probably just wanted to feel like he was still in charge.

Downstairs, Siovon flipped on a few breakers then switched the thermostat to blow out heat. It was only slightly warmer in the cabin than it was outside, but she saw her breath every time she spoke, and with Naomi's open wounds, she had to be freezing as well. She might be impervious to human illnesses, such as catching a cold, but she could still become fevered if exposed for too long.

Entering the storeroom, Siovon took in the wooden shelves. There were dozens upon dozens of bottles, vials, baggies and small ceramic pots, all with written labels on them. There were potions, brews, creams, dried herbs and even a few poisons, all effective against humans, demons and animals. There were chopped logs for firewood, caldron pots and a handful of binders and books containing different recipes for hers and Calysta's mixings.

The cabin had always been Siovon's favorite home of theirs. It was cozy and secluded in the tiny town, not to mention that she loved being close to bodies of water.

All she needed was to step outside and she'd be able to hear the rush of the Mississippi River in the distance.

Siovon eyed the shelves, looking for one particular medicine that would be perfect for Naomi. As was the case with human medicines, there was no one mix that was acceptable by all demons. Where one simple cream could heal a young troll with a scraped knee, it could eat through the skin of a fairy. The reactions were different for everyone.

For Naomi, Siovon had made many mixes over the years. Her eyes landed on a white plastic bottle the size of her hand. She twisted the cap off and peered inside, then gave it a small sniff. Then, she tilted her head and allowed a few small drops to fall into her mouth. The dark liquid was bitter and acrid, causing her to cringe. However, she was thankful that it was missing only two ingredients.

She screwed the cap back on, gathered everything she needed, then headed for the kitchen. It didn't take long for her to place a small round pot on the stove, set it to a low simmer then pour the ingredients into it.

Siovon made a second trip to the storeroom to gather a few logs, then went to build a fire. Satisfied with her work, she figured it had been at least a half-hour since she'd left Naomi upstairs. She dusted her hands on her pants leg and entered the nearest bathroom.

Like the rest of the cabin, the design of the bathroom was nothing special — all wooden interior with an off-white sink and tub. She ran the water to a temperature she was comfortable with and poured a generous amount of liquid soap into the water. The scent of honey and almonds filled the air, making her stomach growl. She rubbed it, standing to go back into the kitchen. She raided the cabinets and pantry for something that wouldn't take long to cook.

Hey, if she didn't have to cook at all, that would be even better.

That was why she almost jumped for joy when she found a large bag of trail mix, a box of peanut butter granola bars and a pack of teriyaki beef jerky. Meat, protein and trail mix with M&Ms for dessert. What a feast. She could brew the hell out of a potion and cook up all kinds of medicines to perfection, but when it came to actual food, she was a complete disaster. Calysta had often joked that if Siovon ever got married, her husband would have to do all the cooking if he wanted a decent meal.

With a humorous snort, Siovon set the items on the countertop. She poured her share of the food onto a plate, stirred Naomi's potion stewing in the pot and went back to the bathroom. She stripped naked and turned off the water. Grabbing her plate of food, she sank into the tub, a small moan of satisfaction slipping past her lips as the steaming hot water blanketed her body.

Finally.

Chapter Twelve

By the time Siovon had finished her bath, another hour had passed. She wrapped herself in a cozy robe that had been hanging on the bathroom door then returned to the kitchen to find that Naomi's medicine was done brewing. She inhaled the minty scent as she poured the hot liquid into a Christmas-themed coffee mug. She gathered the remaining food and strolled upstairs, careful not to spill anything from the tray in her hands.

She'd been so caught up in her relaxation that she'd lost focus on the vibrations in her chest. One had ceased, letting her know that Naomi either had fallen asleep or was sitting still as a mannequin. Lucian's had thinned out but was growing stronger as he neared the cabin. When she made it to Calysta's room, she knocked on the door and waited several seconds before turning the knob.

Though she'd half-expected such to be the case, she was still surprised to see Naomi fast asleep on the bed.

Her chest rose and fell with her gentle breathing. It just went to show how bad her condition was that she'd fallen asleep while under the same roof as a stranger. Naomi would never do anything to lower her guard if she could help it.

Frowning, she set the tray on the nightstand. The potion tasted better when it was hot, but she wouldn't dare wake Naomi up. She'd tried once before and had damn near had her head severed. Besides, Naomi hated being taken care of. Tender gestures and caresses were foreign to her, making her far too uncomfortable.

Siovon backed out of the room, once again closing the door. She yawned as she descended the stairs. She wanted to make sure all the doors and windows were locked before retiring to her own room to sleep until nightfall, not that deadbolts would keep out demons. Plus, she'd feel it if any trespassers crossed her property, but it was old habit she'd never managed to shake.

Siovon was still yawning when she bumped into something hard. Rubbing her sore nose on a grunt, she blinked up into gleaming silver eyes. A tightening in her chest was becoming all-too-familiar when she was around Lucian. With her standing on the bottom step, she was still shorter than him, the top of her head only meeting his nose.

He carried with him the scent of snow and his own musky aroma that had heat pooling in the pit of her stomach. God, he was a beautiful man—tall, dark and handsome with a bite that had her eager to offer a vein.

She'd never experienced a vamp's bite, but she'd heard plenty of stories about how a skilled vampire could bring their donor's pleasure to soaring heights as they fed from them. Siovon had never understood the fascination, but as she stood before Lucian, she wanted to. Good lord, she wanted to so bad.

His gaze roamed over her, taking in the robe that revealed a tantalizing view of her cleavage. It skimmed even lower to see the fabric stopping above her knees.

Siovon's throat went dry as she was frozen in place. Though she'd never taken a lover, she'd perfected techniques of seduction to get people to do what she wanted whenever threats didn't work. Standing before Lucian, however, all knowledge of such a topic disappeared, and she felt every bit an inexperienced virgin.

Just one look in his hungry eyes told her it was okay, though. He knew *exactly* what to do. Hell, the man had almost two thousand years' worth of experience.

He stepped closer to her and brushed her damp bangs from her eyes. "It looks like you've made yourself busy, *fatina*," he murmured.

Siovon gave what she thought was a casual shrug, but it felt stiff and awkward. "What were you doing?"

"Making calls to my clansmen and scouting the premises."

Siovon suppressed an amused smile. She'd been right. Still, she didn't want to burst his bubble by telling him his inspection was unneeded. "I see."

He continued to devour her. He stepped so close that she felt his cool power. "It's only eight a.m., several hours away from sunset. Whatever shall we do to pass the time?"

Siovon licked her dry lips. Good lord, it was embarrassing how much her hands were trembling as she tugged his jacket's zipper down. "I can think of a few things," she whispered.

His chest touched hers as he encircled her waist with his arms. The fact that she didn't pull away must have given him a positive sign, because he leaned down to press his lips to hers. It was a brush, but white-hot desire sparked between them, creating an electric bolt that shot right to her libido. She let out a soft sigh and slid her hands under the folds of his jacket, pressing her palms flat against the hard muscles hidden beneath his black shirt. He plunged his lips over hers, then he shot his tongue past her lips to mingle with her own.

Emboldened, she nipped at his lower lip, causing him to gasp. When she pulled it into her mouth and sucked on the soft flesh, he let out a low sound from deep within his chest. He tightened his hold on her, pulling her so close that there wasn't a single part of their bodies that wasn't touching. He dragged his hands over her ass, giving it a big squeeze. At the same time, he ground his erection against her core, causing the hem of her robe to rise up.

Lucian broke away from her lips to trail hot kisses to her ear. He nipped at her lobe. "I need to taste you, Siovon," he murmured. "I need to have your sweetness drenching my tongue."

Siovon shuddered. She threw her head back as he scraped his fangs down the curve of her throat, flicking his tongue to trace a wet path along her vein. She shivered again. "Yes," she whispered, angling her head to give him better access.

Lucian paused, just enough to let out a low sound of appreciation. He kissed her tender skin but didn't bite her. Instead, Siovon found herself being scooped into his arms. He took off upstairs, and in less than five seconds, he was closing her bedroom door behind them. He tossed her onto the mattress then yanked off his jacket and T-shirt, revealing tan skin stretched over powerful muscles. Siovon sat up on her elbows, admiring the view.

He had a light dusting of dark hair on his pecs and a thin line trailing from his navel and disappearing under the leather pants he was unbuttoning. Siovon's mouth went dry as she took in all that sculpted perfection. When he shed his pants, her eyes flew wide with a tiny bit of fear as his erection popped free. It was tall, proud and massive, just like the rest of him.

Good God, he's going to rip me in half.

Seeing her fearful eyes, Lucian frowned. If she didn't know any better, she could have sworn there was a touch of insecurity in his tone. "Is there something wrong?" he demanded, shifting as though self-conscious.

This arrogant, magnificent specimen embarrassed? Absurd.

She met his gaze before dropping it back to the monster he was working with between his legs. "It's just... I've never seen one so...big."

He lifted a brow, but his sensual lips curved into a grin that was all male. *So much for him being self-conscious.*

He placed his hands on his hips, and with an astonishing twitch of muscle, his dick jerked. She drew in a sharp breath, eliciting a small chuckle from him. "Surely the proud little lady who can take out a master vampire isn't afraid of this?" He made it jump again.

Siovon dropped her mouth, but then she raised her chin to a defiant angle. She'd never been one to shy away from a challenge, no matter how huge and intimidating it could be. "Bring it on, Frosty," she said, all traces of fear subsiding. She reached for the belt of her robe and shrugged out of it, tossing the garment to the floor.

Lucian's eyes were almost black, the pupil expanding to where there was only the thinnest ring of silver. It was his turn to swallow hard as he eyed the smooth, ivory curves of her body, the mounds of her breasts and the triangle of soft curls hiding her dampness. He let out a feral growl and laid her back, covering her body with his much bigger one. When his lips met hers, it was just like it had been in Keegan's apartment, fierce and demanding. Siovon met him, tugging the leather strap from his hair to tangle her fingers in the soft locks.

Lucian placed his hands everywhere, stroking her hips, arms and stomach before at last cupping her breasts. He massaged and kneaded, then used his thumbs and forefingers to toy with her erect nipples. Siovon moaned, sucking his tongue into her mouth as sensations that always managed to escape her with other men burst to life within her. Now that she was free of clothing, Lucian's touch ignited her body more than ever before, something she hadn't thought was possible. He ground his body into hers and more than once his straining dick rubbed against her tender flesh, but he was careful to avoid penetration, as if he wanted to drag the foreplay out for hours. It was utter torture, and with each passing minute, she climbed higher and higher to a peak she was desperate to jump from.

Lucian had his lips on her neck, sucking and kissing and licking while continuing to play with her breasts. When he gave her nipples a rough pinch, her body tightened and colors exploded in her eyes. She released a sharp cry as waves of intense pleasure rippled through her core.

Shaking as her release wound down, she opened her eyes to see Lucian peering at her in wide-eyed amazement.

"Did..." He cleared his throat. "Did you just...?"

Siovon's face went up in flames. She'd just had her first non-self-induced orgasm, and the man hadn't even done more than kiss her and play with her breasts. *How freaking embarrassing.*

"It's been a long time," she protested, knowing full well he'd scent the lie. "I've never...felt anything like that." That part was true. She was sure her cheeks were the color of an apple.

"I'll say," Lucian murmured. He continued kneading her breasts, and to her surprise, her body was once again responding as if it hadn't just had an amazing climax. "Your previous lovers must have been rather impatient."

Siovon looked away from his knowing gaze. There was no judgment in his tone, just fascination, as if enjoying her heated reaction to his touch. It was a wonder her cheeks weren't on fire with her level of embarrassment. "Or nonexistent."

Lucian paused again. When he spoke, his voice was filled with shock. "You are a virgin?"

Siovon bit the inside of her cheek and forced herself to meet his wide eyes. "Yes. I can't..." She grunted. "No one has ever...turned me on like this."

Yeah, good job admitting such stupidity, she silently chided. It wasn't like the man needed his ego inflated even more than it already was.

And that was precisely what her words had done. Again. His eyes filled with arrogance and...something else—some deep emotion she couldn't begin to comprehend.

Lucian slid down her body, kissing every inch of her skin until his lips found her hardened nipples. He replaced his hands with his mouth and nipped the sensitive peaks. Not once did his eyes leave hers. Siovon's breath came out in little pants, and she fisted his loose hair. She was already climbing toward that glorious peak again when he pulled his mouth away from her.

With a wicked grin, he murmured, "We are just getting started, *fatina*."

Lucian couldn't believe anything that was happening.

He pleasured Siovon's dripping wet pussy with his lips and tongue while using his hands to toy with her breasts. In return, she damn near yanked his hair from his scalp. He pressed his aching dick into the mattress for some kind of friction, and every inhale of her sweet arousal only made it swell more with the need to be buried inside her.

Oh, it all felt very, very real.

It was the emotional sensations running through him that made him fear it was all a dream. Hours ago he'd been sure he was going to have to dig deep for some hint of a charming personality to seduce her into submitting to him.

However, when she'd bumped into him on the stairs, somehow he had known it wasn't necessary. The lust in her eyes and the sudden rush of her arousal hitting his nose had told him clear as day that she wanted him just as bad as he desired her.

And now that he'd had a taste of her, it was so much better than anything he could have conjured up. She reacted to his touch with a fevered passion.

Above all, it was her confession of innocence that had damn near sent him spilling his seed far too soon. This beautiful, proud woman had never allowed a man to enter her body, yet she was willing to give him the pleasure of doing so. What male in his right mind wouldn't feel honored? He damn sure was.

With Siovon, things were...different. Special, even. He already cared for her, and he knew that for her to trust him with her past and body, she cared for him too. The ice around his heart was melting at a pace he couldn't keep up with.

He wanted to be her first and last, whether she was his truemate or not. He wanted her all to himself, to lock themselves away in his lair and remain hidden for centuries, taking pleasure only in each other's bodies and company.

It was hard to tell if this level of dangerous thinking was real or due to his state of arousal, but he didn't want to dwell on it any longer. He just wanted to focus on feeling Siovon racing toward another dive over the edge of orgasm. He could taste it on his tongue. She was so close, and he was more than happy to send her there, but then she pulled on his ears to bring him up her body.

"Lucian," she moaned, "I need..."

He obeyed, spreading her legs wide to settle between them. The head of his erection slid between her folds, growing slick. He took the base of his shaft and stroked his length against her, groaning at how good it felt.

Siovon's eyes were half-lidded and glazed with passion that once again almost had him coming before entering her. "Tell me what you need, *fatina*," he groaned, leaning to flick his tongue over her nipple. His fangs were hanging from his mouth, though it didn't seem to deter her in the least bit.

Siovon's cheeks were pink, a light sheen of sweat glistening above her brows. "I need you," she breathed. "I need you inside me."

Merda, that was sexy as hell to hear from her.

Gritting his teeth, Lucian angled the tip of his cock at her entrance. Though every nerve in his body wanted to ram its way inside and take her fast and hard, he refrained. He wanted to drag it out. He was her first lover, and he wanted to send her to heights of pleasure that no other man would ever be able to come close to reaching.

Hell, he didn't want any other man even attempting. He wanted her to be his and his alone.

With painful slowness, he entered her, pushing past the thin barrier of her hymen. Her face pinched with discomfort, but only for a moment. Her beautiful features melted into an expression of pure bliss as he continued to sink inside.

Good…gods.

Nothing, *nothing* had ever felt so damn amazing. She was tight and wet around his girth. Every last one of his muscles was strained to the absolute max at the willpower it took to keep from coming. When he was buried to the hilt, he held his breath and waited for her to tell him she was ready for him to continue.

Instead of speaking, she rolled her hips into him, making them both moan. "By the gods, woman, I'm not going to last," he said through clenched teeth. He pulled out to the tip before sinking back in a smooth motion.

Siovon tilted her head to one side. "Bite."

He slid in and out of her at a slow, steady pace. He managed to lift a brow in question. "What was that?"

Every stroke caused her to release a tiny moan. "Bite," she breathed, smoothing her hands across his chest and over his shoulders. "I want you to bite me."

Lucian's chest tightened and his fangs throbbed. He'd known she wanted his bite when they were downstairs, but to hear her say it out loud...

He groaned and leaned forward, wrapping his arms around her back as he picked up the pace. He pressed his lips to the side of her neck, feeling her racing pulse. He shuddered. "Are you sure you want this, Siovon?"

Please say yes, please say yes, his mind begged.

At that moment he was not a proud clan chief who took what he wanted and dared anyone to defy him. No, he was a desperate man who wanted his woman to submit everything to him. *Everything.*

"I'm sure," she whispered.

It was all he needed.

She gasped when he sank his fangs into her tender skin, following it with a moan as the pleasure of his bite chased away the tiny prick of pain. Likewise, Lucian groaned as her blood flowed onto his tongue. It was unlike anything he'd ever tasted — sweet and smooth with a rush of magical power.

He braced his hands on her hips, shifting so that he was pumping into her at an angle. Siovon arched her back forward, encircling his waist with her legs as he pushed them both to the very edge of pleasure.

"Oh, yes, Lucian," she crooned, digging her nails into his back in a way that made him thrust harder and faster. "Yes, just like that! Please don't stop!"

Stop? A gateway to hell could open in the middle of the room and swallow them both, yet he wouldn't stop. Not until they'd both—

Siovon tensed. She bit into his shoulder to muffle her scream of release. It wasn't hard enough to draw blood, but he almost wished it had been. He'd never before let another woman drink his blood, not unless he was turning her, but with Siovon, he wanted to experience the pleasure of giving a lover his blood. His brethren had often boasted about how gratifying it was, but it required a certain level of trust he'd never given anyone.

Not until that moment. Her core tightened around his cock as her orgasm rippled over him. He withdrew his fangs and licked the twin punctures closed before throwing his head back. He had to bite his lip to keep from shouting as the most intense orgasm of his life tore through him, flowing into Siovon as she lay shaking from her own climax.

When Lucian ceased quivering, he fell onto his side, drawing Siovon close to his chest as they lay there, breathing hard. She slid one arm under him, curling it around his waist so that she was hugging him. A tremendous sense of satisfaction washed over him when her heart rate slowed. Still cradled in his arms, she was fast asleep in moments.

A feeling of peace settled within him—peace and utter happiness.

Lucian let out a wide yawn as his eyelids grew heavy.

Intercourse played a vital role in assuring a vampire whether or not they'd found their truemate. While other signs were evident from the start, sex strengthened the connection between unmated truemates. And if one or both of them drank each other's blood during the process, it made them able to feel one another's presence, sometimes even their emotions.

There was a light fluttering in Lucian's chest that hadn't been there earlier. Siovon was now a part of him. Even in her sleep, he could sense her stress, worries and fears.

Yet above it all was the same sense of his peace and, much to his enjoyment, trust. He felt everything she felt, and perhaps when she woke up, she'd be able to feel him as well.

There was no longer a doubt in his mind. Siovon was his truemate.

At last in his endless life, fate had been generous and gifted him his perfect match.

* * * *

Siovon awoke with a start.

For several confused moments, she didn't understand why her body was vibrating like an unbalanced washing machine, not until she stared up at the open-beamed ceiling of her bedroom and realization dawned on her.

With a gasp, she shot up and dashed to her bedroom closet. She picked out a handful of clothes and donned them, her hands shaking from the near-painful vibrations.

Her sudden movements jarred Lucian awake. He sat up, the fur comforter draped over his waist in a tantalizing way that would have had her salivating had she not been in a rush.

"What's wrong, *fatina*?" Lucian questioned, his voice sexy and rough from a deep slumber. He watched her with a heated gaze.

Despite her urgency, a delicious shiver of excitement washed over her as she recalled their morning of hot, hot sex. *Yum*.

But it was so not the time to dwell on such matters. It took a great deal of willpower to tear her eyes away from him lying there like a beautiful Roman god. "Trespassers," she hissed.

Lucian uttered a series of Italian curses and settled into ice mode, jerking on his clothes. "How many?"

"I don't know, but there's a damn lot of them." She paused, testing the source of the vibrations. "They're surrounding us."

Fully dressed, Lucian moved to the door. "Looks like we're in for a fight. The spells were strong enough to repel even me. There's no way so many should be able to get past at once, unless the spells have weakened."

Siovon didn't say anything because he was right. She had a feeling there were only Rogues out there. They could have tracked Naomi's scent, but that didn't explain how they knew she was in the cabin. The spells were designed to mask anyone's scent once inside the barrier.

But then, what else could it be?

No one knew about the cabin except for her, Naomi and Calysta, and the spells kept out any strays.

With a shake of her head, she looked to Lucian. "They're closing in."

"We'll have to fight our way through them," he muttered. He pulled out his cell phone and sent a text before sliding it back in his pocket. "At least until the cavalry arrives."

Siovon opened her mouth to question what he'd meant by that, but paused as the vibrations almost made her legs go weak. Damn, but she didn't want to fight. Even if they were Rogues, they hadn't asked to be. They'd been transformed into brutal monsters by Mikhail and his entourage. The majority of them had been ordinary people and vampires who happened to be in the wrong place at the wrong time. She wanted to let Lucian handle all the fighting, but that was just wrong. There was no telling how many Rogues were out there. He couldn't take all of them out alone.

Then again, there was Naomi...

No. Naomi was her dear friend, and Lucian was... Well, he'd wiggled his way into her heart somehow. She wouldn't let them risk their lives while she remained inside like a coward. It appeared that she'd once again have to kill for survival.

If she could go at least one full week without breaking her pacifism, her life would be so much simpler. Just once, however, she decided it was for a good cause.

She reached into the top of the closet for the sleek handgun that was already loaded, then darted to her nightstand to pull out a clip in case she ran out. While she was an up-close fighter, silver bullets to the head would put the beasts down faster than using her blades.

Lucian was out of the bedroom seconds before her and stormed downstairs, but Siovon paused at Naomi's room. Before she could lift her hand, the door was jerked open and Naomi stood there with her eyes narrowed above the mask.

"What's the move?" she questioned.

Siovon relayed what was going on, and Naomi nodded, pulling out two blades from the half-dozen strapped to her body. Siovon noticed that her wounds were healed, meaning she'd drunk the potion.

The women joined Lucian, who was peering out of a crack in the shutters covering the windows. "What do you see?" Siovon demanded, rubbing her chest. The vibrations had turned into deep thrums of her heartbeat, meaning the enemy was close and large in numbers. There was no chance for escape.

"At least two dozen Rogues," he responded, his broad shoulders tense.

Naomi peered at Siovon out of the corners of her eyes, and the mask above her mouth crinkled as she smiled with anticipation. "Bring back any memories, Siovon?"

Siovon snorted, flicking the gun's safety. "I can recall at least three similar scenarios. Take your pick."

Naomi twirled a dagger in each hand with precise skill. "I hope your so-called pacifism hasn't affected your skills, *amiga*."

Siovon sighed. "I guess we're about to find out."

"How do you want to do this?"

"I'll take the front door. You take the back."

Lucian turned away from the window to glare at them. "We'll wait here until I give the signal."

Siovon and Naomi looked at him, then each other, then him again. Then, promptly ignoring him, Naomi faced Siovon. "There's likely more at the front, so I want them. I owe these bastards a decapitation or two."

"Whatever you say," Siovon said with a snort, already moving toward the back of the cabin.

"*Cazzo*," Lucian growled. He caught up to Siovon before she reached the door, his expression one of annoyance when he caught her arm. "I said to wait here."

Siovon scowled, poking him in the chest with a finger on her free hand. "And I told you plenty of times that I am neither your slave nor one of your clansmen. You will not order me about and expect me to follow your command."

Lucian frowned right back at her. "No, but you are my lover, and I won't let you rush off into danger."

Siovon rolled her eyes. "A one-night stand hardly makes us lovers."

He sucked in a sharp breath, as if offended. Despite the urgency of their situation, he cupped her chin in a tender gesture. "You say that now, but the way you screamed your release in my arms tells me otherwise."

Siovon's eyes widened as a jolt of heat shot straight to her core. Her reaction was inappropriate, yet she couldn't help her shivers of desire. "Stop that," she murmured.

He brushed his lips over hers in a swift kiss. "Don't ever try to downplay our night of passion as a tedious matter, Siovon, especially not when you and I both know it was so much more than that." He reached past her to palm the doorknob. "It appears we're in for a long fight. Stay close to me."

"Not a chance, Frosty. I'm not some fragile kid who needs protecting. Just don't get yourself killed before I'm done with you."

Lucian's eyes bored into her. "You just can't admit you care about me, can you?"

"I'd be lying to both of us if I said I did," she drawled.

He murmured something under his breath about stubborn women before opening the door and disappearing into the night. Siovon frowned and shook her head to clear it before following.

Of course she cared about the man, and despite her inner claims to not let their morning together be anything more than sex, something had changed in the last several hours. She didn't understand where her feelings stood, but what she did know was that she couldn't get any closer to him.

Once he realized she couldn't heal his brother, he'd crush her heart as his own filled with hate for her.

That is, if he didn't kill her first.

Chapter Thirteen

Siovon fired another round of bullets, taking out the last four Rogues who'd surrounded her. She blew out a loud breath, her heart clenching as the deceased vampires faded to ashes.

She'd gone the last twenty-three years without killing, fighting only to incapacitate. Yet in the last hour she'd broken her hard-earned record by killing seven Rogues. Granted, she'd been merciful and shot them in the head to end their suffering, but the knowledge did nothing to ease her guilt.

Siovon was so lost in her self-deprecation that she hadn't paid any mind to the Rogue sneaking up behind her, not until the crunch of twigs gave it away. Whirling around, she realized too late that her gun was empty. "Shit," she yelped, tossing the weapon to the side. Before she could utter the spell to conjure one of her daggers, the Rogue leaped at her.

The shadows surrounding the forest thickened. Siovon thought it was a mind trick until a form loomed before her, even taller and more imposing than Lucian. Lucian's brother—the Viking—sent a throwing knife through the air. It lodged in the Rogue's forehead. The beast just dropped to the ground with a thud, its forehead sizzling as the silver burned through skin. Within moments, he was reduced to ashes.

Feeling sick to her stomach, Siovon looked up, up, up into dancing pale blue eyes. "Are you okay?" he asked.

Lucian approached them at that point, sheathing his sword.

Siovon planted her hands on her hips, glaring between him and Cassander. "Is this what you meant by the cavalry?" she seethed, angrier with herself than him. "How the hell did he know where to find us?"

Lucian fixed her with a bored stare. "When I was checking the landscape, I called Sal and had him materialize here in the event that we needed to make a quick escape. When we awoke, I sent a text to come for a fight."

Siovon didn't look pleased with his answer. In fact, her fists were clenched, the telltale sign that she was pissed, though Lucian couldn't say he knew what the stubborn woman's problem was. His brothers had been a big help, killing the outer Rogues and working their way inward. If not for them, they would have spent several more hours fighting.

She gave a toss of her head, flicking her bangs from her eyes. Then the violet jewels narrowed. "The Viking isn't the one who can teleport. So there's more than one of them here?"

"Actually, there are three of us," another deep voice called out.

The three of them turned as Julius strolled from the shadows, small dots of blood splattered on his tan face. Lucian frowned when Siovon's eyes widened, and before he knew what he was doing, he moved to her side. He didn't like the way she was all but gawking at the twin.

Like all vampires, Julius was quite a looker. He was tall, like the rest of the Gordano men, with an athletic build and chestnut-brown hair that was shaved into a long mohawk. He had the same Roman features as Lucian, their father's pale blue eyes and a small hoop pierced through his nose.

"Who the hell are you?" Siovon demanded.

So much for her gawking, Lucian thought with glee. Her eyes were mere slits, her lips turned in a curl of annoyance.

Julius flashed a wide smile to reveal teeth as white as the snow around them. He gave a mocking bow at the waist. "Julius Gordano at your service, milady," he drawled, his accent more modern-day Italian than his older brothers, which wasn't surprising, given that Julius, Darius and Andreas had been born many centuries after him, Sal and Cass. They were only some three hundred years old.

"Also known as the animal whisperer," Cass murmured. "He can command animals."

"Terrific." Siovon shook her head, glaring at Lucian. "Did you invite your whole family, or what?"

"Nope, just me, Cass and Sal," Julius crowed, as if she were speaking to him. "The rest of the Gordano clan were otherwise occupied."

"Actually, I only asked for the last two," Lucian drawled. "I'm not sure why *you* are here."

Julius spread his arms wide. "I came to offer my services."

"What services would that be?"

"I've heard about your adventures with a beautiful female. Knowing you, you'd just screw up and scare the poor woman away."

Lucian stiffened in outrage, annoyed that everyone thought he was some barbarian who didn't know how to treat a lady. For the love of the gods, he wasn't an idiot. He was just as civilized as the next man.

Well, for the most part.

Before he could utter a word, Julius continued. "I'm not called the Love Doctor for nothing, you know."

"No one calls you that," Cass said. "If anything I'd say you were *Dr. Doolittle.*"

Julius sputtered and Lucian frowned, wondering what the hell a 'Dr. Doolittle' was. He wasn't as tuned in to the modern Hollywood entertainment as his brothers.

Siovon rolled her eyes and walked away. "Imbeciles," she muttered.

"Hey, where are you going?" Julius called out.

She didn't even look over her shoulder. "I've known you for less than five minutes and already I've decided I dislike you."

Cass coughed to cover a chuckle and Lucian smirked at Julius' shocked expression. Despite the way he and Darius aggravated the living hell out of them all, women tended to find them charming. Lucian had never understood their fascination, but he was pleased to know Siovon was one of the few intelligent women who wasn't succumbing to the foolery.

"Go check the surrounding perimeter," Lucian said to Julius. "I don't want any nasty surprises springing on us again." His younger brother opened his mouth to argue, but Lucian gave him a dark glare.

"Sure thing, Your Highness," Julius teased.

Cass shook his head and fell into step beside Lucian, both maintaining a safe distance behind Siovon. "Have you figured out if she's the one?" his brother questioned.

Lucian didn't have to ask what Cassander was referring to. After spending hours making love to Siovon, he knew she was his truemate. When he'd been buried deep inside her, his heart had exploded with a burst of feelings that wouldn't be banished any time in the near future. He was now bound to her, could feel her annoyance and stress as if they were his own.

Yes, Siovon was the woman who possessed the other half of his soul. After countless years, he'd at last got to experience what so many of his fellow brethren had longed for over their lives. All he had left to do was convince Siovon to accept him.

Something told him it wouldn't be easy. Swallowing a jar of silver nails with serrated edges and no water would be less complicated. Probably less fatal, too, considering Siovon would run to the other side of the Earth if he brought up such a claim.

Lucian had heard plenty of stories where vampires went off the deep end after losing their truemate. Losing one wasn't limited to death. Just meeting a truemate set the bonding process into motion, and until it was completed, the vampire could go mad with longing and turn Rogue. The number of times it had happened was far greater than Lucian was comfortable with.

Realizing Cassander was still waiting on an answer, Lucian nodded. "She is. However, I don't want you or anyone else trying to play matchmaker or putting any ideas into her head. I can woo her on my own."

Cass grunted in disagreement. "The fact that you said 'woo her' like it's the 1800s tells me you have no idea what you're doing."

"And I suppose you do? When was the last time you tried to court a woman since—" Lucian snapped his mouth shut when a haunted look crossed Cassander's hardened features. He breathed a silent curse, not having meant to bring up his brother's past. "*Merda*, brother, I'm sorry. I didn't mean it like that."

"Yeah, I know." Cass shook himself, as if trying to shake the memory of his dead mate, Maria.

Instead of lashing out as Lucian deserved, Cass displayed an immeasurable amount of the patience he'd developed ages ago by straightening, keeping his tone steady. "Your mate is the type of woman who is unaccustomed to having to depend on others for anything, even something as simple as offering to hold a heavy bag for her. You will have to be patient with her. And believe you me, out of us all, patience is something you lack the most. All I'm saying is that you need not hesitate if you ever find yourself unsure of what move to make."

Lucian frowned but gave his brother a grateful nod. Cass wasn't the most outgoing of their family. In fact, he was just short of a recluse. The man spent the majority of his time locked away in his lair, only coming out to participate in family meetings or to oversee the popular fighting cages he owned.

The brothers rounded the corner and paused when Siovon stopped in her tracks. Alarmed, Lucian moved to her side. "What is it?"

Instead of answering, all three of them went silent at the sight several yards away. Dressed in the same black outfit Naomi had worn when Lucian first saw her, she was all long limbs and elegance as she ducked, dodged and parried against Salvator's equally graceful moves. It was like watching a death match between a viper and a cobra. It was impossible to tell which was more dangerous.

When he'd met Naomi earlier in the morning, he'd wanted to kill the wench for attacking Siovon — no ifs, ands or buts. Now that he was able to sit back and watch her move, he had to admit that she was damned skilled. Sal was no enemy to take lightly, but Naomi was remarkable, as she was holding her own against him.

"Who is that?" Cass queried, more curious than worried about their brother.

"My friend Naomi," Siovon answered, staring in obvious awe at the battle.

"If she's not an enemy, why is she fighting our brother?"

"My guess is that your perverted brother didn't bother to mention he wasn't a foe. Naomi is in battle-mode, and all she sees is a man who's threatened her."

"I'm guessing she isn't the dainty, hey-how-are-you type of female," Cass drawled.

"That's an understatement," Lucian groused. "The woman is about as polite as a crocodile with a loose tooth."

Siovon clucked her tongue. "She is not. She's just…misunderstood."

"My ass."

The three of them turned back to watch the scene play out. "Should we intervene?" Cass asked after several more minutes.

"You're more than welcome to try," Siovon murmured, "because I'm sure as hell not getting in her way when she's in the heat of battle."

"You fear she will harm you?" Lucian demanded.

Siovon shrugged. "Anyone in their right mind should fear crossing paths with a fury when she's pissed. Don't you think?"

Lucian sucked in a sharp breath and Cass let out a low curse. "You're kidding, right?"

When Siovon only shook her head, Lucian's tension rose. Furies kept to themselves inside their own little sacred communities. However, that didn't mean they were peaceful, innocent ladies. They were mean, vicious and dangerous as hell when they were angry. *Merda*, it was for the best of demon kind that the shrews stayed in their holes. Very rarely did they travel to the outside world, and almost never alone.

"Hell's bells," Cass breathed.

"Yep."

"Furies have wings," Lucian muttered, eyeing Naomi's slender frame outlined in the skin-tight bodysuit. "I doubt she's able to hide them under her outfit."

"She's a half-blood, so she doesn't have any wings."

"Ah, so she's...lacking."

Siovon glared up at him. Then she gave a smug smile and turned back to the scene. "Ever heard of the Makalu Massacre?"

Lucian frowned, recalling the story that had shaken the demon world several decades before. The mountain trolls living within the Makalu Mountain had been feasting on humans and demons from the nearby towns. The story said that one day an extermination team commanded by the Imperials was sent to detain the trolls, but when they made it to the caves, the trolls were all dead. Heads and limbs were severed, blood stained every inch of the caves and insides were strewn across the floor. There had been rumors of the murderers being assassins, but nothing had ever been proven.

And since the Imperials had already planned on bringing an end to the trolls' evildoings, they hadn't cared to investigate upon discovering someone had beaten their extermination team to the gruesome attack. They'd pretty much treated it like a first-come-first-served situation.

When Siovon's smirk remained in place, Lucian pieced the puzzle together. Even Cassander's eyes were wide with shock. "You mean to tell me she's behind that attack?"

Siovon gave a small chuckle. "She *was* that attack." Her eyes were flashing with humor as she took in Lucian's and Cassander's horrified expressions. "Suddenly she doesn't seem so *lacking*, now does she?"

Ever since first coming across Siovon's scent, his life had consisted of shock after shock. And now he'd discovered her closest friend was a demon who'd slaughtered some of the toughest-skinned creatures in the demon world.

Blood of the gods. Just what the hell did I get into?

Salvator was having the time of his life fighting the slim vixen with gorgeous caramel-colored eyes. It had been many years since he'd fought a competent opponent that wasn't one of his brothers. Granted, he was holding back with the woman before him, but only a little. Even more entertaining was that she was holding back as well. To say he was impressed was an understatement.

There were no meaningless taunts, no tricks, no hidden traps to gain the upper hand, just two skilled fighters going at it in an elegant battle of the blades – him with a claymore dagger, her using custom silver knives with knuckle protectors. Sal realized more than once that the woman had aimed for his heart and neck, intent on killing him. He'd attempted the same at first, but in his peripheral vision he was aware that his brothers and Siovon were watching instead of helping. That let him know that the woman he fought wasn't his enemy, but that didn't make him eager to end their battle. He was having too much fun.

That is, until Lucian called out for him to back off. Sal heaved a long sigh, pushing back a childish urge to throw a tantrum. The woman before him ignored the command, continuing to come after him. Fire flashed in those beautiful eyes of hers. She was feeling the heat of battle, and like any proud warrior, it was near impossible to just stop.

He dodged a swipe to the head and swept out a leg to kick her feet from under her. As expected, she leaped over his leg. He called on his powers and teleported out of sight, reappearing behind her as she landed. She paused, confused as to his sudden disappearance.

Sal used her hesitation to his advantage and slid one arm around her waist to pin her right arm to her side. He caught her other wrist in his free hand, pulling it to rest against her sternum. With their bodies pressed together, he inhaled the scent of rich chocolate. A sudden craving for sweets made his mouth water. He damned near groaned aloud as his body hardened with the flush of heat swimming through him.

Her inability to use her weapons didn't deter her in the least bit. She brought one leg forward and dropped her weight to throw him off balance. Sal spread his legs to keep from falling forward, but he lost momentum.

That one second cost him, however, as the sly demon bent her legs and jumped, flinging them both backward. Startled by the move and strength, he released her as they both fell back into the snow. Before he could twitch a muscle, the woman perched over his chest with the tip of her knife a mere breath away from his throat, so close that if he swallowed, the silver blade would burn him.

Not that he could move, regardless. He stared up at the woman in complete awe.

In their scuffle, the black mask that had covered the lower half of her face had slid to bunch around her neck. He'd already been drawn in by her eyes. Her heart-shaped face was all angles and sharp perfection and her lips held a sexy pout.

However, it was clear what the mask was intended to hide. A white scar in the shape of an X had been carved into both of her cheeks. He couldn't imagine her deliberately marring such perfect features, which made him wonder what had happened to her. Yet even with the flawed skin, she was...perfect, far more beautiful than any woman he'd seen in a very long time.

And as a man who had taken countless beautiful lovers over the nearly a thousand years of life, that was saying something.

Moving in what seemed like slow motion, Sal reached up to her. He was mesmerized to the point where he paid no mind to the sizzling burn of the silver blade touching his throat. Her eyes shifted over him, as if she were unsure of his motives. They were so expressive that he wondered if she'd ever be able to hide her feelings.

Sal palmed her cheek. "So beautiful," he whispered, stroking the ridged skin over one scar.

Sal frowned at the haunting pain that flashed across her features. She shoved off him, backing away several feet. She jerked the mask back over her face and ran through the trees to retrieve her fallen weapons from the piles of ashes that had once been Rogues.

Sal stood, still frowning after her. He'd only taken a step when a literal gut-wrenching pain tore through his abdomen, breaking whatever spell he was under. He tried to suck in a deep breath, but the pain made it impossible on the first few tries. When he was able to breathe again, he glared at the tiny siren whose violet eyes were burning with rage.

"What the hell was that for?" he growled, clenching his hand to his stomach. *Gods above.* The woman might be little, but she had one hell of a punch. He feared that single contact had ruptured his spleen – or worse.

"What the hell did you say to her?" she demanded, raising her fists to deliver another blow.

Sal could dodge it with his speed and engage in a match with Siovon, but Lucian would kick his ass if he so much as flicked a strand of hair on her head. She was his truemate, and Lucian had shown some damn aggressive signs back in the high-rise apartment. That alone let Sal know Luc was fond of the woman.

Fortunately he didn't have to do anything. Lucian appeared at his woman's side, capturing her dainty little hand in his. He grunted, and Sal had a feeling that stopping her fist had taken more strength than the man let on.

"I only told her she was beautiful," Sal grumbled, turning to peer through the dark forest where his opponent had disappeared to.

"You bastard," Siovon snarled. She tried — and failed — to tug her hand from Luc. When she made to throw her other fist at Sal, Lucian wrapped both arms around her, pinning her in place. She settled for glaring daggers at Sal. "How could you be so cruel to mock her for something she's insecure about?"

Sal blinked in genuine confusion. "Mock her? It was an earnest compliment," he objected. He softened his tone. "She is stunning."

Siovon glared at him for several tense moments, as if contemplating whether or not he was telling the truth. He was. The caramel-eyed woman was alluring. Her imperfections were what made her perfect. She was a delicious temptation and Sal licked his lips as he felt a desire to have a taste — or two, or three. Something told him the tall female would never be an easy seduction. She would challenge his charms.

After a while, Siovon's tension drained as she gave a stiff nod. "Fine," she muttered. "Naomi may be a badass, but she's all woman at heart. Don't stare at her, and you sure as shit better not say a damn thing about her scars. And wipe that disgusting look off your face."

Sal scoffed. "Disgusting look?" He knew very well he possessed the beauty all vampires had. Disgusting had never, ever been a word used to describe him.

"You heard me, you perverted leech. You're practically drooling at the mouth. If you do anything to make her feel any more uncomfortable, I'll feed your 'little friend' down there to Thor for breakfast."

Sal blanched, and someone—Julius, to be exact—barked out a laugh. Cass let out a humorous noise as well, but he covered it with a fake cough. Sal didn't know who the hell Thor was, but he didn't doubt for one moment she wouldn't deliver her threat to his 'little friend'. And judging by the power in her punch, the tiny woman wasn't half as delicate as she looked.

"What's a Thor?" Julius questioned as he joined them.

Luc answered, sounding exasperated. "Believe me, you do not want to know, *fratello*."

Siovon stabbed Lucian with a glare over her shoulder. "You can put me down now, Frosty. I won't attack him...yet."

Luc's eyes twinkled when he looked down at Siovon. *Yep*, Sal thought, *Luc is head-over-heels for her*. He'd never looked at anyone the way he was looking at her.

"Think pacifist thoughts, *fatina*," he murmured.

And a cute little pet name. Sal smirked. His brother was so lost. He shook his head in pity.

"Okay," Julius said, narrowing his eyes on Lucian with suspicion. "Who the hell are you and what have you done with the real Lucian?"

Sal only continued to smirk, and Cass had a faint smile on his face. "My thoughts as well, Julius," Sal murmured.

Julius' eyes were filled with uncertainty as he looked between Siovon and Lucian. Sal knew the exact moment realization struck his younger brother. The eyes that were a mirror image of their own widened and his mouth split into a wide grin. "Hot damn, brother. You've found your truemate—"

Cass slapped his palm over Julius' mouth, silencing the idiot from spilling a secret Lucian didn't want to be told.

It was too late, of course. Siovon frowned at Sal, Julius and Cass. Then Luc, whose expression was guarded. "What's a truemate?"

Neither Julius nor Darius knew when to keep their big mouths shut, so Sal was quite shocked when Julius looked at the glares from each of his brothers and decided not to reveal the truth. Instead, he gave Siovon an easy smile. "Um...truemate? Sorry, I meant to say *teammate*. Since you're working together. Ha ha. I was dropped on my head as a babe, you see. I tend to get my words mixed up. A verbal-dyslexia type of thing, and my English isn't very good. Forgive me."

Sal rolled his eyes. He supposed their one saving grace was that Darius had stayed in Chicago. Separated, the twins were loads of trouble. The two of them together were walking, talking migraines.

Changing the subject, Lucian released Siovon, but he didn't allow her to move more than a few steps from him. New truemates tended to be possessive of one another, especially if they were natural predators like vampires and shifters.

Gods... Sal recalled all too well how annoying Marc had been around Ava. He'd snap and growl at any of them if they got too close to her, even knowing they were all siblings. He was better now, but there were still times when vamps who weren't in their family had cast lingering glances at Ava, only to find themselves tossed out of a window or over the balcony of their father's upper floors by a pissed off were-cougar.

"We should have left one of the Rogues alive," Lucian said, rubbing a hand across the back of his neck.

Siovon turned to him. "Why? It's not like you can get them to tell you anything useful. They're Rogues."

"No, but my sister would have been able to see into their memories. We could have learned something useful."

Sal frowned and looked at Cass and Julius. Cass gave his head a shake of denial, so small and swift that most people would have never even seen it.

Lucian, however, didn't miss a thing with his hawk-like eyes. He scowled, knowing they were keeping something from him. "What is it?"

Sal and the others looked over each other once more, but Cass was the one to step forward. "Ava is…unable to help right now."

As expected, Lucian stiffened. For as long as they'd known their youngest sister, Lucian had been the most protective of her. Her being absent for decades hadn't changed a thing.

His face turned to stone as he fixed the three of them with a hard look. "What's happened?"

They hesitated another moment before Sal sighed. "She's Purging. There have been some minor complications back home."

All the air in Lucian's body seemed to come out in one breath. He glanced at Siovon, who was watching them with a deep frown, trying to figure out what they were talking about. The four of them stared back at her. Smart enough to know this was a family conversation, she lifted her hands in annoyance. "Fine. I'll go." She strolled away, grumbling to herself. "Freaking hulking giants and their secrets. I didn't want to know anyway."

Sal's lips twitched in amusement as Lucian watched her go with a laser focus. "For such a tiny thing, she's quite the fireball," Sal drawled.

A corner of Luc's lips lifted, pride clear in his tone. "She's amazing, isn't she?"

"You're one lucky bastard, I'll admit," Julius said with a resigned sigh. "Although I find great humor in the knowledge that she's the total opposite of the women you prefer. She's mouthy, brave and won't deal with your less-than-appealing attitude." He then straightened, his eyes twinkling. "Her friend is single, though, right? I like women who are less deadly with a blade, but I'll make an exception. She was pretty freaking hot."

Sal frowned as an uncomfortable feeling tightened his gut. He shook himself, though, telling himself that it was a lingering effect of Siovon's punch. It couldn't be something so tedious as jealousy. That word wasn't even in his vocabulary.

Lucian frowned, turning back to his brothers. "All jokes aside, tell me what's happened to Ava."

Chapter Fourteen

"Ava and Marc found an abandoned child last night," Julius explained to Lucian. "Her name is Anais, and she's ten years old."

It was one of those rare times when Julius showed his true colors, his ability to focus and reveal his intelligence. He and Darius, as frustrating as they could be, had been scholars once upon a time. They had to be in order for Darius to own one of the most popular five-star restaurants in Chicago and for Julius to own an art gallery that had the wealthiest names in the world coming to view and purchase his works.

Lucian shifted his weight to one leg. "They were already planning to open their home to orphans. It doesn't surprise me that they found one so soon."

Julius shook his head. "No, but I bet this will. Anais is a Royal."

Lucian's jaw went slack. He stared at his brothers.

He and his family were the only Royals left in the world. The others had long ago died away. In the early

500s, the Plague of Justinian had broken out and affected most of the Mediterranean port cities, which had been home to thousands of vampires — mostly Royals, as they'd preferred to live in clusters for safety. In just one year, the plague had devastated millions of humans who were their primary food source. Diseased blood didn't make them sick, but it lacked the nutrients vampires needed to survive. As the disease spread and humans began to die, so did the vampires of the region. They'd starved, which had led to them turning Rogue. That was, if they hadn't killed each other first.

The vampire population had greatly decreased in number. Those who'd survived had traveled far to break away from the diseased areas, and starvation had become less critical. However, centuries later, another strand of the Bubonic Plague had torn through the continents. Famine once again had struck their people, as the human death toll had grown to alarming heights. For years and years on end, Lucian, Cass, Sal and Cyrus had been powerless to do anything except watch their people suffer and wither away to nothing but bones and ashes. Royals, Aristocrats and Turnbloods had all become reduced to a small populace scattered around the world.

There was no fear of extinction, as they could always breed with or convert healthier humans into Turnbloods, but there was no salvation for Royals. They were the pureblood descendants of the Ancients, and only a handful of them outside the Gordanos had survived.

Cyrus had found his second mate, a Royal named Anna, who had given birth to the twins. Years later, they'd taken a newborn Andreas in as their own, despite his unknown origins. As the years had passed, the last of the Royals died out, and only the Gordanos remained. Lucian knew that because, for centuries, they'd had eyes all over the world, searching for any who lived, but never there had there been any signs or even a whisper of other Royals out there.

And with no other pureblood Royals to carry on the rich bloodline, there would come a day when the Royals would be nothing but an old tale passed down through the vampires.

Lucian wasn't buying any of the bullshit his brothers claimed. "That's impossible."

Julius shook his head, his tone solemn. "Believe me, Lucian. We all said the same thing. However, you have to admit that a lot of things we long thought impossible have proven us wrong. Sirens were thought to be extinct centuries ago, and yet there is Siovon, along with her sister, and not too long ago Lila. We never thought we'd see Ava again. Hell, we all thought she was dead, and yet we were reunited. Even Marc is a mixblood, and up until a few months ago, we never even knew they were real, but now—"

"All right, dammit. I get your point," Lucian growled. Good grief, he hated being proven wrong. He didn't need anyone throwing it back in his face. "Okay, so this child is a Royal. I won't believe it until I see it for myself, but where did she come from? Who are her parents?"

His brothers hesitated again. This time Cass spoke up. "She escaped from some mysterious 'master', whom she's terrified of. She has no family, and she can read souls, apparently. We don't know much more about her other than that. Marc drove straight to Father's home, and he was hysterical because the moment the child touched Ava, she started her Purge."

Lucian frowned. Purging was the name they'd given to label Ava's 'episodes'.

As Ava had once explained it to them, her powers gave her the ability to absorb the feelings of those she touched into herself. There were people like Cyrus, who had a vast amount of 'dark energy' in them. Over the course of that person's life, if they'd experienced an immense amount of pain and anguish, it would sit and fester until it became an almost tangible force within their hearts and minds. When Ava touched someone who was filled with dark energy, for even just a few seconds, that darkness would flow into her body, filling her until she became nothing more than a hollow shell. Her consciousness would be forced to the recesses of her mind while the memories and feelings that had caused the darkness would replay over and over again. She'd stay like that for days, even weeks at a time, until her own aura was able to 'purge' the dark energy.

It had happened only a handful of times, but it always made their family sick to their stomachs with worry over whether or not she'd come back from her episodes.

"Luc," Sal said, running a hand through his hair. "It's really bad this time. It's the worst we've seen."

Lucian frowned. "How is that possible from a mere child?"

Sal kicked at the snow on the ground, the ends of his silver ponytail trailing over his shoulder. "I have no idea, but whatever the girl went through is horrible. Ava won't feed, and any time anyone gets close to her, she freaks out and tries to harm herself. We had to strap her down to the bed and place an IV in her arm to keep her nourished and sedated, but at this rate, there's no telling how long it'll be before she comes back."

"Yeah, and Marc isn't any better," Julius added. "He can't feel her through their bond anymore, so he's on edge."

"What of the girl?" Lucian questioned, worrying she could have been a trap.

As if reading his thoughts, Cass shook his head. "She is too afraid to let anyone near her other than Marc or Ava. Last we checked, Father was trying to ease her into trusting him, but he wasn't making much progress."

"*Cazzo*, what awful timing. Anything else happening that I should know about? How's Andreas?"

His brothers shared another look before shrugging. "He's been sleeping a lot. It's all he can do to keep up his strength these days," Julius answered.

"Lucian," Sal said, straightening a black silk tie that complemented his smoky-gray Armani suit. *By the gods.* Lucian had told him to come prepared for a battle, yet the man was wearing a fancy-ass suit. "I hate to be the bearer of bad news, but I have to admit I'm concerned."

Lucian frowned, not at all liking that serious tone. "What concern would that be?"

Sal contemplated his words. "Do you think Siovon will be able to heal Andreas? I know you said she is able to create powerful medicines, but do you truly think anything she makes will be effective, compared to using her sister's ability?"

Lucian looked to the dark sky. The snow clouds were thick, and he didn't need to look at the news forecast to know a bad storm wasn't too far off. He could sense it in the air as the wind whipped around them. His brother's words had pissed him off, but he couldn't be angry. Instead of searching for Calysta, he'd lingered with Siovon, even spending a week tracking her scent for no other reason than to satisfy his curiosity. He could argue that her ability to sense magic was helpful or that he was keeping her prisoner because she'd taken part in Mikhail's plots, but they all knew it was a lie. He'd been bewitched the moment he'd caught her scent, and now that they knew she was his truemate, of course his brothers would question his judgement.

Hell, *he* questioned his judgement. He wanted to find a cure for Andreas, yet instead of searching for the one surefire way they all knew would work, he'd trusted Siovon's words that she could heal him, even though he'd heard the uncertainty in her voice.

Family came before everything. He'd always lived by those words. Family first, then his clan. Anything else was debatable.

Just what the hell am I doing?

Even as he doubted himself, he still met his brothers' looks with grim determination. With a confidence he didn't feel, he said, "She can heal him."

Sal frowned. "But—"

"She will," Lucian cut in. "I don't want to hear another word about this. I know what I'm doing."

Cass spoke. "Originally, yes. But no one knows when they will meet their truemate, so when it happens, your judgment can become clouded." He then shook his head, the ends of his braids swishing around his lower back. "Just remember that, brother. I like your mate, but we cannot ignore the fact that her blood is what created these Rogues in the first place." Lucian opened his mouth, but Cass held up a hand. "And yes, I know she was forced into doing so. That can be forgiven, but in the end, it's Father's decision. He is still our king, and someone needs to be brought to justice."

"That's just it," Lucian said in frustration. "There *is* someone to be brought in. Mikhail has a son by the name of Jarek."

All three of his brothers took a step back in shock. "What?" Julius questioned.

Lucian nodded. He needed a distraction. He didn't want to think about what his father would think of Siovon or whether or not she could heal Andreas. It should be his primary focus, but gods help him, it wasn't. Not anymore. "Mikhail had a dark wizard help him use Siovon's powers to create Rogues that he could control, and he had imps who would use portals to aid him. He killed them all, but he had a son meant to carry out his plans."

Julius sucked in a sharp breath. "That must be why it was so easy to kill him in the Apennines. He knew he would die, but he had a backup plan."

"Precisely. It's possible his son is meant to launch an attack on my clan. Yesterday he was hiding in a town outside of Des Moines. I believe he is behind sending these Rogues after me."

"Wait," Sal cut in. "How do we know this Jarek even exists? For all we know, Siovon could be leading you—"

Lucian took a threatening step forward. "I can smell her every lie, Salvator. That is the last time you will accuse her of any wrongdoing."

Sal rolled his eyes but didn't say anything further. *Smart man.* Though his family could spend days arguing with each other over petty matters, there was a hierarchy they followed. Lucian was the eldest sibling. Not only that, but he was their clan chief and future king. When he put his foot down, that was the end of a conversation. "Twice now I've had Rogues sent through portals after me, and when we went through the imp's computer, we found a video of her sister. Calysta said Jarek was following her, so she was going to hide here for a while." He told them everything they had gone through from the moment he'd met Siovon to now, making sure to go over every detail, in case they caught something he didn't. Of course, he left out the tidbits where the two of them had shared intimate moments. That knowledge was for him and him alone.

When he'd finished, his brothers had contemplative looks on their faces. "There's something missing here," Sal murmured. At Lucian's annoyed look, he held up a slender hand. "Pull your fangs in, brother. I'm not accusing your woman this time. I'm saying it feels like there's a piece of the puzzle missing. We killed Mikhail months ago, and weeks before that, Siovon escaped him. Why wait until now to make a move? You'd think Jarek would have been wise enough to just disappear, yet somehow he knew exactly where you were each time he sent the Rogues. And now" — he waved his hand to indicate the ashes around them — "it's clear this was a trap. If Siovon is innocent in all of this, then who else could have known your locations?"

Lucian grimaced, not liking the implications being voiced. His first thought was that Naomi was behind things, but he dismissed it. The bond between the two women was far too strong. He didn't detect a shred of deceit from her — maybe contempt for him and a desire to rip his heart out, but nothing against Siovon.

Then he thought of the only other possibility of how someone knew where they would be. "Her sister."

"My thoughts too," Cass muttered. "However, it's too soon to make assumptions. This…pet of your truemate, Thor, is scouting the schoolhouse now, correct? Let's wait until she receives word from him before venturing out."

"Yes. Plus, it'll take hours before your clan members make it to Des Moines," Julius murmured. "They have an additional three-hour drive compared to us. If Jarek is waiting on us to close in and make a move, at least we'll have more firepower to back us up."

Lucian nodded. "Right." He'd already called several of his clansmen early that morning and let them know where to meet him. They were a healthy mix of Turnbloods and Aristocrats, so he'd told them to wait until sunset to head out. There was no sense in wasting any of the strength they might need.

He peered through the forestry when he sensed the two women making a return. Sal's eyes flashed with desire when he caught sight of Naomi in the distance. "I'd be careful with that one, *fratello*," Lucian warned in a quiet tone.

Sal raised a slim silver brow. "I beg your pardon?"

Lucian shrugged. "She's dangerous."

"The most beautiful women always are."

That's true, Lucian thought. Siovon was the prettiest woman he'd ever seen, and, despite her desire to be passive, she was a lethal warrior.

"Remember the story of the Makalu Massacre?" Cassander asked.

As expected, Sal's eyes widened. "Really? *She* did that?" When Cass nodded, Sal let out a low whistle of appreciation. Then he got a wicked gleam in his eyes. "All the more reason why seducing her will be fun."

Lucian rolled his eyes. He should have known that wouldn't deter Sal in the least bit. The man liked his women beautiful and deadly, and it couldn't get much deadlier than ripping apart mountain trolls. "Suit yourself, but we warned you. And if she doesn't kill you, Siovon will."

Sal grimaced, once again clutching his abdomen where Siovon had struck him. "I feel like you're right on that one."

Lucian gave a feral grin, turning toward the cabin. "I always am."

* * * *

If Siovon had been told a week ago that she would be standing in a room full of vampires and not feel her skin crawl — and even offering them warm beverages like a gracious hostess — she would have laughed it off and replied that it would happen only when Hell froze over.

Well, the cold December air of Iowa must have seeped into the underworld, because there she was, standing in the opening separating the stairs from the living room, watching the four brothers make themselves comfortable in her house. The cabin felt pretty darn small compared to their tall, muscular physiques.

Julius was near the fireplace, his hands clasped behind his back as he studied the framed painting of a valley landscape she'd made years ago. He'd been in that exact position for the last ten minutes. Sal was sitting in the armchair with one ankle crossed over his knee, looking far too elegant for the rustic interior. Cass and Lucian were on opposite ends of the couch, both tapping away at their phones. Next to her, Naomi leaned against the wall, twirling her dagger. Every so often she'd send Sal a lethal glare that should have caused him to cower. Instead, he'd flash a charming grin right back at her.

Siovon watched the interaction with narrowed eyes but didn't comment on it. So long as Naomi didn't decide to leap across the room and stake the silver vamp, everything was fine.

Well, as fine as a group of demons waiting around a cabin could be. Thor hadn't yet contacted her, and since Lucian's men were still little over an hour away from their rendezvous point in Davenport, they'd come inside to work out the details of their plan until meeting the other vamps there.

"I really like this painting," Julius commented. He looked over his shoulder at Siovon. "The colors blend beautifully, and you detailed even the tiniest blades of grass, as well as placed correct shadows caused by the sun's angle. It's remarkable."

Siovon lifted a brow, surprised that he'd noticed such a thing.

"Julius is the artist of the family," Salvator elaborated. "He owns the largest art gallery in downtown Chicago."

Siovon gave an absent nod. Of course he did. She wouldn't be surprised if every last one of the Gordano brats owned some fancy business. Both times she'd met Sal, he'd been dressed like some business tycoon. He probably had his own line of expensive clothing called *Forever Young*. Or *Bloody Outfitters*. Or, better yet, *Salvator's Secret*.

"Do you have any others?" Julius asked. "I'd love to see more of your work."

Siovon pointed a thumb over her shoulder. "I hang all my paintings in my room. I'll take you —"

Lucian jumped to his feet. "That's not necessary," he growled. Then, he cleared his throat. "I mean, he can stay right here. There's no need for him to wander off."

Siovon frowned. "It's just upstairs. I'm sure he's looking to pass the time."

"Yeah, Luc, that's all," Julius chirped. "I only want to see her skills."

Something about Julius' tone went right over Siovon's head, but it made Lucian tense. "What?"

"Oh dear," Sal murmured with amusement. "Best you choose your words carefully, Julius. Lucian has marked his territory."

Julius' playful expression remained in place as he glanced past Lucian to wink at Siovon. "If you're up for it, we can even work on a project together. I'd be more than happy to show you my...art kit."

Siovon lifted her brow once more. *Ah, I get it*, she thought. Julius was goading Lucian by flirting with her.

She shouldn't care. She should shrug it off and try to harden her heart against feeling anything for Lucian. However, she just couldn't help defending him. Giving a tilt of her head, Siovon blinked innocent eyes at Julius. "Thanks for the offer, but judging by the size of your boots, I'd say your 'art kit' couldn't come close to being as impressive as Lucian's."

Sal, who had been in the middle of taking a sip of the herbal tea she'd brewed, spewed the drink in a spray of mist at her words. Cass tossed his head back and chuckled, though he covered it with a cough. Lucian grinned, squaring his shoulders with pride. Naomi shook her head in dismay, though she was hiding a smile. Julius' tan face turned the color of strawberries.

"T-that's so not true!" he stammered. "It's been proven that foot size has no direct correlation to the size of a penis. Tell her, Cassander."

The Viking rolled his big shoulders, stretching his leg out to peer at his sasquatch-sized boot. "Given that I wear a size fourteen, I can't say I can relate to your inadequacy, *fratello*."

Julius tried — and failed — to get his brothers to validate his arguments. Lucian beamed with male arrogance, looking like he'd won some sort of valuable prize. Siovon was amused, but not for long. She had to admit that she was envious of the brothers. Despite the way they bickered, it was clear there was nothing but love between them.

She'd never had that kind of sibling bond growing up. It had always been her and her mentor. She had Calysta now, but they were total opposites, and there was still so much they kept from each other, Siovon more so. Her sister knew her past was a touchy subject, so she was always patient and understanding, never forcing her to open up about anything she wasn't ready to talk about. In truth, Siovon just didn't want to burden Caly. She was always so bright and gentle.

Lucian was lucky. He had six siblings and a father who all adored each other. Hell, he was shirking his duties as a clan chief to find a cure that didn't exist for his youngest brother. How much love and devotion did it take to do something like that?

With a sigh, she almost jumped out of her skin when a static buzzed in her head. Recognizing it for what it was, she straightened. She did her best to clear her thoughts, focusing on the mental thread connecting her mind to Thor. *"Thor, is that you?"* she called out.

"But of course, a chara," Thor responded. *"Who else could it be?"*

Siovon snorted. Sarcasm was a language that the tiny dragon was fluent in. He was an asshole more often than not, but he was charming in his own way. She adored him for it. *"What have you found?"* she asked.

There was another buzz of static, as if they were speaking through a phone with terrible service. Even in her mind, she had to strain to hear his voice. *"The place is empty."*

Siovon frowned. "What do you mean 'empty'?"

She'd spoken the words aloud and became aware of everyone in the room eyeing her. Julius looked around, confused. "Um, who is she talking to?"

Naomi 'shh'ed him. "She's communicating with Thor. Do not disturb her."

The brothers looked among each other. "Telepathically? That seems...weird."

Naomi shrugged but didn't comment further. Siovon ignored them all and moved toward the kitchen where it was quieter. She gave up speaking mentally altogether. It was easier to talk aloud. "Thor, what do you mean, it's empty?"

"I mean, when I woke up, the Rogues were all crowding into the back of a huge moving truck, with Jarek and his female driving."

"Why drive, when after all this time they've been traveling through portals?" It didn't make any sense. Unless... "Christ, they must have known you were spying and that you can track portals." Lucian started toward her, no doubt taking in her distress.

"That was my thought too, Siovon. However, I know I wasn't spotted. Someone must have tipped them off."

"That's impossible," she murmured. "No one knows you were going there except..." A chill crept down Siovon's spine. She turned and met Naomi's narrowed eyes. Naomi had been there. She'd known Jarek's location and she'd known Thor was heading her way. Siovon had told her so. But then, Naomi would never betray her. Naomi had so much honor, and she had never once turned her back on Siovon. Hell, she'd been the one to help her escape Mikhail, risking her own life in the process. Besides, Siovon had saved Naomi many years ago from a dark, twisted fate. Naomi would slit her own throat before turning traitor.

So who else could have known?

"I don't know, Siovon, but they left Keegan behind."

"Keegan? Are you sure?" Lucian tensed, growing impatient as he waited for her conversation to end. She waved him away.

"Positive, a chara. *He is in very poor condition. He looks like he was a scratching and feeding post for the Rogues."*

"Is he dead?"

"No, he is alive...but barely."

"Damn," Siovon muttered. "Did you see Calysta?" When Thor was silent for a long time, her worry climbed a few notches. "Thor, did you see her?" she asked again.

"No. But, Siovon...something isn't right."

Siovon frowned. "What do you mean?"

Thor hesitated again, and she knew without looking at him that his tail was twitching in agitation. *"When you first sent me to join Naomi, you told me that in Calysta's video, she said Jarek was following her."*

Siovon snapped her eyebrows together, recalling the video word for word. "She said she *thinks* he was following her, and if he caught Keegan, then she was correct."

Thor grunted. *"Now, Siovon, you know I've spent a lot of time with Calysta and Naomi while you were locked away."*

"Yes," Siovon drawled, a ball of dread twisting in her gut. "I'm aware of that."

"I could be wrong. Actually, I hope to God I am wrong, but you did not tell Naomi and me about Jarek until after she rescued you from Mikhail."

"Yes," she repeated, the dark feeling intensifying. "I told you guys everything. It's why Naomi decided to track him down."

"I know," Thor said with slow caution. *"But by that point, none of us had seen Calysta in years. How could she have known who Jarek was, if neither you, Naomi nor I told her about him?"*

All the blood in Siovon's body seemed to drop to her toes. Lucian wrapped an arm around her shoulders, but she didn't feel a thing. She was frozen in place. Even the simple act of breathing seemed to be a struggle.

"Siovon?" Thor called, his voice filled with concern.

"I'm here, Thor," she said, her voice shaking. "We will be there in a few hours. Keep an eye on Keegan and let me know if his condition changes."

Thor hesitated again, before responding. *"I will."* Then their mental connection ended.

For several minutes, Siovon stood there, staring straight ahead as words of betrayal bounced around in her head. Even as she tried to deny everything, to make up some sort of excuse that there was no way Calysta would ever turn against her, it was growing difficult to believe it when the signs were all there, clear as day. She knew all too well that family and friends could betray each other. Even the most unlikely of candidates could turn out to be monsters. She'd seen it far too many times.

Lucian peered into Siovon's eyes. She blinked, staring into his. She wanted to be sucked into those metal depths, to be absorbed until she and Lucian became one and the same. At their proximity, it was as though he was lending her his strength, giving her an anchor in the sea of despair she was drowning in. When he swept her bangs to the side with his fingertips, she blinked again.

"Don't lose yourself, *fatina*," he murmured. "Whatever Thor told you, we will work through it. You have to stay strong."

Swallowing the lump in her throat, she gave a jerky nod at his faint smile. When they returned to the living room, Naomi straightened. "What's happened?"

Siovon relayed the details of her conversation to the rest of them. Amusement left the brothers. When she told them about Calysta's possible role, Naomi's eyes widened, shock and horror crossing her features.

Her brows knitted together. "No. Calysta wouldn't do something like this."

Siovon ran a hand through her hair. "I don't want to believe it either, Naomi, but the signs are all there. She knew I'd be searching for her and would come across Keegan's apartment and find her video. She knew I'd travel here to Buffalo without anyone else being able to figure it out, and since there's no way those Rogues could have tracked your scent past the repulsion spells, that means someone had already sent them here to attack as soon as I got settled in."

Beneath her mask, Naomi clenched her jaw, frustration in her eyes. As much as Siovon hated the thought of Caly turning traitor, they both knew it could happen to anyone. Naomi let out a string of Spanish curses, sheathing her knife. "I guess the only way we'll know for sure is if we question the imp."

Siovon nodded. "Agreed." She faced the vamps, who were on their feet, watching. "Your men should be close to Davenport by now. While you head there, Naomi and I will get a head start and go to Alleman."

Lucian, stubborn as ever, crossed his arms. "No. We'll all go together."

Siovon mimicked his movement. "Again with this crap. I'm not traveling in some crowded vehicle with a bunch of freaking leeches."

"Seconded," Naomi murmured behind her.

"You are staying with me," Lucian commanded in a tone suggesting his word was final.

"A better plan would be for Naomi and me to ride together to Alleman, while the rest of you go to Davenport," Sal suggested with a wink.

Naomi's eyes narrowed. "In your dreams, bloodsucker."

Sal's smile widened. "And what lovely dreams they are, slayer."

"We don't have time for this," Siovon growled. "I'd like to get to the imp *today*, if you don't mind."

"I do mind," Lucian growled back. "Jarek left the imp behind as an obvious trap to bait you, and you're about to walk into it with no sense."

"I know very well what I'll be walking into. I know a trap when I see one. I'm not as stupid as you seem to think. I outsmarted you, didn't I?"

Before he could say anything else to damage her pride, Naomi stepped forward. When she spoke, it was full of arrogance. "Siovon may be a pacifist now — "

Sal choked out a curse of disbelief. "My ass," he grumbled.

"But she wasn't offered the title of guild master for nothing. She knows what she's doing, so back off."

The four brothers looked astonished at that bit of news, and Siovon resisted the urge to twiddle her thumbs. It wasn't like it was a big secret. All her old comrades knew of the promotion. Hell, a good number of them, including Naomi, had looked up to her long before that. Her leadership skills had been superb, and her ability to swiftly think through any situation had aided in successful missions. Their praise had made her feel honored, but after meeting Calysta and Lila, she'd turned down the offer. She'd known for many years that she wanted to be more than an assassin, but — like many of them — it had been the only life she knew.

Which was why her desire to be a pacifist and refrain from violence was so important to her. She didn't want to be seen in that kind of light anymore. Though she and Naomi were alike in so many ways, the biggest difference between them was that Naomi had become an assassin to be free of her bindings, while leaving the guild had allowed Siovon to be free of hers. She craved to live a life of peace, but it seemed her years of killing were catching up to her, making her desires a mere pipe dream. Maybe she really was meant to be a killing machine. After all, her sister and mother were the only reasons she'd left that life in the past. Lila was gone, and if Calysta had turned against her, what the hell did she have left to live for?

Lucian's face appeared in her mind, making her heart clench. She forced it away. She didn't want to think about those strange feelings. After making love to him, she'd felt so close, connected in a way that had felt so…right. Which was wrong, because she'd lied to him, and when he discovered the truth, there would never be a future for them together.

She turned her back to him, nudging Naomi toward the door. "Frosty, I understand your concern, but it's unnecessary. Between Naomi and me, very few stand a chance." She paused to glare over her shoulder. "Vampires included."

Lucian clearly wanted to argue further, but then all three of his brothers were surrounding him. With a swift movement, Julius swiped his hand out and tossed something in the air. Siovon heard jingling before catching the keys.

"Take the Jag, ladies. We'll meet you in Alleman," Julius chirped. Lucian's eyes went wide, and he tried to shake his brothers off. However, Sal flashed all four of them out of sight.

Surprised, Siovon and Naomi looked between each other for several beats. Then, they both grinned. "Rock, paper, scissors you for the wheel?" Naomi suggested, her eyes gleaming.

Siovon chuckled, handing her the keys. "Go for it. I have yet to learn to operate a stick."

Naomi lifted a brow. "From what I gathered this morning, it seems you know how to work a stick very well."

Siovon's cheeks flamed at Naomi's blunt words. "Y-you…heard us?"

Naomi snorted. "I'm only a half-breed, but I'm still a succubus, *amiga*. I can always tell when someone nearby is having sex."

Siovon shook her head, not even sure how to respond. She'd forgotten that bit of information, mostly because she'd never had sex before Lucian, thus she'd never had to worry about Naomi being close enough to sense it. And, oh, what amazing sex it had been. The man wasn't at all cold like she'd first thought. There had been nothing but hot, sweet passion. Even now, her body was ready to go another round with him.

Down, girl, she commanded herself. She had to remember to keep her distance.

Naomi studied Siovon. "You've already fallen for him, haven't you?"

Siovon could deny it. She could deny, deny, deny until the cows came home, but what good would it do? She'd only be lying to herself.

She sighed. "What am I going to do? There's no way we can ever be together. Hell, before I met him I never even thought of settling down. I was content with the thought that I'd be a virgin spinster for the rest of my life."

Naomi lifted her hands. "Don't look at me, honey. You're treading waters I've never been in and don't ever plan to ever be in." She straightened, shaking her head. "Never would I have thought I'd hear you say these words. I still say we should have knocked him out when we had the chance — or, better yet, killed him."

Siovon scoffed with humor. "That's your answer to everything. You can't kill all your problems."

Naomi shrugged and opened the door. "That, my friend, is a matter of opinion."

While Naomi started up Lucian's car, Siovon went to the storeroom to fill her backpack with several different medications, including a couple of healing potions effective for imps. She hoped one of them would be useful to Keegan — or at least keep him lucid enough to provide her with some answers.

While she was still battling against her inner turmoil, she forced it all to the back of her mind. She needed to be the level-headed Siovon that her mentor had raised her to be. To be calm and detached, so that even if her suspicions about Calysta were proven true, she would have the backbone needed to handle business.

Same goes with Lucian.

Whenever he figured she was no longer useful to him, so long as she kept her heart locked away, he couldn't hurt her when he'd turn his back on her.

Chapter Fifteen

Naomi parked them in front of a closed mechanic's shop. Siovon frowned at the storm clouds that were continuing to thicken. The wind was brutal as it whipped around them, making Siovon tighten the hood of her coat over her head. Naomi was still wearing her skin-tight suit, and Siovon didn't understand how in the world her friend managed to stand there without so much as a shiver. She had to be freezing.

"This storm is going to be hell," Naomi commented.

Even her voice was calm, as if she spent her days rolling around in the snow for fun. That only made Siovon curse her fey bloodline, because she'd spent over twenty years training in the Siberian Mountains, yet the cold still bothered her. "Yes," Siovon responded, her teeth chattering. "It'll hit in a few hours at the most."

Not that she needed to voice the obvious. The weather forecast had said it multiple times on the radio, urging people to take shelter indoors, lest they get caught in a potential blizzard.

"We're going to need somewhere to lie low until it blows over." Naomi shook her head, the end of her ponytail sweeping side to side. "I, for one, do not plan on being trapped in a house full of leeches."

"It wouldn't be all bad," Siovon offered with a sly smile. "I'm sure Salvator wouldn't mind keeping you warm."

Naomi took an unconscious step back, flustered. She then narrowed her eyes to hide her embarrassment. "I would never let that cretin touch me."

Siovon chuckled, though she hid her shock. For as long as she'd known Naomi, she'd never been so worked up over a male. It was interesting, to say the least. "Never say never, Naomi."

"Never! Just looking at that creep makes my skin crawl."

Siovon shook her head, still smiling. Despite her disgusted words, Naomi couldn't hide that she was attracted to Sal. Who wouldn't be? He was graceful, elegant and beyond beautiful.

It was funny, though, how he didn't do anything for Siovon. He was worthy of a good bit of mouth-watering, but he wasn't Lucian.

Still, Siovon didn't blame Naomi for her prejudice. It wasn't that she hated the entire race of vampires — just men like Sal, and with good reason.

Men *exactly* like Sal.

Naomi had only just reached maturity when Siovon had met her. When it had been discovered that she wasn't a pureblood fury, she'd been shunned by her own people. Her mother had been killed while she'd been sold into demon slavery. She'd been terrified and vulnerable to her newfound succubus needs. When she was bought by a vampire who was rich and beautiful, she'd thought Prince Charming had come to rescue her from a cruel existence.

Little did she know... The man had turned out to be a monster and had made Naomi's life hell. It wasn't that he looked like Sal, but it was the way he'd carried himself. It was like a trigger in Naomi's mind, a red flag to stay far away from those types of men.

The wind around them made the nearby trees bow and twist under its force. "Come on," Siovon murmured. "Let's hurry before we get snowed in."

Though Siovon didn't know where to go, she listened to Naomi's directions as they made their way through a desolate town. There were no streetlights, and the houses were so far apart that not even the distant porchlights offered any help to pierce the darkness. Since Naomi couldn't see in the dark, she relied on Siovon to keep a lookout for anything amiss.

Wherever one of them was lacking, the other made up for it. When they went on missions together, Siovon had been the eyes while Naomi's other senses were much stronger. They made one hell of a team.

They came to a stop at the edge of the tree line when Siovon spotted the small schoolhouse. She regarded the boarded-up structure with disdain. "Christ, it's like something out of a horror flick."

"It doesn't look much better in the daylight, believe me."

Siovon fumbled through her mind until she could find the thread tying her to Thor. She gave a mental tug on it to open the connection to him. "Thor, are you there?" she whispered aloud.

There was a brief, quiet static before he answered. *"Aye, I'm here."*

"Can you sense anyone lingering inside?"

"No, but I wouldn't be surprised if Jarek had left some of his zombies behind to keep watch."

"Yeah, that would have been the smart thing to do," she muttered. Then again, from what she'd learned about Jarek, he wasn't all that bright. Hell, she'd seen pigeons with more intelligence than him. "I'll be in shortly, Thor."

Their connection ended and Siovon faced Naomi. "No one else is inside, but we should scout the area first."

Naomi tilted her head back before rolling her eyes in annoyance. "No need, *amiga*. Your parasite is here."

Siovon opened her mouth but paused when the air around them dropped to the negatives. She shivered as frost inched over her boots, sealing her in place. She glanced up to see Naomi retreating several feet away. "Hey, wait—"

Just then, a looming form detached itself from the darkness, and Siovon was hauled against the sturdy chest of one pissed-off vampire.

She reared her leg back and placed what she thought was a powerful kick to Lucian's shin. He grunted but squeezed his arms tighter around her. "Put me down," she commanded, digging her nails into his forearms.

Yeah, because that always works in the movies.

Lucian buried his face in the curve of her neck. His body shook, as if her very scent caused excited shivers to travel through him. "Never. Do. That. Again."

Siovon closed her eyes and savored the feel of his arms around her for just a moment. She was going to miss it. She hadn't known the man for more than a few days, yet she was accustomed to his touch and presence. Oh, he was *so* going to break her heart.

She struggled against him once more. "You can blame your brothers on that one."

"Oh, trust me. He did," Sal grumbled, stepping out of the tree line to stand before them. "Two and a half hours of sneering, idle threats and growling at us. It was true agony, my dear."

Siovon lifted a brow. "Then why pull that disappearing stunt if you knew he'd be pissed?"

Sal rolled his eyes. "He would have stayed in that cabin all night arguing over who was riding with whom, so we did what was necessary."

"Ah. Fair enough." Siovon delivered another kick to Lucian's shin, though there wasn't as much force in it. "Put me down, Lucian. There's work to be done, and I don't want to be caught in this storm."

Lucian growled, but set her on her feet with obvious reluctance. He didn't let her get far, however. Every time she took a step, he was right there on her heels like some clingy pup.

"Let's go."

* * * *

When Siovon and Lucian entered the classroom filled with the scent of burnt lemons, a flap of wings sounded. "Finally, *a chara*. I was beginning to think the nasty wind blew you away."

Siovon smiled at Thor, who was perched on the edge of a dusty wooden desk. Her smile disappeared when she caught sight of the figure lying face-down, still as death. The imp was naked, save for a pair of boxer briefs that lay in tatters across his butt cheeks. With everything else on display, she froze. There wasn't much skin that wasn't covered in blood. It was just as Thor had warned. Keegan looked like he'd been used as a scratching post for mountain lions. With the pool of blood surrounding him, she was shocked he was even still breathing.

Lucian stood close by as she crouched beside Keegan, sliding her backpack off her shoulders. She dug around until she pulled out a vial of medicine and a small ceramic pot of healing cream. She hoped he wasn't too far gone for it to work.

She unscrewed the top of the cream and scooped out a small portion. She smoothed it over one major wound but paused with upraised eyebrows at Lucian's dark growl.

"What is it now?" she demanded.

As per usual, he was scowling, looking between her and the unconscious imp. "Must you touch him like that?"

"What?"

He gestured between them with his hands. "The intimate way you're touching him seems unnecessary."

Siovon blinked...then blinked again. She looked down at Keegan's flayed, bloodied body, then back at Lucian. She blinked one more time. "Are you serious right now?" Instead of responding, he straightened to his full height, setting his mouth in a hard line while continuing to glare. Siovon shook her head. "Would you prefer to do this instead? I need him conscious."

"I would prefer it if we just leave him here," Lucian drawled. "The world will survive with one less imp."

Siovon rolled her eyes, continuing to spread the cream over Keegan's body. When she was finished with his backside, she urged Lucian to help her turn him over. He reluctantly did so, but he used the tip of his boot to roll him as if he were roadkill. "You're such a child," she groused.

Thor's tail twitched. "He is a leech, Siovon. They all have loose screws."

Lucian turned his glare to the tiny dragon. "Watch it, lizard, or I'll show you exactly how many screws are loose."

"Don't start, you two," Siovon said on a sigh. *Jeez, it's like babysitting two bratty toddlers who can't get along.*

She continued to smooth the cream over Keegan's legs, chest, neck and face until the container was emptied. Then she lifted his head into her lap and pried his mouth open enough to pour the liquid inside, little by little. She had to massage his throat to coax him into swallowing, so he wouldn't choke, but once the potion was all gone, she exhaled a small sigh of relief when the wounds started stitching themselves closed.

Lucian tapped his foot, making his annoyance loud and clear. It didn't help that Siovon was ignoring him. She didn't care about his misplaced jealousy.

Okay, she cared a little. It was kind of cute, knowing that a powerful, arrogant commander was throwing a little tantrum over something so tedious. Still, she didn't let it show.

After several minutes of silence, Keegan's eyes fluttered open. "Calysta?" he whispered.

Siovon flicked her bangs out of her eyes. "Not quite. I'm her sister."

Keegan blinked, his eyes coming into focus. "Her sister? You must be Siovon."

Siovon lifted her brows. "She told you about me?"

He gave a weak smile that turned into a cough. "She bragged about you all the time."

That made Siovon's heart swell, which in turn made her even more upset over the possibility of her sister turning against her. "How did you meet her?"

Keegan coughed again, trying to sit up, but he was too weak to do so. "Where is Calysta? Is she okay?"

Siovon placed her hands on his shoulders to keep him steady. When he made to lift his head from her lap, she said, "You need to relax. The medicine I gave you is coursing through your body, but it won't do any good if you open your wounds any further." He settled down, though his muscles were still clenched. "We don't know where she is. Jarek and the others abandoned this place when the sun set, but they left you behind, presumably to die. I need to ask you a few questions."

His jaw tightened, but he gave a small nod. "Sure."

"How did you meet Calysta?" she repeated.

"I met her about two years ago. She came into my pub one night looking dejected, so I gave her a free drink."

"Seems awfully kind of you," she said with no small amount of suspicion. Imps were not known for their generosity. Most of them would sell their own mothers for a profit. Nothing they did was free.

Keegan gave a sheepish smile, his straight teeth stained red with blood. "Well, she was the hottest woman I'd seen in a long time, especially in my pub, so I wanted to...talk to her." When he noticed Siovon's eyes narrowing, he rushed to say, "She turned me down before I could make a move on her, but we conversed a lot."

Siovon was glad to hear his voice getting stronger as the medicine kicked in. He'd be healed in a few hours and strong enough to stand in less time.

"She was really down in the dumps, but she wouldn't tell me what was bothering her. Of course, now that I know, I understand the secrecy. Anyway, she got fucked up off the drinks, so I let her crash at my place. Nothing happened, I swear. I didn't even sleep in the same room as her. When she woke up, we talked some more, and she said she was going to stay in the city for a while to make some money before continuing on with her travels. She told me she was some sort of healer and that she made natural remedies, but she couldn't sell them on the UBM because she was 'lying low for a while'. Again, I didn't understand what she meant, but I struck a deal with her. I'd sell her potions and let her work at the pub as a waitress, but only if she split the profits with me."

Siovon rolled her eyes. "Of course."

Keegan snorted at her derisive tone. "Hey, with a business that was going nowhere, the extra money was a great help. So, we became business partners."

Lucian took a step forward. "You said you allowed her to work as a waitress, but the rumors said you had a siren singing for you whose voice could heal."

Keegan's eyes darkened and he licked his cracked lips. "That's false." He looked up at Siovon. "Allow me to explain."

Lucian glared down at him. "It looks like the medicine has given you more than enough strength. You can sit up now."

Siovon glared at him. Keegan looked confused but did as he'd been told. She helped push him into a sitting position. He murmured his thanks then leaned against the desk for support.

"While Calysta and I worked together, we became good friends. She eventually told me what she was.

Mind you, before then her earrings made her come across as a simple fairy."

Thor scoffed in disbelief. "You are an imp. How could you have thought she was some lesser fey?"

Keegan shrugged. "To be honest, I knew she was more than what she appeared, but I never asked. I didn't want to pressure her into thinking she had to tell me her secrets, you know?"

"And ruin your flow of income."

"At first, yeah, it was just about the money, but as I mentioned, we became good friends. She was someone I could trust, and I wanted her to feel the same." He shook his head, his hair matted in place. "She was feeling down again, got super drunk and told me everything—about what she really was, about her curse, about you, about how much of a failure she felt because she couldn't save you."

Siovon recalled the last time she'd ever seen Calysta. She'd taken a pretty nasty spell from Mikhail's dark wizard after trying to save Siovon, so Siovon had made her take a blood oath to never attempt it again. Calysta had been distraught, but Siovon had just wanted to ensure her sister's safety. "Is that why she betrayed me? She was angry that I made her leave me alone?" Siovon whispered, tears pricking her eyes.

She blinked. *Tears?* Holy crap, she hadn't cried since…hell, since her mentor had left her in the middle of the night.

"She didn't betray you, Siovon, not of her own free will."

Lucian growled and crouched beside them. "Explain yourself."

Keegan glared at him, but his eyes softened on Siovon. "I hated that she was cursed, but it had happened so long ago that I thought surely there was a new spell that had been discovered over the years that could free her from it. When I suggested this to her, she didn't have much hope, but she joined me on a hunt to look for one. For the past year or so, we've been traveling all across the continent, bribing and trading what we had to get some useful info out of magic users. We had a few leads about a djinn whose magic could break all curses for the right price."

Siovon met Lucian with wide eyes. "A djinn? I've never met one."

Lucian grunted. "That's because most of them prefer to remain in Tartarus."

Siovon frowned. Tartarus was one of the more popular realms of Hell where most nonhumanoid demons resided, but it was impossible to get in and out without a 'pass' from the Imperials. Obtaining one, Siovon had heard, was even harder to get than it was to become a Raptor. Sacrifices and unspeakable deeds had to be done, and in most cases, outsiders who ventured there almost never left, whether it was by choice or not. "Jesus," she muttered.

Keegan nodded. "Calysta and I had learned that one lived here in the human world, so we've been trying to track her. We'd almost caught up with her until that bitch ruined everything."

Siovon leaned forward with anticipation. "Jarek?"

He shook his head. "Sierra, the imp he's screwing."

Siovon and Lucian shared another look. Naomi had told her a little about the half-naked female imp who'd come to fight her before she'd escaped. "What happened?"

"One night while we were investigating a townhouse where the djinn was staying, Sierra came to us, pretending to be some sorceress who'd heard about our travels. She offered to help us for a cheap price. Of course, neither one of us believed that bullshit, and we could sense she was using dark magic, so we declined and made to leave. Too late, though, we realized we were surrounded by Rogues, too many for either of us to fight. I tried to make a portal, but the sons of bitches were too fast. Sierra must have placed some sort of enchantment spell on Calysta, because the next thing I knew, she had complete power over her. Calysta followed her every command with blind obedience."

He curled his hands into fists. "The bitch used her like some kind of puppet, and nothing I could do would bring her to focus. That was about three weeks ago, I think. It's hard to tell time in here. As for those singing rumors, it never happened. I wouldn't have allowed it with her curse."

Siovon's temper rose with each of his words, but it wasn't directed at him. One look at Sierra and Jarek — and at herself for not being better at protecting her sister.

"This is still confusing to me," Siovon remarked. "It's clear that Jarek spread those rumors about Calysta, knowing I'd come to look for her, then he made Calysta record that video for me. But at the same time, he should have known you and your family would search for her in order to heal your brother. Since his father wanted him to carry out his plans for getting revenge on your family, it's hard to tell which of us is the true target of whatever his plan is."

Lucian grunted in agreement. Thor flapped his wings. "You think Jarek was intelligent enough to believe the vamps would team up with you to find

Calysta? That way he can kill two birds with one stone, so to speak?"

Siovon frowned. "No. Jarek is dumb as a rock. Literally. There's no way he could have come to that conclusion. Hell, even I would have never seen this coming." She glanced at Lucian. "No offense."

Lucian's eyes twinkled with humor. "None taken, *fatina*."

Keegan also frowned. "Hold on, guys. Jarek isn't behind any of this."

"What?" Siovon, Lucian and Thor asked at once.

"Jarek is even deeper under an enchantment spell than Calysta. Every time I saw him, the spell was so thick that it was almost tangible. The only way that can happen is if—"

"He's been enthralled for years," Siovon breathed, finishing the statement for him. Her heart fluttered as realization struck her. "Christ, it all makes sense now."

Lucian scowled. "Care to elaborate, Siovon? I'm afraid none of this magical business is making much sense."

Thor snorted. "That's because—"

"Don't even say it," Lucian growled to him.

Thor grinned but closed his mouth.

Siovon explained. "Enchantment spells are just that. You cast a spell, and the object you are enchanting is bound to you. Likewise, it can be placed on a living creature—human or demon—if the caster is strong enough to wield such power, or if the other person has weak mental stability." Lucian nodded, and she continued. "As I told you before, all enchanted items need to be refilled every few months or years to maintain their strength, otherwise the magic will wear off. However, the more you refill that magic, the longer it lasts and the stronger it gets.

"When I was locked away, I met Jarek a handful of times, but it was less and less in the last few years. I knew he was afraid of me, but I was paralyzed more often than not. Even then, it's like he was always too afraid to come near me. I always thought it was strange, but if what Keegan is saying is true, then I would have seen Jarek's enchantment right away, yet Mikhail would have been blind to it."

Lucian, proving once again that his two-thousand-year-old brain possessed far more intelligence than the average person, was able to piece together the rest of her words. "Jarek must have been ordered not to go near you, in the event that you would inform Mikhail."

Siovon nodded. "Precisely. Or that I had the power to break the enchantment and cast my own on him."

He shook his head. "I hate magic." He rocked back on his heels and stood. "So from what I am understanding, for many years Jarek has been a mere puppet being controlled by someone."

"Sierra, no doubt," Thor said. "She certainly seemed to be running the show, from what I saw. She stayed right under Jarek, and every time she said something to him, he'd announce it to the Rogues and they would obey."

Lucian pondered that. "So she has direct control over Jarek but not the Rogues. Yet it is through Jarek that she can control the Rogues."

"Okay, so that means she's behind everything," Siovon murmured. "It still doesn't make sense. She used Calysta to lure me out into the open, but why? Mikhail had taken lovers before, but I never saw or heard of him using a female imp, and I've never met anyone named Sierra, so what gives?"

The four of them looked up as Julius and Cassander strolled into the classroom. "Did you hear any of that?" Lucian asked them.

Julius was the one to answer. "We heard enough to piece together what's going on." He peered at Siovon. "Can you tell how old Jarek is?"

Siovon's lips turned down at the corners. "That's a weird question. Does it matter?"

He shrugged. "It might. I have a theory."

Siovon thought it over. "I'm certain he's younger than me. There was an almost…immaturity to his behavior, and his powers weren't as developed as one would think. If I had to guess, I'd say he's no more than fifty."

Julius gave a wide smile. "That works just fine with me."

Cass lifted a brow. "What's your theory?"

"And for the love of the gods, if you say something idiotic, I will toss you out the window," Lucian growled.

Julius waved that away. "Bear with me, class. No offense, Siovon, but let's forget your theory for a moment. From what we know, Mikhail had only one other child, which is his daughter who died, like a thousand years ago. That's what started this whole grudge he had against father. Jump several centuries forward in time. As Mikhail gets closer to carrying out his grand plan, he comes to the realization that he will not survive once he sets his plan into motion. Therefore, he needs a backup. He needs someone to carry on his legacy and continue his plot by controlling Rogues. However, he learns that the Rogues are bound only to his blood, so he cannot transfer that control to an outsider. So, as the very last Nilsen left alive, how is he supposed to find someone with his blood in their veins?"

"Make one," Keegan answered.

Julius pointed a finger at him, grinning. "Bingo. He finds some unlucky woman and knocks her up. Nine months later, out pops baby Jarek, aka Mini-Mikhail. Mikhail raises this child, making him believe the world is better off without Gordanos and all that mumbo-jumbo. Unfortunately for Mikhail, this child he placed all his hopes and dreams into turns out to be a major disappointment. Jarek's shortcomings make Mikhail realize that all his hard work will be for nothing. But he's running out of time, so it's not like he can create another Mini-Mikhail. So what's the next best thing?"

Keegan answered once again. "Get someone he trusts to control his son."

"Another bingo for the man-fairy," Julius drawled.

Keegan narrowed his eyes. "Imp. Not a damn fairy."

Julius shrugged. Siovon stared up at him, rather impressed with his hypothesis, inelegant as it might be. Reading her shocked expression, Cass' lips quirked in a tiny ghost of a smile. "He and his twin have their moments."

"Devil's balls, there's two of them?" Thor demanded in disgust.

Julius frowned, looking around the room in confusion. "Is there an Irish ghost in here, or am I going crazy?"

Thor fluttered his wings. "I'm no ghost, ya stook, but this Irishman will batter your arse till you really are mad as a box of frogs."

Julius narrowed his eyes on where Thor perched on the desk, then let out an honest-to-God squeal. "What the hell is that thing?"

Thor rose into the air. "Oh, now you're asking for it."

When Thor made to fly across the room, Lucian caught him by the tail. "Calm yourself, little demon."

By that point Julius was hiding behind Cass, peeking over his shoulder with wide eyes. "Hell's freaking bells, Siovon. You could have warned someone you had a gremlin in here."

"He's a dragon," she muttered, holding her arm out for Thor. Lucian let him go, and he settled on her arm, much like a falcon would its master. "His temper is even shorter than mine, so you might want to consider your words."

Julius stepped back in place beside Cass, brushing invisible lint off his shoulder as if he hadn't screamed and hidden behind his brother like some frightened little girl. Cass eyed him with a look of utter disbelief. "Really?"

Julius pouted and cast wary glances at Thor. "I didn't think it would be an actual freaking dragon."

"Did you expect a two-foot-tall dwarf?" Lucian demanded.

"Well...yeah. I did."

Siovon rolled her eyes, lowering her arm to let Thor settle in her lap. He folded his wings against his body, flicking his long tail back and forth in anger. "It's bad enough you befriended one leech, Siovon, but the whole clan? Ridiculous."

Siovon stroked her fingers along his scaly neck. "Let's get back on topic," she muttered. "If Sierra is someone Mikhail trusted enough to pass his leadership on to, then we still don't know what she wants."

Cassander shrugged. "Perhaps she wants to use you to make Rogues who are bound to her instead."

Siovon frowned. "But she's not a vampire, so she can't turn anyone. Rogue blood is poisonous if ingested, so they can't turn anyone either."

"No, but Jarek can."

That caused her eyes to widen.

Keegan shook his head. "Sick, twisted bitch."

"Okay, so that makes sense as to why she wants you," Julius remarked, "but it doesn't seem like she's made a move against us. It's like you said. She should have known we would send others out to find Calysta, so I wonder what her plan was for us if she is to carry out Mikhail's wishes."

"She could be on her way now to attack your city," Thor offered with an evil smile. "They seemed to be in a rush to leave this evening."

Julius glared at him, but Lucian frowned, already using his phone to send out text messages. "I will warn my clansmen to be on the lookout, as well as notify Father that he may have trouble heading his way."

"Trouble has already struck," Salvator gritted, entering the room. Naomi was several feet behind him, moving to lean against a corner away from everyone. All traces of playfulness were absent from his grim features as he pulled his cell phone away from his ear.

All three of his brothers stiffened. "What's happened?" Lucian demanded.

"We need to go home. Now. Ava is missing."

Julius sucked in a sharp breath, Cassander went stiff as a board and Lucian turned a shade whiter. Worry clenched deep within Siovon's heart, fear becoming lodged in her throat. However, she knew they weren't her own feelings. They were Lucian's. Somehow she could feel his emotions as if they were her own.

It confused the hell out of her, but she was more concerned for him. She stood and touched his arm. "Ava is your sister, right?"

He swallowed audibly, but he couldn't speak. Sal was the one who explained. "Yes, she's our younger sister. We were reunited with her just a few months ago."

Siovon frowned, remembering Mikhail talking about the half-breed daughter Cyrus didn't deserve to have. "Did she run away? Or maybe she just left to go to the store or something—"

"No," Lucian growled, his voice dark. Siovon shivered at the haunted look in his eyes. "She would never run away. Not again." He shook his head, turning back to Sal. "Marc can track her through their bond, can't he?"

Sal gave a helpless shrug. "Their connection is faint. Marc isn't doing too good right now. On top of not being able to sense her, this storm is about to hit hard, and with her being pregnant—"

"Yeah," Cass breathed. "If Sierra and her troop are heading that way and they end up coming across her..."

Siovon glanced at Keegan, who appeared as out of place as she felt. "You guys should go look for your sister. I'll stay here with Keegan until—"

"Not a chance," Lucian growled, grabbing her hand. "You'll both come with us."

"And be locked in some crusty leech dungeon again?" Keegan demanded. He stood. "I don't fucking think so."

Siovon was surprised. He was much taller than she'd expected.

Then again, most people were taller than her. "I won't let them put you in a cell," she promised, jerking her hand from Lucian's grip. She glared at him while guarding Keegan. She should have looked ridiculous, being the second tiniest creature in the room standing up to the second tallest, but she didn't care. They all knew that she could kick his ass if it came down to it. Even if his brothers wanted to join in, Naomi had her back. And that was someone they'd be wise not to piss off. "Since you're a friend of Calysta's, you will not be a prisoner."

Lucian gave her a hard look, his jaw clenched. Between his anger at her and worry for his sister, it was a wonder the room wasn't covered in ice. "Everything in Minnesota, Wisconsin, Iowa, Illinois, Indiana, Michigan and Ohio falls under the Chicago clan territory. That means every demon — vampire or not — answers to me, so long as they are on *my* turf. Every decision I make is final." He leaned down to be nose to nose with her. "That means *you* are under my direct command, and disobedience is not tolerated."

Despite her inner bitch that begged to be let free, she had to admit he was right. Curse his rotten soul to hell, but he was correct. Though his clan's HQ was stationed in Chicago, his control extended across the borders of different states. It was the same with the other three clan chiefs in the US. One controlled almost all the western states, one had most of the southern states and the other one owned everything in the northeast. She and Calysta had chosen their homes in the smallest towns and cities that were considered free territory, but in Alleman, just north of Des Moines, Lucian had every right by demon law to do away with her as he saw fit.

From the corner of her eye, she saw Naomi push off the wall, sliding two long daggers out of their sheaths. It didn't matter how many vampires they were up against or how powerful the ones in the room were, Naomi was the most fearless person Siovon had ever met. Even if she knew there was a battle she couldn't survive, she would fight until her very last breath.

Siovon flicked her fingers, a silent sign to tell her friend to stand down. She focused on Lucian and lowered her voice. "I'm asking as a personal favor that you not treat Keegan as a prisoner. If you do, I will not forgive you, Lucian. I will see you as nothing more than my enemy."

A muscle ticked in his jaw, but she didn't miss the flash of worry in his eyes. "Are you threatening me, Siovon?"

She stiffened her resolve. "It's my promise to you. You will be nothing to me. *Nothing*."

For several minutes they stared at each other, the tension so thick in the air that it was almost suffocating. Siovon didn't need to look at the others to know they were each holding their breath, waiting to see what would happen next. Peaceful resolution or a civil war?

Thank God the former became the result, because Lucian closed his eyes, schooling his expression to be one of pure ice. "You and Keegan will join us at my father's house to be treated as guests." He turned to Sal before either of them could respond. "Teleport us home."

"Siovon, are you sure?" Naomi snarled, still clutching the hilt of her weapon.

Siovon nodded. "You and Thor can stay here. I'll call if anything happens."

Naomi didn't like it, but she gave a reluctant nod, returning to her corner as Sal first teleported Julius and Cass home, then returned for Lucian, Siovon and Keegan.

Chapter Sixteen

The guest bedroom in Cyrus Gordano's monastery-sized house was so large that Siovon could run laps around the place and burn off an assload of calories. She glanced at the clock on the nightstand for what seemed like the hundredth time. Lucian had been gone for the last four hours. The snowstorm was in full force. Though he'd told her the cold didn't affect him, she was still concerned — not just for him, but for his sister as well.

Which was ridiculous. She'd never met the woman, but for her to be pregnant out there in that weather, it was no wonder the Gordano men were all filled with fear. Even Cyrus had left the comfort of his home to go look for his daughter. Siovon half-expected to hear the news blaring out warnings that crazy-strong men were rampaging and tearing the city apart.

Standing near the massive floor-to-ceiling window, she tugged the thick curtains open. The sun would soon rise, but there weren't even the tiniest of rays piercing through the dark clouds. It was almost ominous, in a way.

The wind slammed against the frosted windowpanes, howling into the darkness and threatening to rip the nearby trees from their roots. She groaned in frustration and resumed pacing. She checked the time again. Only two minutes had passed.

She jerked her hands through her hair, not at all liking the coldness throbbing in her chest. While waiting on Lucian to return, she'd showered, watched TV, eaten from the platter of food that had been delivered to her door, watched more TV, called Naomi and Thor to check on them and explored every nook and cranny of the vast room.

Still no Lucian. When she'd tried to leave the room, she'd discovered some vamp guarding her door. Lucian had assured her that she was a guest in his father's home, but the vamp refusing to let her leave the room had made it clear that he'd lied. Though the room was beautiful and filled with the lushest of comforts, it was just a lovely way to disguise the fact that she was nothing more than a prisoner.

This was just another cell she was trapped in, and once again, the vamps were her captors.

Siovon was very close to going into a full-blown panic, but she paused when something pulled at her insides. Like fingers strumming the strings of a guitar, it was as if the same was being done deep within her gut. She didn't know where the hell it was coming from. It didn't hurt, but it wasn't comfortable either. It was almost like something was calling out to her.

As if being led by some invisible force, she took blind steps toward the door as the tugging on her core propelled her forward. She paused with her hand outstretched, however, she remembered the vamp who'd be waiting for her on the other side.

Scanning the room, she weighed her options. Going outside was a hell no. She doubted there'd be any guards under her window in this weather. Regardless, it was too cold for her. She'd get swept away in no time. Thor had stayed behind with Naomi, so she couldn't use him as a diversion.

She chewed on her nail as she paced. "Come on, dammit. Think."

Two seconds later she paused dead in her tracks, a small smile curving her lips.

She couldn't use Thor, but she could make another little minion. She rummaged through the nightstand and picked up an unused notepad and ink pen that had been placed there. *Just like a regular freaking hotel,* she thought with glee. She tore off six sheets of paper and lined them up, side by side. With a grin, she sketched out two long rows of wavy lines, then connected both ends. She threw in a few stripes and small details to make the creature look authentic.

Once satisfied with her rough sketch, she unsheathed a dagger from her boot and sliced a shallow cut along her palm. Fat droplets of blood dotted the paper, and she used a finger on her free hand to smear it, tracing over the length of the snake. Once finished, Siovon chanted the words Lila had taught her long ago—the spell that would tie her creations to her.

In a show she had seen dozens of times, the image she'd drawn slithered to life, its body solidifying until it became a two-foot-long garter snake. Its blank little eyes stared up at her, waiting for a command.

Siovon chuckled. "I hope this works." She carried the snake to the door, then set it on the floor. "You know what to do, little guy," she whispered. The snake didn't give any indication that it knew what the hell she was saying, but the connection she felt to it let her know it would follow her silent commands.

Schooling her expression to one of petulance, she cracked the door open. As expected, the vampire standing guard turned to her with expressionless eyes. "What now?" he demanded.

Siovon wrinkled her nose. "Are all vampires this sour or do you have a personal grudge against me?"

The male gave a slow, uninterested blink. "What do you want?"

Siovon forced a pout and folded her arms under her breasts. After her shower, she'd dressed in everything except her hoodie, so she stood in just a thin tank top and her jeans. The movement had her pushing her bosom up, and the male's eyes dropped there before returning to her face. While he continued to look at her with boredom, he couldn't hide the flare of his nostrils that showed he wasn't as impervious as he pretended to be. "I'm lonely in here by myself," she murmured, forcing her tone to sound whiny, but flirty.

The vamp narrowed his eyes. "Lord Lucian will return. You won't be alone much longer."

Siovon used her foot to urge her snake out of the door. In the meantime, she kept the guard distracted by throwing her head back like a child throwing a tantrum, giving him what she hoped was an enticing view of her neck. "That's no help at all." She straightened, making a mental note of the way his fangs lengthened. Or perhaps it was the scent of her blood that had him aroused. "I'm so bored in there, and I'm sure you are out here. Surely you can spare a few minutes to entertain me?"

The vamp grunted and observed her slender frame. When he started to lean forward, he shook himself, as if trying to clear his mind from her attempt at seducing him and he took a step back. When he spoke, his voice was rough with lust, though it was evident he wasn't falling for her tricks. "As tempting as you are, Lucian will rip my throat out for even thinking such things. And I, for one, do not have a death wish. Return to your room or I will be forced to lock you in the dungeon until everyone returns."

Siovon dropped her arms to her sides. Her snake was out of the door, so she let go of all pretenses of teasing him. "Very well," she said with a false grudge. She stepped back and flashed him a faint smile. "Your loyalty is pretty admirable. Keep up the good work."

When the vamp snorted and turned his back on her, Siovon closed the door. She didn't move away, however. She waited a few more minutes, closing her eyes as she focused on the thread tying her to the snake. When she felt the time was right, she commanded it to bite the vamp on the leg. The man yelped a curse.

"It's a fucking snake," he cried. She sent her creation down the hall, hoping her trap would work.

It did. The vamp was silent as he gave chase to her minion. She snorted. "Not the brightest crayon in the box." Then again, as far as she knew, only Lucian knew of her capabilities. No doubt her guard had no idea she could give life to her drawings.

Siovon cracked the door open and peeked around to make sure the coast was clear. She didn't have long before the vamp would catch up to the snake. And if he 'killed' it, he'd see her minion turn back into its 2D form.

Focusing on the strange tug on her core, she followed it in the opposite direction the vamp had gone. When the connection between her and the snake snapped, she willed herself to move faster. It wouldn't take long before he figured out she was no longer in her room.

Twice she had to stop when she detected guards patrolling the mansion. She found another set of stairs and made her way to the third-floor landing, pausing again to avoid being caught. Then she continued through the winding halls. Christ, she had no idea how anyone learned to navigate this freaking place. It was a big-ass maze, and if not for the invisible force tugging her along, she would have been sure she was lost.

After what seemed like half an hour, she came to a halt outside a wooden door with intricate carvings. She didn't have time to admire the beautiful designs, though. She sensed more vamps coming, so she opened the door and ducked inside.

The first thing she noticed was the scent of death that was thick in the air. Not like rotting flesh, but, beneath the smell of sanitizer and disinfectant, there was a sickly-sweet odor of rotted fruit. As if in slow motion, she turned to peer into the room.

A bit larger than the guest room she'd been in, it was shrouded in darkness with only the faint glow of a dying fire in the fireplace. She froze when she spotted someone tucked under the comforter of the four-poster bed decorated in varying shades of gray and black. The man was lying still as death, and in the silence of the night, she heard raspy breathing.

Keeping her eyes on the motionless man, she took leaden steps toward him. An eternity seemed to pass before she was at his side. She peered down at him and gulped.

He was a vampire, one who would have been as beautiful as the others had he been in full health. As it was, the man's skin was gray in color. The comforter was halfway down his body, revealing a jagged scar where some creature had sliced into him. He was well-built, but the disease plaguing his body must have eaten away at him from the inside, leaving a good bit of his skin loose and hanging in flaps. His broad chest rose and fell, though his breathing sounded awful. The skin around his face was stretched tight, his cheeks were sunken and he had large dark circles where his eyes lay closed. Even his hair hung in lifeless black strips across his forehead.

Oh, dear God, she thought in horror.

Siovon knew without a doubt that the man was Andreas — Lucian's youngest brother, the one who'd been cursed by an abaddon. Tears stung her eyes as she observed him, her heart ripping in half. She touched the amulet around his neck, the cold metal a heavy weight in her hand. Lucian said a handful of magic users had embedded it with a combination of their powers, prolonging Andreas' life for a little while. However, there wasn't a drop of magic left in the brass piece. It was impossible to tell how long he had left to live. *Weeks? Days? Hours?*

Will he even survive the night?

That was easy. No. He wouldn't. His life was fading as the disease ate its way through his body. "You poor thing," she whispered, tears sliding down her face.

She wondered if Lucian, his family or anyone knew the magic had left the amulet.

More tears filled her eyes and she wept for their loss. Even without Calysta's curse, she doubted her sister's voice could heal him. He was too far gone.

Siovon squeezed her eyes shut and she sank onto the bed beside Andreas, careful not to disturb his sleep. She covered her face with her hands and quietly sobbed into them. She didn't care about how weak and vulnerable doing so made her feel. She didn't care about her pride, that she didn't owe this family anything or that she didn't even know this man.

All she could think of was how crushed Lucian would be.

That steady thrumming in her gut that had led her here pulsed again. She wiped her eyes, blinking several times to clear her vision. She looked over at Andreas once more. Well, if he was already going to die, it wouldn't hurt to at least try. She didn't hold much hope that she could do anything for him, but would doing nothing really be better than not?

With a deep sigh, Siovon thought over every formula for her medicines she could think of. The abaddon had inflicted an internal disease, one that destroyed its host from the inside out.

That narrowed it down, but not by much. There were tons of different internal diseases. Heart, lungs, digestive system...

She leaned forward to press her ear just above Andreas' heart. She listened for several moments.

Heartbeat weak but steady. Lungs...

Ahh, it's a respiratory disease, she concluded, listening to the rattling of his lungs with every inhale and exhale.

She stood. *Okay, so a vampire with a lung disease. Do I know a medicine for that?*

She hadn't treated any vampires before. They were one of the few demons in the world who didn't get sick, even with demon diseases. No doubt it was why the abaddon had used such a strong plague on Andreas.

Any others would have healed after enough fresh blood.

Siovon entered the connecting bathroom. She turned the light on and dug through each of the drawers and cabinets, looking for anything that could help. Water, herbal essences, Epsom salts and creams made by demon doctors. She shuffled through them, reading the ingredients scrawled across the labels.

She grimaced. "Bat secretion? Crushed cobra scales? Lizard urine! These are supposed to be healing creams?" She cringed and returned the containers to their place. None of those could be ingested, and even if they could, she wouldn't feed them to Andreas. He was suffering enough as it was.

She tapped an impatient finger across her chin. She'd left her bag in the classroom back in Alleman, much to her dismay. She'd made sure to stuff a handful of common ingredients inside. She was always prepared in the event that she had to brew a quick potion, but she'd been too caught up in the excitement to remember to grab it. And she couldn't very well wait on Lucian to get back. Even if he got Salvator to teleport there, it might be hours before they returned from their search for their sister. Andreas didn't have that long.

She glanced at him and gasped when she was met with dull amber eyes staring at her. She was frozen in place, but his half-lidded gaze was focused on her. "Who...are...you?" he rasped between words, every word filled with pain.

Siovon inched out of the bathroom. "I'm Siovon," she said, clearing her throat. "I've been working with Lucian."

Andreas' cracked lips twitched in amusement. "He's...an ass...isn't he?"

Siovon forced herself to relax and moved farther toward him. She smiled. "Yes, but he's not all bad. He's sweet and considerate when he chooses to be."

Andreas closed his eyes. "He...must...like you...then." He opened them again, but it was obvious it took a great deal of strength. "You...like...him?"

Siovon thought about lying but chose not to. There was no sense in hiding it. "I care about him...more than I should."

His lips twitched again. "He...needs...that." Despite the dull look in his eyes, he seemed like he could see her clear as day. "He...blames...himself...for what...happened...to me."

Siovon sat on the bed beside him. She hesitated, but then placed her hand over his resting at his side. She frowned at how cold his skin was. "He really cares about you guys, doesn't he?"

"Hmm. My...family...will be...crushed...when...I die."

Siovon gently squeezed his hand. "You aren't going to die, Andreas."

He screwed up his face as if in pain. Then, with his eyes still closed, a tear slid down from one corner. "I can...feel it. I...didn't...want...to tell...them."

Siovon's eyes brimmed with tears yet again. "Andreas—"

"Siovon," he wheezed. "Don't...let them...fall...apart... Please. They...need...each other."

Her tears fell when his hand went limp. The thrumming in her core lessened, as though mocking Andreas' fading life. Panic rose, lodging itself in her throat.

"God," she whispered, shifting her body on the bed, "I haven't asked for much in my life. I doubt if you will hear this request, but please, *please*, let this work."

With that, Siovon pulled a blade from the sheath at her calf and sliced her wrist open. The biting pain stung like hell, but she ignored it as she held her arm over Andreas' mouth. With her free hand, she pulled his chin to part his lips. Several drops fell onto his tongue, but most of her blood slid down his cheeks to pool at his neck. "Come on, Andreas. Drink."

When the wound stitched itself closed, she sliced it open with enough force for the blade to nick her vein. She hissed in pain, but then pressed her wrist flat against his lips. At first, nothing happened. Then she felt it. It had been faint, but he'd swallowed.

"That's it," she whispered, still praying it would work. As a vampire, drinking her blood from the source should be far more effective than her mixing it into medicine.

Actually, she didn't have the slightest clue if that were true or not, but she hoped to God it was — and that it wasn't too late.

Something sharp touched her inner wrist, and she blinked up to see that Andreas' fangs had lengthened. Without giving herself time for second-guessing, she pierced her inner wrist with the sharp tips. Andreas let out a guttural noise, like a weak moan, and latched on to her. There was no rush of pleasure like she'd experienced with Lucian, only pain. This was the true bite of a vampire.

Still, she let him drink. With each pull of her blood, his movements grew stronger. Black dots danced before her eyes and the world started to spin.

"Andreas," she murmured, trying to pull her arm away, but she had no more strength.

He clamped his hands around her arm, holding her in place while he continued to feed.

Siovon squinted her eyes to focus on Andreas, taking in how the gray had faded from his skin, and his cheeks had begun to show a healthy glow. She twisted her lips with grim humor.

It looked like God had answered her prayer. Her blood had worked on healing Andreas, yet the cost was her life.

How laughable.

* * * *

After spending hours traveling through the snowstorm in search of Ava, Lucian growled in frustration as he came to a stop in the middle of a small field. Several feet away, Marc was in his demon form — a pony-sized cougar with dark brown fur and golden eyes. He paced back and forth, snarling as he searched for his missing mate.

Lucian frowned, feeling his own chest constrict with the need to return to Siovon's side. The truemate bond tying them together was still new to him. It was torture staying away from her for so long, which was why he'd been a total ass throughout the car ride from Davenport to Alleman with his brothers. Of the four of them, only Cass understood how powerful the truemate call was. Lucian had witnessed his clansmen go through it over the centuries. He'd often thought to himself how he'd never sink that low, even over a truemate. He'd been so sure that nothing would change.

Yet over the past week, he'd learned how gullible he had been to believe such nonsense. He'd fallen...hard. Every fiber in his being ached to be next to Siovon, to pull her into his arms and kiss every delectable inch of her small frame until she was screaming in pleasure as he gave her release after release.

Then he just wanted to hold her. After making love to her, he'd held her in his arms while he slept. And by the gods above, it had been the best sleep he'd had in his life.

Lucian shook his head at Marc's pained whine. "We'll find her, *fratello*," he assured. The storm didn't look like it would let up any time soon, and even with his superior vision, he couldn't see more than a few feet ahead of him.

Marc scratched at the snow around his paws. Lucian was just as worried. From the time when Ava was thirteen up until when she'd run away at age twenty-five, she'd been his best friend, despite the fact that he was a thousand-plus years her senior. He'd been close to his brothers as well while they'd grown up, but he'd been absent a lot. The times had been different back then. Their people were still going to war with each other, and Lucian had journeyed far and wide, along with other hunters and clan leaders, to establish order under his father's rule.

By the time Ava had come to them, vampire-kind hadn't been much different than it was in modern times. Though there had still been many outlanders and Rogues running around, at least clans had been formed and the chiefs were allowed to hash out their differences on their own. It was then that Lucian had journeyed home to Tuscany to be closer to his family. His brothers were all grown and had ventured out to explore their own paths of life, but they'd all come together after learning they had a little sister.

Though only a half-blood, it hadn't mattered in the slightest. She was a Gordano, and before they knew it, their little family had been completed. When she'd run away, they had all been devastated, but Lucian had taken it to heart.

And when she'd come back to them almost a century later, a piece of him had returned.

However, the little piece was threatening to be ripped away again. At the time, no one had known why Ava had left, so they all had blamed each other for a while. But now, once again, she was gone, and no one knew why. There had been no note, no letter, no ransom calls. She was just...gone. Whether by choice or by force, no one knew, but they had to get her back. With Andreas' life hanging by a thread and Ava's whereabouts unknown, Lucian feared his family would never be able to recover.

Marc paused in his pacing, twitching his ears this way and that. While he had a laser-focus, Lucian stiffened as well, but he couldn't sense anything. "What is it?" he demanded.

Marc was quiet for several more moments. Then, with a mewl, he dashed forward. Lucian followed, making sure not to get lost in the thick snowfall. The farther they ran, the louder water flowing from the nearby river could be heard. They ran along the snowy bank until, at last, a lone silhouette could be seen facing the water.

Marc released a loud, pained noise. As they neared, Lucian breathed a sigh of relief when he recognized his sister's scent. While Marc ran, he transformed, his bones snapping and popping until he was on two legs again. In his human form, he was stark naked, but he didn't seem to care in the slightest. He ran up to Ava and pulled her into a tight, possessive hug.

"Ava," he whispered, his voice rough with emotion. "Good God, woman, I was worried sick to my stomach."

"We," Lucian corrected, joining them. He looked at Marc, whose expression was filled with agony. Lucian almost wished he'd never met Siovon. Sooner or later he'd need to explain to her that she was his truemate, and if she denied him or disappeared... Well, Marc going crazy over missing Ava was just the beginning of the pain Lucian would go through if he couldn't claim Siovon. That is, if he didn't turn Rogue. "She's still in her Purge, so she won't be very responsive."

To his shock, Ava spoke up. "I can respond just fine, thank you," she murmured. Still pressed against her mate, Ava turned her head to peer at Lucian. Her bright green eyes were distant, but she was lucid.

Lucian widened his eyes. He stepped forward but paused at Marc's warning growl. The man was not only a new shifter, he was also a demon who'd found his mate a short while before. He was still in beast mode, in a way, concerned only with protecting his female. Though Marc's subconsciousness would recognize that Lucian was Ava's brother, on the outside he just saw another man moving too close to what was his. Lucian just held his hands up, taking no offense.

"How are you able to respond to me right now?" he asked Ava. "All the other times of your Purge, it was like you weren't there."

"That's because I wasn't," she answered. She wrapped her arms around Marc's waist, and though she was dressed in thick winter clothes, she was shivering. "I used to go to a dark place in my mind and stay there until it was over."

Lucian frowned, not quite understanding. "So, the dark energy is gone?"

Ava's eyes darkened. "No, not even close. But somehow I am able to cope this way."

Lucian looked between her and Marc. "It could be your mating," he murmured. "Since you two can feel each other's presence, it's possible he's able to absorb everything you feel, so you don't have to go through it alone."

Surprise flashed across her features, and she placed her chin on Marc's bare chest to look up at him. "You can feel it?" she asked.

Marc's face was set in grim lines. "I couldn't feel you at first. It was like something was blocking our connection, but now I can sense you. It's just faint for now."

"I'm sorry I didn't tell you about this sooner," she whispered. "It has only happened a few times when I saw my father's memories."

Marc placed a loving kiss on her forehead. "Don't apologize, love. We're mates now. I'll accept everything about you. However, you scared the hell out of me. I thought I was losing you."

Ava rested her head back on his chest. "Never," she promised.

Damn, all this sweet shit was giving Lucian a cavity. Still, he was relieved Ava had been found. "Why did you run away, *piccolina*?" he asked, taking in their surroundings.

Ava blinked and pulled away from Marc. Well, tried to. He growled and tightened his arms, refusing to let her go. She sighed and pointed at a spot between her eyebrows. "Anais' memories kept playing over and over in my head. It's...horrifying. It's really bad, Luc. She's only ten."

Lucian shook his head. After dropping Siovon off in the guest room, he'd set out to join Marc and the others. He'd known the little girl they'd found was somewhere in the mansion, but he hadn't given her much thought after that. "What did you see?"

"Hell."

Lucian frowned. "I understand it was awful, but that doesn't really give us any information."

"No," she said, shaking her head. She pulled back to peer at him and Marc with wide eyes. "I mean I saw *Hell*. Tartarus. That's where Anais came from." Her eyes darted between Marc and Lucian, who shared equal expressions of shock and confusion. "Her Royal power is to cross over worlds. Worlds, Lucian — not just teleport like Sal."

"Wait a minute," Marc said, pulling back from Ava just a bit. "Love, what do you mean she came from Hell? And what does that have to do with you running away?"

Ava clung to Marc as she shivered. "I wanted to find a way to go there."

Both men stiffened. "What?" Lucian demanded, his voice tight.

Ava's face twisted into one of pure fury. "I need to find the man she called 'master', Luc. I need to find him and kill him."

Marc's arms tightened around her as if afraid she was going to slip away and forever be out of reach. "Ava, what are you talking about?"

Ava pushed against Marc once more. She must have used her demon strength that time because he stumbled back a step. "The memories are all jumbled, but what I do know is that Anais is a pureblood Royal and she is only ten years old. That means that up until a decade ago, the Gordanos have not been the only Royals alive, like we thought. There are others, and this mysterious 'master' has enslaved them. He's been killing and feeding off them for ages, but we never knew because he does so in a different realm." She peered at Lucian, who had gone still the moment she'd said the little girl could cross worlds. "Do you know what that means?"

"*Cazzo,*" he breathed, tugging his hands through his hair. "Our people didn't die from starvation all those years ago. They were taken. That is so…strange." He dropped his hands. "We will work through everything later. For now, Ava, we need to get you back indoors and out of this nasty weather."

When she looked like she wanted to argue, Marc took her hands in his. "Please, love. Think of our child and Anais. We believe you, but right now, she needs us. Let's get everything at home settled first, then we will all figure this out—whatever it is—together."

Ava parted her lips, but then swallowed her words and gave a small nod. "Okay."

And just like that, Lucian's respect for his brother-in-law ratcheted up several more notches. He'd more than proved he was worthy of being Ava's mate months ago when they'd battled Mikhail. Despite living all his life as a human, he didn't look shaken in the slightest over the fact that the child they wanted to adopt had literally come from Hell. He just rolled with the flow, adapting to the new world he'd been brought into.

Marc scooped Ava into his arms and took off at a speed that belied he was anything but human. Lucian sent out a mass text to his father, brothers and their clansmen to let them know Ava was safe and that they were heading back to the mansion. Despite the running around they'd done for the past several hours, they weren't at all far from Cyrus' home. Hell, they were less than a mile away.

Though Ava's words and the child worried Lucian, he pushed it to the back of his mind as he focused on getting back to Siovon. Four hours was far too long to be away from her. He needed to have her heat and scent wrapped around him in the comforting embrace he'd become familiar with. For the moment, he wanted to forget all the stress and worry plaguing him.

With their speed, it took less than fifteen minutes for Lucian, Marc and Ava to meet the others in the large foyer. At once, Darius, Julius, Sal, Cass and Cyrus crowded Ava, all clucking like mother hens and chiding her for making them worry so much.

Despite the darkness that was still inside her, Ava smiled up at them and apologized in soft tones. At once, all five went silent.

"Ava, you can talk," Cyrus breathed, his eyes softening as he looked her over. "But you were in the Purge."

Ava nodded, tightening her hand in Marc's. "Lucian thinks it's because Marc and my bond is balancing the dark energy between us so I don't have to bear it alone."

Cyrus' eyes widened, but then he nodded. "Ah, that makes sense. The truemate bond is a beautiful thing, is it not?"

There was some pain in his words, but Lucian knew his father said them with genuine joy. Ava's expression grew solemn. "There's something I need to tell you all, but first I need to see Anais."

Cyrus tilted his head. Lucian moved out of the foyer, intent on joining Siovon upstairs. However, he paused when the scent of sweet cherry blossoms filled the air. That, and blood that was potent enough to have his fangs descending.

"Oh my gods. What is that?" Darius questioned in a dreamy tone. "It smells...delicious."

"Siovon," Lucian growled. He hadn't even finished saying her name when he was darting up the stairs, his body a blur as he sped down the winding halls. He sensed his family following him, but he focused only on Siovon's scent. He paused outside her room, glaring at the guard standing in the open doorway. "Where is she?"

The younger vamp's eyes widened, and he bowed his head in regret. "She escaped, my lord. Please forgive me for my failure."

Lucian would have sent the younger vampire flying across the hall if he hadn't been struck with fear for Siovon. A siren in a house full of vampires who would be drawn to her delightful scent.

Merda, *I should have known better!*

"She couldn't have gone far," Cass soothed.

"No," Lucian growled in frustration. "She..." He paused, tilting his head back to focus on the thin connection that had formed after he'd made love to Siovon. She was still nearby, though above him somewhere. "Andreas' room," he murmured, once again taking off with his family in tow.

He knew his way through his father's mansion as well as he knew his own, so it didn't take long before he was pushing past Andreas' door. Someone flipped the light switch, and Lucian's eyes flew wide in horror at the sight of an unconscious Siovon lying on the bed while Andreas had his lips clamped around her wrist.

"*No!*" Lucian roared, dashing across the room to tear Siovon away from his brother. The loss of contact made Andreas gasp. Shock and horror soon filled the confused look in his eyes.

Lucian carried Siovon far across the room, away from everyone else. He stroked his fingers over her face, hair and neck with feather-soft touches. Her skin was pale and cool, but her heart was still beating. Andreas hadn't drained her all the way.

"Wake up, *fatina*," he urged, his voice tight with pain. After two thousand years of being alone, he couldn't lose the one bit of joy he'd found. The pain was unbearable as it was.

She let out a small moan, and her lashes fluttered but didn't open. He exhaled a breath of relief, though his muscles were still clenched. He rested his head on hers, rocking back and forth as he sent a silent thanks to whatever gods were listening for letting him come to her in time. Otherwise, his brother would have...

"Luc, I'm so fucking sorry," Andreas said, his deep voice holding a slight edge of panic. "I... She..."

Someone gasped. "Andreas," Ava murmured. "Your wound is healed!"

Everyone, including Lucian, looked at Andreas in shock. For the past several months, the jagged scar from the abaddon had refused to heal, no matter how many demon creams or medicines they'd used. As Andreas stood before them, wearing only pajama bottoms, his scar had been reduced to the thinnest, faintest of white lines that marred the smooth skin of his chest, as if he'd been injured and healed years ago.

What was more, his skin was its usual fair color, his cheeks no longer looked skeletal and the dark circles around his eyes were gone. Even his hair looked restored.

He would have to build back up the muscles he'd lost over the past few months, but other than that, he looked healthy.

"Oh, my God," Marc whispered. "It's a miracle."

"Andreas," Cyrus murmured, moving to stand before his youngest son. Dressed in his traditional toga, he tilted Andreas' head this way and that. "How do you feel?"

Andreas looked down at his hands. "I feel...alive. Siovon's blood cured me." He peered at Lucian, his amber eyes turning sad. "She saved my life."

Cyrus clapped him on the back, hugging Andreas in a tight embrace before pulling away. "*Si*, she did." He turned to Lucian, his pale eyes sparkling with unshed tears. "Now it's time we save hers."

Chapter Seventeen

Siovon felt like crap, a steaming hot pile of crap that had been run over by a freaking semi. Her body felt heavy, so much so that it took a great amount of effort just to raise her eyelids. It took several moments for the grogginess to clear from her vision, and a massive headache was threatening to split open her skull. Above her, she could see a fancy canopy draping over the bed, the same one from the room she'd been placed in by Lucian.

Confusion swamped her. She didn't remember going to sleep. *Christ, what the hell happened?*

With a pained groan, she mustered up enough strength to push herself into a sitting position. The bed beside her dipped, and a cool rush of power caressed her skin.

"Siovon," someone breathed. It was Lucian. She was sure that even if she stood blindfolded among a crowd of people, she'd recognize his deep timbre with ease. "You're awake."

Siovon grunted, placing her head in her palms. "Yeah, Frosty, I'm awake," she grumbled, her voice hoarse. She smacked her tongue a few times, trying to search her mouth for any kind of moisture. "Water."

Lucian moved away from her, but only for a few seconds. Something opened and closed—the mini fridge, no doubt. Then the bed dipped again and a cold plastic bottle was placed in her hands. "Here, *fatina*. Anything else you need?" The concern in his voice touched her, but it only added to her confusion. She shook her head in denial.

With her eyes still shut, she downed half the bottle of chilled water before clearing her throat. It still felt scratchy, but there was a bit of relief. She opened her eyes, squinting through the pain. "I'm good. Thanks." She looked at him, and in the soft glow from the fireplace, she saw shadows across Lucian's face. She frowned, taking in the haunted look in his glistening eyes.

Glistening eyes? Has he been crying? This proud, arrogant chief? No way.

"What happened?" she questioned. He was dressed in a clean black T-shirt and denim jeans, but the shadow along his jaw made it look as if he hadn't shaved in days, making her frown even more. It had only been a few hours since she'd seen him.

Pain rippled across his features. He picked her hand up, and for the first time, Siovon noticed the white bandages wrapped around her wrists. "Andreas nearly drained you dry," he growled.

Siovon tilted her head, suddenly remembering the sight of Andreas looking like a skeleton as he lay on his deathbed. She gasped. "How is he? Did he..." She swallowed, her heart thumping. "Did he make it through the night?"

Lucian's eyes narrowed. "He survived, but I would have killed him myself for attacking you if he wasn't of my blood."

Confusion swamped her as she took in the hurt in Lucian's eyes. "Lucian, Andreas didn't attack me."

His brows snapped together. "I came into the room and he was covered in your blood. Had I not arrived in time, you would be dead right now."

Siovon shifted to face him. The more conscious she became, the more bearable the pain. She had a high tolerance, after all.

"As a part of my healing blood," she explained, "I can sense when someone close is nearing death through sickness. It's like a beacon calling to me. While I was waiting for you to return, I felt it and sought it out. It was Andreas. Just one look at him and I knew he wouldn't survive the next hour. So I did the only thing I could think of at that moment. I opened my vein to get him to drink, but he wouldn't take it at first. That's why he was covered in my blood, but on the second try, he gained enough strength to feed on his own. By then I'd already lost a good amount of blood, but the more he drank, the better he felt."

As she relayed the events to him, Lucian's eyes became less hardened. When she finished, the sheen of unshed tears caught in the firelight. "So" — he cleared his throat — "you offered your blood to him?"

She nodded.

"Why?"

Siovon unwrapped the bandage from her arm and tossed the white cloth to the side. Someone had cleaned her wrist, leaving the skin smooth and healed from where she'd sliced through it. Well, healed save for the small old scars marring her hands and arms from ages ago. "I couldn't watch him die," she whispered.

"Because of our deal?"

She could lie and say yes. Or she could say it was due to her pacifism. It was on the tip of her tongue, but in the end, only the truth came out. "I didn't want you to suffer through the pain of losing him."

Lucian drew in a sharp breath, but Siovon kept her eyes fixed on her hands clasped in her lap. Several moments of silence ticked by. Then his next words made her tense.

"You didn't believe you could heal him, did you?"

Siovon swallowed, dread forming an ice-cold lump in her stomach. Again, she could lie. Hell, she *should* lie. But she couldn't — not to him, not anymore. She sighed and closed her eyes. "No. I'm sorry. I was just so...desperate to find Calysta that I was willing to suffer the wrath of your people when you discovered I failed in saving Andreas."

Several more moments passed by, each one making her shoulders tense more and more. Lucian had every right to despise her or want to kill her for not being truthful in their oath. And so she sat there, waiting with resignation for him to lash out at her, or curse her, or even throw her into the dungeons to await some horrible fate.

What she wasn't prepared for was for Lucian wrapping his strong arms around her, pulling her to his chest for a bone-crushing hug. "Lucian — "

"I had a feeling you were unsure of yourself," he said, making her gasp in surprise. "All my life my family has been the most important thing in the world to me. I've never once hesitated to kill, torture or double-cross anyone, so long as my family's wellbeing was ensured. I knew all along you probably wouldn't have been able to save Andreas. I should have continued to find your sister and do what was needed to make her heal Andreas before it was too late, but gods forgive me, I couldn't, not after I came across you."

A lump formed in Siovon's throat, making it difficult to breathe. "Lucian... What are you saying?"

He tilted her chin so he could press a tender kiss to her lips. The touch was soft, but the intense emotions behind it filled her with warmth. He pulled back to gaze into her eyes. "You are my truemate, Siovon."

Still dazed from the heart-wrenching kiss, she frowned. "Julius mentioned that before. What is a truemate?"

"Every vampire has a destined mate that fate has chosen for them. When the two cross paths, a powerful bond is instantly formed, and the two are drawn to each other in a way that is impossible to ignore. They can fight it, but it will only bring them both pain in the end."

"I don't understand," Siovon murmured, the implications making her heart squeeze. "You think I am your truemate?"

He shook his head. "I don't think, Siovon. I know. I can feel it." He placed her hand above his breastbone, flat above his heart. "Since I first caught your scent, I felt a need to be by your side, no matter the cost. I have felt...things that I've never felt before. And after we made love, I knew without a doubt that you were the one. I can feel your very presence inside me, as you can now feel mine. There are many signs that point to a truemate, but this connection, the ability to feel one another, is the one sure way a vampire knows they have found their mate."

Siovon pulled her hand away, touching her own chest. She'd already known she could feel Lucian, even when he had been away from the mansion, even when they'd been separated before meeting up in Alleman. She hadn't understood what it meant, but the feeling was there, a constant presence in her heart that provided her with comfort.

She chewed her lower lip, dozens of thoughts going through her head at a hundred miles per hour. She didn't know much about mating between other demons. Some mated for life, while others were able to take several mates at once. There were others, like sirens, who didn't mate at all. As far as she knew for her kind, there was no such thing as predestined mates. They fell in love and married whomever they wanted, much like humans. "So what happens next?"

Lucian's gaze remained guarded, as if he feared her response to everything. "Vampires only mate once in their lifetime. If a vampire's truemate dies, very, very rarely are they fortunate enough to find another, though it can take centuries, if not millennia, to find one. In all my years, I have never found my truemate until you. There will never be another for me. No other woman will be able to excite me or make me feel the way I feel for you. Should we consummate our mating, you will carry my mark and the mating will be complete. You will be respected and protected by everyone under my clan, and I will give you anything you ask of me. However, should you reject me" — he paused, swallowing several times as if his next words pained him — "then you will be free to go your own way. Since you are not a vampire and aren't tied to the inner workings of finding a truemate, you are free to do whatever you please, including taking other lovers."

Siovon tilted her head to the side at the pain in his voice. "What happens to you if I say no?"

He jerked his head away, staring at the far wall before turning back to her. His eyes seemed to be made of steel, a stony mask falling into place to hide any trace of emotion. "There have been stories of my brethren falling Rogue for not being able to claim their mate, but others are able to move through it and carry on with their lives over time. It's hard, but it's possible."

A tidal wave of feelings raged through Siovon, far too many for her to sort out. She cared about Lucian. Hell, as she'd admitted to Naomi, she'd already fallen for him. For the first time, she'd met someone who set her body on fire, someone who ignited her desire to scorching degrees and touched her body and heart in a way that she'd never experienced from another man. And while she had Calysta, Thor and Naomi, she'd still always felt a pang of loneliness. She'd long ago accepted that perhaps she was meant to live the life of a spinster. After years and years of killing strangers with cold calculation, she didn't deserve any such thing as love and happiness. However, she'd still longed for a family of her own—a cute little house with a white picket fence, a pet and an adoring husband.

According to Lucian, he was offering her just that. Well, money-wise he'd give her everything she wanted. And, as his mate, she and Calysta would be protected from outsiders. They might be able to live in peace.

But did Lucian care about her of his own accord or did he only want her because of this 'truemate' business? Did he even want children—and could he love them as she would? As promising as it sounded, she didn't know anything about his kind or their rituals. For all she knew, agreeing to be his mate could be imprisoning. And God knew she'd had enough of being caged.

As odd as it was, though, she wanted Lucian to love and care for her of his own will, not because of some magical connection binding them together. Sure, the sex was beyond incredible, but was it selfish of her to want more than that? She wanted him to love all her flaws and to accept her for *her*. How could she mate him not knowing whether or not he liked her as a person?

With a deep sigh, Lucian kissed her forehead before standing. "Do not rush to make a decision right now," he said. His features were still hard, but his tone was reassuring. Well, as reassuring as he could be. "Take some time to think about it, but for now, let's focus on finding Calysta. I'll have your answer after that."

Siovon nodded, still gazing up at him. He was so beautiful. Tall and imposing and powerful, yet unbeknownst to others, he had a softer side that was tender and affectionate.

And he was all hers, should she say yes.

Instead, she crawled across the bed to stand as well, a bit shaky at first. "Have your clansmen located them?"

"Several of my hunters are tracking down the truck they used to get around. I have others on high alert throughout the territory who will notify me the moment even one Rogue turns up."

Siovon's shoulders sagged at that information, but she nodded anyway. The sooner she found her sister, the less worry she would have plaguing her mind. Just a week ago, the only thing that had mattered to her was finding Calysta and getting back to their regular lives.

Yet somewhere along the way, a vampire had managed to wriggle his way to the top of that list.

"So what do we do until then?" she asked, rubbing at her bare arms. "Sit here and hope we get a response soon?"

Lucian's eyes softened at her frustrated tone. "I'm afraid it's all we can do for now, *fatina*. At least until sundown."

Siovon blinked in surprise, turning her gaze to the digital alarm clock on the nightstand closer to her, frowning at the time. "It's two in the afternoon?" she demanded, bewildered. It had been dark by the time she had gone to Andreas, and her body was trained to require only a few hours of sleep.

Lucian's lips twisted. "You lost a lot of blood, Siovon. Even with a transfusion and your natural healing, your body needed the extra rest to recover what was lost. I expected you to sleep much longer than this." He nodded to the attached bathroom door. "Get yourself cleaned up and I will bring you something to eat to build up your strength."

Despite Siovon's strange mood, she smiled. "So commanding. What are you, my mom?"

Lucian's own lips curled upward, and in the blink of an eye, he was standing before her, his nose a breath away from hers. Siovon inhaled his scent, her body heating at his proximity. He brushed his lips over hers. "The things I want to do to you are far from motherly."

A soft sigh of pleasure fell from her lips. Much too soon, Lucian pulled back, though it was clear it took a great deal of restraint for him to do so. "Do not be alarmed, but my father has requested your presence."

How he thought his words wouldn't frighten her was beyond comprehension. Siovon stiffened, her eyes flying wide with panic. "Your father? Cyrus, the king? W-why?"

Well, that was a dumb question. He was the freaking king of the vampires, and she'd spent ten years held captive by his latest enemy. What was more, her blood was the very thing that had turned Mikhail's Rogues into...well, some kind of super-rogues, able to comprehend thought and follow commands. Of course he would want to question her. Hell, she'd be flipping lucky if he didn't smite her on the spot with his legendary powers.

Lucian swept her bangs out of her eyes. "Calm down, Siovon. He only wants to hear your side of the story of what Mikhail has done. He is well aware that you were the victim in this."

Siovon nodded, but she still felt fear settling in her gut. Lucian squeezed her hand in reassurance and nudged her toward the bathroom door. "Go get cleaned up."

Siovon was numb as she set her shower to a comfortable temperature. She hoped the hot water would wash away some of the dread inside her.

Good Lord. First, she had been told she was the destined mate of a powerful vampire chief. Now she had to suffer through a private meeting with his even more powerful father.

Freaking. Terrific.

* * * *

Siovon sat in an armchair across from Cyrus, king of the freaking universe. His private library was an impressive two-story structure with a high, domed roof that held beautiful paintings of angels, cherubs, fairies and other fey frolicking through the meadows. Thousands of leather-bound books, old scrolls and other items lined tall shelves separated by fluted columns. With the white and gold interior design of the room, it certainly looked fit for a king.

Cyrus looked as if he'd been teleported right out of the height of the Roman Empire. He was tall and imposing, with raven hair pulled into a ponytail that fell past his waist and broad muscles hidden beneath a fancy purple and gold toga. His eyes were the same intense pale blue that matched his sons'. His expression was stern, and though Siovon was good at reading people, it was impossible to figure out what the king was thinking as she finished telling him her side of the story regarding Mikhail. She was honest and open, relaying every detail to him so he wouldn't suspect her of lying.

Several minutes of silence ticked by, and Siovon spent the entire time trying to focus on anything besides the nervous beads of sweat sliding down her temples. Cyrus' gaze on her was penetrating, making her think she was a third-grader in trouble with the principal — only this principal could let out a single breath and his powers would fry her on the spot.

When he spoke at last, his deep voice startled her, making her damn near jump out of her skin. "You are pardoned."

Siovon placed a hand to her racing her heart. "I'm sorry. I'm *what*?"

His lips twitched in suppressed amusement. "I am pardoning you, Siovon. You were an unwilling victim in Mikhail's plan, and, though your blood is what created these Rogues we must deal with, I will not hold you accountable for your part in this."

Siovon released a deep breath, relief flowing through her. She dipped her head. "Thank you, Your Majesty."

Cyrus snorted. "Cyrus," he corrected. "There's no need to be so formal. You have risked your life to save Andreas, and in return, you are now under my protection. Should you ever find yourself in need of anything — anything at all — so long as it is in my power, I will offer you my assistance."

Siovon lifted her head, meeting his eyes with caution. "I appreciate it, but that's not nec — "

She trailed off when he held his hand up. "This is not up for debate. Regardless of you being Lucian's truemate, the Gordanos are forever in your debt, Siovon. Thank you."

Siovon didn't know what else to say, so she nodded, glancing past him when there was a loud knock at the double doors. One of them swung open, and a handful of vampires led by Cassander strolled in. Following him was Julius and a man who was identical to him, though he had a full head of hair cut into a short style. She sat straighter when she saw Andreas behind them, walking with the support of a cane. She stood and approached him.

"Andreas," she breathed, taking in his pale, though healthy, color. His eyes were brighter, with only faint dark circles under them. His hair was brushed away from his face, revealing features that were handsome now that he wasn't on his deathbed. "How are you feeling?" She touched his cheek, then his forehead.

His cheeks turned pink. "I'm so sorry," he whispered. "I didn't mean to… I mean, I…"

Siovon gave him a warm smile and dropped her hands. "We're both alive and well. There's no need to be sorry. I'd do the same thing a thousand times over if it meant saving your life — any one of you."

His eyes brimmed with tears, but he smiled, exhaling with relief. "Thank you." Before Siovon could guess his intentions, he pulled her in for a tight hug. The strength behind it surprised her more than the actual act. "I'm declaring myself your personal bodyguard for the rest of my days."

Siovon chuckled and pulled away from him. "Just focus on building your strength back, then we'll talk."

Smiling, she looked around at the rest of the Gordano men, who returned her gaze with gratitude and awe. She frowned. "Where are Lucian and Sal?"

Cass spoke as he moved toward one of the couches. "Lucian is out meeting with his clansmen, and we're here to keep you company until he returns. Sal is…"

Siovon frowned, glancing between him and the snickering twins. "Sal is *what*?"

Julius turned to her with mischief dancing in his eyes. "He's returned to Alleman to look for more clues."

The way he used his fingers to air quote 'look for more clues' had Siovon narrowing her eyes, because something deep in her gut told her the silver-haired vamp had only returned to Alleman to seek out Naomi.

Chapter Eighteen

Any man in his right mind would not be grinning like a clown with a sharp dagger pressed to his jugular.

Well, slap some paint on his face and call him Bozo, because that was exactly what Salvator was doing. Smiling while caramel-colored eyes glared down at him with such disdain that anyone else would have been frightened for their life, Sal only lay on his back, his hands clasped behind his head as Naomi perched atop his chest.

"What the hell are you doing here?" she demanded. Gods, even her voice was beautiful. It was husky, giving one the impression of her letting out sexy groans while being pleasured. Add to that, there was a light Hispanic accent to her words, and Sal was lost in a fantasy of having her writhing naked underneath him, murmuring Spanish praises while he kissed every inch of her skin.

Feeling the blade threaten to break through his skin, Sal blinked at her. At this proximity, he could see her nostrils flaring beneath her half-mask, taking in the scent of his arousal. If he wasn't mistaken, he saw a flicker of red flash into her eyes before disappearing.

Odd. What was that?

"What are you doing here?" she demanded again, though it was through gritted teeth.

Gods, and her scent... She smelled like chocolate, making his mouth water for a bite. He'd never met a woman with such an intoxicating aroma. He flashed her a charming smile. "I've come to assist you, sweet Naomi."

She didn't look pleased. "I don't need help with anything, certainly not from some bloodsucker."

Well, that's rude. He'd already gotten the impression she was far from sociable. She was also independent and capable of taking care of herself, which only added to Sal's desire for her. The gods above knew he liked his women dangerous.

"Then consider it a command from my clan chief," he said, though it was a lie. No one had even suggested he return to Alleman. Lucian already had several of his other clan members scouting the nearby areas and tracking down the Rogues, so his presence was unneeded. It was just a tiny white lie that he didn't feel bad about in the slightest. He had one reason and one reason only for being there.

Naomi had him eager to seduce her into submission. All he needed was to crook his finger in another woman's direction and he'd have them ready to please him. Naomi wasn't half as easy as that, and it was thrilling to know she provided a challenge.

She shoved off him, backing away several feet, as if the need to put distance between them was mandatory. She kept her back facing the wall, away from the doors and windows. *Smart woman.* She also didn't sheathe her dagger. She twirled it between her fingers while glaring at him. "Well, tell your chief he can take his command and shove it up his — "

She gasped when Sal teleported. One moment he was lying on the ground, the next he was upright, using his body to press her into the wall. He caught her wrists and held them at her sides, his lower body pressing her legs to the wall. She was trapped, and though she was pretty damn strong, Sal was stronger.

Her eyes were wide as she stared at him, still shocked at his powers. Then anger set in and she tried to free herself. All her wiggling was doing was making her body rub more against his, and he bit back a groan.

"Let me go, you bastard," she growled, a touch of urgency in her tone.

Sal smiled at her, inhaling her rich scent. "Sorry, my sweet, but no one is allowed to speak ill of my clan chief without repercussions."

"Pinning me to the wall is repercussion?"

"No, this is." He pressed his lips to hers through her mask. The fabric was pitch black, but it was so thin that it may as well have been nonexistent. Naomi sucked in a sharp breath, her entire body going stiff as a board. Still, Sal kissed her and nipped at her plump lower lip.

Owning several nightclubs and having lived well over a thousand years, Sal knew the potent attraction certain demon pheromones had on those in the vicinity. The tingling sensation that crawled over his body heading straight for his groin was nothing new. The pheromones sprouting through the air, however, were different. Potent. They called to him, making him harden until he damn near exploded.

He sucked in a surprised breath and pulled back. Gone were the pretty caramel irises. In their place was a glowing dark-red color that caught and held his attention, pulling him in. "Naomi—"

"Go away," she croaked, squeezing her eyes shut.

Sal frowned, stepping back at the pain in her voice. "Naomi, what is it? What's wrong?"

No longer restrained, she doubled over with her hands clenching her stomach. Sal was torn between concern for her and wariness that it was just a maneuver to get him to lower his guard so she could attack. The woman was crafty, so he wouldn't put it past her to use a cheap move like pretending to be in pain.

She gasped in short breaths. "Sh... Sh..."

"What?"

"Siovon... Need...medicine."

Sal frowned. *Siovon needs medicine? Wait. Naomi needs medicine from Siovon.*

"You're sick?" He felt rather dumb for not understanding what was happening.

Naomi groaned, stumbling to get away from him. "Go...away."

Frustration and concern warred within Sal. He contemplated flashing to his father's house and bringing Siovon back, but, of course, Lucian would be pressed to come along. The fewer vampires that were around Naomi, the more at ease she would feel.

Not that Sal should care one way or the other, but if she was comfortable with just him around, he had a better chance at seducing her.

Pulling out a cell phone from an inside pocket on his jacket, he scrolled through his contacts and dialed Luc's number. As expected, his brother answered on the first ring. "What is it?"

"A proper greeting works wonders, you know," Sal drawled. His eldest brother never bothered with a preamble. "Where is Siovon?"

Sal didn't need to be standing next to Luc to know he'd gone still. Suspicion was loud and clear in his tone. "Why?" It was a demand, not a question. The whole possession thing over truemates was damned annoying.

Sal rolled his eyes. "Naomi here seems to be in pain, and I suppose she receives some kind of medicine from Siovon for her ailment."

Lucian breathed a curse. "Hold on." There was a series of clicks and beeps, then a dial tone. Three seconds later, Sal received an incoming call.

"Hello?" he answered.

Siovon responded. "Sal? What's going on with Naomi? I swear...if you did something to hurt her —"

"I didn't," he said in exasperation. His temper flared. He understood Siovon was just trying to protect her friend, but good gods, he didn't hurt women, not unless it was to save his own life — or to punish them in the bedroom if they asked for it. Sure, he was a renowned lover of women, but he wasn't a heartbreaker.

Darius, however, was another story. *That* was the one who women cried and fought over.

"We were just...talking."

There was a brief pause. "Talking?" Siovon asked with no small amount of suspicion.

Sal shifted his weight. There were very, very few things Sal feared these days, and Siovon's wrath happened to be the newest on the list. Tiny as she was, the woman packed one hell of a punch and Sal was certain that wasn't even a quarter of the damage she could do. He'd seen the way Lynx and Caesar had looked after their encounter with her. "Well, perhaps there was a teensy...tiny...very brief touch of the lips."

There was another pause. "You kissed her?"

The shriek made him wince and pull the phone away from his sensitive ears. "I'd hardly call it a kiss. Her mask was still in place."

Siovon let out a string of curses in another language. *Russian?* He was almost positive she was cursing him in Russian. "Were you turned on?" she demanded, with no shame whatsoever.

Sal shifted again, turning away from Naomi to hide his embarrassment. "That's a rather personal question, Siovon."

She growled at him. "You were, weren't you?" When he still didn't answer, she let out more curses, her Russian accent growing heavier. If that was where she was from, she was damn good at hiding her true dialect. She'd sounded like a full-blown northeastern American. "You idiot. *You're* the reason why she's in pain."

Sal frowned, knitting his brows together. "I beg your pardon?" he demanded in outrage. Was she insinuating that his kiss was revolting? By the gods, he'd known the woman all of three days, and already she'd insulted and humiliated him more than anyone he'd ever come across. If she wanted to damage his well-built manhood, she was doing a damn fine job of it.

There was another muffling of voices, and Sal assumed Siovon had pulled the phone away from her mouth, covering the speaker so she could relay the details to Cassander. After waiting for them to finish going back and forth, Sal tapped his foot with impatience. He glanced over his shoulder at Naomi, frowning to see she'd made her way toward the open doorway of the classroom. "Hey, where are you going?"

"Go away," she growled again. "I need...Chè."

"Sal? How bad is it?" Siovon questioned.

He frowned. "She said she needs Chè. What the devil is that?"

"Shit," Siovon murmured. "It's really freaking bad. I knew she needed to recharge."

Sal didn't know what the hell was going on, and that annoyed him more than anything. "What are you talking about? Recharge? What is a Chè?"

Siovon paused as if reluctant to answer. Then, no doubt out of concern for her friend, she heaved a long sigh. "Not what. It's who. Naomi is half-fury, half-succubus."

Sal's eyes flew wide and he whirled around to see Naomi leaning against the doorjamb. *Half-succubus? Devil's spit, no wonder she's throwing off some powerful pheromones.*

Siovon continued. "Because she's only half, her needs aren't as strong as a full-blood, but if she goes too long without sex, her body begins to turn on her."

Sal's frown deepened. That happened with full-blooded succubi and incubi. However, they needed sex every day to live. Most of them multiple times a day. "I see."

"There's a certain type of medicine I give her to push her needs back, but that's only temporary. And if she senses when someone nearby is...aroused, her body responds. Since it's been so long for her and I just gave her medicine yesterday, she needs the real thing."

Interesting, Sal thought. His eyes widened further when Naomi arched her back, thrusting her breasts forward. As if unable to help themselves, her hands shook as she cupped the mounds, and Sal's dick hardened. He damn near dropped his phone. "The real thing, huh," he managed to choke out.

Naomi's gaze was filled with lust as it landed on him. She walked toward him with slow, seductive steps. Her eyes never once left his as she inched forward, like a tigress stalking her prey. Sal swallowed and he nearly dropped his phone again with the trembling of his hands. Excitement raced through his body because, for the first time in his whole life, he didn't feel like the predator.

"Salvator," Siovon warned through the phone, already forgotten, "Chè is a man we used to work with and someone who can help Naomi. If you can get her to call him—"

"Another man?" Sal demanded, stiffening in outrage. Another man touching Naomi's delicious body when Sal was there hard and aching for her? *Like. Hell.* "I'll take care of her." He didn't wait for her response. He cut his phone off and dropped it back into his pocket as he kept his eyes trained on Naomi's. "You're not going to accuse me of taking advantage of you after this, are you?"

"You should be more worried about me taking advantage of you," she said in a low, sexy voice.

Sal shrugged out of his jacket, tossing it to the side without a care. Naomi was in arm's reach, and the last thing that was on his mind was dirtying the expensive piece of clothing. Hell, she could rip the rest of his outfit off him and he wouldn't mind.

Naomi finger-walked up his silky shirt from his waist to his neckline. With a tug, she had the top button undone…then the next one…and the next. Half of his shirt was gaping open as she dipped both hands inside to splay across his torso. He growled low in his throat at the unexpected pleasure. Blood of the gods, all she'd done was brush her fingers across his skin, yet it felt so damn good.

With her sultry eyes still holding his gaze, she leaned forward and flicked her tongue across one nipple, then the other. Sal hissed, reaching for her ponytail while she continued to torture him with her tongue. He wrapped the long mass around his fist, wishing it was undone so the silky strands could be flowing around her. When she nipped at his tender flesh, he choked out a curse and almost lost all control.

With more force than Sal had intended, he tugged her head back, snatched the mask off her face and crushed his lips to hers. Someone growled, though he hadn't the slightest clue if it was her or him. Hell, it was probably both of them. Her lips felt good on his. He outlined their full shape with his tongue before darting inside the warmth of her mouth. Her tongue met his, and this time it was he who let out a low sound in the back of his throat. She tasted as good as she smelled — sweet and strong.

Sal needed more, much more. Her pheromones filled the room and Sal could only respond, his muscles tightening until he felt he was going to spill himself right then and there. And holy hell, he was a man who had endless patience in the bedroom, even when he'd made love to other succubi.

Sal popped his eyes open in surprise when he found himself being pushed toward the dusty old teacher's desk. The edge of it bit into his thighs, but he paid it no mind as he whirled Naomi around. He lifted her by her soft ass and placed her on the desk, stepping between her legs. He ran his hands everywhere, stroking her hair, fondling her breasts, cupping her waist. Likewise, she scratched and tugged at him in frantic need. When she reached for the leather belt holding his pants up, she brushed her hands against the bulge straining against the material, and Sal bucked his hips as he almost lost himself.

It was fucking pathetic, but he couldn't give a damn at that moment. His brain was shrouded with the most potent cloud of lust he'd ever experienced. He helped Naomi with his buckle. When at last they had his pants unbuttoned and pushed down his thighs, she took his cock in her hands and he swore his knees went weak.

"Naomi," he gasped in desperation she glided her hands up and down the length of his shaft. "*Cazzo*, Naomi, I need you," he growled.

Naomi licked her swollen lips. "Then take me, Salvator."

Without a moment's hesitation, Sal dipped his hands between her legs. He fisted the spandex material and tore it open with a quick jerk to reveal the bare skin waiting beneath. He leaned forward and inhaled her sex, growling at the sweet scent of rich chocolate. Unable to help himself, he squeezed her muscled thighs and licked her soaking wet pussy. Naomi arched forward and moaned. She tangled her hands in his hair, urging him to continue.

And he did. By the gods, he did. He licked and sucked her clit, then dipped his tongue inside her, taking turns between pleasuring the two. Naomi cried out, writhing and grinding her hips in tune with the thrusts of his tongue. "Now, Sal," she breathed, tugging at his hair to pull him to her. "Take me *now*."

He didn't need to be told twice. Her desire fueled his, and Sal needed to be buried inside her ASAP. None-too-gently, he thrust inside, pausing for a moment to throw his head back as her tight center clenched around him. *Merda*, he was in trouble. She felt so fucking amazing. So right.

Judging by the way she panted in need, there was no time to take things slow and drag it out like he wanted to. On any other given day, with anyone else, he was patient. With his age, sex had become dull, so, of course, he'd had to find new and creative ways to keep himself entertained.

With Naomi, he was learning that he couldn't hold out. As much as he desired to pleasure her through the last hours of sunlight, his need for her didn't allow that luxury. Each time he'd seen her, he'd ached to be buried inside her, and it had been twice as bad when he'd been away from her.

Sal pounded away, enjoying the way her small breasts jiggled each time he slammed into her. Her eyes were closed, her brows pulled together as she gasped and moaned beneath him. She was so damn gorgeous. Even the scars marring the perfection of her face did nothing to deter him. If anything, they enhanced her looks, and the fact that she was insecure about them revealed a vulnerability that made him want to hold her close.

Which was something Sal never did. He didn't stay for cuddling or any such tender things. That wasn't his style, so the fact that something ached within him to do that for Naomi shocked the hell out of him. It was unwelcome.

Gritting his teeth, he focused on bringing them both to orgasm, leaning forward to brace one hand on the desk beside her head. He gripped her waist with his other hand, tilting her body so she could take more of him. When he shifted one of her legs over his arms to angle himself deeper, she arched her back off the desk and screamed her release. With her sex clasping around him, he threw his head back and went still, his hips jerking as spasm after spasm shook him to his very core.

Their combined orgasm seemed to go on forever, turning moments into an eternity. When at last they both came down from their intense release, both of their bodies went limp. Sal peered at Naomi to find she'd fallen asleep. Right there on the desk, her legs wide open with Sal still buried inside her.

The sight made him smile, and an odd feeling settled in his chest. Despite his prior musings on not holding his partners, Sal tucked his semi-erect cock inside his pants, then gathered Naomi into his arms and located his discarded jacket. He settled on the cold floor and leaned his back against the wall, Naomi snuggled against him. He managed to get an arm free and used it to lay his jacket over her. He didn't know if her kind were vulnerable to the elements like humans and some demons, but he wanted her to be comfortable.

Of course, he could just flash them to his bedroom in his private lair, but somehow he got the feeling she wouldn't be too pleased at waking up in a foreign room.

His eyes grew heavy as he stared down at Naomi sleeping in his arms. Awake, she looked like a proud and dangerous adversary, her narrowed eyes always wary and alert. She never let her guard down, and she moved like a snake, always ready to strike. Asleep, however, she was the total opposite. She looked vulnerable and sweet and serene. It was a combination that tugged at something deep within him.

Sal frowned. The pressure that had settled in his chest was...odd. Like a constant aura of peace, it provided him with a comfort he didn't understand. He'd never felt anything like it, and he was almost certain it had everything to do with Naomi. With a grim twist of his lips, he leaned his head back against the wall, disliking the implication that jumped to mind.

Truemate.

Naomi couldn't be his. He didn't want to experience any of those annoying symptoms his father and siblings had gone through upon discovering their truemates, nor did he ever want to experience the pain that came with losing one. They'd almost lost their father after his second mate had died, and when Maria had passed, Cassander had become so withdrawn that they'd all feared he was lost to them forever.

Sal shook his head. No, Naomi was *not* his truemate. No one was. He didn't want one. He was fine with only taking lovers. He didn't want to get hurt that way. He couldn't, if he didn't form emotional attachments. No doubt after the hot sex they'd just had, Naomi's tough shell would be gone and she would want to continue to be one of his lovers. He'd be glad to offer her that until one or both of them were ready to go their separate ways. No strings, no complicated feelings, no mating... Just two demons sating each other's desires the way countless beings had done since the beginning of time.

Sal closed his eyes, inhaling deeply of Naomi's sweet chocolaty scent as he settled into a light slumber.

She'd been so determined to kick his ass and deny him since they met, and now that she had gotten a taste of what making love with him was like, she'd be hooked. It was the way of women in his life. The ones who were hard to get didn't stay that way for long. Eventually they'd desire something more serious, and he'd be forced to gently turn them down and move on. Naomi wouldn't be any different.

At least, that was what he told himself.

* * * *

Despite the worry nagging her, Siovon found herself enjoying being around Lucian's family. They were...*hmm, what's the word I'm looking for?* 'Strange' was a good fit, but that was too simple.

And there was nothing *simple* about the Gordanos, at least not the ones she'd met so far. She had yet to meet Ava, though the brothers assured her that she and her mate were spending time with their new daughter. Siovon knew they weren't telling her the full truth, but she didn't question it.

Still in Cyrus' library, she sat on the loveseat closest to the fireplace while listening to Darius and Julius relay the details of one bar-fight they'd gotten into with a small group of shifters. In a lighter air, she found Julius wasn't as annoying as she'd first thought. Well, he and his twin were still annoying, but in a charming, likable way.

Both were handsome as well, almost identical in looks. Like the other Gordano men—excluding Lucian and Andreas—they had the same pale blue eyes that glittered in the dark. However, they both had chestnut brown hair instead of blond or black. Julius' was shaved into a long mohawk that was in a neat manbun, while Darius' was much shorter in a professional style. However, he had a tongue piercing and two tiny hoops pierced in one eyebrow, whereas Julius only had one small black hoop pierced through his nose. Both wore shirts that revealed an array of colorful tattoos lining one or both of their arms.

Cassander sat on the couch next to Andreas, who kept glancing at her with puppy eyes that were filled with feelings of regret and gratitude.

Siovon smiled in reassurance that she wasn't angry with him. She no longer felt out of place among Lucian's family, but she didn't dare allow herself to become too comfortable — not while Calysta was still out there under Sierra's control and not while she wasn't ready to accept or deny Lucian's proposal to her.

She didn't want to sit around waiting. Patience had always been something that came to her naturally, but it was lost at that moment. She wanted to be hunting down Sierra and ending her control over Calysta.

Something caught her attention out of the corner of her eye, and she blinked in question at Darius, who waved his arms in her direction. She blinked again, only then realizing he'd been speaking to her. "Sorry, what?"

He grinned, something he'd been doing the entire time she'd known him. She was growing used to it, but it had made her uncomfortable at first. The man was *always* smiling.

"I asked what type of potions you can make," he said, his Italian accent lilting each word.

Siovon lifted a shoulder. "That's a loaded question. Given the right ingredients, I can make just about anything—potions for sleep, healing, pain relief, muscle relaxers, hallucinogenic, energizers... The list is endless." She paused, tilting her head to the side. A fond smile curved her lips. "Actually, I'm still learning as I go. Calysta—my sister—has been studying medicine since she first learned to read. Most of the things I know now are because of her. You can ask her any question related to healing and she can tell you without hesitation."

Andreas let out a low whistle. "She sounds rather impressive." He blushed. "Not to say you aren't! Your powers are amazing."

Siovon gave another small shrug. "The capabilities of our blood are still a mystery, even to us. Calysta and I are the last sirens, as far as we know, so we didn't have the opportunity to be taught our full potential by others like us. The information we do know is very limited, and most of it we learn as we continue on with our lives."

"Let me ask you this," Cass said, spreading his legs and leaning back against the couch he sat on. He looked out of place on the elegant furniture with his black hoodie, casual ripped jeans and gruff Viking features. Siovon was willing to bet everything she owned that the furniture had to be custom-made to support his bulk. "And this is purely hypothetical. Since Mikhail was able to use your blood to create Rogues he could control through magic, do you think there is a way for you to reverse its effects?"

Siovon frowned, thinking it over. "I have no idea. I didn't even know Mikhail would be able to use me to create Rogues. However, Calysta is able to wield magic, so she would know far more about binding spells than me. If we can find a way to break or reverse the magic, then it's possible the Rogues would no longer be under anyone's control."

"What about finding a way to convert Rogues back to their normal selves?" Cyrus asked, leaning with his elbows on his knees. He lifted a raven brow at her. "Hypothetically, of course, if the magic is broken, would there be a way for you to create a potion to bring them back?"

Siovon's eyes widened at the notion. She'd never even thought of such a thing. She'd only been concerned with finding her sister. "Well, Rogues are kind of like schizophrenics — that's a human disorder, by the way. They're suffering from a mental breakdown somewhere in their mind. Except they're vampires, and for most of you guys, even demon medicines are ineffective, since your natural healing abilities are far greater than most others." It was a fact, not a compliment, yet all five of the men in the room sat up straighter, as if she were praising them. *Arrogant asses.* She tapped a finger against her cheek in thought. "If someone were given the opportunity to look into it, they would need to create some kind of mentally calming potion that's powerful enough to relax the Rogues in order to run tests and do some in-depth research on them. With modern science and the variety of different types of magic out there, it could be possible for a cure to be found. Hey, we learned that healing sirens can destroy an abaddon's disease, so the potential for success is limitless."

The men looked astounded, peering at one another as if she'd told them where to find a leprechaun's pot of gold. There seemed to be some kind of silent communication going on until Cyrus leaned forward again, his pale eyes shining bright with determination.

"When all this is settled and after we rescue your sister, what do you think about being hired as the king's trusted scientist?" Cyrus enquired.

Siovon raised her eyebrows in shock. "Your scientist? I thought we were just talking hypotheticals?"

Cyrus shrugged his wide shoulders. "Before taking the role as king, it was my greatest wish to unite all my brothers and sisters as one, no matter what class. I wish to establish peace among my people. However, too many of our brethren fall victim to Rogues each year. As you stated, it is a mental breakdown they go through. Too much pain, whether physical or mental, can destroy them. When one vampire turns Rogue, their loved ones experience the pain of losing a family member."

His eyes lowered in sadness, and Siovon recalled the story of how he'd had to put down Mikhail's teenaged daughter after she'd turned Rogue. She wondered how many other times he'd had to do the same to people he'd once called a friend.

He continued. "However, if your hypothesis turns out to be correct and you are successful in creating an elixir that can prevent and reverse the effects of...Rogueism, then you would save the lives of not only vampires, but also those victims of other species as well. Humans especially, since they are the most vulnerable."

Andreas turned to her with wide eyes. "He's right," he murmured, rubbing at his chest hidden underneath a thick terrycloth robe. "Not to mention that, as the king's employee, you will forever be protected and respected by vampires everywhere. Well, you will be anyway, once I regain my strength." He held up his arm at an angle and attempted to flex his loose muscles, frowning at the result.

"Plus, with Father paying you," Julius chimed in, "you'll be freaking rich in no time."

Siovon snorted. "I don't know. It's a nice notion, but there's no guarantee that I'll be successful. I don't want you all to get your hopes up only for me to fail."

Cyrus gave her a comforting smile. "Believe me when I say I know it's a long shot, Siovon. I am in no way putting any kind of pressure on you. You're even free to work on whatever other projects you desire, whenever you want. I can get you set up in your own personal lab. Tools, ingredients, decorations — whatever you need, I'll ensure your comfort. Your knowledge and skills are insurmountable, and it would be an honor to work with you."

A flare of excitement raced through Siovon. It was so much to take in at once. First, the truemate business, and now the vamp king wanted to hire her. Was this all some kind of cruel cosmic joke meant to offer her happiness, only to snatch it away when she lowered her guard?

The offers were tempting, so tempting that it was on the tip of her tongue to say yes to everything. But she didn't. She couldn't. Not yet. "Do you mind if I take some time to think about it? It's just…a lot right now."

Cyrus flashed an understanding smile. "Take as long as you need, Siovon. The offer will always be there, whenever you're ready."

Siovon nodded with gratitude and excused herself. It was only a couple of hours after sunset, and while she enjoyed the company of the Gordanos, she just wanted a quiet place to relax. She had a lot of thinking to do, but first and foremost, she needed to strengthen her mind before looking for Caly. She was thankful Sal had returned her backpack to her before he'd gone searching for Naomi. She'd go to her room to burn incense and meditate until her inner thoughts were once again at peace. She hoped by then that Lucian would have some good news.

As Siovon made her way past the foyer to the large stairs, she paused when the front door flew open. A disgruntled Salvator stood there with his silk shirt ripped in half. His neat and immaculate hair was astray, and his expensive pants were soiled with dust. His eyes were angry as he stormed right up to her.

Siovon turned defensive, tensing in preparation for a fight. She knew the silver vamp wasn't foolish enough to hurt her, but still... Better safe than dead.

"What happened to you?" she drawled.

Sal narrowed his eyes. "Where is she?"

Siovon frowned. She already knew who *she* was. "Why are you asking me? You're the one who was with her last." And Siovon was still unhappy about that. If Sal had done anything to hurt Naomi, Siovon wouldn't hesitate to throw her pacifism right out of the window and tear him a new ass.

Sal growled in annoyance. "Yes, and when I awoke, she was gone."

Siovon lifted an eyebrow. "Didn't you try to track her scent?"

"Of course I did, but she got into Luc's Jag and left, so I lost her."

Siovon shrugged, unconcerned. "Then she's not in any danger. What are you so pissy about?"

Sal crossed his arms like a petulant child. "She should have..." He grunted. "Forget it." Then he stormed away, slamming the door shut on his way out of the mansion.

Siovon frowned after him in confusion. *What the hell was that about?* she asked herself. *Is the proud, womanizing, hedonistic Salvator Gordano throwing a fit because Naomi screwed him and left while he was asleep?* His brothers had told her tales of how he'd done the same thing to women, pleasuring them then leaving in the middle of the night so he wouldn't have to stay and cuddle.

The thought caused an evil grin to curl Siovon's lips as she continued up the stairs to her room.

Karma was an ugly bitch that way. If Sal was that upset over Naomi disappearing on him, he was going to be in a world of hurt once he realized he was never going to see her again. Siovon knew Naomi well enough to know she would do everything in her power to avoid ever crossing paths with him.

Chapter Nineteen

After lighting a handful of incense and sitting in front of the blazing fireplace, a sense of peace settled on Siovon's mind as she opened her eyes.

It was a peace that was shattered when a faint, familiar tingling danced along her ear.

With a gasp, she touched the earring that had once connected her to Calysta and Lila. She'd given it a bit of magic back in the cabin, just enough to get it working for a few days until she could give it a full recharge. While she hadn't expected Calysta to have hers done as well, there had been a tiny flicker of hope that it would work.

Siovon squeezed the earring, her heart clenching when she felt the resounding buzz, signaling that Calysta had done the same. She closed her eyes. The connecting earrings acted as a homing device that could allow the sisters to track each other, no matter where in the world they were. Though the buzzing was faint, Calysta was north of them. Several miles away, perhaps in Wisconsin, but still close.

Siovon paced. She knew full well that it was a set-up. If Calysta was under Sierra's spell, then it would be difficult for her to escape, especially if she was surrounded by Rogues. The only logical explanation for her earring to work again out of nowhere was that Sierra had coerced her into doing so to lure Siovon.

Siovon knew that, but everything in her was screaming to get to her sister. The longer the days stretched, the more anxious she became. Knowing someone out there had a mental hold over Calysta set Siovon's teeth on edge, and she couldn't wait for Lucian and his people to get ready. If she told them she could find Calysta, he'd want to wait and form some kind of plan before moving out. And if Sierra grew alert to an army of vampires heading her way, she'd balk and take off again with Caly.

For all she knew, it could take many more weeks before the imp made another move. After all, she'd been rather patient this long—spending weeks prior keeping an eye on Siovon's cabin in Buffalo, getting Calysta to make that video at Keegan's office and spending even longer spreading rumors about Calysta's singing to bait Siovon.

The woman was cunning. Then again, so was Siovon.

Devising a plan, she weighed her options. Lucian would disapprove—no ifs, ands or buts. He'd rather wait until his clansmen contacted him, not to mention he'd do everything in his power to try to keep her in the room while he went out and played hero.

She scribbled a note to him and tucked it into her pants pocket, threw on a light jacket over her sweater and exited the room. She walked fast, though not in a way that would alert anyone who was watching.

And they were definitely watching. She sensed several vampires lurking nearby, though it was impossible to pinpoint them all. It was just one of those annoying vampy perks, she supposed, but she continued onward, relaxing her features to show curiosity, as if she were exploring the sights in the mansion.

She jogged downstairs and headed for the 'guest' room where Keegan was being held. As expected, there was a vampire standing outside his door, one Siovon recognized. The man Lucian referred to as Lynx spotted her, his handsome face turning into a deep scowl.

He was an impressive sight — tall and slender but with a physique that spoke of hours upon hours of hardcore training, dark eyes of oriental descent, straight black hair that fell just short of his shoulders and a collection of shimmering scale-like tattoos lining the base of his throat. Two handguns rested in the belt wrapped around his hips, and a third was present in his ankle holster.

Siovon felt like a bunny strolling up to a lion as she flashed him a sweet smile. He merely narrowed his eyes. "Good evening, Lynx. We meet again."

"Third time's the charm," he drawled, his voice making it clear that he wasn't pleased with the sight of her.

She nodded at the door. "I need to see Keegan."

Lynx folded his arms, standing tall. "The imp isn't allowed any visitors."

"Oh? It was my understanding that he is a guest here, not a prisoner."

Lynx shrugged, unconcerned. "I have my orders."

"Orders from who?"

At his silence, it was impossible to tell whether or not he was lying. There wasn't so much as a twitch of muscle to belie his words. Still, Siovon knew better.

She placed a hand on her hip. "I'll ask you just this once, vampire. Step aside and allow me to speak with Keegan. It's regarding my sister."

Lynx remained in place. "You may have bested me twice, siren, but not again. Here you are in my master's domain, surrounded by vampires who will descend upon you the moment you try to attack me. I know what you are capable of now, and I am prepared."

Arrogance shone in Lynx's dark eyes, his lips curving into a triumphant smile. Siovon lifted an eyebrow.

Taking a step back, she raised her hand. Lynx tensed, thinking she was going to hit him. Instead, she brought her palm across her own cheek. A loud smack rang out, and Lynx's mouth dropped open. Siovon did it again, the mild sting not affecting her in the least.

"What the hell are you doing, you psycho?"

Siovon slapped herself again. "You know I am Lucian's truemate, correct?"

"Of course I do," he growled, annoyed. "Everyone in this mansion knows. What does that—?"

Siovon paused long enough to peer at him with determination. She might be a pacifist but she wasn't above using manipulation to reach her goal. "Then you know that Lucian will see my bruised cheek and become pissed. He will be pressed to seek vengeance, as the bond between us will urge him to protect me. Now, I can make up some believable excuse and calm him down, or..." She gave a dramatic pause, nodding at the realization dawning on Lynx's face. "Or I can tell him there was one vampire in particular who wanted revenge because I roughed him up a little bit. And we both know he will be too heated to be rational. The choice is yours, Lynx." For added measure, she slapped herself once more.

Lynx bared his fangs at her, though he'd gone a shade paler at the realization that she was right. It was a lose-lose situation for him. "Damn you," he growled.

Siovon shrugged. "Like you said, third time's a charm. Guess that means I'm the lucky winner, right?"

Lynx eyed her for several moments, as if unsure what to do. Then, a tiny smile twisted his lips. "You are a very dangerous woman, siren," he murmured, shaking his head in bewilderment. "I don't know whether to be envious or sympathetic toward Lucian." He stepped to the side, opening the door just enough for her to enter. "You have ten minutes. The imp is to stay in the room until my lord can question him."

Siovon gave a grateful nod and moved past him, waiting until the door had closed before moving farther inside. "Keegan?" she questioned.

The room was smaller than hers, but still decorated with beautiful furniture. Keegan sat up on the bed, his eyes widening at the sight of her. He scrambled to his feet. "Good lord. I was beginning to think the leeches had ripped you apart."

Siovon snorted but waved it away. She lowered her voice in the event that Lynx was listening to their conversation on the other side of the door. "Never mind that. Can you create a portal for me?"

"Why?"

Siovon shifted her weight to one leg. "I don't have time to explain. I need to leave before Lucian or someone else discovers I'm gone. I can feel Calysta's location, but I can't risk Lucian and the others scaring her away, nor can I leave these grounds without anyone following my scent. If Sierra thinks I'm alone, she'll probably try to kidnap me, and she'll have to take me to their hideout, which is probably where Calysta is. If that happens and she thinks I'm vulnerable, I may be able to reach out to Thor and have him lead everyone to our location before they can escape. Lucian saves me, does what he has to do with Sierra and Jarek and Calysta is returned to me. Boom! Everybody's happy."

Keegan didn't look impressed. "Those are a lot of 'ifs' and 'probablys', Siovon. You're risking a lot over this."

Siovon worried her lip. "I get that, Keegan, but the longer it takes to find them, the more I worry about Caly. Sure, she's under an enchantment spell, but who knows what they're doing to her? I can't sit around and take it. I have to do something. *Now*."

Keegan ran his fingers through his hair. Showered and clean from blood and dirt, it was a thick, healthy blond that gave him a rather charming appearance. "Shit. The vamps are going to kill me if I do this."

Siovon pulled out her folded letter and placed it in his hands. "Give this to Lucian. He'll know I'm not giving you a choice, and since you've had a close encounter with Sierra and her Rogues, they'll need you to relay every detail. You're safe. I promise."

Keegan grumbled and paced away from her, clutching the note in his hand. "Okay, fine, but I can't open a portal here. Cyrus has this entire place hexed so that no one can open portals to get in or out of here. Even Salvator has to step outside to teleport."

Siovon shouldn't have been surprised. Of course the king would take all measures to prevent people from popping in and out of his home. She pointed at the window. "What about out there?" she questioned, peering outside. In the distance, she spotted a few vamps guarding the gates, but if she and Keegan moved fast enough, maybe no one would see them.

"Yes, but we have to move quickly."

Siovon nodded, unlocked the high window then pushed it open. She leaped outside, her feet landing with a soft crunch in the snow. Keegan landed beside her. After a few moments, he whispered a curse. "We're still too close to the house. We need to move farther away."

Siovon stayed low to the ground as she led the way. She stopped to peer at Keegan. "How about here?" she questioned, looking around to make sure no one had noticed them.

Keegan closed his eyes then waved his hand around in a cardinal direction. "The hexes are strong, but I can manage a portal for a few moments."

"I need to go north from here. As close to Wisconsin as you can."

Keegan nodded, concentrating on forming a portal. A shimmering pool of sparks floated in the air between them. "There. It'll hold, but you need to move your ass," he murmured.

Siovon nodded and stepped forward. They both froze when someone shouted out in the distance. "Shit," she muttered.

"Go," Keegan demanded. "And please be careful, Siovon."

"Right," she said and stepped into the portal. A burst of color exploded around her and the air shifted, making her feel as if she were sliding down a kaleidoscope's tube. The travel took all of ten seconds, but when she emerged on the other side, she landed flat on her bottom with an 'oomph.' Siovon looked up as the portal closed with another shimmer of sparkles.

Standing, she dusted the snow off her backside and took in her surroundings. She was in the middle of some small field surrounded by trees, but she was able to pick up the sounds of multiple cars on a nearby highway. She retrieved her cell phone and sent a coded text message to Naomi. Then she pulled up the GPS to pinpoint her exact location. She was only a few yards from the Illinois-Wisconsin border, just as she'd hoped.

She placed her fingertips on the earring, pausing for several moments to get a reading on Calysta. The connection was stronger, though the farther north she moved, the better she'd be able to find her.

Just as she started jogging, she paused when her thigh vibrated. It was a call that she answered right away. "Naomi?"

"*Si*. What's going on?" Naomi's voice came out gruff, as if she were annoyed.

Siovon frowned, but she knew better than to ask her friend about her time alone with Sal. Naomi would be too embarrassed to tell her anything about him. Instead, she relayed a brief rundown of her plan.

By the time she'd finished, Naomi growled. "Are you crazy? What possessed you to leave the safety of the leeches to do something so...so...stupid?"

Siovon grunted, keeping her eyes peeled for anything that might be lurking in the shadows of the forest. "I thought, of all people, you would be encouraging me to leave them behind. Hell, just recently you insisted we kill Lucian."

This time Naomi grunted. "On any other day, *si*. However, we don't even know the full extent of Sierra's plan or what she's capable of, but at least you were protected."

"Naomi Sofia Morales, are you *actually* concerned for my wellbeing?" Siovon asked with mock surprise.

Naomi was quiet for several moments but Siovon knew the other woman was blushing. As hard as Naomi portrayed herself to be, there was a softie inside that rough shell.

"I'm just saying," Naomi grumbled. She sighed deeply. "It's a stupid plan. This is obviously a trap to bait you."

"I'm aware of that, but I need to see Calysta with my own eyes. I need to make sure she's okay. After what they did to Keegan when we found him..." She trailed off, swallowing hard as pain cut through her heart.

"Yeah...I get it. What do you need me to do?"

Always ready for a fight, Siovon thought with a small smile. "Keep an eye on my phone's location. In the event I'm not able to maintain a connection with Thor, someone is going to need to lead Lucian and the others to my whereabouts." Siovon was met with silence. "Naomi, are you there?"

After several awkward minutes, she could have sworn her friend's voice sounded tight. "Um, what?"

Siovon frowned. "I'll need you to reach out to Lucian and the others to give them my location. You and I can't fight all those Rogues alone, nor can we fight someone wielding dark magic we know nothing about."

"*Si*, I understand the meaning of your words...but you want *me* to work with *them*?"

"Well, if you don't want to, then I suppose being paralyzed from Darkmist while an evil bitch drains me of my blood for the next ten years is my alternative. I don't know about you, but that scenario has already been scratched off my bucket list." Siovon paused, a nagging sense of suspicion welling within her. "Is it because of Sal?"

Naomi ignored her. "Fine. I'll notify the leeches, but if they so much as breathe in my direction, I'm shoving garlic down each of their throats."

A laugh tore itself from Siovon's mouth, because she knew Naomi meant every word. "Fair enough." After rattling off Lucian's cell phone number — which he'd given her to memorize before he'd left — Siovon disconnected the call and continued her jog.

Siovon hadn't the slightest clue what Sierra was planning, but even with her Rogues, she couldn't expect to take on Lucian's entire clan. If that were the case, the woman had a death wish. Even a hundred Rogues weren't a match for a fraction of the Chicago clan.

So does she really intend to fight the Gordanos? Siovon wondered. *Surely that's what Mikhail wanted, but how?*

A little over two hours had passed when Siovon came to a stop at an old gas station smack-dab in the middle of nowhere. It was closed for the night, but she leaned against the building to catch her breath. The farther she traveled, the stronger her connection to Calysta grew, but the temperature outside was dropping. Her blood pumping kept her warm, but the wind stung her eyes as she ran.

Through the faint bond she had with Lucian, she'd known the exact moment he'd grown enraged. It had felt like her own, followed by equal amounts of worry and loneliness. It had been intense enough that she'd almost turned around and caught a ride back to Chicago.

Being away from him for hours had created a hole in her chest, one that was growing larger with each step she took. It made her realize that in his arms was exactly where she wanted to be, where she *needed* to be. Just as soon as everything was all over — always assuming she would survive the night — she was going to find out how he felt about her before deciding to become his mate. She needed to know if his feelings for her went beyond their truemate bond.

With a sigh, she pushed away from the building and had taken all of three steps when she felt the familiar tingling of a portal opening nearby. It was an inner sense most fey had, an automatic response to the call of magic being wielded. While there was no way of knowing who or what creature was using the portal, Siovon didn't take any chances. She ducked behind the store, peeking around the corner to see who or what had appeared.

At first, no one came into view. But then a collection of raspy breathing could be heard. She pressed farther into the wall in an attempt to blend in with the shadows when several Rogues exited the surrounding trees. Siovon conjured up her short sword, a cold bead of sweat sliding down her temple when a few of them tilted their heads back to scent the air.

Then a half-dozen red eyes snapped in her direction. *Shit.* With her free hand, she pulled her phone out and dialed Naomi's number.

At once, the Rogues dashed toward her with extended fangs and outstretched claws. Siovon stood her ground, setting her feet to fight them off. When the nearest one swiped at her, she leaped back and drew her sword up to block it. When the next one made another move, she turned and sliced in an arc, grimacing at the feel of the blade cutting through the Rogue's wrist. It cried out, a piercing sound that sent the animals of the forest scurrying away in fear.

With a speed that had earned her credibility in the past, she continued to fight the Rogues, landing blows that were meant to maim rather than kill. Even though they'd rip her to shreds without hesitation, she was still reluctant to kill the beasts. They hadn't asked to be what they were. They'd all been people before being forced into a life of mindless servitude.

Because of her blood.

Siovon ducked under the arm of another Rogue, and with a silent prayer to not fail, she slid her opened phone into the Rogue's pants pocket. The result ended in her having the beast's claws rip through her clothing and scrape her back, but she bit back her cry of pain. She'd done what she'd needed to do.

"Enough," a nasally male voice called from the distance.

The Rogues formed a semicircle around her, but they didn't attack. Siovon glanced up to see Jarek Nilsen emerging from the shadows.

He looked the worse for wear, despite having a well-groomed appearance. He had the same pale Slavic features as Mikhail, complete with soulless black eyes and fair hair. Siovon frowned as her ability to see magic picked up the golden spiderweb crisscrossing his body. Keegan was right. The man was far too deep under the enchantment spell to function on his own. Hell, even if she couldn't see magic, she'd know something was up, due to the dull, lifeless look in his eyes.

Clinging to his arm was who Siovon assumed to be Sierra. The imp wore a sheer hot-pink slip with hideous fur boots of the same color. The getup revealed more than it covered, and the woman *had* to have been birthed in the cold to wear something like that without so much as a shiver. She was beautiful, with fair hair and skin, bright blue eyes and pink-tinted lips curved into a pleased smile.

Well, she would've been if not for the cold malice in her eyes. That type of evil could transform even the most beautiful of creatures into something ugly.

When the couple stopped a few feet away, Sierra cast Siovon a dismissive look. "People have always said sirens were the angels among us 'lesser fey' with their beauty, but I can see that was an obvious exaggeration."

First time meeting the woman and that's the best she can do? Siovon snorted but didn't give her a rebuttal, not when a single command could have Siovon ripped to pieces in a flash. "Where is Calysta?"

Sierra only kept her smug smile in place as she stroked a loving hand over Jarek's chest. "It's rather amusing. Mikhail often stressed over your intelligence, always worrying that you'd outsmart him and ruin his plans and *blah-blah-blah*. And yet here you so readily fell for the simplest of traps."

Siovon cocked a brow, not about to point out that she'd 'fallen' for such an obvious trick on purpose. "Yeah, how could I have been so blind? Woe is me. Now, where is she?"

"Oh, you'll see her soon enough. First things first." She reached into her bosom and pulled out a syringe filled with a gray liquid. She tossed it across the few yards separating them. "Dose yourself."

Siovon reeled back as the syringe landed at her feet, a cold knot forming in her belly. "No," she growled. "I'll come along compliantly, but I'm not shooting that shit in my blood again."

Sierra studied her manicured nails in boredom. "Nice try, but unlike you, I'm not stupid enough to risk letting you go. Dose yourself or I'll kill Calysta. Then I will kill you. Simple."

Siovon gritted her teeth, rage sparking inside her. She glared down at the offensive piece of plastic. The Darkmist not only paralyzed fey, but it blocked their magic, including the connection she had with Thor. She wouldn't be able to reach out to him afterward, and there was no telling what it would do to her bond with Lucian. Her only reliable resource was to hope Naomi had kept track on her phone before the battery died.

"Time's ticking, siren," Sierra huffed.

"Damn you," Siovon muttered before snatching the syringe off the ground. Still crouching, she pretended to lose her balance and fell forward. She emptied half the tube into the snow and covered it before anyone took notice, then forced herself into a sitting position. She shoved back her sleeves and jammed the needle into her inner forearm. Before the container was fully empty, she cried out in pain as the poison spread through her arm, up her shoulders, into her chest and throughout the rest of her body.

No longer able to support herself, she fell forward, the snow numb against her cheek as the poison worked its magic and rendered her immobile. She closed her eyes as everything inside her melted away to nothingness. Oddly, though, her last thoughts weren't about her sister, where they were going to take her or if she'd even wake up afterward.

The last thing that flashed in her mind was the beautiful silver gaze of the man she'd fallen in love with.

* * * *

Lucian was going crazy, the need to get to Siovon tearing him apart. Had he really thought that he could continue with his chief duties if she turned him down? *Ha! What a load of horseshit.* Every nerve in his body was screaming to get to her.

When he'd returned from meeting his clansmen in Chicago, he'd felt the moment Siovon had left his father's home. The bond between had stretched, telling him that she'd been teleported a great distance away. It didn't help that he'd felt her body go weak, as if she'd been rendered unconscious — or, worse, poisoned with the Darkmist she'd told him about.

It was only the strength of his brothers holding him back that kept him from ripping Keegan to shreds upon learning that he'd help her escape. The imp had been frightened but hadn't cowered, which only made Lucian more pissed.

Keegan had gotten lucky when he'd passed along a note from Siovon that told Lucian where she was going and why, and she'd pleaded for him not to harm the imp. Once he got to the infuriating female, however, he was going to have a long, *long* chat about disobeying his orders and rushing off into danger without him at her side.

Well, assuming he could get to her in time. While the bond between them allowed him to follow her location, it would be impossible to keep up with her if Sierra used magic to send them through portals.

And so he bounced his leg up and down with impatience, glaring at Cassander as he drove the blacked-out SUV across state lines. "Can't you go any faster?" he demanded.

Cass sent Lucian an irritated glare. "For the last time… I'm driving as fast as I can without sending us sliding across these icy roads."

There was a line of eight similar vehicles, each filled with armed vampires ready for war. Marc, who sat in one of the back seats, along with Darius, Sal and Keegan, spoke up. "We'll get to her, brother. You just need to keep your head cool."

Lucian grunted at the pun, crossing his arms. "That's what I told you just a few months ago in Tuscany. You can eat those words, Whiskers."

Marc chuckled. "Now you know how I felt when you said them. They don't help at all."

Lucian flipped him the bird. "Why are you even here? I was sure you'd be stuck under Ava at this point."

"Yeah, well, when I took her as my mate, I took you assholes as my family too. When one goes to war, we all do. Besides, I'm fine knowing she's safe at home with Cyrus and his Guard."

"Right."

"In other news, what are we going to do about Anais?" Darius asked, popping a stick of gum in his mouth. He offered one to everyone else, and only Marc accepted. "This is some weird shit."

"She's only ten," Sal murmured. He was in as much disbelief as the rest of them. "If she's from Tartarus, who's to say how many others are down there—and who's holding them?"

"Father is going to petition the Imperials to hold a meeting," Cass muttered. "Somehow, though, I have a feeling they won't tell us shit."

"If anything, they'll want to examine Anais herself to see if she—"

"No," Marc growled. "She's been through enough goddamn torment already. I won't let them cause any more distress for her."

There was a collective pause among them, and Lucian turned in his seat to peer at his brother-in-law. "The Imperials are the most powerful demons, Marc. If they demand to see the child, there is nothing you can do."

Marc bared his teeth. "'The child is my and Ava's daughter now, as well as your niece. I don't care what anyone has to say about it. We will *not* hand her over to some high-and-mighty demons to treat her like a lab rat." It was clear he was struggling to contain the beast inside him, so he sat back, chewing his gum with far more force than was necessary. His face remained in a stubborn scowl. "We've been talking anyway. We think it'll be best if Anais' memory is…altered."

"You can't be serious," Darius scoffed.

Marc peered out of the darkened window. "As much as I hate the thought of tampering with someone's mind, it's for the best. She can't even sleep for five minutes without waking up screaming. She's blind, but the memories plaguing her remain the only things she sees. It's temporary until she's much older and better able to handle what she's been through, but for now, it's all we can think to do to give her some peace—to at least have some kind of a pleasant childhood. Otherwise, she'll be haunted for the rest of her life."

After a long, stretched-out silence, Lucian nodded. "I think that is a wise decision as well."

"But what about when she's older and finds out the truth?" Darius demanded, growing angry. "What if she feels betrayed for having her memory altered against her will?"

Marc sighed. "We've talked about that too. Anais said herself that she wants the memories gone. We will fulfill her wish, and when the time comes that she is old enough to decide if she wants them back, we won't keep the truth from her. We can only hope to provide her with enough love and care to keep her...sane."

"You'd better do it before the Imperials find out," Cass said. He glanced at Marc through the rearview mirror before returning his eyes to the road. "It would be nice, though, if we had some kind of connection to Tartarus that could give us some insight on what the devil is going on — or if other Royals truly are being held captive."

Lucian grunted, turning back around in his seat. "I just wish I had a way to get in touch with Siovon's adoptive father. I'd bet that bastard knows a thing or two."

Cass raised a brow. "He's from Tartarus?"

Lucian shook his head. "Better. He's a Raptor."

Lucian could feel everyone's wide eyes on him as silence descended among the men.

"Jesus Christ," Keegan breathed.

"Is there no end to the surprises revolving around your mate?" Sal commented.

Lucian shrugged, rubbing at the ache in his chest. "I doubt it. She was raised by a goddamned Raptor, and shortly after she reached maturity, he left and never contacted her again."

"That's fucked up," Darius grunted. "It explains her fighting skills, though."

"Trust me, *fratello*, that's merely the tip of the iceberg." Even as he said it, he was proud that his truemate wasn't some weakling. Granted, he'd once wanted a woman that way — meek and easy to control. Not anymore, however. Siovon was perfect in every sense of the word.

"Excuse me, but what the hell is a Raptor? Some kind of dinosaur?" Marc demanded.

Darius faced Marc. "Very simply put, Raptors are the bogeymen of the demon world. What makes them so terrifying is that they're super-assassins employed by the Imperials. They make John Wick and Jason Bourne look like Girl Scouts. Hell, even Batman — "

"I get it, dude," Marc cut in. "So, he gets a free pass into Tartarus since he's a Raptor?"

Sal shifted in his seat as well. "Pretty much. Whichever realm the Imperials want them to go, they get a free pass. That, and the fact that if anyone would know anything dealing with Imperial business, it would be a Raptor. It's unfortunate that he left her alone all those years ago, though. Do you know why?"

Lucian shrugged, his anger welling at the memory of Siovon's crestfallen face after telling him her story. "No, but she said — " Lucian's phone began to ring, and he pulled it out. He'd hoped to see one of his clansmen's contacts pop up, but instead, it was a blocked number. Frowning, he answered the call. "Speak," he demanded.

"Hello to you too, leech," an annoyed female responded.

Lucian's eyebrows shot up at the familiar tone. "Naomi? How did you get my number?"

Lucian didn't miss the way Sal perked up like a puppy, but he dismissed it. He had no interest in his brothers' sexual relationships. "Siovon gave it to me," Naomi said, "and before you start nagging, believe me when I say I was against her stupid plan to begin with."

"So you know about it?" he questioned, feeling his gut clench with worry.

"*Si*, and she asked for me to keep a tracker on her phone since she knew she would be taken by them. She managed to slip it into one of the Rogue's pockets, and I was able to hear the conversation between her and Sierra. That bitch is definitely planning something, but—"

"But what?" Lucian prompted.

Naomi sighed in frustration. "She made Siovon dose herself with Darkmist, but from the way she spoke, I don't think Sierra has any interest in your family."

Lucian straightened in his seat. "What do you mean by that? We assumed she was carrying out Mikhail's plans to bring down my family."

"Maybe she was meant to do that at first, but I'm not so sure anymore. Again, I could be wrong, but by the way Sierra spoke, she sounded jealous. She kept going on and on about Mikhail obsessing over Siovon's blood. I think... I think she's envious of the attention he gave to Siovon."

"Nonsense. If that's so, then what's the purpose in capturing her alive? Or even using Jarek to command the Rogues?"

"Protection, maybe? Mikhail knew of Siovon's guild status, and even though it's been years since she left, only a fool would think any less of her. Sierra must have known as well. Plus, Calysta isn't so harmless. Though she dedicates her life to healing others, she can cast some powerful-ass spells to defend herself. Knowing that, even if Sierra used her dark magic, there's no way she alone would have been a match against a siren."

Lucian scowled as he tapped his foot against the floor. "I still don't think —"

"Look at it this way," Naomi cut in, obviously running low on patience. "Sierra caught Calysta and spread those rumors about her singing powers. Why? Why would she go through all those complications to only *possibly* get your family's attention, when instead she could have just sent an anonymous message straight to your doorstep? Or why not spread the rumors in your own territory, hmm? All it would take is a small command to send a Rogue to do her bidding if you were her true target."

Lucian shifted again, his heart beginning to race.

Naomi continued. "Furthermore, the video of Calysta at Keegan's apartment? The ambush at their cabin in Buffalo? Unless the bitch can see into the future, there is no damn way she could have known you would be with Siovon all this time. When she saw you were there as well, just after I escaped my encounter with her, it's likely she got scared and bolted the moment she learned you and your clan had discovered their location."

"*Merda*, you're right," he growled, curling his hands into fists. "So if Siovon was her true target this entire time, then why capture her alive? She could have dosed her with the Darkmist and killed her right then."

Naomi sighed. "I don't know, leech. Maybe she wants Siovon's blood for herself. Whatever it is, I'm almost positive she has no intentions on keeping Siovon alive."

"*Cazzo*," he growled again, urging Cass to drive faster with a silent gesture. "Where is she now?"

"Her signal jumped from Clinton to Rochester, Minnesota."

"Rochester? You're kidding me. It'll be fucking daylight before we get there."

"I'm just the messenger," Naomi snapped back. Her tone hardened. "I'll get there before you, but understand one thing, bloodsucker. If Siovon dies because of your failure to protect her in the first place, you'd better pray your clan is powerful enough to save you from me." With a sharp click, she disconnected the line.

Lucian breathed a slow exhale and sent out mass text messages to his fellow clansmen who were traveling with them. More than half of them were Turnbloods, so they couldn't step foot in the sun, meaning they'd have to find a hole to hide in until the sun set again.

He turned a glare on Sal. "Can you teleport us to Rochester?"

Sal shook his head in regret. "I've never been there, so no."

Cursing, Lucian turned back to the road, his grip on the armrest tightening until he almost ripped it from its post.

Naomi's threat rang out in his mind, sending a chill down his spine. He didn't have the slightest doubt that she meant her dark words. The woman was protective of Siovon, despite her detached attitude. Not to mention that after the story of her slaughtering the mountain trolls decades ago, Naomi was someone he didn't want on his bad side.

Still, it wasn't her threat on his life that had him breaking out in a cold sweat. It was the sheer knowledge that if something fatal happened to Siovon before he got to her, he knew full well he couldn't carry on with his life without her. Death would be far more merciful than him turning Rogue.

Chapter Twenty

"Siovon."

The whispery voice floated over Siovon, causing her eyes to flutter open. Teary eyes similar to her own peered down at her. A single drop slid from those eyes, sliding down a pointed chin before falling to Siovon's cheek. She blinked away the grogginess in her mind, the memories of last night — *is it still night?* — filling her mind.

"Calysta?"

More tears fell from Calysta's eyes, pain and sorrow swirling deep in their midst. She brought up a dainty hand and touched Siovon's cheek with a familiar gentleness. "I'm so sorry."

Siovon frowned. She peered closely at her sister, able to see the web of magic crisscrossing her body, just as it had been with Jarek. The fine threads glowed gold, signaling that a command had been given. "What —?"

Calysta rammed a knife through Siovon's thigh, causing her to cry out in pain. "Calysta —" she barked, only to cut it off with another loud scream when a second blade was stabbed through her shoulder. *Holy crap.* Someone had removed her outer clothing, leaving her wearing nothing more than a thin T-shirt and panties.

"I'm sorry, Siovon," Calysta sobbed, bringing up another blade. "I can't stop it." She slammed that one down into Siovon's side, almost nicking her kidney.

When Siovon was able to suck in a shaky breath, she glanced up at her sister. "I know, Caly," she rasped. "Sierra is forcing you."

Calysta squeezed her eyes shut, the magic threads losing their glow. Heels clopping against wood sounded, and Siovon turned her head to see Sierra strolling toward them in the same hideous pink outfit as before. Her lips were curved into a cruel smile that mirrored the darkness in her eyes.

"Aren't you wondering how you're able to feel pain despite being paralyzed from the Darkmist?" she asked in a sultry voice meant to have men drooling. Unfortunately for her, Siovon was neither a man, nor did she drool.

Siovon cast her a bored look. "I wasn't, but clearly you altered it. It doesn't take a genius to figure that out."

An annoyed look crossed Sierra's features at the sarcasm.

What did she expect me to do? Recoil in terror? Beg for mercy and freedom? Pledge eternal servitude? Yeah, right.

Though the knives still lodged in her body hurt like a bitch, it wasn't anything new to Siovon. Back at the guild, if someone refused a kill or screwed up a mission, the consequences were far more terrifying and painful than a mere stabbing. A few stabs were nothing compared to those days. Plus, it was hard to be terrified of someone who looked like the love child of a yeti and a flamingo with all that pink fur on.

"I'd watch your tone if I were you," Sierra said. She stopped a few feet away from Siovon and picked up a rather sinister-looking tool that was curved like an 'S'. "Your life is in my hands right now."

Siovon snorted. "I have no reason to fear some imp."

Red rose into Sierra's cheeks, and with a quick movement, she sliced a deep cut into Siovon's forearm. Siovon hissed and the scent of burned flesh filled her nose. The damn weapon was made of iron, curse it all.

"You will respect me as your superior," Sierra growled, slicing another deep gash into Siovon. "You are just a low-down" —*slice*— "annoying" —*slice*— "pathetic creature, who is beneath me." This time, she stabbed the blade deep into Siovon's gut, the hissing of her flesh being singed drowned out by Siovon's sharp cry.

Siovon coughed up blood, willing her fingers to move. Though she'd only dosed herself with half the syringe, it was still one hell of a poison that lingered in her system. Sierra's eyes were wide, her cool composure lost to her rage. It was common in dark fey. Dark magic was a double-edged sword for all demons and humans. Once they delved into it, their darkest desires fueled them, making them crazed with the need to satiate it.

In Sierra's case, she wanted blood.

When Siovon spoke, it was through gasps of breath. "What...is your problem...with me? What...have I...ever...done...to you?"

Sierra's face twisted even further, turning her beautiful features into something ugly. "What have you done? You stupid bitch!" She raised her hand high and punched Siovon hard enough for her to see stars. The room around her blurred as she struggled to maintain consciousness. "You took away the only man I've ever loved."

Siovon frowned in confusion. *Took away the man she loved? Who the hell is that?*

It had been almost a century since she'd last killed a target besides the seven Rogues from the other night, and she'd always made sure to cover her tracks in the event someone sought vengeance. Had he been one of the stray demons who'd tried to capture her and Calysta for the slave trade? They'd encountered several of those types over the decades, and while Siovon had been working on her pacifism, she'd still been forced to kill a lot. She just didn't know who the hell Sierra was to any of them. She never forgot a face.

"You still have no fucking clue," Sierra growled. She took Siovon's jaw in a bruising grip, the tips of her nails digging into her cheeks. "Mikhail... You took Mikhail from me."

Siovon furrowed her forehead even more. "I didn't...kill him."

The other woman leaned forward until her nose was an inch away. "No, but you stole his attention from me. I've been at his side since his exile, have given and done everything he asked of me. Even when we captured that bitch Lila, it was us against the world. Yet the moment he realized he needed another siren — *you* — he...changed."

Sadness flashed in her eyes and she shoved away from Siovon, turning her back to them. "When he found you, all he talked about was *you*. Your blood this, your powers that... Big fucking deal! I'm far more powerful and beautiful than you will ever be." She made a sound of disgust and whirled on Siovon, her eyes burning with fury. "You stole his attention from me, making him cast me aside like some piece of filth, and he died before he could ever see his mistake."

She snatched up another iron blade and slammed it into Siovon's upper thigh. Instead of screaming, the pain was so great that Siovon's eyes rolled into the back of her head, unconsciousness briefly taking over her. When she awakened, her vision was far too blurred for her to see anything, and the voices around her sounded far away.

"There are intruders approaching," Sierra said to Calysta. "I'll take care of them. You stay here. Make her bleed. The tub beneath her needs to be filled before I can bring back Mikhail."

"Yes, Master," Calysta said with no emotion. Rapid footsteps sounded afterward, followed by a distant door slamming shut.

Siovon heard metal scraping metal. She squeezed her eyes shut, working her mouth to form words. "C...Caly...sta."

The scraping stopped, but only for a moment before sounding up again. Siovon opened her eyes and it took several blinks before she was able to force back the blurriness. She watched as her sister tinkered with the cart of blades near the table Siovon lay on. "Calysta, please," she rasped. "Don't do this."

"Master has given orders," came the monotone response. Calysta faced her with blank eyes. The magic around her was glowing bright again.

"She's not your master," Siovon said, fighting to stay awake. "You're my sister, and we serve no one. Remember?"

Calysta paused, blinking in confusion. "Sister?" She then shook her head, the dead look returning to her eyes. "No, I live only to serve my Master." She continued forward with a wicked-looking dagger held in her hand.

What a load of garbage, Siovon thought. Sierra was too obsessed with the whole superior-inferior thing. "Caly...you're more than that. Remember Lila?" Her steps faltered, making Siovon's heart lurch. "Yes, you remember her, right? Our mother. She loved us so much."

Calysta battled the enchantment as the magic bonds faded in and out. Though Caly was pure of heart, she was far stronger than most people guessed. Even Siovon had made the mistake of thinking it a couple of times over the years. "Calysta, I need you. You can fight this spell. You're stronger than Sierra." She paused, her eyes tearing up. "Stronger than I'll ever be. Please fight it."

Calysta's eyes closed, her brows pulling together as she fought to gain control of herself once more. At the same time, Siovon's vision blacked out again, though she was still awake. With each second that passed, however, she realized she wouldn't be for long. She'd already lost so much blood, and the iron blade still embedded in her was sending her closer to that eternal darkness.

Please, Calysta, Siovon whispered in her mind since her voice no longer worked. She could die today and be okay with that. Well, that wasn't true. She regretted not telling Lucian how she felt or having the opportunity to spend a lifetime with him. But dammit, if she were going to die, she didn't want Calysta to be stuck serving anyone, especially not someone with a massive superiority complex. Nor did she want her sister feeling guilty over killing her.

Siovon heard the sound of metal falling to the ground, followed by a sharp gasp. "Siovon? Oh, goddess! What have I done?" She pulled out the blades protruding from Siovon, apologizing over and over until each one was gone.

Siovon didn't feel a thing, however. Her body was numb. When she tried to speak, nothing would come out. She coughed, almost choking on her own blood.

"No-no-no-no," Calysta cried, squeezing Siovon's hand. "Siovon, I'm sorry. Please stay with me."

The pain in her voice broke Siovon's heart, because she couldn't even tell her that it was okay, that she knew it was Sierra's fault. She couldn't say a thing.

As Siovon floated closer to the endless dark tunnel, she could have sworn she heard the voices of angels singing. No, not angels. *An* angel.

Warmth spread through her body, searing away all traces of pain. She sighed, basking in the feeling of sunlight on her skin as the voice continued to wash over her.

Is this what heaven feels like? she wondered. A floating cloud as an everlasting warmth filled her. Hell, if she'd known it was this good, she would have given in to death's call a long time ago. The good Lord knew she'd been avoiding it for far too long.

The angel's voice grew louder, and she smiled as peace settled in her heart. She opened her eyes in an attempt to locate the source of the beautiful singing. She expected to see herself lying on a cloud as she ascended high above the earth. She expected to see the pearly gates and golden city spoken of in religion. Hell, she even expected to see a creature with large wings and a face so beautiful that it was impossible to look them in the eye without weeping.

What she was met with instead was an open-beam ceiling with rotted wood, and a dark, dank chamber with a faint glow from a nearby furnace. It wasn't even close to what she'd pictured heaven to be. Or maybe she was on her way to Hell and the peaceful feeling in her heart was a cruel teaser of something she would never again be able to experience.

Siovon blinked in confusion, turning her head toward the source of the soft singing. The woman was beautiful enough to be an angel, but her clothes and skin were marred with blood and dirt.

Then it hit her. She hadn't died, and that wasn't an angel singing. It was Calysta using her powers. Her face was twisted in pain, her skin turning pale as a fine sheen of sweat lined her forehead. Horror settled in Siovon's gut and she slapped her palm across Calysta's mouth.

Caly's eyes flew wide with shock, and she tried to pry Siovon's hand away, but to no avail. "No, Calysta. Stop," she pleaded. "Don't make another sound."

Calysta got a good grip on Siovon's wrist and pulled it away, frowning. "But you're hurt, Siovon. I need to —"

"Look at me," Siovon said, waving her free hand down her body. "You've already healed me, Caly." She wiped away the wet blood on her belly. There was a small open wound, but it was stitching itself closed as Calysta's singing powers had healed most of the internal damage. "With proper rest, I'll be good to go in no time."

Calysta didn't look convinced, but she didn't try singing. Siovon refused to let her activate the curse again. She was just pleased to see that every trace of Sierra's magic was gone, meaning that Calysta had managed to break the enchantment spell.

Caly sighed in relief, using her sleeves to wipe her eyes. "I can't believe... Sierra just... I'm so sorry."

Siovon slid off the table and used it to brace herself as a wave of dizzying nausea overcame her. When it passed, she pulled her sister in for a tight hug. Despite her sister being half-naked and covered in wet blood, Calysta didn't seem to mind as she wrapped her arms around Siovon. They stayed like that for several minutes, crying into each other.

Siovon inhaled a deep breath as she was at last reunited with the one bit of flesh and blood she had left. She pulled back, framing her sister's face. "We need to get out of here," she murmured, looking around. "Wherever here is."

"Rochester," Calysta murmured, wiping the tears from her eyes. "I overheard Sierra saying this was an old factory one of Mikhail's dead servants owned decades ago. We're downstairs in a storage room."

Siovon frowned as the one window she saw was boarded up. "What time is it?"

Calysta shrugged. "A few hours past noon, maybe? Or it could be nearing sunset. I don't know."

Meaning Thor would still be asleep by now. Siovon rubbed her chest, the dull hole that had been present ever since being separated from Lucian growing smaller. She hoped it meant he was nearby or getting closer to their location.

Siovon was still too weak to conjure up one of her weapons, so she grabbed a long silver knife off the tray and motioned for Calysta to do the same. "Come on.

Help is on the way, but we need to leave before Sierra realizes the danger she's in and tries to flee."

Calysta picked up a dagger. "How do you know someone's coming? Who is it?"

Siovon just gave a soft smile. "I always have a plan, Caly. And trust me. It's a long story."

Calysta grunted and followed Siovon up the basement stairs. Siovon was freezing, but the adrenaline coursing through her took away most of the chill. She wished she had a jacket or some socks to throw on, but oh well. She was just going to have to go without.

As expected, the door at the top of the stairs was unlocked. As bright as Sierra was, she'd made the crucial mistake of thinking she was invincible. No doubt she'd been positive that her enchantment was strong enough to force Calysta to continue to do her bidding without fail.

The entire floor was dark, but if it was sunlight outside, then all the Rogues would be hiding somewhere. They tended to sleep during the day, but they'd wake up if food was nearby.

And with Siovon and Calysta both covered in fresh siren blood, they would definitely be considered food.

Siovon tensed at the sound of gunshots echoing off the walls, followed by growls, curses and shrieks of pain. Grabbing hold of Calysta's hand, she took off in that direction, traveling down several corners and backtracking before, at last, coming to what looked like an indoor battlefield. Rogues were fighting off other vampires and Siovon recognized some of them as Lucian's brothers.

Sunlight shone from several broken-in windows, burning each Rogue that got too close to it. Naomi was far across the room, firing rounds of bullets into skulls, a huge were-cougar was chewing through the enemy as if they were ragdolls and Keegan was throwing magical fireballs, though he was careful to avoid hitting the 'good' vamps. It was obvious that the Rogues didn't have the upper hand as their numbers dwindled. When a Rogue noticed the two sisters, Siovon planted her foot and struck out with her knife, plunging it into the beast's heart with one clean motion.

She didn't have time to dwell on the guilt that bubbled within her as it faded to ashes. Her main concern was putting an end to Sierra before she escaped.

"Outside," Calysta breathed as if reading her mind. Siovon looked toward the nearest window where she could sense magic being wielded.

She nodded and weaved through the melee, fighting her way through the Rogues before making it to the wide window. She leaped out of the frame, shivering when her bare feet touched the snow. It wasn't the weather that made her shiver, though. Lucian's powers were thick in the air, sending frost across the concrete structure of the walls.

She huffed as her weakened state caught up to her. While Calysta's powers had healed most of her, she still needed to rest to regain what she'd lost. When they rounded a corner, Jarek and Sierra were double-teaming Lucian. Jarek kept Lucian from taking notice of Sierra, who was in the middle of casting an enchantment spell on him.

"No," Siovon whispered, preparing to run at the woman.

Instead, Calysta took off before her. In her free hand, Calysta was forming a spell of her own, sparks of red and yellow shooting out. She threw the ball at the unsuspecting Sierra, singeing the side of her head. Sierra cried out and dropped to her knees. When Calysta reached her, she leaped at the woman and brought her blade down hard, stabbing Sierra in the heart.

Siovon winced, shocked that Calysta hadn't even hesitated. She'd seen Calysta kill before, but only twice, and both times had been mercy kills. Her sister had been even more remorseful than Siovon.

This is one kill Caly won't regret, Siovon thought.

Calysta pulled the blade free of Sierra's chest. "That one's from me," she said. "This is for my sister." She plunged the blade into Sierra's chest again and twisted. The imp's pained scream cut off as her body was reduced to sparkly ashes.

With the enchantment spell broken, Jarek stopped fighting, looking around in a daze. When he saw Sierra's remains, his face warped with rage. "No!" He turned to attack Calysta but hadn't even taken a step when Lucian knocked him on the side of his head with the broad end of his sword. The lesser vampire's eyes rolled into his head as he dropped, unconscious.

Siovon blinked in surprise. "Well...hell," she muttered, dropping her knife. Lucian glanced at her, relief relaxing his tight features. In half a second, he was standing before her, crushing her body to his in a hug tight enough to make breathing a struggle. Still, Siovon only hugged his neck with the same fierce need that had been plaguing her since she'd left.

"Siovon," he murmured against her neck, "my love. Please don't do something so stupid ever again. I can't bear the thought of losing you."

Siovon smiled and pulled back enough to frame his face in her hands. His silver eyes were filled with all the emotions she felt inside herself. Worry, relief, pleasure...love. "You'll never lose me, Lucian," she whispered. "I'm here to stay...forever."

She knew her words shocked and pleased him by the way the bond between them flared to life with emotion. "I love you," he murmured, leaning to press his lips to hers. Siovon's toes curled in the snow, warmth spreading through her body that made her desperate to be even closer to Lucian. She needed him just as she could feel he needed her.

He planted a kiss on her forehead.

Siovon cleared her throat. "For the record, Frosty, it may have been a stupid plan, but it worked."

Lucian snorted, tightening his arms around her waist. "You are going to be the death of me, *fatina*. I just know it."

"Yes, well, truemates are all about till death do us part', right? You'd better get used to it." Lucian stiffened in her arms. She smiled up at him, taking one of his hands in her own. "My answer is yes, Lucian. I want to be your mate."

Lucian's eyes closed, his relief and happiness filling her. "Thank you, Siovon." He looked down at her, only then seeming to notice her lack of clothing. He scowled and snatched off his leather jacket. He wrapped it around her and zipped it up to her neck. "What the devil made you come to a fight wearing only a shirt?"

His jacket swallowed her whole, falling past her knees. She pushed the sleeves up to free her hands, which she placed on her hips. "Do you think this a was a decision I made freely?" With the adrenaline died down, she could feel the snow settling on her feet. "I don't suppose you have an extra pair of socks on you?"

"Nope." He swept her off her feet and cradled her close to his chest.

Someone cleared their throat, and Siovon spotted Calysta watching them with a mix of humor and wariness. "Lucian, this is my sister, Calysta. Caly, this is Lucian, my..."

"Mate," Lucian offered with a prideful smile. "Soon-to-be mate."

Siovon's cheeks heated, but Calysta smiled with delight. "I'm happy you've finally found someone to make you happy, Siovon. You deserve it."

"Their crazy asses deserve each other, that's for damn sure," a familiar voice grouched.

All three of them turned to find Keegan approaching. Calysta gasped, running to throw her arms around his neck. "Keegan, you're alive," she exclaimed.

Keegan stumbled back several steps, looking rather pleased. He hugged her in a lingering embrace. "Yeah. Don't get all mushy on me, kid."

Calysta chuckled and pulled back. The others came to join them, all looking a bit rough, though uninjured. Someone announced that all of the Rogues had been disposed of.

Siovon frowned when she saw everyone except her dear friend. "Where's Naomi?"

Darius snorted. "The badass hottie who stole all my kills? She took off after the last of the Rogues were killed. Sal went to go look for her." His ever-present grin widened into one that was suspiciously close to the Cheshire Cat's. "She must be the one giving him a run for his money."

Siovon shook her head, sending her best wishes to Naomi. No doubt Sal was the only reason she'd taken off so soon, which meant she was running from her own feelings.

Keegan opened a portal. "Where the hell do you think you're going?" Lucian demanded.

Keegan gave a one-finger salute to all of them. "It's been fun, vamps, but my job here is done." He held his hand out to Calysta. "Wanna ditch these losers?"

"Wait, Calysta—"

Keegan cut off Siovon with a warm smile. "Don't worry. We'll meet you back in St. Charles before the sun rises tomorrow. After all, I'm sure your vampire is eager to have some alone time with you."

At Lucian's grateful nod, Siovon found Calysta smiling at her. "Don't worry, sis. No offense to the rest of you, but I'd rather stick with the demon I do know— the lesser of two evils sort of deal. See you at sunrise." With that, the two disappeared through the portal.

With a deep sigh, Siovon leaned into Lucian as he walked past his brothers and clansmen toward a row of SUVs parked in the distance. "I've got shotgun!" Julius yelled after them.

Lucian turned his head over his shoulder. "Find your own ride. We're going to a hotel so Siovon can...rest."

At Lucian's words, an immediate rush of heat head straight toward Siovon's core. They both knew full well there would be very little resting once she had showered and cleaned herself up.

She wrapped her arms around his neck. "So, mate-to-be, if you're having second thoughts, you'd better spit them out now, because I don't want to hear you say you're tired of me in fifty years."

Lucian chuckled, picking up the pace. "Any hesitation I may have had was lost since the day I first caught your scent in St. Louis."

Chapter Twenty-One

Due to being an accomplice in his father's nefarious plans, Jarek Nilsen was brought before the Imperials to be judged. His execution wasn't a pretty one, nor was it painless. While Cyrus had every right to dispose of the traitor's son how he saw fit, he'd preferred to hand him over to the Imperials to deal with.

Vampire-kind was once again safe — well, as safe as it had been before Mikhail's threat hung over them. Now they had a new problem on their hands, one that they didn't even know how to begin figuring out.

The Gordanos were no longer the only Royals alive. Anais was a Royal child, and from her memories, Ava had seen there was an entire community of Royals being held captive in Tartarus. Not only that, but the mysterious 'master' they were enslaved to was a creature who fed off them like livestock.

Cyrus had petitioned the Imperials for a meeting, though that wouldn't take place for a handful of weeks. It would take longer for them to investigate the issue.

The king had been working hard, going through all his distant contacts and allies for any information.

In the meantime, there was nothing more any of them could do besides wait. The main threat was terminated, so a celebration was in order. Not only had they defeated an enemy that had caused them all such grief, but the oldest Gordano son had also found his truemate, their sister was home and growing the next generation of their family and Salvator's latest club was continuing to rise through the charts as the most popular demon club in Chicago.

Life was great.

Well, it should have been. To say Sal was in a shitty mood was the biggest understatement of the century.

He was annoyed. He was grumpy. Above all, he was downright insulted that the one woman who'd brought him to his knees in pleasure had disappeared out of his life without a trace. Twice.

Tossing back another shot of aged whiskey, he slammed the glass down on the top of his desk, pissed that the odd feeling of loneliness refused to leave his chest.

What the hell is the matter with me? he growled in thought.

So what if Naomi didn't want to be bothered with him. There were dozens, hell, hundreds of women out there who would be willing to take her place. Actually, one of his favorites was on the way to take care of his primal needs.

It was Naomi's loss, after all. He was a phenomenal lover with a long line of groupies to prove it. He'd had her shivering and screaming in pleasure as he'd taken her with a fierceness that had rocked his world. By the gods, she should have been smitten, begging for his touch over and over again.

And yet the ungrateful woman had disappeared on him without so much as a wave goodbye.

He'd chased her after their last battle with the Rogues. He'd been working his way toward her side, determined to be close to her for a moment to speak, yet the damned beasts had kept coming until he'd been far too distracted in his fight. When it was over, he'd noticed she was no longer around, having fled the old factory.

Sal had followed her scent all the way until he realized she'd gotten into a car and left. Need had driven him to follow her tracks in the snowy road until they'd disappeared on the highway with tons of other cars.

Since then…

Well, since then he'd been in a shitty mood. Siovon wouldn't tell him how to locate the woman, which had annoyed him even further. His sister-in-law was pretty damn cruel.

A knock sounded on Sal's door, and he knew who it was long before a beautiful nymph entered his office. Wearing nothing more than a silky black robe and high heels, she sashayed her way across the floor, her rounded hips swinging back and forth as she drew near. With a mane of golden-blonde hair, bright green eyes and a figure that most women would kill to have, she was one to draw heads everywhere she went.

Sal leaned back in his seat as he enjoyed the sight of her, though the usual excitement he felt over seeing a beautiful woman didn't flare to life, no doubt due to his sour mood.

"I was beginning to fear you'd forgotten me, Salvator," the nymph stated with a pout as she came around his desk. She sat on the edge, the short robe hiking up several inches to reveal a tantalizing view of a creamy thigh.

Sal touched her knee, walking his fingers across her skin. "How could I ever forget such beauty, *cara*? Yours is one to put all others to shame."

Tilly gave a toss of her curls, baring her slender neck. Her eyes twinkled with mischief and desire. "You sure know how to sweet talk a lady," she murmured.

Apparently not well enough, a voice grumbled in the back of his mind. Sal forced it away, ignoring the taunts. He had every intention of forgetting Naomi. If she wanted nothing to do with him, so be it.

Tilly rose to her feet and tugged on a lock of Sal's loose hair. "You look down in the dumps, Sal. Has something happened?"

Yes. "No," he lied. "I just need a distraction. Can you help me with that?"

Tilly's lips formed a small smile. She reached for the knot holding her robe together. "I believe I can." She freed herself from the robe, letting the soft garment fall from her body. "Is this a good enough distraction?"

Sal peered at the expanse of naked flesh standing before him—full breasts with rosy nipples, a narrow waist flaring out into wide hips and bare skin already damp with arousal.

All that beauty before him, yet nothing happened for Sal. Tilly moved to stand behind him, running her hands over his shoulders and chest. She leaned forward, the smell of her excitement thick in the air. "I'm ready for you, Sal," she whispered in his ear before licking a trail down the side of his neck.

Still, nothing happened. There was not even a twitch from his cock as he sat there, unresponsive as a gorgeous woman was eager to please him.

With a sound of disgust aimed toward himself, he stood and turned his back on her. "I've changed my mind, Tilly. I'm not in the mood tonight."

There was a shocked silence between them. "Not in the mood?" she echoed, offended. "Have you not taken a look at me?"

Sal half turned, waving her away. "Yes. I'm sorry. Put your clothes back on."

Tilly's mouth parted, her eyes filled with confusion and disbelief. Then anger. Lots and lots of anger. "You bastard," she growled, snatching up her robe before stomping toward the door. "You aren't the only man who wants me, you know. I can have my pick, but I chose you, and yet you treat me as if I am nothing."

"Tilly, I'm tired. Please just go."

She made a sound of annoyance. "Fine. When you're ready to apologize, you have my number." With that, she exited his office, slamming the door.

Sal heaved a deep sigh and sank into his chair. He poured himself two more shots and tossed them back.

Cazzo, that was a first. Never before had he been utterly flaccid when in the company of a woman who was willing to please him. When he looked at Tilly, all he could see was how she wasn't Naomi. No woman was.

He leaned forward on his elbows and placed his head in his hands.

"*Merda*, I *am* in trouble," he murmured to the empty room.

**Want to see more from this author?
Here's a taster for you to enjoy!**

The Royal Gordanos:
Craving a Royal
Makayla Roberts

Excerpt

The suburb in the village of Hinsdale just west of Chicago was the type of neighborhood that made Naomi cringe. Each house she passed was bigger and more lavish than the last, as if the residents were in competition to show off who had the most fortune.

And it was clear that the owner of the sprawling mansion at the very end of a private road won the award for Top Over-Compensator.

Beyond the large wrought-iron gates was a Mediterranean-style mansion that looked like it'd been plucked straight from the Hamptons. It stretched over a piece of property that could house an entire subdivision of equally large homes. And stepping out of the elegant double doors making up the entrance was a mere waif of a woman who looked as out of place as Naomi felt.

Her closest friend and ex-comrade of many years wore plain yellow scrubs and a white lab coat that was far too big for her small frame. The sight made Naomi snort behind the mask that covered the lower half of her face. She stepped out of the rental car as Siovon strolled up to her.

"You look comfortable," Naomi drawled.

Siovon grinned. "I wouldn't live here if I couldn't feel comfortable in my own home." She waved a slender hand toward the entrance. "Come in. I'm surprised you showed up this time."

Naomi snorted again, following Siovon with caution. It wasn't that she didn't trust her. Quite the contrary, in fact. Siovon was like a sister to her, one she trusted with her life.

No... Her hesitancy had everything to do with the fact that Siovon wasn't alone in that mausoleum of a home. She was the mate of Lucian Gordano—a powerful clan chief who ruled more than a fourth of the United States. Not only was he a ruthless badass whose very word was law, but he was also the firstborn child of Cyrus Gordano, the almighty vampire king. That made him one of the most feared demons around.

And with that grand title came a horde of devoted clansmen assigned to protect every inch of his property. While they were good about staying out of sight—no doubt following Siovon's commands—Naomi still sensed their eyes on her. She'd never ventured to a vampire's lair, not unless it had been to kill one of them.

Something she'd promised Siovon not to do tonight. *Damn it all.*

"It's not like you gave me much of a choice," Naomi grumbled, studying the layout of the grand mansion. She lightened her voice to mimic a higher pitch. *"Come over and get the medicine yourself. I have sooo much work to do, what with pleasing my hubby and groveling at his feet."*

Siovon chortled. "First off, I do *not* sound like that, nor have I ever said any such nonsense. Second, I wanted you to see my lab. The contractors just finished the repairs last week, and Cyrus ordered a shipment of all sorts of herbs and ingredients and... Well, everything, really." She led them down one hall that had a single door at the end. "And the best part? No one is allowed to enter without my or Calysta's permission — not even Lucian." She punched in a series of numbers on the touchpad. Seconds later, a metal latch unlocked and she swung the door open.

Naomi raised her brows, amused at her friend's excitement. The vast room was like a laboratory from a sci-fi movie. Multiple shelves lined the perimeter, all filled with large glasses of herbs, plants and other earthy products. A portion of another wall contained a refrigerator with glass doors that held all sorts of vials. The steel door next to it was what she assumed to be a walk-in freezer. There were also a half dozen rolling tables, metal slabs jutting from the walls and glass cabinets encompassing cauldrons, ceramic pots, beakers and lots of scientific equipment that was clean and ready for use.

"This is impressive, Siovon," Naomi murmured in earnest. "Frosty really went all out for you, didn't he?"

Siovon beamed with pride. Her hair was styled in the same short pixie cut she'd had when Naomi had first met her decades prior. That, plus her short stature, dainty features and wide eyes, made her look like she couldn't harm a fly if it bit her on the nose.

Unbeknownst to others, she was all warrior, despite her wish to be peaceful. The battle with Sierra and her zombie Rogues a few months prior had proved that Siovon's new life of peace hadn't corrupted her deadly skills. Since then, her life had just...evolved.

For the better, of course.

She had been reunited with her sister after a ten-year absence, found the love of her life — in a vampire, of all things — moved into a lavish house and had her mate's family to call her own. It wasn't too bad for someone who'd once been an empty shell of an assassin.

Naomi was happy for her. She truly was, but she couldn't halt the twinge of envy that always pierced her heart every time she spoke to Siovon. Naomi didn't have any illusions of a perfect life with a perfect mate and an even-more-perfect family. Still, she couldn't help but wish she could trade spots with her dear friend, if only for a day.

Hell, for just an hour.

She wondered how it felt to be worshipped by a loving companion, someone who'd dedicate his entire existence to pleasing her and keeping her happy.

An image of silver hair and pale-blue eyes flashed in her mind, followed by a longing that she ruthlessly squashed.

I am not *going there*, she growled to herself. *I am* so *not going there. Not again.*

Shaking off the depressing feelings she'd been forcing away for weeks, she hopped onto one of the steel slabs. Her feet dangled from the floor as she waited for Siovon to retrieve the vial of medicine she'd come for.

When Siovon paused with a raised eyebrow to look over her shoulder, Naomi only then realized that her friend had been talking the whole time. She gave a slow blink. "What did you say?"

Siovon huffed. "Are you listening to me?"

Naomi shrugged. "No. Sorry."

"I asked if you wanted to stay for dinner. Calysta is still with Keegan, looking for a jinn, and Lucian will be working late."

Naomi widened her eyes in mock surprise. "The leech isn't going to be glued to your side? I'm shocked."

"Oh, trust me. It wasn't his choice. I told him he'd have to find somewhere else to sleep if he shirks his duties again."

"Ah, the old no-cooch-for-the-pooch threat. Works every time." Naomi glanced around the room. "Thanks for the offer, but I have things to do. Maybe next time."

"A job, huh?"

"Nah. My contract ended a week ago."

Siovon looked shocked and froze in the middle of pouring some kind of liquid into a vial. "Really? Why didn't you tell me?"

Naomi shrugged. "It's not a big deal."

Liar, her mind whispered.

The assassin's guild had been her home since age nineteen. Though their methods of dealing with insubordination and failed missions were rather gruesome and painful, they'd saved her life. The vigorous training she'd endured had helped her become stronger, bringing her a long way from that frightened, weak little girl she'd once been. Killing targets for a living had become the only life she knew. And for a while, she'd been content, though that wasn't something she wanted to do forever.

Oh, she didn't share Siovon's tender heart that craved a life of harmony and cupcakes and rainbows, not even a little.

Her past held a noose around her neck, and it was high time she faced it.

"Are you going to sign another contract?" Siovon asked.

"Probably not."

"Well, what are you going to do?"

Naomi shrugged again. "Dunno."

Siovon let out an annoyed huff. "You should consider working with me and Caly. We're going to open a clinic-slash-pharmacy soon, so extra hands are always welcome. In the meantime, Cyrus is paying us an assload of money to find a way to reverse Rogueism among vampires."

Naomi lifted an eyebrow. "You think you can do that?" Rogues were the class of vampires who had given in to their bloodlust. They were nothing short of rabid beasts, and since there was no way of restoring their sanity, Cyrus' law demanded the execution of them on sight. Siovon had conveyed her surprise to Naomi about his request for her to seek a solution that would help those lost souls find their way back to their former way of being.

Frustration caused Siovon to frown as she glanced at a table holding several beakers containing different color liquids. "I'm not holding my breath on it, but I'm doing my best. From what I've learned about Rogues, there's always some kind of trigger to make them snap—losing a mate, starving from lack of blood, being tortured, et cetera. I think it's a brain function that clouds the mind with only the most basic needs remaining—hunger and attack mode, like how rabid animals are. I hope I can create some kind of anti-rabies vaccine and modify it to work the same for Rogues. If I can—"

Naomi opened her mouth on a wide, obnoxious yawn. "I get it. Nerd talk here, rabid Rogues there. Let's skip the schematics."

Siovon tsked. "Well, you asked."

Several minutes ticked by while Siovon worked the finishing touches on Naomi's medicine. It was a mix that suppressed her succubus needs. While she didn't require daily sex to survive, like full-blooded succubi, if she went more than a couple of days without it, her body would start to turn on itself.

She always chose to suffer through it until the pain became too unbearable. She'd rather that than to give into the needs that had caused her so much misery in life.

Yeah, a sex demon who hates sex. Go freaking figure.

"I'm done," Siovon murmured. She plugged a cork into the opening of the bottle and handed it to Naomi. "Seriously… What are you going to do now that your contract is over? You can teach a martial arts class, you know — show others how to fight and defend themselves. Luc's brother Cassander owns a popular demon gym that's always looking for skilled instructors. They even have cage matches once a month that have large-award prizes. Well, those fights are for men, but I'm sure I can talk Cass into at least considering holding some for women."

When Naomi said nothing, only stared at the six-inch bottle in her hand, Siovon's smile faded. She was calculating, and it wouldn't be long before she found whatever it was she was looking for.

"Something's wrong, isn't it?" Siovon questioned.

Naomi pulled a small piece of paper from her pocket and handed it to Siovon.

She studied the drawing with a frown, twisting and turning it several ways before glancing up. "What am I looking at?"

Naomi returned the paper to her pocket. She didn't even have to glance at it. She'd spent countless hours eyeing the image, trying to figure out its meaning. It was an eye of Horus, the ancient Egyptian symbol for peace and prosperity. However, the eye itself was backward and flipped in a way that made it near impossible to tell which side was correct.

"It's a symbol." Dread settled like a cold weight in her gut. "A few years ago, I came across a man who had it tattooed on his shoulder. We were after the same target, so of course, he and I got into a brawl. I won, in case you're wondering, but he ran away before I could get any information out of him. I just let it go."

She tapped at the paper tucked away in her pocket. "My last mark had the exact same tattoo on her inner wrist. She was a member of some demon group that was distributing goods on the black market."

Siovon tilted her head. "Okay, so she and that guy had the same tattoos. They could have been from the same group and that symbol is their insignia. But what does that have to do with *you*?" She narrowed her eyes in suspicion. "Don't tell me you want in on the underworld scam. The black market has some pretty twisted shit going on, Naomi."

Naomi snorted. "I may be a killer, but I have morals — hypocritical as that may sound." She shook her head. "I thought perhaps it was all just a coincidence — and maybe it still is — but I've seen this symbol years ago." She sucked in a deep breath, steeling her nerves for the worst part of her revelation. "My mother had a pendant just like it."

For several long moments, the two of them just stared at each other in silence. Siovon's shock had been expected.

Naomi had once lived with her mother in a small corner of Tartarus that was solely inhabited by furies. All furies were female and pureblood, so long as they reproduced with humans, yet Naomi was an anomaly. Her mother had been impregnated with incubus sperm, though no one had known the truth until Naomi had reached maturity and her succubus side had come out. Her mother had been deemed a traitor to their kind and had been executed, while Naomi had been sold into demon slavery.

She'd been a snooping child when she'd found the pendant, but her mother had scolded her with a strict demand to never bring it up again. However, after coming across the same mark on people who might or might not be tied to a group of black marketers, she had to know if it was all tied together.

"I don't know what to say," Siovon murmured.

Naomi blinked up at her with a wry smile. "If you say something pitiful, like you're sorry for my loss, I will hit you."

Siovon flicked her bangs out of her eyes. "This is bizarre. Are you sure it's the same symbol? If your mother was associated with outsiders—"

"Then it's likely her death wasn't because of me being born."

"That's not what I meant. If you go down this path, you might discover answers that are better left covered."

"I'm aware of that." She hopped off the table. "Siovon, I have lived with guilt for so long. I've spent years blaming myself for her death. I need closure or else I'll never be able to move on. And even if don't find the answers I'm looking for, at least I can say I tried."

Siovon flattened her palm over her heart. "Naomi Sofia Morales, that was the longest I've ever heard you talk without mentioning death, torture or kicking someone's ass. I'm so proud of you."

Naomi rolled her eyes, though her lips twitched in amusement. "I'm serious. I need to find the truth."

Siovon nodded and shrugged out of her lab coat. "Very well. I'll go with you. It could be dangerous."

"Oh, no, you're not."

Siovon paused mid-strip. "Why not?"

"Is that a serious question? For one, you have your own life here, and if we come across any danger, you'll only sulk and complain if you have to ruin your newfound pacifism. For two, the moment you step foot outside Chicago, your pet vampire will come after us with his entire clan—and I, for one, have no desire to be in the company of Frosty throwing another one of his temper tantrums."

Siovon's cheeks tinted pink as she gave a small smile. "I suppose he can be a bit overbearing at times." Her smile waned. "I just don't think you should go alone. There's a chance that other furies are involved, and if they catch you snooping around for answers, they may try to kill you."

Naomi already knew that but hearing the words aloud stung. The only family she'd ever known had turned their backs on her when she'd needed help and guidance the most. After her exile, the council had threatened her demise if she ever tried to return—not that she'd wanted to anyway. There was nothing left for her there.

Good riddance to every one of those bastards.

"Don't worry about me," she said on her way out of the door. She pocketed her medicine and threw her hand up in a casual wave. "'Careful' is my middle name."

"The hell it is," Siovon grumbled, following her. They walked side-by-side until they were back on the driveway.

Naomi used the key fob to unlock her car door. "Have you ever heard of The Lotus? Chè tracked down an elf who's a frequent customer there. He wears the same symbol. I'm on my way to see if I can locate him."

"The Lotus?" Siovon asked incredulously. "That's—" She broke off her words, a strange expression crossing her delicate features. It had been there one minute and was gone the next, far too fast for Naomi to analyze it. Siovon then smiled and stepped back. "I've heard of the place. It's a popular nightclub that was opened a few months ago."

Naomi narrowed her eyes. Siovon's smile sent chills down her spine. It was far too wide, her tone overly sweet, as if she were plotting something. "I mean it, Siovon. You'd better not try to join me."

Siovon laughed, waving her away. "I promise I won't. Be careful and call if you need anything."

Naomi still didn't trust her friend's sudden change of heart, but she nodded and slid behind the steering wheel. Seconds later, she was headed down the long drive toward the outer gate.

Siovon's smile fell when Naomi's taillights were no longer in sight. Still, she stood on the gravel of the wraparound driveway, staring off into space.

Fear and worry became a living force in her chest, but not because she doubted Naomi could protect herself. No, it was because her friend had been through so much hurt and betrayal that her journey could quite possibly be the one to tip her over the edge of sanity.

However, there was no use trying to change her mind. Naomi would forever be tormented by her past, and if facing her people was her way of finding peace at last, then Siovon had no right to try to intrude.

Still, the voice of reason always won in those types of situations. Naomi was her closest and dearest friend. She couldn't sit back and let her endanger her life on a mission that could take a turn for the worse. There was no talking her out of it, and she'd just given her word to not interfere.

But someone else can.

"Please, don't let me regret this," she grouched as she retrieved her cell phone. She scrolled through her contacts until she found the number she needed. She swallowed her pride and crossed her eyes in frustration. "*Please*." Then, she hit Call.

A suave voice that could charm the scales off a snake answered on the second ring. "Yes, sister-in-law. How can I help you?"

She rolled her eyes at his sarcasm, knowing full well her mate's brother had been annoyed with her the last few months. However, she needed his help, and she knew he above all others would see to Naomi's protection.

She drew in a deep breath before letting it out. With false cheeriness, she said, "Salvator, darling, how would you like to be reunited with my dear friend Naomi?"

Home of Erotic Romance

Sign up for our newsletter and find out about all our romance book releases, eBook sales and promotions, sneak peeks and FREE romance books!

About the Author

Makayla's love for reading began at the age of twelve when her mother introduced her to the world of mystical creatures. From then on, she discovered a talent for turning her own imagination into words. From fanfictions to short stories to full-length novels and novellas, if she wasn't focused on school activities, she was either reading or writing.

Raised on the coast of Mississippi, Makayla juggles her everyday life between work and being a mom. In her free time, she enjoys binge watching criminal suspense shows, shopping, painting, wood burning, and of course, working on her books.

Makayla enjoys writing stories with strong elements of romance, adventure, and paranormal. Vampires, shifters, fairies, dragons — she loves them all!

Makayla loves to hear from readers. You can find her contact information, website details and author profile page at https://www.totallybound.com